"A beautifully written and masterful work of character-driven crime fiction. One of the most fascinating and compelling main characters I've read in a long time. A bad guy real enough to smell. A plot that fits together like a puzzle. As soon as I started *Lost Dog,* my heart began to beat faster. This was the book I'd been craving. Not only does he give us a knock-out plot, he gives us real people in real settings. He gives us characters we care about, characters we know and want to know. And like real life, the darkest moments often contain humor. I laughed out loud several times. *Lost Dog* is a heart-stopping, tightly woven debut by a remarkable new crime fiction writer. Thank you, Bill Cameron."

—Anne Frasier, *USA Today* bestselling author
of *Hush, Play Dead,* and *Pale Immortal*

"Engaging and unique, *Lost Dog* features an unlikely but compelling hero. Peter McKrall is a complete original. A gritty yet witty tale with a cast of offbeat characters you want to spend more time with and the unexpected twists kept me turning the pages. I can honestly say Bill Cameron is an author who kept me up all night long!"

—Sandra Ruttan,
author of *Suspicious Circumstances*

"In the chill of Portland at Christmastime, Bill Cameron weaves a story of murder, human frailty, and the frightening reality of coincidence . . . Bill writes a compelling, layered tale with graceful prose, realistic scenery, and dead-on dialogue. I really enjoyed *Lost Dog*. Bill Cameron can add me to his list of fans."

—Julia Buckley,
author of *The Dark Backward*

LOST DOG

bill cameron

MIDNIGHT INK
WOODBURY, MINNESOTA

FIRST EDITION
First Printing, 2007

Book design by Donna Burch
Cover design by Lisa Novak
Cover photograph © Danny Bright / Photonica / Getty Images

Midnight Ink, an imprint of Llewellyn Publications

Library of Congress Cataloging-in-Publication Data
Cameron, Bill 1963–
    Lost dog / Bill Cameron.—1st ed.
        p. cm.
    ISBN-13: 978-0-7387-0966-6 (alk. paper)
    ISBN-10: 0-7387-0966-2 (alk. paper)
        I. Title.

PS3603.A4475L67 2007
813'.6—dc22

2006047070

Midnight Ink
Llewellyn Publications
2143 Wooddale Drive, Dept. 0-7387-0966-2
Woodbury, MN 55125-2989, U.S.A.
www.midnightinkbooks.com

Printed in the United States of America

To my J's, Justin, Jessica, and Jill
(and I can't leave out Jasmine and
the non-J's, Nene and Mr. Glubber)

PROLOGUE

SWIRLING SNOW BIT HIS cheeks, snapped at his blinking eyes. It was starting to stick to the ground. *No good.* Snow meant footprints, and cops got all over footprints. Just the other night, Jake watched a show where they busted some guy from his frigging sneaker. Nailed the sucker to the wall. The ground was mostly bark chips, which wouldn't take a print for shit so long as he beat the snow. Just had to hurry.

The wind felt like a jagged blade at his back. Jake bent down and grasped the woman under her bony shoulders, pulled her toward the low concrete wall behind him. It was late, dark, colder than nobody's business. Still, no telling who might show up outta nowhere at just the wrong moment. Some loon who wanted to play on the swings in the middle of the night, something like that. Had to get her out of sight. They'd find her anyway, but no reason to make it easy. If he was lucky, the snow might fall thick enough to help him out a little. Didn't need much. Just time to get away and clean up. Maybe throw away his shoes. Then they could find her.

He dragged her through the gap in the wall, looking for the right spot. Plenty of options. Big ol' concrete tubes the kids climbed on. A surge of wind rushed through the trees and kicked dead leaves and thickening snow along the ground. Teeter-totter creaked in the cold. He shuddered at the sound—pretty creepy for a playground, but maybe it was different by day. He stuffed the woman into one of the larger tubes, head first. Her shoes, black leather and heels, came off as he wrestled her legs into the narrow space. He tried to slip the shoes back onto her stiffening feet but ended up tossing them into the tube beyond her head. They'd think it meant something if he took her shoes, but he didn't want to chance being found with them. He stood up, caught his breath. Wiped his eyes.

A line of dark houses crowded the fence at the edge of the park, seemed to hunker down against the cold. No sign of life. *Good.* A single lamppost beyond the swings cast a silvery pall over the playground. He couldn't make out much on the ground. No telling what kind of evidence he was leaving. The cops on TV could make a case out of anything. Broken twig could mean the chair. But there wasn't a whole lot he could do about it, short of making himself scarce. He shuffled his feet back and forth to obscure his tracks, then brushed out the gouge in the bark chips left by the woman's feet. He couldn't tell if she'd bled much on the ground, though he knew her blood had gotten on his pants and coat. He'd be up half the night doing the wash.

He saw her purse at the foot of the slide. Grabbed it, dug through the contents. He found a wallet with a hefty wad of cash, a single key on a rabbit's foot keychain. *So much for good luck.* He giggled, kept digging. Make-up … cigarettes … box of rubbers. He put it all into his pockets along with the stuff she'd thrown at him—a beer bottle and bits of junk she must've found on the ground as she scrambled around trying to get away. *Evidence.* He set the empty purse back near her tube. Make them think the whole thing was a robbery gone sour. He'd dump the wallet and anything else not worth keeping on the way home.

The wind died down, the thin snow now drifting softly out of the blackness above. He took a breath, let it out. Then he reached into his inside pocket and pulled out the gun. Empty now, it felt lighter. He wouldn't have thought six measly bullets would make much difference, but they did. He tilted his head back and stared into the dark sky, stretched his arms over his head. He had to get going, but he couldn't bring himself to move. She was safe now—he'd made sure of that. It was time to go, but the snow was falling and the air felt clean and crisp, and he wanted to look at her again. Touch her one more time.

He crept back through the gap in the wall, kneeled at the opening of her tube. It was dark, too dark to see more than an indistinct hump where she lay. He pulled off his gloves, reached out and felt her calf, her thigh, her skin. Still warm, barely. He stroked her legs and felt himself tremble in the darkness. What would they do with her? Would they understand what had happened? Why it *had* to happen? He felt his eyes water. *Go home, Jake.* But he couldn't just yet. He wanted to lie down next to her for just a little while.

Except that would be really frigging stupid. He shook his head sharply and used the sleeve of his coat to smudge any fingerprints on her bare skin. He knew from TV that fingerprints didn't last long on skin, but you couldn't be too careful. He cast about and found a couple sheets of newspaper tossed up against the tube by the wind, carefully spread them over her. Couldn't have said why. Not like she wouldn't be found anyway. Hell, he *wanted* her to be found. He stood, thrust his hands into his pockets. Turned away.

Long walk home. Way too late for a bus, but that would have been stupid anyway, him covered in blood. He kept to shadows, dodged headlights. Took the Steel Bridge across the river, dropped her wallet mid-span. Kept the cash. He didn't think about her, concentrated instead on not being seen. He started to feel a little proud of himself, really, gliding like a ghost through the sleeping city. If anyone saw him, they'd wonder if he was even real. *Heh.*

It wasn't till he was home, halfway through the laundry and feeling especially slick, that he realized he'd left his fucking gloves on the ground next to her dead body.

ONE

NOT THAT HE PARTICULARLY cared for his sister's incessant nagging, but if Peter McKrall had known he would find a dead woman in the park that morning, he'd have stayed home and listened to Abby bitch instead. The day started typically enough: Peter on the porch staring into the dreary morning sky, working out excuses. He'd overslept, and the sun was already up behind a colorless overcast. Snow crusted the grass and rhododendrons in the front yard, but the walk and street were too warm for the snow to stick. Peter expected this sort of thing back in *Kain-tuck-ee*, but since moving to Portland he'd never seen snow before New Year's, and seldom afterward. Normally they kept the white stuff out in the sticks, where it belonged.

Rain. That'd be an excuse. He bent and stretched and thought about his niece, Julie, asleep in the guest room. His sister and her husband, David, had come with Julie for Christmas and to check up on the house. Peter had been renting the place from them on the cheap since they moved to Seattle a couple years before, an arrangement originally intended to be temporary but which had grown permanent through the power of Peter's inertia and the pleasure Abby took in having Peter in her debt.

He wondered how Julie had slept without Patch. Not well, probably. Shapeless, furless, one-eyed Patch, only one day younger than Julie herself. He'd bought Patch in the hospital gift shop when he came to see Abby the morning after Julie was born. The cashier, blue-haired and suspicious, had glared at him as he wandered the shop. All he'd wanted were some mints, but the cashier's attention aroused his *screw-you-bitch* itch. Before he knew it, he had an insipid crystal figurine of an angel tucked inside his coat and Patch in his hand. "For my brand-new niece," he said to the cashier, feeling the heat and satisfaction of his petty crime in his belly. He smiled and paid cash. "Altoids, too, please." The woman took his money, but he knew she'd be counting figurines the moment he left, in spite of the stuffed dog and brand-new niece. He left the angel on the sink in the men's room, his pleasure in the theft already faded. But Patch he presented ceremoniously to Abby and child, as if he'd intended to give the gift all along. In those days, four years earlier, Patch had been fuzzy and tan with a brown spot around one button eye. Years of Julie's affection had transformed the hound. She'd hugged and chewed him down to his woven skin, now gray and mottled from an endless succession of drool and wash-rinse-spin cycles.

The night before, when Patch turned up missing, Julie wept dime-sized tears. The Christmas presents she'd opened that morning did little to comfort her. Peter, Abby, and David crawled under beds, peered behind plants, pawed through the trash. No Patch. Then Peter remembered he and Julie had pushed Patch on the swings during an afternoon jaunt to the park. No one recalled Patch coming home. By the time they realized what must have happened, night had fallen and a Columbia Gorge wind had kicked up out of the east, bitter cold and pushing snow. Too cold to be outside, and besides, while Irving Park held a certain daylight appeal, it wasn't a place for after-dark forays. Peter promised Julie he'd look for Patch when he went out for his morning run.

If he went out for his run. He was still working on excuses.

The front door opened behind him and Abby appeared, wrapped in her new Christmas robe, hair a brown-blond nest, one cheek blotchy with an impression of crinkled pillowcase.

"My God, it's only seven," Peter said. "I didn't expect to see Her Majesty till noon."

She stuck her tongue out at him. "I heard a noise in the living room. I wanted to make sure it wasn't Julie sticking forks in electrical outlets."

"That was me. About fifteen minutes ago." He raised an eyebrow. "Your parental vigilance is an inspiration, Sis."

"Don't call me Sis," she said, "or I'll break your fucking arm." She peered out at the leaden sky. "Aren't you going to run?"

"What's it to you?" A hint of defensiveness in his voice. But then he shrugged. "I suppose, sure, if nothing else comes up."

"Lots of distractions this time of morning."

"I was hoping for a monsoon, or maybe martial law. Killer asteroid. Something."

Abby studied him. "Peter? How are you feeling?"

He felt himself flinch. "So you're my doc now, too? Gonna check to make sure I'm taking my meds?"

"She's got you on medication now?"

"Jesus, Abby. What do you think?"

"I don't know what to think."

"Can't a guy just be a smart-ass? Jesus!"

"Don't be that way. I'm worried about you."

He shrugged again, looked away. "Sorry."

"It's just a job. You'll find another one."

He shook his head. "It's not that. Hell, I don't even know if I *want* to find another one. I don't know what I want to do. Maybe I want to go back to school. Or travel from small town to small town solving local mysteries. Or go be a hermit in the mountains."

"You're already a hermit in this house. Peter, there's no rush. Take your time. Listen, I talked to Dave, and we're okay with letting you skip the rent for a couple of months."

Peter's cheeks grew warm. "Thanks. Hopefully not for too long." He hated to have to ask for help from his sister.

"There's one condition," she continued. "You've got to stop the drinking binges—"

The heat in his cheeks suddenly surged down into his chest. "That was one time, Abby!" he snapped. "I just lost my fucking job. I think I'm entitled—"

She reached up and put a finger to his lips. "You're the one with no job and a two-day hangover for Christmas—not me. If you're going to throw your money away in seedy little bars, you can't expect Dave and me to subsidize the rent. You need to take care of yourself."

He pulled his head back, scowling. Even worse than accepting help from Abby was admitting when she was right. He could hardly afford to make a habit of barhopping, seedy or otherwise, especially if he spent money the way he had the other night. Certainly his wallet had been lighter than expected when he checked it the next morning—probably overgenerously tipping the bartender and cab driver. Not that he could remember. "We can fight this out later," he muttered.

Abby lowered her hand. "I'll win. I always win. Break your arm if I have to."

He didn't react, just stared out at the sky, knowing she was right. Some things never changed. If he had the balls God gave a gopher, he'd tell her to fuck off. Move out, let her deal with the hassle of finding a real tenant. *She'd beat the living shit out of me*, he thought, and chuckled.

Abby tilted her head and narrowed her eyes. "What's so funny?"

"Just easily amused." He clapped his hands. "Okay, time to run. Doc says exercise, by God I'm gonna exercise."

She rolled her eyes and started back inside, then stopped. "What about Patch?"

"Don't worry. I'll look for him while I'm out."

"Her. Patch is a her."

"Right. Her. She's always been a boy to me."

Abby smiled and pulled her robe tight. "Run hard. Don't fret. Find Patch." She patted him on the cheek, then slipped inside and closed the door.

Blizzard. That'd be an excuse. It was Sunday. If he looked first and found Patch, he could put him—her, it, whatever—inside before Julie woke up, and still have time to run before the traffic started. Not like he ever managed to run very far. Besides, he wouldn't feel like searching after his run. He'd feel like drinking coffee and staring into space and begging his sister to rub his feet. Not that she would. She'd stop charging rent, but she wouldn't rub his fucking feet.

Patch then. His breath billowed white behind him as he trotted down the steps and headed up the street. As he passed the tidy little houses to either side, he imagined they stared at him with dark windows. Peter had lived on this street for two and a half years, but he still didn't know most of his neighbors. Portland Mole People, he called them, huddled inside their Portland bungalows, wrapped in Portland earth-tone clothes, with their groomed yards and flower beds filled with purple and green kale. He seldom saw them, though when he did, most were friendly enough in a distant *I'll-say-Hi-but-won't-tell-you-my-name* sort of way. This distinction served to remind him that he didn't live in Lexington anymore, where a careless hello bought you a cup of instant coffee and insight into a stranger's family history going back four generations.

Half a block up from his house, Peter came to a break in the kale-clad yards, a little shrub and posy-lined path called the Klickitat Mall, which formed the east entrance to Irving Park. The asphalt path ran west through the park between two soccer fields, then turned south and rose among tall cedars, firs, maples, and elms. At the end of the path, where Ninth abutted the south edge of the park, huddled the bark-chip-floored playground.

The park was empty. A breeze kicked up at his back, remnants of the east wind. He was dressed for running—sweats, gloves, earmuffs. He rubbed his arms and hoped he'd find Patch quickly. Juniper bushes sheathed in glassy ice lined the path near the playground.

The trees had broken up the snowfall so that only a light dusting covered the ground. Numerous lumps that might be a stuffed animal hid under the snow. Peter thought back to what he and Julie had done the day before. Mostly they'd stuck to the play structure, which served alternately as sailboat or castle, or to the swings—a tremulous endeavor as Peter suffered the final dregs of his extended hangover. Under the play structure, he found an empty forty-ouncer and a sheaf of rolling papers he hadn't noticed the day before. A pack of matches with the heads all burnt. A condom wrapper. But no Patch. The swings looked no more promising. Peter kicked through the bark chips as the wind blew glittering spirals of snow off the trees above. It might have been pretty if he didn't feel so damned cold.

At the edge of the playground, over a fence that separated the park from someone's back yard, Peter saw a big yellow mutt staring at him. Bored with his search, Peter stared back. "Have you seen Patch?" he said. "She's a dog, too." The mutt stared, motionless. "Hello-o-o-o, pooch. Bark-bark?"

"Hey, bud! You harassing my dog?" Peter jumped as an old man appeared on the back porch of the house. He fixed Peter with a scowl, his forehead wrinkled, white caterpillar eyebrows bunched beneath a bald, liver-spotted pate. He was dressed in a bulky parka and rubber hip waders. The dog didn't move.

"I was just—" Peter lost his words beneath the weight of the old man's glower.

But then the old man grinned. "Had ya there!" he said, and laughed. He whistled. "Come on, Bo! Going fishing!" The dog released a clipped bark, then bounded onto the porch. The old man tussled its head and neck. "Hope you find Paunch, bud!" Without another word, man and dog disappeared into the house.

Peter stood staring at the empty porch for a moment. *Crazy old man. That might be an excuse.* He turned his attention back to the playground. Time to find that damn Patch before he froze his ass off.

They'd skipped the slide. Julie didn't like the height, and besides, it smelled like someone had pissed in the landing zone. The teeter-totters were hopeless. Julie wanted to ride, but Peter's 180 pounds threatened to launch her 35 into orbit. Still, Julie had wandered over that way once, so Peter nosed around them for a moment or two. Cigarette butts. But no Patch. He himself had vetoed the merry-go-round. "You wouldn't want Uncle Pete to toss your mommy's Christmas cookies, would you?" *No, Unker Pete.* With diminishing hope, Peter looked under the play structure again. He found old Popsicle sticks and the end of a half-eaten candy cane. Still no Patch.

He considered returning later with Julie, putting her Patch-radar to work. Then he recalled that as their time had crept to an end the day before, Julie had drifted toward the far end of the playground to a big jumble of concrete cylinders, sections of sewer pipe painted playful colors. Some stood on end, some lay on their sides, all different lengths and diameters, all big enough for a four-year-old to crawl through. A low wall encircled them with an opening that faced the playground. Peter had been tired—no way could he keep up with the hummingbird energy of a preschooler—but he'd let Julie explore for a few minutes before he coaxed her back to the house.

Frostbite. Not nuclear winter, but Abby could hardly argue. Some of the pipes were three or four feet around and as much as ten feet long. The wall had captured no end of dead leaves and old newspapers tossed by the Gorge wind. An extra thick layer of blown snow had collected as well. He found a brown leather purse, nothing inside, and a pair of mucked-up gloves. He kicked up a doll head and a mud-caked pink bandana. No Patch. The pipes cut the wind, and the exertion of clambering among them warmed him up a little. At the end of one long tube, his foot slid on ice. Then the ice cracked and his foot sank into a puddle. Thick, dark fluid welled up and soaked the snow black. He lifted his shoe. The fluid left a dark purple stain on the dingy white leather.

"Damn it," he grumbled. He was starting to wonder if Patch was worth all this. A couple sheets of newspaper covered a heap of trash or something inside the tube. He made out ads for car dealerships and home furnishings. After-Christmas sales. Bargains, bargains, bargains. Sticking out from under the newspaper at the end of the pipe he saw a round protrusion of grayish brown cloth.

"Finally," he muttered, grabbing the cloth. He abruptly let go. It wasn't Patch. It was firm and cold and it resisted his tug. He gazed at the newspaper. He knew transients often slept in the park. The pipe might offer shelter from the nasty east wind, but maybe not enough on a really cold night. A bubbling, watery feeling filled his gut. He looked around helplessly, but no one was there. Not even the crazy old man and his dog.

"This is such bullshit," he said. He lifted the newspaper anyway. Morbid curiosity pushed him that far. One nylon-clad foot was tucked under the other, both shoeless. Another sheet of newspaper covered the upper half of the body, but he saw a red skirt hiked up to a contorted waist, pale underwear ripped at the seams. Two pallid, blotchy hands, their painted fingernails split, protruded from under the paper and seemed to grope toward the knees. Nylons down around the ankles, legs blue-white and twisted. A red-black hole below the hip. Dark blood had drained from the hole, down out of the lip of the pipe and frozen. He'd stepped in it. From the size of the flow, Peter felt certain there were more holes in the woman. Lots of them, maybe. *Jesus.* The watery feeling dropped through his bowels into his legs, and he tried to stand. Gravity resisted his effort. Vaguely, he decided to leave the other piece of newspaper in place. Morbid curiosity was one thing. Gazing at a pale, dead face was something else altogether.

But, hey, dead body. *That* was an excuse.

TWO

PETER WAITED BESIDE DETECTIVE Kadash and watched two uniformed police officers string yellow tape around the west end of the playground. *Police Line—Do Not Cross.* No one was around to cross except him and Kadash, and they'd already crossed. Peter supposed the uniformed officers were allowed to cross, too. They seemed remarkably unconcerned by the presence of the corpse just a few feet away. Kadash turned to him. "You want some coffee or something? I got a thermos in the car."

I got a thermos in the cupboard in my kitchen, Peter thought. *Big deal.*

"Can't offer you no donuts. Hope you weren't after donuts." Kadash laughed, a sour, raspy sound. "Don't even like donuts, not like them TV cops. I'm a strudel man myself."

"I can believe it," Peter said. Kadash chuckled, unperturbed. He was a short, potato-shaped man, thin gray hair on top, rumpled brown suit underneath. A red patch of skin flaked at his neck and quivered when he tipped his head back to drink. Peter thought of the blue skin on the dead woman's thigh. The cherry patch on Kadash's neck pulsed in florid contrast. Peter shuddered and turned away.

"Sorry to make you wait," Kadash said. "I'd take your statement, but my partner'll be here soon and she's better at it—doesn't scare the chickies."

"I already told you everything."

Kadash smiled. "Yeah, well, she'll wanna talk to you anyway. She's funny that way."

"I don't mind waiting," Peter lied. He wasn't going to admit to Kadash that he was pretty sure he'd feel the same about any cop who asked him questions.

"Yeah, sure." Kadash slurped his coffee. "Nobody likes waitin' for the detective when they got a story like yours gurgling in their belly."

Peter's story wasn't gurgling under his belt. It resided somewhere deeper, a coiled snake in his bowel. On the Seventh Avenue side of the park, he saw a dark gray sedan pull up. A slender woman in a dark raincoat, jeans, and white cross-trainers got out and walked toward them past the tennis courts. She tilted her head into the wind and crossed the police line without hesitation. No one stopped her. Her raincoat hung open and she had her hands half tucked into her jeans pockets. Peter saw a gold badge clipped to her belt. She'd scraped her dusty blond hair back into a loose ponytail. One of the officers nodded to her and she nodded back. She ignored the concrete pipes and came straight up to Peter and Kadash.

Kadash tossed the last of his coffee onto the bark chips. "Morning, Susan."

"Little careless with your coffee in a crime scene." She took her hands out of her pockets and pulled her raincoat closed.

Kadash colored and gestured toward the pipes. "All the action's over there."

"Be glad the DA isn't here yet." She glanced around. "In any case, good morning."

"Not very, I suppose." Kadash cleared his throat. "This is Peter McKrall. He found the stiff." Kadash turned to Peter. "This is my partner, Detective Mulvaney."

Peter nodded, attempted a smile. It felt more like a grimace.

Mulvaney nodded back. A morning of nods. "Why don't you bring me up to date, Sarge?"

Kadash dug into the pocket of his suit coat and fished out a leather-bound notepad. "Let's see here." He flipped through a couple of pages. "9-1-1 receives an emergency call at 7:22 a.m., Sunday, December 26, from one Peter McKrall of 3351 Northeast Eleventh. That's you." He eyed Peter over his notebook. "Caller reports a body in the playground at Irving Park, and reluctantly agrees to meet a cruiser at the southwest corner of the park near the tennis courts. Two cruisers arrive at the park at 7:33 a.m. and Mister McKrall shows the officers to the scene. Officer Kietz notes that the victim is beyond resuscitation. A Popsicle. Scene secured by 7:38 a.m. Detective Skin Kadash—that's me—" He bobbed his furry eyebrows. "—arrives at 7:45 a.m. I confirm the scene is in fact secure and in no immediate danger of being disturbed by weather or other effects. I perform my initial examination of the area and comfort the witness." A guttural chuckle. "At 8:06 a.m., Detective Susan Mulvaney—" He looked over his notebook at Mulvaney. "—that's you—"

"Thank you."

"—Detective Mulvaney arrives at the scene and takes charge. Weather overcast and colder than a Baptist granny at a sock hop. Kietz is getting the temperature."

"ETA on Ident?"

"They'll be here any minute. And the ME, too. Huxley's the call-out from the DA."

"Okay, thanks. Why don't you take a look around, check in with the others?"

Kadash winked at Peter. "No prob." He ambled off and Mulvaney turned to Peter. "Mister McKrall, I'm sorry we have to meet under these circumstances."

Peter shrugged.

"Please tell me what happened. What brought you to the park so early?"

She was direct, this one. None of that chatting-you-up, pretending-to-be-friends bullshit. He cleared his throat. "I was looking for my niece's stuffed animal." Mulvaney didn't say anything, and after a moment Peter continued. "Julie—she's four—and I were playing here yesterday. Last night, we found out she had lost her little dog and we thought she might have left it here. It was too dark to look last night so I came when I woke up this morning."

"Who's 'we'? Julie's parents?" Mulvaney's face was mostly expressionless. Her eyes were green and comforting in a distant sort of way. But sharp, too, rapidly bouncing from spot to spot. Taking everything in. Definitely a cop. Her cheeks were high and smooth, and her nose straight and her lips thin, adding a touch of severity to an otherwise pleasant face.

"My sister Abby and her husband are staying with me. Well, it's their house, actually, but I'm renting from them. They came on Christmas Eve."

"Where from?"

"Seattle. They're going home tonight."

"Did they see this?"

"No. I told them what I found. Not a lot of details, but they woke up while I was calling 9-1-1 and wanted to know what was going on. They stayed home with Julie." More like Abby caught him puking in the toilet and, after squeezing the story out of him, badgered him into calling 9-1-1. But whatever. It's not like he wanted some kids to head to the park for a little after-Christmas fun and end up with blood on their shoes instead.

"I don't blame them," Mulvaney said. She paused and looked him over. Her intense green gaze made Peter uncomfortable. He wanted to be somewhere else. Anywhere else. Her eyes paused at the stain on his shoe. "You're a runner?" she said.

The chatting-you-up part. "Sort of. I mean, I try. I haven't been at it long."

"I try myself. It's hard to want to get out in weather like this." He guessed she'd said that because she wanted him to relax a little. She didn't seem to Peter like the kind of person who let a little cold or snow keep her off the road.

"So what happened when you got to the park?"

"I already explained this to Detective Kadash."

She tilted her head sideways and smiled a little. "Well, we have to hear it over and over again. You know how cops are."

"What do you mean by that?" Peter said, too quickly.

19

Her smile faded. She gazed at him impassively, and he immediately regretted his question. The moment stretched between them, then she looked away and shrugged. "The thing is, Mr. McKrall, we ask a lot of the same questions over and over again because often people recall something the second or third time that slipped their minds the first."

Which Peter already knew. His sticky fingers had resulted in a lifetime's share of one-on-one time with the police. *Just talk to the woman*, he told himself, *and get it over with*. Yet he wondered why in hell he couldn't stand up to Abby once in a frigging blue moon. Would it have been so bad to let someone else find the woman? If Abby was so goddamn eager, why didn't she get her ass out here herself to freeze and get grilled by cops?

Peter sucked air while Mulvaney waited. "Well, I was poking around trying to remember all the places Julie and I had been," he said at last. "I figured finding Patch was going to be a pain, because of the snow."

"Did you see anyone else in the park this morning?"

"Not exactly." Peter gestured toward the fence. "There was an old guy who came out onto his porch there to let his dog in. He asked me what I was doing and I told him. He said good luck and something about going fishing, then he and the dog went back in."

Mulvaney glanced toward the fence. "He didn't say anything to suggest he knew about the body?"

"No. He was kind of jovial, cracking jokes and stuff."

"Some people can joke about anything."

"You don't really think that old coot had something to do with this," Peter said.

Mulvaney raised her shoulders. "Probably not. He may have heard or seen something, though. Detective Kadash and I'll talk to him." She paused and gazed at the house for a moment. "Did you see any footprints in the snow when you got here?"

"I didn't really pay attention to that."

"But you walked around a lot."

"Well, yeah. My search was a lot of back and forth."

"Okay. Well, that tells us something. Go on."

"I was looking around those pipes"—Peter waved vaguely toward the playground—"when I saw what looked like the end of one of Patch's legs sticking out from under some newspapers. When I grabbed it I realized it wasn't Patch. It was her toe. Then I thought maybe it was a transient who'd fallen asleep under the newspaper. It was so cold that I worried maybe they'd frozen to death. But when I lifted the papers, I saw all the blood."

"You only touched her toe?"

"Yeah. And the newspaper."

"Why do you think you mistook her toe for your little dog?"

"Well, she was wearing stockings or pantyhose, I think. Stockings, I guess. They were grayish, like Patch."

Mulvaney nodded thoughtfully. "Okay. What did you do then?"

"I ran home and called you guys." Approximately.

"Did you touch anything else on the body?"

"No. I mean, all the blood, and the bullet hole. And her skin was so pale. I was sure she was dead. I mean, I guess I could have checked, but she was so, I don't know—"

"I understand. Sometimes there's just no doubt." She paused. "Was there snow on the newspapers before you lifted them?"

21

He thought about it. "Well, I wasn't paying much attention at the time. But I think there was, where they stuck out of the pipe. I didn't see the—the body at first because of the papers. God, I stepped in her blood, before I realized she was there." He felt moistness in his eyes and looked away. When he looked back at her, everything seemed a little darker.

"Do you feel okay?" she said.

"I—" Peter hesitated. The question surprised him. He wasn't used to cops asking questions like that. Without warning, the snake in his belly uncoiled. Mulvaney's features blurred. The world went crystalline gray and his stomach rumbled. Bitter acid rose in his throat. His head swam. He started to sway. Suddenly he felt a cool, soft hand on the back of his neck. "Close your eyes," Mulvaney said quietly. "Take slow deep breaths. Put your hands on your knees if you need to." He closed his eyes and that helped a little, but his gut lurched and filled his mouth with bile. He swallowed reflexively, but his stomach tried to fight its way up through his throat.

"I feel like I'm going to be sick."

"Try to breathe. I'll walk you over to the picnic table so you can sit down."

"I don't think—I don't think I can walk." Peter lowered his head and propped himself up with his hands on his knees. He breathed. For a long, spinning moment, he thought he would topple over, or puke, or both. But then the dizziness began to pass and his stomach climbed back down out of his throat.

"You can sit down right here if you need to," she said.

"I'll be all right." He raised his head and opened his eyes. Mulvaney stared at him. "You're sure?" she said. At that moment, the bile surged upward again. He managed to drop his chin before a thin yellow jet squirted between his lips and splashed onto Mulvaney's shoes. He gasped. In an instant, a wave of dizziness and nausea swept through him and fled.

"Shit. I'm sorry." He wondered if the vomit would stain her shoes.

She seemed to be wondering the same thing. She peered downward, lips tight. But then she looked up and said, "Feel better?"

He took a breath. Puking appeared to be just what he'd needed. "Uh. Yeah, sure." He thought he'd emptied the reservoir at the house. Hopefully this was the last of it.

"Let's go sit down," she said.

Mulvaney led him to a picnic bench at the edge of the playground. She rubbed her shoes in the grass, then said, "Sit and rest for a few minutes. I'll need to get some more details from you, but that can wait for the moment. I'm going to look things over and I'll get back with you, okay?"

"Fine." Peter glanced toward the pipes, the body, then back at Mulvaney. "I suppose you see a lot of this sort of thing."

She paused a moment, then said, "It's my job, so, yes, I do."

"Well…I don't."

She searched his face with her green eyes. "I would hope not." She glanced toward Kadash and the others. "I'll be back. Walk around some, or go sit in my car if you're cold." She motioned vaguely over her shoulder toward Seventh. "The gray Sentra. It's unlocked."

"I'm fine." Like he was going to voluntarily get into a cop's car.

She joined Kadash and one of the uniformed officers among the pipes. A van pulled up at Seventh and parked. A woman and a man got out and pulled large black cases from the back of the van, carried them through the police line, and set them beside the wall encircling the pipes. Peter stood and stretched and walked up onto the asphalt path. He half considered taking up Mulvaney's offer of the car, but only because it was so frigging cold.

What he really wanted was to go home. Find Patch and take her back to Julie and have none of this happen. He moved slowly, staring at his feet, arms folded across his chest. Probably Patch would turn up at the house, way back behind the toilet, or stuffed into Julie's coat sleeve. Peter sighed again. A morning of nods, a morning of sighs. The snow was starting to melt at the edge of the path. Overhead, through the branches of a tall cedar, the gray, shapeless sky went on forever. He found the view of his feet more comforting.

He turned his back to the playground and gazed restlessly up the slope between the boles of the cedars. Snow-dusted junipers sprawled across the muddy ground. After a long sightless moment, Peter realized a figure stood just beyond the shrubs, a young man peering back at him.

For a moment their eyes locked. The young man seemed small and thin in a blue wool coat that looked a size or two too large for him. His hair was short and dark and combed to one side, his eyes large and unblinking. His hands pressed into his coat pockets. Peter sensed an unsettled air about him. Suddenly he felt very exposed. He turned to look for Mulvaney.

Nobody near. Mulvaney stood at the far end of the playground, Kadash out of sight. Peter looked back up the slope but in the barest moment he'd turned away, the young man had vanished. Peter scanned the slope. He saw no one, no movement. He half wondered if he'd imagined the fellow, manufactured him out of his listless melancholy. But that seemed crazy. Probably just a rubbernecker who decided to duck the attention of the police. Maybe he even thought Peter was a cop himself. Peter could sympathize. He'd flee, too, if he could. He shook his head. If the cops wanted to talk to the guy, the cops could chase him down on their own. *None of my business anyway.* None of it was.

More cars came and parked on Seventh. Grave men and women wandered through the playground, prodding at things with pencils. Gawkers gathered at the yellow police tape, murmuring solemnly to each other. Early risers from the neighborhood, maybe even from the houses adjoining the park. One woman still in her bathrobe. Peter wondered if any of them had seen anything or heard anything, or if any of them knew the dead woman. Did someone miss her? Had one of those people awakened to a cold empty spot in his bed, or perhaps decided it was time to start sleeping alone? Was there a killer in the crowd, or was it just an anonymous group of anybodies abuzz with the break in routine? Probably Detective Mulvaney wondered the same, and would get around to them before too much time passed. For the moment, her attention seemed fixed on the concrete pipes.

Another van, the words *Multnomah County Medical Examiner* on its side, pulled off Seventh onto the grass and drove slowly past the tennis courts. It stopped next to the shelter house. A man in a navy jacket climbed out and went to stand with Mulvaney. They talked. Every once in a while, Mulvaney looked in his direction. As far as Peter could tell, no one touched anything, except with their pencils.

He walked back to the picnic table and sat down. At one point he heard a voice call, "Thirty-five degrees." In his reverie he had all but forgotten the cold, or perhaps it had settled into him so thoroughly that he no longer distinguished between the temperature of his body and that of the air around him. He glanced at the blood-stain on his shoe and shuddered.

"Mister McKrall?" Peter looked up and saw a cop, one of the two who'd responded to his 9-1-1. "They need you over there." The cop headed back toward Mulvaney and the man in the navy jacket. Peter followed slowly.

Mulvaney nodded as he approached. "This is Dan Halley," she said. "He's a deputy medical examiner. He has a few questions."

Halley was a thick, sturdy-looking man with short salt-and-pepper hair. Peter accepted his extended hand with conspicuous reluctance. "Don't worry, friend," Halley said. "I haven't touched her yet." Kadash laughed and Halley grinned as Peter searched fruitlessly for a response. "Okay," Halley went on, "just a couple of things to get straight. You were climbing around on the pipes, stepped in a puddle of blood—which you didn't at first recognize as blood—"

"It was black."

"Right. Black. Sometimes is. Okay, stepped in the blood, grabbed the toe, lifted the newspaper, saw the corpse. In that order. Did I leave anything out?"

Peter looked at Mulvaney. She gazed back expressionlessly. "No. That was it."

"Touch anything else?"

Peter shook his head.

"Not the leg or anything?" Halley said. "It was a nice leg." Peter felt his stomach rumble anew. Halley raised an eyebrow. "Felt her up, maybe?" he added. Kadash guffawed and others snickered quietly.

Peter shifted uncomfortably. "Listen, I already explained this."

Halley grunted. "So? Explain it again."

Peter fought down a rising wave of indignation. *It's not gonna help to get pissed off.* He sucked in a deep breath. "I might have put my hand on one of the pipes for balance or something, but I didn't touch anything on the body except—what you mentioned."

"The toe. That's what I mentioned. Did you have those gloves on?"

"Yes."

"And you just touched the toe."

"Yes. The toe. I touched the toe! That's it!" Peter managed to keep from raising his voice, but just barely. "I just found her," he said. The faintly dubious look on Halley's face caused Peter's anger to swell again. "Listen, I didn't ask to find her, and I didn't grope her after I did, nice leg or not!" Halley's eyes widened as Peter added, "If you think she was so hot why don't *you* go feel her up?" Even as the words left his mouth he regretted them. No one spoke for a long, tight moment. Peter heard someone cough.

"You got spirit, friend," Halley said at last. Then he grinned. "Great. Thanks." He clapped Peter roughly on the shoulder and turned to Mulvaney. "Just had to make sure. Hate to get back to the lab and find this guy's hair all over her, no telling how it got there. I'll bag her hands and work out a preliminary TOD, then Ident can fly at it."

"Thank you," Mulvaney said to him. Halley headed off. Mulvaney said to Peter, "In spite of what you might be thinking, he's good at what he does."

"His mother must be so proud," Peter said.

Mulvaney raised her eyebrows briefly and shook her head. "I'm going to be busy for a while," she said, "so I'd like you to go over what happened again with Detective Kadash. I know it seems tiresome, but there's no telling what little detail might later prove important. He'll see to it you get a ride back home."

Pretty eager to get me into a cop car. Peter pictured Kadash's cherry-colored neck quaking as he talked. He grimaced.

Mulvaney caught the look on Peter's face. "Don't mind Kadash," she said. "He's no Dan Halley. He won't bite. He's been doing this a long time, and many years ago he lost what little couth he may once have possessed. But he's harmless."

Mulvaney called Kadash over and told him what she wanted. "Come on down to the car, bud," Kadash said. "I want some more coffee. We'll chat down there." Mulvaney turned away. Peter followed Kadash past the police line. At the street, he saw a car with a Fox 12 News logo on the side. A blond woman in trench coat and sneakers, a pair of high heels in one hand, stood talking to one of the police officers. The officer pointed to Kadash and Peter as they came down the slope past the tennis courts. A man pulling equipment out of the car tossed the woman a microphone. Kadash was already shaking his head and waving his hands as she approached. "Forget it. I'm not giving you anything," he said.

She looked past Kadash. "Do you really have a body up there, Skin?"

"Well, I guess you know that, don't you? Otherwise, why the hell are you here?"

"Did he find the body?" She waved her heels at Peter.

Kadash sighed and looked back up the slope toward the playground. Mulvaney was out of sight. "None of your fucking business, *Mizz Norris.*"

She flashed a big-toothed smile at Peter. "Hi. I'm Kelly Norris. Fox 12 News." She said to Kadash, "Just give me five minutes. Okay?"

She shot a glance over her shoulder and shook the microphone. "Frankie, can you get me some juice in this thing?"

"Two seconds!"

Norris toed her sneakers off and slipped the heels on one after the other. The effort gained her three inches and a view down onto Kadash's shaking head. "You know better than that, Kelly. It's gotta come from the Information Officer first."

"What about you?" she said to Peter. "He can't stop you from talking."

"I can arrest him," Kadash said.

"Give it a rest, Skin." She rolled her eyes at Kadash, then turned to Peter. "What's your name?"

Peter looked at Kadash, who glared at Norris. "You can't have him till I'm through with him," Kadash grumbled.

Kelly's assistant appeared at her back with camera poised. "Go ahead," he said.

"Just tell me what you found," she said to Peter, ignoring Kadash's glower.

Peter didn't respond. Kadash took him by the arm and pulled him toward the car, and Peter found himself reluctantly following. The microphone sagged in Kelly's hand. "Shit," she said to the cameraman, "Well, grab some tape of them getting into the car."

Peter hesitated. *Jesus.* He could just imagine the news report: "*Detectives questioned Peter McKrall, seen here in the back of an unmarked police cruiser, in connection with the killing...*" Abby would skewer him—by phone, by e-mail, by ESP if she could manage it. He wouldn't be able to get her to shut up about it for days. Kadash tugged impatiently at his arm. Peter pulled his arm free of Kadash's grasp, turned back to Norris. "What do you want to know?"

She grinned, raised the microphone. "You found a body, right? Tell me what you saw, what brought you to the park so early. How you felt about it. That sort of thing."

"Damn it, Kelly," Kadash said, "you know better than to interfere—"

"He'll get with you when I'm through," Kelly said with obvious satisfaction.

Kadash opened his mouth to protest, then seemed to think better of it. Without further comment, he moved over to his car, got out his thermos, and struggled with the cap.

The light of the video camera shone in Peter's eyes and the microphone hovered before his lips. Kelly Norris stared at him, her eyes gleaming. Could be a good story for her, he guessed—body discovered in an urban park by an early morning jogger. *Blood in the snow.* Might even turn out to be someone important. People might watch the news to find out about this one. Maybe even remember her name as the one who reported it. You never knew.

"How I felt about it," he said. Now that it came to the point, he wasn't sure how to proceed. Most likely he'd say something he'd regret. Or something Abby would make him regret.

"Yes. What did you think when you saw the body?"

Peter realized she knew nothing about what had happened. Maybe not even that it was a woman lying up there half buried under newspapers. He thought of Kadash and Halley, and the others. Even Mulvaney had a cold edge to her. *A cop is a cop*, he thought. He gazed at Norris and her cameraman, at Kadash with the thermos. His eyes wandered up beyond the tennis courts to the strip of yellow tape flapping in the breeze, over to the onlookers and their troubled, yet blatantly curious faces. Most of the snow had melted and the grass and bark dust now looked sodden and dank. He felt surrounded by vultures. "I felt—" he began. *Felt her up? Jesus, no!* Was that so hard to believe? He turned back to the camera. A flood of words rose to his lips, but he held them back for a bare moment. *How do I feel about it?* But that wasn't the right question. He looked at all those around him and thought, *How do* you *people fucking feel about it? What's a dead body in the park to you?*

THREE

THE TELEVISION WAS THE only light in the room, blue-white and a little spooky. As the screen shimmered, gray shadows leaped around a haphazard collection of furniture—an old, sprung couch, a black vinyl beanbag chair, a coffee table dotted with cigarette burns, a milk-crate shelf filled with crack-backed paperbacks and video tapes with handwritten labels like *Bunch of Simpsons* and *Mulder Missing X-Files*. The table was bare except for a half-eaten Hostess Apple Pie on a napkin and his gun, an anonymous thirty-two caliber revolver. The TV sat on its own milk crate, rabbit ears wrapped in foil. Through a dark doorway at one end of the couch came the blue gleam of the pilot light from a gas stove. Despite its battered and mismatched quality, the room looked tidy in the ghostly light. The books stood upright on the shelves, not a crumb dirtied the tabletop. Even the fruit pie was carefully centered on the napkin. Jake sat on the couch and scowled at the Sunday evening news, his body wrapped in an old blanket. He clutched a mug of instant coffee in both hands. On television, the guy, Peter Something-or-other, resident of the inner northeast Irvington neighborhood, told Jake and whoever else was watching how upset he was by that morning's murder. "It was horrible," he said, for about the one-millionth time. "... it doesn't even seem possible."

On screen, the guy huffed and puffed. Behind him, Jake saw the tennis courts of Irving Park. They looked different on TV. But it was the guy himself who had Jake's attention. He was thin, with red cheeks and a bump on his nose. One of Jake's foster moms had once told him his nose was as smooth as a ski jump, but not this guy's. Round, obvious eyes and flat ears. Brownish hair, kinda wavy, mussed. "You mostly stay out of the park at night," the guy said, "but not because you think something like this will happen."

"Who cares what you think, jerkwad?" Jake muttered. "You never seen a stupid dead body before?" He felt annoyed. This was the guy, after all. The guy who found her, the guy who puked on the lady cop. But not just that. Jake recognized him. He had seen him before—and not just that morning at the park. Somewhere else.

"What does this do to the neighborhood?" the reporter asked.

The guy shook his head. "No one else from the neighborhood is dead and dumped in the park. No one else is being gaped at and prodded like a piece of mea—" He stopped and ran his hand through his messy hair. *Geez, you'd think it was his sister or something.* "The only thing I can say is that I don't care if it's about drugs or what," the man continued. "I hope they nail this psycho to the wall."

Jake flinched. "Nail yourself to the wall!" he blurted. In his mind, unbeckoned, flashed a half-forgotten memory. The dark, dark room, the half-open door, light streaming in. Low, guttural sounds from the next room, and the voice. The big, booming voice. Jake shook his head. "Damn it," he muttered. "Damn it." He slurped coffee, then set the cup down and grabbed the gun. The blued steel was pitted and black along the short barrel and around the hammer. The gun smelled of burnt powder. As the scene on TV shifted to another view of the park, he stuck the barrel into his mouth and rolled it around on his tongue. He liked the harsh, medicinal flavor of old machine oil and spent gunpowder.

The reporter said, "Police have not speculated on the motive for the killing, though some observers have noted that gang activity recently increased in the area, and Irving Park has been known for drug trafficking in the past. So far, no witnesses to the fatal shooting have been identified, nor has the victim herself. If you have information relating to this case, contact the Portland Police, or call CrimeStoppers at 823-HELP. From Irving Park, this is Kelly Norris for Fox 12 News."

Jake pulled the gun out of this mouth. "Gang related. What do they know?" He tossed the gun onto the coffee table and stood up. The abrupt motion tipped the table and the mug bounced, splashing coffee. The pie and the gun slid off the edge of the table. Jake's body tensed as the weapon hit the floor with a clatter. The blanket fell off his shoulders and onto the couch. He went around the table and looked down at the gun. The impact had forced the hammer into the cocked position. "Oh, boy oh boy." He gingerly picked the gun up and waved it at the TV. The news anchor had gone on to a story about the state budget. "Who cares?" he muttered. "The budget ain't murdered in the park, *heh*." He carefully released the hammer and set the gun down. The pie, now partly mushed, had landed on the napkin. That was something, at least. He wolfed it down, then grabbed a clean sponge from the kitchen. He wiped the sides of the mug and blotted the spilled coffee on the table. Tossed back the last of the coffee. Then he snatched up the gun and went to the window beside the TV. He pushed the drab brown curtain aside a couple of inches. He was in a corner basement apartment. The window faced the alley. Outside, it was already dark and a misty rain fell, half mixed with snow. He saw no one outside.

Across the alley stood another apartment building. Some of the windows on the upper floors had window boxes filled with kale. He stared at the basement window straight across. No window box there. The window was dark. "Stay dark," he said. He held the gun at his side. He wanted to lift it and point it at the window and shoot, but what if someone showed up at just that second? Maybe even a cop. They'd nail him to the wall then, wouldn't they? He shuddered to think of it. He thought about that TV guy—Peter Whatever-His-Name-Was. Peter Head, *heh*. Jake giggled. "I could shoot you," he murmured. "That'll teach you to stare, monkey fracker." He let the curtain fall shut.

He went into the kitchen to wash the mug and the sponge. Or just toss the sponge, get out a new one. He flipped the light switch and a weak fluorescent glow flickered to life. "Peter McStaringhead," he said. Jake giggled again, but then a cold feeling swept over him. *Where had he seen him before?* He pictured Peter moving through the playground. It was weird, the way he'd hunted around, almost as if he was looking for her, as if he *knew* she was there. Jake watched from under the trees, and Peter searched until he found her. *Did you know?* Then he was gone, run off like a pussy. That gave Jake a chance to grab the gloves, at least, before Peter came back with the cops. No worries about footprints, either, the way Peter Head had kicked around in the dusty snow. But later, while the cops did their thing, Jake slipped out to see better. There was Peter, staring back at him. Could anyone else have seen? He and Peter were away from the others, and no one seemed to pay any attention. But maybe they were just pretending not to notice. Maybe they were looking for Jake right now—all because of Peter Head.

Jake saw the phone sitting on the kitchen counter. He considered it for a minute, his thoughts rolling around at a slow but determined pace. Needed more coffee, maybe. Perk his brain up. He set the gun and cup on the counter and pulled open a drawer beneath the phone. The phone book was buried beneath a heap of pizza coupons. *What the hell did that guy think he was staring at anyway?* He got the phone book and flipped through the pages. "What did they say? What was his last name?" McSomething, Peter McSomething. He stopped on the Mc's and thought carefully. "It'll be in the morning newspaper," he said. They got the a.m. edition at the Plaid Pantry by four or so. But Jake wanted to know now. "Nail me to the wall? Nosiree, Bob." The monkey fracker seemed to know *she* was there and he seemed to know Jake was there, and he *stared*. If only Jake could remember where he knew him from. Jake looked at the names on the page. McGuire. McIlvain. McIver. Wasn't that a TV show, something like that? *Heh.* McKean. McKeever. Something like that. He looked up and stared into empty space, tried to picture the news story in his mind. Peter Mc—McWhat? Peter McChicken. He laughed again softly, but a little nervously now, because the more he thought about it, the more he couldn't get the staring and the searching out of his head. Searching. Staring. Finding. He flipped the page. Inner Northeast. Irvington. He looked down and saw it. *McKrall.* Peter McKrall, the only McKrall in the book. "Stupid name." Sounded like some kind of fish. He lifted the receiver off the cradle and dialed the number. It rang twice.

"Hello," a voice said. Jake didn't respond. He tried to imagine the face on the other end of the line. "Hello? . . . Is someone there?" Yeah, that was the voice from the TV all right. Right name, right voice. The address kinda made sense, though Jake hadn't paid much attention to where he'd been, and couldn't have said that Irving Park lay south of Fremont between Seventh and Eleventh if his life depended on it. But he could walk there if he had to . . . or if he wanted to. "Is anyone there? . . . Hello?"

Jake hung up. Suddenly he remembered. The memory popped into his head as abruptly as a bullet. Peter McHead had been with *her*—Jake had seen them just the other night, coming out of that joint together. Couple nights before Christmas. She was being all loud, hanging off of Peter like he owned her.

Jake grabbed the gun. Suddenly he didn't need any more coffee. *Peterhead knew her.*

Jake's thoughts began to swirl: Peterhead leaving the bar with *her*. Peterhead searching the playground. Staring at Jake. On television—"I hope they nail this psycho to the wall." It was all because of her. Had to be. What the hell else could he have been looking for? Jake had thought he'd fixed everything, thought he had made everything all right at last. But it wasn't over. Peterhead was the unexpected wildcard.

Jake swept into the living room. His mind felt swollen and hot. *Peterhead knew something—but he couldn't know everything, could he?* Because he had only stared—he hadn't yelled for the cops. He *knew* her, somehow, he *knew* she was there in the playground. Some kind of psychic, maybe. Picking up vibrations or something. But, so far, he hadn't picked up vibrations about Jake. Not exactly—but he was wondering, wasn't he? Because otherwise why had he stared like that? He was trying to figure things out. And if Jake wasn't careful, maybe Peterhead *would* figure things out. And then what?

Nailed to the wall.

Except Jake wasn't going to let that happen. He was gonna trump the wildcard. He grabbed his coat out of the front closet. It was still kind of damp. He'd washed it twice, and the driers in the laundry room weren't too good. Didn't matter. What with the rain and snow, coat'd be soaked in no time. And if the cop movies were right, he'd probably have to wash it again anyway. Maybe even get rid of it, like his shoes. They could find blood on anything these days, if the movies were right. He returned to the kitchen. He looked at the phone book again and wrote Peterhead's address on the back of his hand with a ball-point pen. *Near the park, near the park*, he thought.

He put the gun in his pocket and went to the front door. Then he remembered he'd shot all the bullets. He'd hidden the extras behind a row of paperbacks on the bottom shelf of the bookcase. He pulled them out and went to the couch. He released the cylinder and let the spent shells drop out. They clattered onto the coffee table with a sound like dropped coins. He carefully loaded six fresh bullets and snapped the cylinder shut, finger-rolled it like they did in the old westerns. He put the empty shells into the ammo box and hid it again behind the books. Then he grabbed her box of rubbers from where he'd hidden it behind the picture of the woman with the bald guy on the top of the bookshelf. Didn't know what he'd do with them—didn't have a plan at all, really—but something would come to him. Peterhead would wish he'd never messed with Jake, that was for sure. He stuffed the gun and the rubbers into his coat pocket, and went to the door, listened. No sound from the hallway. He opened the door and looked out, didn't see anyone in the hallway. He left the TV and lights on. Make them think someone was home all night. *Heh*. He took the side door out of the building into the alley and slipped away into the wet darkness.

FOUR

THE PHONE RANG SHORTLY after the late news ended. Peter snapped out of a fitful doze and sat up. He'd slumped to his side on the couch with the TV remote in one hand and an empty water glass in the other. All the lights in the living room were on. He muted an infomercial for an electronic device that claimed to duplicate the effect of a face-lift without the bother of surgery—*how much would you pay?*—and grabbed the phone off the end table.

"We're home at last," Abby said breathlessly. "Safe and sound. Barely."

He glanced at his watch. "What happened?" he asked, not really interested. "I expected you to call a couple of hours ago."

"The weather's a beast. Freezing rain and snow most of the way. We could only drive about thirty miles an hour. People were spinning out all over the highway."

"Sorry I missed it. I watered the plants and potted the amaryllis bulbs Hank sent me. Trimmed the quince."

"Peter, if you took care of yourself half as well as you do those plants … did you do anything else, for heaven's sake?"

"Not really."

"No barhopping or drunken binging?"

"Jesus! I watched *Columbo* on A&E! Does that satisfy you?"

Abby ignored his churlishness. "Is it too late to trade places with you? Julie was fussy all the way from Centralia. 'Where's Patch? Where's Patch? I want Patch,'" Abby cleared her throat. "And of course, all the maniacs in their four-by-fours were trying to drive like it was the Indy 500. They slid around like everyone else."

"So much for four-wheel drive."

Abby chuckled. "Ours worked well enough, for a wimpy little station wagon. But I thought Dave was going to have an aneurysm, he was so tense. If it keeps up like this all night, nobody's going to work tomorrow."

"I wasn't going myself, but that's the magic of unemployment. Just think—if you'd known about the snow you could have had another day here in bright and cheerful Portland. Maybe find your own corpse."

Abby didn't respond. He could imagine her pursed lips, the disapproval on her face. After a moment she said, "Is it snowing there?"

"More slush than snow, but it's sticking. I'm about to break out the skis."

"Yeah, right. What skis?"

"I watched some guy on cross-country skis go through the park earlier. I could hit him in the head with a rock and take his. He must not have seen the news. 'Course, he didn't go up by the playground."

There was a long pause. He'd been expecting a long pause at some point during the call. He heard the static of bad weather on the line. "Are you okay, Peter?" Abby said at last.

He shrugged, indifferent to the fact that she couldn't see him. "I'm fine."

"You sure? I would have stayed, you know."

"Yeah, I know. I'll be okay. I'm not the one with the problem. I'm still breathing. With healthy lungs even."

Another pause. "Peter, it wasn't Mom, okay? It wasn't the same thing at all."

"I never said it was Mom." He felt his face grow warm. Too quickly, he added, "Did I even once suggest that it had anything to do with Mom?"

"No. Of course not. You never *say* it."

Well you never shut up about it, Peter thought. But he kept his trap shut. Despite his sudden agitation, he didn't want to turn the conversation into a fight.

"Mmm, yeah, well—" Her voice trailed off. After a moment, Abby drew a noisy breath, then said, "Did you watch the news?"

Let him off the hook. Maybe she didn't want to fight, either. "Must be a slow day. It was the lead story on 12 and 8."

"What was the lead on the other channels?"

"Bill Clinton buying pornography from the gay children of Senate Republicans. Shit, I don't know. But the murder came up, and me with it. My Warhol moment. I was pretty shrill, especially on channel 12. And man, what a slant they put on it. 'Man Freaked Out by Murder in Park.' Like how I felt had anything to do with it at all."

"Well, Kelly Norris is an idiot, and it's not the first time she told the wrong story. At least you had a chance to calm down before the guy from 8 showed up."

"Thank God for small favors. They still haven't identified her."

"That's terrible. I wonder if she had any family anywhere. You'd think someone would be worrying about her."

"You'd think."

Abby breathed into the phone. "So what are the police making of it?"

"Like I know."

"You watched the news. What did they say?"

"They are considering robbery as a possible motive, though they're not ruling out anything. I still can't believe it even happened. You always said Irving Park was kind of rough, but this sort of brought it home, you know?"

"Peter, this isn't Irving Park. Irving Park is small-time drug deals and teenage boys lipping off to each other. I don't deny that in days gone by I might've heard what sounded like gunshots from the park, but far more often than not they were firecrackers, not cold-blooded killings. Children play soccer and Little League there."

"Last night they weren't firecrackers."

"I know, Peter." Abby sighed. "Listen, you're probably worn out. I know I am. This has been a hard day after a long weekend. Why don't you get some sleep?"

"Such a good parent. Actually I was dozing when you called."

"Then hit the sack. I'm heading that way myself. Dave and Julie have both already passed out. I'll call you in the morning."

Don't do me any favors, he thought. But he only said, "G'night."

He cradled the phone. On TV, a grinning woman who clearly didn't need it ran the electro-face-lifter over one side of her face. Her cheek twitched in galvanic delight. An 800-number flashed on screen. *Just three easy payments and you can look younger, too.* Peter watched in mindless fascination, sound still muted. After a moment, unswayed by the lure of taut flesh, he shook his head and thumbed the remote. The house seemed especially quiet. He left the water glass on the arm of the couch and went from room to room flipping off lights and pulling shades. He stopped in the darkened dining room and gazed out the back window. The snow had changed to freezing rain, then tapered off. No skiers out now. Mercury-vapor lights throughout the park lit the frozen snow with a pallid spectral glow. Peter stared out the window for a long time. "Are you out there, Patch?" he said. Hiding in the bark chips? Consorting with baby doll heads and condom wrappers? Buried under ice-glazed snow? Maybe it would be spring before the old hound turned up again, like some mountain hiker who wandered off the path.

Peter lowered the blind. He gave a quick once-over to the shelves of plants on either side of the window, then trudged into his bedroom. There, he kicked off his shoes and jeans and slid into bed. When he closed his eyes, an image came to mind of white, twisted legs. He shook his head and tried to think of anything else, but the image returned, pushing away even thoughts of the woman's gleeful rictus from the infomercial. After a time, he drifted into an uneasy sleep and dreamed of pale, disembodied legs racing ahead of him through the park, somehow contriving to hide Patch over and over again, no matter how close he came to finding the tattered hound.

An abrupt sound—a dull, heavy *clunk*—dragged him out of his dark slumber. He listened for a moment, but the sound didn't repeat. Part of another dream perhaps. *Tumbling legs, falling bodies.* He lay in stillness, waiting, but the silence pressed around him like a blanket. He just started to doze off again when the jangling of the telephone jerked him upright. He lurched out of bed and stumbled toward the hallway, then stopped and turned. The phone rang again. He felt around on his bedside table and finally found the receiver. "Hello?"

There was no response. "Hello?" He caught a glimpse of the red numbers of the clock glowing in the darkness. 2:24. "Hello? Who's there? Hello?" The sound of falling rain greeted him. "Great," he said. "Thank you for waking me up. Call again anytime." He dropped the phone carelessly onto the hook. It was the second such call that night. Kadash had warned him he might get crank calls, with his name and face appearing on TV. He flopped back onto his bed and debated taking the phone off the hook or letting the answering machine get it. Before he could make up his mind, the phone rang again. He reached over and clicked the light on. He glared at the phone. 2:28 now. A dull throb of anger pulsed at the base of his neck. He picked up the receiver. "Hello," he said through his teeth. No one answered. "Talk, goddammit." Far away he heard the faint, staccato chatter of distant conversations, and maybe the sound of soft breathing. "Listen, I don't know who the hell you are but it's time to amuse yourself with someone else's phone number." *Definitely take the phone off the hook.*

"I'm sorry," a hushed voice said. "I'm sorry." He heard quiet weeping. The sound reminded him of Julie and Patch. His anger faded, replaced by abrupt unease. "Who's there?" he said. "Is that you, Abby?"

"I—I—" The voice hesitated. "I shouldn't have called. I'm sorry."

Not Abby. Female, but definitely not Abby. The voice was too raspy, too breathy. The realization provided a sharp measure of relief. He wasn't sure he was up to Abby weeping on the phone. "Who is this?" he said.

There was the briefest hesitation, then, "Darla." He heard a shallow cough. "My name is Darla. I was—I mean, I'm—" The voice faltered again. A young woman, an older girl? He couldn't quite tell. He heard another soft cough. "That was my mother you found in the park."

Heat surged through his feet and hands. "Jesus," he said. "Jesus." He stood up. "How do you know that?"

The weeping grew stronger. "I know it's my mom," she gasped. "I know it is."

"Oh my God." Peter started to pace within the narrow range of the phone cord, struggling for something to say. Unexpectedly, the faces of Mulvaney and Kadash appeared in his mind and he blurted, "Have you talked to the police?"

The weeping stopped. "I ain't talking to no cops."

"Listen, I can understa—"

"No frigging *cops!*" Peter heard a loud slam and the connection severed. He held the receiver against his ear for a moment, then hung up.

"Oh, holy shit," he muttered. He sat down on the edge of the bed and ran his hand through his hair. It was damp with sweat. The clock showed 2:30. He stared at the red numbers until they changed to 2:35 ... 2:36.

"Darla," he said aloud. The name sounded strange against the stiff silence of late night. *All I wanted was to find Patch. Not to talk to people whose mothers might be dead.* He didn't want to even think about mothers who might be dead. Peter realized he had already come to think of the woman as a cipher. No history, no family. Half a mannequin, discarded in the park. But with an unexpected phone call, legs became a mother with a daughter—maybe with other daughters, maybe sons, maybe a husband. People who didn't want to hear she'd been murdered. People who wanted her to come home.

"I don't have anything to do with this," he said, looking at the phone. "Why the fuck did you call me?" He supposed he ought to tell Kadash and Mulvaney about the call as soon as possible. It would be the good citizen thing to do, and all that. He suspected they wouldn't even mind if he called tonight. He didn't know how the phones worked exactly, but there'd be computer records or something, at least temporary ones, and knowing sooner rather than later would probably help them out. Like he cared about helping out cops. Of course, they'd fuck with him if they found out he'd gotten this call without telling them. Sighing, he got up and headed for the living room to find Mulvaney's card.

He hesitated in the hallway. So the call is traced—then what? The police find this Darla, learn her mother's identity. That was probably important, perhaps key to finding her killer. But Darla could have as easily called the police, and the fact that she hadn't troubled Peter. If she was involved in the murder somehow, it seemed all the more important that he call Mulvaney. On the other hand, Darla might have a perfectly good reason for avoiding the cops. Outstanding parking tickets, a phobia of men in uniform. A keen disinterest in being fucked over. Anything. As far as Peter was concerned, Kadash alone served as reason enough. Maybe he should just leave it alone. Let the police do their job and stay the hell out of it. He'd found the mother, hadn't he? Let the cops find the daughter.

The phone rang, jarring electronic chirps from the living room and bedroom that raised an unnerving clamor in stereo. *Let it ring or talk to her?* Maybe he could learn something, something to tell the cops. Or maybe he could let the machine get it and get the hell on with his life. For all he knew, she was the killer. He always found it hard to let a phone ring, one of many compulsions. Yet he stood in the hallway, stood his ground. Abby would be proud. After the fourth ring he heard a beep and his own voice—*leave a message after the tone.*

"I'm sorry," he heard her say, brassy but clear enough through the answering machine speaker. "I'm sorry. Please answer. I won't get mad again."

Involuntarily, he took a step. Was she trying to work him, or was the forlorn desperation in her voice genuine? He found himself wondering what Abby would do in his place. Sure. Abby would assume the caller was the killer, and be on the phone to the cops as fast as she could think of it. That was enough for Peter. He went into the living room and picked up the extension from the end table. "Darla." Abby could say what she wanted—she wasn't the one who found the body.

Hesitation. Then, "I shouldn't have gone off on you like that."

Stay calm, he thought. *Listen. Take notes, string her along, whatever. Just stay calm.* "It happens," Peter said. It wasn't always safe to mention the cops around him, either. "What can I do for you?"

"You found my mom."

"What makes you think it was your mom?"

She started crying again. "It can't be nobody else. It's got to be her."

"How do you know? The police don't even know who it was."

"I know it was my mom. I saw her." Great wet sobs broke against his ear. "She left that place last night, right near the park. But I never saw her go home. Do you see? She never went home! That's how I know it was her."

"Okay," he said. "I understand." He didn't, but he doubted her ability to make herself any clearer. "What do you want me to do?"

"I—I've got to talk to you about her. I got to hear about her. I mean, I want you to tell me what you found." She choked on a sob. "Do you understand what I mean? I got to know what happened," she finished, her voice edged with misery.

A nervous shiver ran down Peter's back. Was she asking for a chance to make some kind of confession? His connection to the dead woman couldn't be more tenuous. He took a deep breath and said, "Darla, listen. Don't hang up, okay? This is important, if you want me to keep talking to you. I need to know why you won't talk to the police."

Her voice took on a hard edge. "I can't talk to the police."

"Why not?"

"All they want to do is screw you over, okay? I'm tired of being screwed over by cops!" The outburst came in a guttural hiss, and for a moment the thin traces of femininity in her voice were lost. "Don't talk to me about the cops, okay?"

"Okay, okay," he said quietly, hoping his soft voice would soothe her. "No cops. Makes sense to me." *Perfect sense*, he thought. "But why me? I don't have anything to do with this."

"You *found* her," she said, her voice plaintive again. "I saw you on TV. You said it was horrible that someone could do that to someone." She paused for a beat. "Were you lying?"

The question surprised him. He found himself pacing back and forth along the edge of the couch. "No, I guess I wasn't."

"I want you to meet me, okay? Please? I want to hear about my mom. Please?"

A small hot knot tightened in his gut. "Wait. No. I can't do that." He stopped pacing, sagged onto the couch. "Darla, I never even knew her."

But her voice pleaded. "*No*body knew her. She didn't have any friends. You're the closest thing to someone who gave a shit about her that I know. I mean, I don't know you, but, well, I mean you said it was horrible. Didn't you say that?"

He sighed. "Yeah, I guess I said that." The knot wouldn't unclench.

"Nobody else is gonna think what happened to my mom was horrible."

"Don't you have a friend or someone else you can talk to? Someone other than—"

Her weeping returned with renewed vigor. "I got no friends, neither. I—I just wanna talk to you about her. Okay?"

Peter hesitated. "I don't know what to say. Maybe you should call a crisis center—"

"I'm *at* a crisis center, for Christ's sake. All they say is, 'I know it hurts. I honor your pain.' I don't need that crap." She continued to sob. Peter listened in stupefied silence. Finally, her sobs subsided. "Please meet me, okay?"

"This is crazy, Darla. What's wrong with the phone?"

"I'll pay you. Okay? I don't have a lot of money, but I'll give you what I got. Maybe I can borrow some from someone. Just meet me. Okay? Please?"

He felt dull and weak, just imagining this desperate voice handing him money. "You want to pay me."

"Would that make you come?" Her voice climbed an octave. "How much do you want?"

"You don't have to pay me, Darla … Jesus."

"But you'll meet me. Okay?"

"This is crazy."

There was a long pause. Peter tried to picture this woman of wild emotional turns at the other end of an anonymous phone line. The only image that came to mind was of pale legs and newspaper. He heard a long, deep sigh. "Look," Darla said, "the cops want to know who she is, right?"

"I suppose. Probably."

"Well, I *know* who she is. Okay? But I'm not telling them! I'll tell you, and you can tell them if you want to, but only if you meet me. I want to hear about my mom, and I want to see your face when you're telling me. Then I'll tell you who she is. Okay?" He heard another cough, and she added, "Please. It's my mom. Okay? I want to hear about my mom."

"Why don't we talk right now?"

"Because it's—because I'm not supposed to be using the phone. If they find out, I'll lose my coffee privileges. I need to get back to my room. You understand?"

"No." He rested his forehead against his palm, elbow on his knee. The skin of his face felt moist and tight. "Where do you want to meet?" That sounded like a decision to him. At exactly which point in the conversation had he lost his mind?

"You know Uncommon Cup? The coffee shop?"

"Wait a second." He took a breath, thought for a moment. He had an idea. "Listen, if I'm going to meet you, I want to pick the spot."

"You don't understand—"

"No, wait. This is crazy enough. You gotta meet me halfway if you expect me to meet you at all." Abby would be proud, except she'd think he was an idiot to begin with. *You win some, you lose some.*

"I can't go very far. I—I'm kind of limited in my movement." He wondered what that meant. Was she hurt? In a wheelchair, something like that? Or what? "Uncommon Cup is public," she said, "and I can go there. There aren't too many places I can go to that are public like that, with people around." She paused, then added, "You'll be safe. Okay?"

He rubbed his eyes. "Listen, if I agree to this—"

"I won't bother you no more," she said quickly. "I promise."

He was crazy. That was the only explanation. Abby would have him committed if she heard about this. "Where is it? This Uncommon Cup."

"It's on the corner of Sandy and Ash. Southeast."

"Okay. I don't get down that way much, but I guess I can find it." Crazy.

"Can you meet me there in the morning?"

Peter felt as though he was tying a weight around his neck. If he went to this meeting, it'd be like jumping into a river—the weight would pull him all the way down. "What time?"

"Eight-thirty? Nine o'clock? Is that okay? Do you have to work or something? I can try to get there earlier, I think."

"No. That's fine. I'll meet you there at nine. Uncommon Cup."

"Please don't tell the cops. I can't talk to them. Promise me you won't call the cops."

Peter swallowed. The weight tugged on his neck, but he heard her shaky breathing and thought of the weeping. "I promise," he said.

"Okay," she said. "Thanks." He thought she was going to hang up, but then she added, "Now if you call the cops, you'll be a liar."

Peter almost laughed. God, Abby would have a field day with this. "I won't call them," he said thickly.

"I'll see you." She hung up. Peter knew he should just call Mulvaney at once. Skip the charge of obstructing justice or whatever they'd come up with to punish him for not telling. His petty thieveries had gotten him into enough cop trouble. No need to add to it here. But, of course, he'd made a promise, and while he'd broken promises before, none of them had been to a woman whose mother he'd found murdered in the park.

FIVE

The rain continued off and on through the night. At some point the temperature rose just enough to melt most of the ice off the streets. By early Monday morning, what ice remained lay in greasy black patches that tangled traffic in all the usual spots: on the Sunset Highway between Sylvan and the zoo, inbound on the Banfield, I-5 southbound from Delta Park. Peter listened to the traffic report on NPR while he dressed. It gave him something to think about. The weather followed traffic and he listened with rapt fascination to reports of small craft advisories at the coast, fog up the Willamette Valley and sub-zero temperatures in the Central Oregon high desert. He didn't expect to make it to either the coast or the high desert anytime soon, but you just never knew. Fore-warned is forearmed, blah blah blah. When he finished dressing he sat on the bed and looked at the telephone. *Don't be an idiot—call Mulvaney*. Let her meet Darla and if Darla didn't like it, too damn bad. He'd be out of it, which was precisely where he belonged.

The telephone rang. The sound startled him, but he grabbed the phone before the second ring. "Hello?" Silence. Peter felt he was getting used to it. "Hello, Darla."

He waited. She'd talk when she was ready, he supposed. He could hear breathing, and the sound of a television or radio in the background. "I'm coming," he said. "Don't worry, okay? I'll be there." He didn't like the way his mouth made decisions for him.

A man's voice, high in pitch but definitely a man's, said, "Is Darla your girlfriend?"

"Who is this?"

Peter heard a brief chuckle. "What'd you say your name was, mister?" the voice said.

"What? Who *is this*?"

"Sorry. Wrong number." He heard a click, and cradled the receiver. Definitely time to let the answering machine take care of the calls. He switched off the radio and went into the kitchen to drink some juice while he checked his TriMet map for the bus route. The coffee shop wasn't too far, just across Burnside in Southeast. He'd only have to make one transfer.

The rain had tapered off to a sprinkly drizzle, Portland's most prevalent weather condition. Abby called it "Portland Spittle." Peter looked up at the gray sky and thought, *say it, don't spray it.* But the spit kept falling. He trudged up Klickitat to the bus stop at Fifteenth. When it came, the bus was steamy and full of commuters, and he had to stand all the way to the Lloyd Center mall. His transfer dropped him at the corner of Southeast Eleventh and Ash, two blocks from the café. The clouds above started to break, but the rain continued in fits. As he plodded down the street, it seeped into his shoes.

Most of the buildings in the area were of a type—brick edifices housing hardware and auto body shops, contract bakeries, with an occasional errant farmhouse or Old Portland bungalow to stir the mix. The coffee shop was a one-story addition to a two-story warehouse that took up most of the southeast block at Sandy and Ash. From the outside, Uncommon Cup didn't look like much. White-painted cinder block with big plate glass windows and a teal awning. Small round tables sat to either side of the door. Several women huddled at one table, braving the spittle to drink coffee and smoke cigarettes. At the other table, an older teenage girl sat, heavy red scarf wound tight around her throat and thin, fingerless-gloved hands clutching a steaming cup. Inside, he saw a couple of guys sitting at a table near the window. He checked his watch. Five after nine. Maybe he could just bail. Missed the bus, sorry. But then the girl at the table caught his eye.

He took a deep breath and walked up to the table. "Darla? Hi... I'm Peter."

The girl gazed at him from under coal-black bangs and took a sip of her drink. "So? You want a medal?"

Peter felt the dull ache of his wet feet and the chill of rain on his neck. "Wait a minute. Are you—"

"I'm not Darla," the girl said. "Go hassle someone else, dickhead." She looked away.

Peter shrank away. He glanced at the women at the other table, but none showed any interest in him. Feeling hot-faced and helpless, he lurched toward the door to the café.

Bells on the door jingled as he entered. A dark walnut counter extended across the back of the tiny shop. Behind it, against the wall, stood a row of matching bins and above them hung a shelf filled with glasses and mugs. On one side of the counter sat a broad display case, and the center was dominated by an espresso machine. The Drip Option of the Day, according to the blackboard above the rear shelf, was Jamaican Blend. A woman stood behind the counter filling small paper bags with coffee beans from one of the bins. She smiled when Peter came in. Almost immediately, he felt the relief of warm air and the aroma of brewed coffee.

"What can I get for you?" the counter woman said. Her face was round and cheerful, with blue eyes and a deep pair of dimples.

Peter scanned the blackboard. "Just a tall latte," he said.

"Good choice—the lattes are excellent today. For here?"

"Yeah." He remembered his short night. "Better make it a double."

"Livin' on the edge." She grabbed a glass mug from the shelf behind her. He heard a hiss and steam rose from the espresso machine. "You want anything to go with that? Coffee cake? Biscotti? Something?" She nodded to her left at the display case. Peter peered through the glass at pastries, muffins, and scones.

"What's a beignet?" he said.

"It's a Bavarian creme donut in which they traded the hole for an expensive French name. Lots of sugar, fat, and cream. Instant heart death. Which is to say, *mmmm delicious!*"

"Sounds like way too much of a good time," he said. "A prune Danish is fine."

"Man who cares about his colon." She set his drink on the counter, put the Danish on a small glass plate, and set it beside the drink. "Four-fifty," she said.

Peter handed her a ten. As she made change, he said, "Do you happen to know a woman named Darla? A regular, maybe." She returned five ones and a couple of quarters. He dropped a one into the tip jar in front of the cash register. Living large.

"That oughta jog my memory." She grinned. "What does she look like?"

"I don't know. I've never seen her before. I'm supposed to meet her here."

"You picked a great spot for a blind date. I highly approve." She blew noisily through pursed lips. "Darla … I can't say as I can attach the name to a face. But as you can see, we're not busy. You missed the rush, so if she shows up, you're not liable to miss her in the crowd." She leaned over the counter. "Either of you two guys named Darla?" she called to the two men sitting at the window.

"That'd be me," one said. Both chuckled.

The woman grinned and turned back to Peter. "What's your name?" she said.

"Peter."

"Just Peter? Never mind. I'm Ruby Jane. Tell you what—anyone comes looking for Peter, I'll point you out."

"Thanks."

"No sweat. Enjoy your coffee. Best in Portland."

Peter took his drink and Danish to a table by the window. A few sections of the morning *Oregonian* lay half opened on the table and he picked through it. The story was on the front page of the Metro section, under the fold. He read through it and was pleased to see he hadn't been quoted. Just a brief mention: "The body was discovered by Peter McKrall, area resident, during his morning jog." After the heavy evening news coverage, he guessed the *Oregonian* didn't feel his bleatings were worth repeating. There was no new information. The body remained unidentified as of press time.

The newspaper moved in a sudden rush of cold air and he heard the door bells ring. He lowered the paper and saw her enter. She looked young, early twenties maybe, but worn beyond her years. Her hair was long and red and frizzy, and stuck out from beneath a dirty black watch cap. Her tattered army jacket was soaked with rain. She'd knotted bandanas above her knees. She wore black leather boots scuffed gray, fingerless wool gloves. But it was her face that told him who she was. Her eyes were sunken into cheeks laced with fine red capillary lines. Her skin was blotchy and dry, her lips cracked. A thin scar ran along her jaw line on the left side of her face. He kept returning to her eyes. Steel black in the middle, swollen red around the edges. But nervous. They darted around fretfully, glanced over at him and looked away. She'd been crying. He could believe she'd been crying all night.

She went to the counter. He could barely make out her muted voice when she ordered. As Ruby Jane mixed her drink, Darla said something else. He heard Ruby Jane say, "Yep. He's sitting right over there." She pointed to Peter. Darla turned and looked quickly, her cheek twitching. She said something else and Ruby Jane nodded. "No problem." Darla took her drink and walked nervously over to where Peter sat.

"You're Peter McKrall," she said. She didn't quite make eye contact. Her voice sounded flatter and harsher than it had on the phone. He caught the scent of stale tobacco.

"Yeah. That's me."

"I thought so. You looked fatter on TV."

"Thanks. I think." He hesitated as she stood there looking from one side of his head to the other. "Go ahead and sit down," he said.

She set her drink down and slid into the seat opposite him. "Did you read what they said in the paper this morning?" she said.

He nodded.

"They didn't have anything you said. None of that stuff about how horrible you thought it was. About …"

"I know."

"I don't know if I'd've called you if that was all I heard. Just the stuff in the paper. I mean, all that stuff on TV really got to me, I guess."

I should have kept my trap shut, he thought. But all he said was, "I guess it did."

She took a noisy sip of her coffee and cleared her throat. "I—I feel kinda weird."

"I didn't call the police," he said. "I probably should have. But I made you a promise and I kept it. And now I'm here."

"Thanks," she mumbled. "I appreciate it."

He waited for her to speak, but when she didn't, he said, "Maybe you regret getting me here. Maybe you wish you hadn't shown up, or that *I* hadn't shown up, or something."

"I—well, I don't know. I was really upset last night, but …" She dropped her hands in her lap and stared at them. "… maybe it wasn't my mom after all."

Peter perked up. "Why do you say that? Have you seen your mother?"

She shook her head. "No. I don't know. I mean, she still hasn't gone home." She looked up at Peter for half a second, then back down at her hands. "Who am I kidding? It's her. I know it's her."

She sipped her coffee. Peter inhaled slowly, deeply. It was growing more painfully obvious he shouldn't have come. Darla seemed sullen and agitated, and he felt helpless beside her. Still—as long as he was here—maybe he could learn something that Mulvaney and Kadash would find useful. Keep them from being too pissed off when he finally called. Maybe they wouldn't arrest him. "Did you see something?" he said at last.

"What do you mean?"

"Well, you said something about how she left some place near the park, but she never went home. How do you know that?"

Darla inhaled slowly through her nose. "I was watching her. I followed her."

"Why?"

"I don't know!" Darla took a sip and looked up at him over the rim of her mug. "You got a cigarette?" she said suddenly.

"I don't smoke."

"Of course not. None of you people ever do."

Peter didn't understand that. "I used to smoke. My dad and mom both died of lung cancer." That wasn't strictly true, but Peter didn't feel like going into it. Darla would never know the difference anyway. "I quit," he said.

"Jesus, that's even worse. *Used* to smoke. I bet you think you're pretty special."

Peter sighed and shook his head. This was pointless, and he wasn't up to fighting Darla's obvious feelings of persecution. "I tell you what—I agreed to meet you because I felt bad for you. I obviously shouldn't have. This situation doesn't have anything to do with me, and I'm beginning to think it should stay that way." He started to push himself to his feet.

Panic registered in her eyes. She reached out and grabbed his hand. Reflexively, he pulled back, but she didn't seem to notice.

"Wait," she said. "You're right. I'm sorry. I shouldn't've said that." She shook her head. "Hell, I'd have to go outside anyway, and it's too damn cold." She held his hand for a moment, and he settled uneasily back into his chair.

"Maybe this was just a mistake," he said. "We could just go our separate ways right now, and forget everything. I won't even tell the cops I met you. Okay?"

She seemed to consider his words. "I—I want to hear about my mom. I got to know what happened. Please just tell me what happened."

Peter sighed again. "Darla, I wasn't there. I don't know what happened."

"You found her! You saw what was done to her. I want to know about it!"

The two guys at the other table looked up. Peter glanced at them nervously. "Calm down," he said. "I just don't know how I can help. What do you want to know?"

She rested her face in her hands for a moment, then pushed her hair back behind her ears. "I don't know. I mean, what you saw. What you found..." She hesitated, then added, "What she looked like."

"Okay. But it isn't much." He tersely described the scene in the park, the search for Patch, the snow. How he found the body. She listened without expression, sipping her coffee, staring out the window past him. He told her about the pipes and the newspaper and how he thought he'd found Patch at first. "What was she wearing?" she asked.

"I didn't see much. A red skirt."

Darla looked back at him abruptly, her eyes suddenly focused. "The skirt," she murmured. She pressed both hands palm downward on the table. "What else did you see? What did she look like?"

"I only saw her legs, Darla. I didn't look any further."

"Why the hell not?"

Peter took a breath. The two men at the other table got up and stretched and said something to Ruby Jane. "See ya tomorrow, fellows," she said. She glanced at Peter and Darla and then went back to filling bags with coffee beans. "Darla, I don't know. I guess I didn't want to see any more than I had to. I just wanted to get out of there. Does that make sense to you?"

"Yeah, I guess so." She snatched her cup and took a final pull of her coffee, then set the empty mug down in front of her. "Are you going to eat that?" She pointed to the Danish. He thought he caught an anxious glint in her eye—he wondered when she had last eaten.

"No. Go ahead." She slid the plate over and took a big bite. "You said you followed her," he said in an effort to turn the conversation around. "Tell me what you saw. Maybe there's something there that will help the police."

"Why the hell should I want to help the police?"

"It was your mother, or at least you think it was. Don't you want them to find her killer?" She didn't answer, took another bite of Danish. "What's the problem?" he added.

She continued to eat in silence, staring past him, always past him. At the counter, Ruby Jane stopped filling the bags and started weighing them and writing prices on them with a marker. A woman came in, got a large coffee to go. Darla finished the Danish. "She was at this bar," she said at last. "A place down on Broadway called the 747 Lounge. You know where I mean?"

He didn't answer. He was familiar with a few bars down on Broadway. Some of them were pretty nice, but lately he had been more drawn to the small, dingy taverns, places that smelled of old beer and cigarettes. Anonymous joints thick with comforting indifference. He'd wandered into a few in recent weeks. The 747 was one of them—he'd last been there the night before Abby and family came down. No telling why, just another in a long series of stupid decisions that seemed to make sense at the time. When he wandered out again, he could barely walk. Abby had given him shit about it all weekend.

"It's one of the places she goes sometimes," Darla continued. "I saw her leave with a guy. They walked around the corner and got in his car. The car started and they sat there for a while. Then my mom got out and the guy drove off."

"He left her there? Why?"

She turned her stare on Peter, her eyes dark voids rimmed in red. "She's a whore, that's why! My mom's a fucking whore and she probably sucked the guy off for fifteen bucks. Then he went home to his wife and kids and left her there."

Peter looked away, his face awash with sudden heat. "Jesus."

"Jesus didn't have nothing to do with it," Darla growled. She pulled her hat off and tossed it onto the table, ran her fingers through oily hair.

There'd been a woman there the night he'd gone to the tavern. Flirting hard with the guys at the bar. Flirting with him, even. Could it have been Darla's mother, working the crowd at one of the places she went sometimes? He didn't even want to consider the possibility. "Darla . . . I don't know what to say."

"'Course not. Don't smoke. Don't know what to say. All you people are the same." She stood up suddenly and turned to Ruby Jane. "Can I have the key to the bathroom?"

Ruby Jane reached under the counter and held out a large silver ring with a key dangling from it. "You know where it is?" Darla nodded abruptly. She took the key and stalked through a doorway at the far end of the counter.

Peter couldn't remember the last time he'd felt on such uncertain ground. He gazed at Darla's cap for a long moment, then felt his hands sliding toward it. He suddenly pictured it in his pocket. What would she think if she came back and found it missing? Would she even notice? His hands crept across the table until his fingertips brushed the fabric. It felt warm and coarse. *What would it smell like?* Tobacco and musk, body odor. The thought of it seemed almost alluring. He could just slide it across the table, slip it in his pocket, play dumb when she came back. Just play dumb. Give him something else to think about besides a seedy bar and the possibility he'd met a dead woman. He took the cap into his hands, curled his fingers into the fabric.

Jesus.

A shudder passed through him. What on earth was he thinking? He abruptly pushed the hat away. It slid to the edge of the table. *What a fucking idiot*, he thought. Why was he even here? Because he never thought anything through. *Jesus.*

Peter looked at Ruby Jane, who was gazing at him. "Got anything stronger than coffee back there?"

"Still waiting on my liquor license. Haven't figured out who to bribe at the Oregon Liquor Control Commission yet."

"All of them, probably."

"Yeah, and their brothers and cousins, too." She glanced over at the doorway Darla had disappeared through. "Not a blind date after all, eh?"

He shook his head. "Maybe this is my chance to escape."

"The suspect fled on foot," Ruby Jane said. She set a bag of beans on the counter. "It's pretty tight in here—you know what I mean. Small quarters. When she comes back, I'm going to suddenly discover something I need to do in the back. That way you'll have a little privacy. I'll hear the bells if anyone comes in."

Peter smiled weakly. "Thanks. I think."

"Don't worry. I won't go far."

Darla returned and sat down heavily. Ruby Jane gathered dirty glasses and mugs onto a tray and disappeared with it through the doorway behind the counter.

Darla's face had taken on a firm set, her mouth a hard line and her brows furrowed above her nose. "Okay," she said. "I know how the cops work, okay? So I'm going to tell you what I know and then I'm outta here. You can tell them whatever the hell you want."

Peter nodded. Nervously, he pinched his lower lip between the index and middle fingers of his left hand.

"Here's the deal. I ain't seen my mom in a while. We been outta touch. I've been working up the nerve to talk to her again, and I actually thought I'd go see her Saturday night, just to—I don't know. Just to say 'Hi.' It was stupid. When I got to her place she was leaving. I was still up the street when she came out, so she didn't see me. But I saw her. She had her red skirt on, and this fur jacket thing she wears when she goes out to work."

"I see." Peter shifted in his chair nervously.

"Yeah. I bet you do. Anyhow, when I saw her dressed like that I got mad and decided I wasn't going to talk to her. She walked down to the bus stop and waited, and when the bus came she got on it. I ran up and got on after her."

"Didn't she recognize you when you—?"

Darla interrupted. "When she's going to work, she doesn't look twice at a woman, okay? All she wants is a man that needs a hand, okay?"

"But, you're her daughter."

"Shit. I don't know. She coulda been wasted. I haven't met a hooker yet that wasn't a junkie, too. Okay?"

"Okay. I guess I understand." He shifted again, fingered his coffee cup.

"So she goes to this bar. I went in and made sure she was staying, but I didn't want to hang in there and watch her go at it, so I went outside. I hung around for a while and that's when I saw her come out with the guy and go to his car. After he left, she went back inside and I knew it was gonna be a long night. I wasn't gonna hang around for that."

"But before that you just waited outside in the cold? It was freezing Saturday night."

"Yeah. I just waited outside. I'm used to waiting in the cold, okay?"

"Sure. Whatever you say."

"I went back to her place and waited a while. In the cold. Outside. But she never came back. Okay? She didn't come back on Sunday, and she's still not back. She had a red skirt on, and she's a fucking pro, and she was getting in cars with guys all night long just a few blocks down from that park. And so that's her, okay? Now all the goddamn police gotta do is find all the guys in Portland that bought a suck or a hand job on Saturday night and ask them which one did it. But they can leave me out of it." She rubbed her eyes with both hands and looked past him again.

"I'm sorry about your mother, Darla. I really am."

Tears formed in the dark black wells of her eyes. "You know what?" she said. "I believe you. I believe you because of that shit you said on TV. No one ever makes a fuss about an old whore. I know you didn't know that's what she was, but the cops probably know by now and they're not gonna make a fuss over her. Not much of one anyway. Maybe you can get them to. I don't know."

"Darla, I'll try. I'll do the best I can."

She nodded and the tears slipped down her face. "I'm leaving now," she said. "I don't know you, but you seem like the kind of guy that's gonna get up and try to stop me. Try to get me to talk this out or whatever. But I said my piece. You go talk to the police now and tell them that dead woman is Carlotta Younger and she's a professional cocksucker. But tell them they can leave me the fuck alone." She stood up and picked up her cap.

"Wait," he said. "How do I get in touch with you?"

She smiled grimly through her tears. "What the hell makes you think you'll want to get in touch with me?" She shook her head. "You'll be glad you got rid of me so easy. Just give it a few minutes."

She walked out the door. He half stood and watched her through the glass. She headed around the corner of the building and disappeared. He settled back into his chair and sat staring at his empty

Danish plate, at his full coffee mug. *Should've called Mulvaney.* He was just not made of tough enough stuff to deal with this. *Jesus Christ.*

"You haven't touched your coffee. It must be cold."

Peter looked up and saw Ruby Jane. "Oh. Yeah. I guess so."

She dimpled. "I'll fix you a fresh one."

"No, that's okay."

"How about I steam it again? Just to warm it up, then?"

"Well, okay. Thanks."

She took his cup back behind the counter. He heard a gurgle and a hiss. White steam framed her face for an instant. She glanced up at him and smiled again. Then she brought the cup back out and set it in front of him, sat down in the seat Darla had vacated.

"Darla said you were paying for her coffee," she said.

"What? Oh. Yeah. Might as well." He leaned back to dig around in his pocket, pulled out the change she gave him earlier. He slid the four ones across the table. "That enough?"

"Sure. Plenty. You want the change?"

He shook his head. "That's okay."

"It's a lot of change." When he didn't say anything, she said, "Thanks." She cocked her head to one side, looked at him with slight narrowed eyebrows. "How do you know Darla?"

"Did you recognize her?"

"Yeah—once I saw her. She used to come in a lot, six months ago or more. Not lately though. I'd forgotten her name was Darla. Or maybe I never knew."

"Well I just met her. She called me last night and asked me to meet her here."

"Really. She get your number off a bathroom wall?"

Peter took a sip of his coffee. "What do you know about her?"

"Nothing, really. I hardly know her. She's one of about five or six women that used to come in most mornings and order caramel lattes and sit out front smoking cigarettes. Some of them still come, and different ones, too. They're from a women's halfway house that's a couple of blocks on the other side of Sandy. Most of 'em are drug offenders, and most of 'em are pretty brittle. Darla obviously didn't have an uplifting chat with you, and you don't seem to have come out of it too well, either. So I thought I'd snoop."

"Hmmm." Peter wasn't particularly interested in being snooped. Still, he lifted his eyes for a moment to regard her face. Her eyes were bright and probing, yet also warm. She didn't blink as she stared back at him. She had medium-length, reddish-brown hair, capped by a sapphire beret. She wore a matching blue sweater under a red vest printed in metallic gold with moons, stars, and suns. A button on her vest declared, "I Wear a Brown Coat." No brown coat in sight, however. The overall effect was downright perky. Peter couldn't decide whether to be annoyed or smitten.

"You don't want me to snoop, do you?"

He shrugged. "Not really."

"Occupational hazard. I'm back behind the counter all day, and I end up listening when I'm not supposed to and intruding where I'm not wanted. Can't help myself."

"What does your boss think of all this?"

She dimpled. "I am the boss."

"Ah." He took a long swallow of coffee, then pushed the half-empty cup away. He suddenly felt a headache coming on. He guessed he was more annoyed than smitten. Or maybe he just had a lot on his mind. In any case, time to go. He leaned forward and started to stand, but Ruby Jane reached out and put a hand on his forearm. The contact startled him and he hesitated.

"Listen…" For a moment she seemed to search for words. Her eyelids narrowed and she glanced away for an instant. "…listen, I hardly know Darla, and I don't know you at all," she said. "But I can say she was asking you to do right by her. That's all."

He regarded her across the table. A gust of wind slapped rain against the windows, and out of the corner of his eye he saw the smoking women grab their cups and scatter. Inside, Ruby Jane bit her lower lip and met his gaze. He couldn't imagine ever being so direct with a stranger. He could barely imagine being so direct with someone he knew. His instinct, under other circumstances, would have been to snap at her. *Thanks for the insight*, only pissier. But either because of her disarming warmth or because his encounter with Darla had worn down his habitual defensiveness, he said, "I'll do what I can." He pushed himself to his feet. Managed a weak, uncertain smile. "I don't know what that is, and it may not be much. But I'll do what I can."

It sounded hollow to him. Repeating himself like an infomercial hawker to reinforce a sincerity he wasn't sure he felt. But she grinned and stood as well. "Good," she said. "I'm glad." He zipped his jacket up to his neck against the rain and moved toward the door. She collected the cups and plates and headed back behind the counter. As he pushed through the door, she called out, "Hey! Come back, if you like. After all, I make the best coffee in Portland."

SIX

PETER SAW THE FIRST police car as he came up Eleventh less than a block from his house. He'd walked all the way from Uncommon Cup, maybe a mile and a half, maybe two miles. Not a difficult walk, but rigorous enough to take the edge off two shots of espresso. The Portland sky stopped spitting by the time he passed Lloyd Center, but the air remained cold. He kept his feet moving briskly to fend off the chill. He tried to keep his mind clear, but an unsettled feeling stuck with him. He felt battered and uncertain. And not just because of his meeting with Darla. It was everything. The body, the police, the reporters—everything. He'd let things get out of hand, let events sweep him up and carry him out of familiar territory. Now, he needed to think about something else—to relax. Catch his breath and move on. Hell, maybe even think about looking for a job.

The sight of the police car gave him his first serious pause since the coffee shop. Not just one, but three cruisers were parked along Eleventh at the Klickitat Mall. He saw a uniformed cop kneeling before a Japanese maple in the corner of the yard nearest the start of the Mall. A strip of telltale yellow tape fluttered from one of the limbs. The tape had broken, and the officer was retying it. Peter continued slowly up the sidewalk.

The small, tidy house on the south side of the mall was getting all the attention. It sat on a gentle rise, separated from the street and from Klickitat by twenty feet or so of lawn. The front door stood open, but all the activity seemed to be outside. Peter saw a cluster of somber-faced men and women, some in uniform, some in plain clothes, staring into the bushes along the side of the house. The snow on the lawn had retreated like a transient glacier, but a patch still remained in front of the bushes.

As Peter approached, the officer working on the tape looked up. "Nothing to see here, sir. Best if you went on home."

"What happened?"

The officer stopped what he was doing and eyed Peter. "You're the fellow who found the body in the park yesterday."

Peter shifted his feet and looked away. "Yeah. So?"

"What are you doing here now?"

"This is my neighborhood." Peter gestured down the street. "I live a few houses down. I was out for a walk."

"Pretty shitty day for walking," the cop said. *Like it's any of your business*, Peter thought. The cop eyed the gray overcast. "Keep moving. There's nothing to see here. Catch it on the news, if you're so interested."

Peter bit back a snotty remark. *Why did cops always have to be so fucking difficult?* He moved away without further comment. As he continued down the sidewalk, he couldn't resist looking over his shoulder to try to see what was going on, what lay hidden by the bushes. He really didn't want to know, not specifically. Yet the activity around the house unaccountably drew his eyes. He continued a few steps past the cop and paused. With dismay, he recognized Mulvaney among the cluster of onlookers at the bushes. She looked much the same as the day before—same dark raincoat, same white cross-trainers. She glanced toward him briefly but didn't appear to recognize him. A sudden thin sun break warmed the air around him, but the chill had settled into him and the sun couldn't penetrate it. He thought of Mulvaney's card. *Detective, Homicide Detail.* There could be only one reason she'd be here. There had to be another body behind the cluster of police officers. He suddenly felt caught in a spotlight, as though to move would only draw attention to himself. Yet to stay was no better. Uncertainly, he peered at the house. It was a yellow bungalow with well-kept flower beds and religiously trimmed rhododendrons. He remembered that an elderly woman lived there. Alone, he thought. In the summers, she yelled at kids who cut across the lawn with their bikes on their way into the park.

Mulvaney walked around the corner of the house to the front. One of the other cops said something and she looked back around for a moment. Peter turned away abruptly. He wasn't ready to face her, especially in the presence of another corpse. The story of Darla could wait. He took a couple of quick steps but had barely crossed Klickitat when he caught sight of the medical examiner van approaching from farther down the block. As it passed, he felt himself shrink away, half expecting Dan Halley to burst out. But the van rolled by without stopping. Peter thrust his hands into his jacket pockets and continued on. In his mind, he counted down the houses until his own, four lawns to safety. Then he stopped. Parked in front of his house he saw a Fox 12 News van. Kelly Norris and her cameraman stood in his front yard. Norris gesticulated wildly while the cameraman fiddled with equipment on the ground at his feet. As Peter watched, he saw Detective Kadash step down off of his porch and join Norris on the lawn. She spun away from the cameraman and raised her microphone toward him but he waved both hands and shook his head.

A creeping sense of dread crept over him like a cold hand clutching his chest. *What have I gotten myself into?* he thought. Slowly, almost without realizing it, Peter began inching backward. His stomach hurt.

"Hey, pal? You gonna move it, or what?"

Peter jerked and spun around. The cop stood behind him, hands on his hips, eyebrows lowered in agitation. Over the cop's shoulder, Peter saw the ME van parked in the street, a navy-jacketed man digging around in the back. He felt penned in. Mulvaney on one side, Kadash and the abhorrent Kelly Norris on another. The last thing Peter needed was another close encounter with the TV news. No telling who'd come crawling out of the woodwork a second time. He twisted his head around, looking for a way out. The only escape seemed to be the paved path of the Klickitat Mall and the park.

The cop said, "You got anything to say for yourself?"

Peter looked at him. Awash in anxiety, he nevertheless felt a sudden wave of anger flood him. "What the hell are you talking about?" he blurted out.

The cop drew himself up. "Listen," he said, "I asked you to move along. Now are you gonna move along or what?"

"Thought I'd go to the park instead," Peter muttered. Clouds drifted in front of the sun and turned the street gray again. Lowering his head, Peter trudged past the cop and the yellow house with its grave cluster of attendants, hoping Mulvaney wouldn't see him and call out. He could only guess why Kadash had been on his porch. Could they have some idea of the existence of Darla, or was it just routine questions? *Well, Mr. McKrall we got another carcass up the street and wondered if you could pitch a fit about it.* He was glad that the cop who'd hassled him apparently hadn't known Kadash had just been at Peter's door. He might not have been so quick to shoo Peter off.

He hesitated only a moment before entering the park. His lack of reluctance surprised him. Only the day before he thought he'd never go back. But today, the place seemed unchanged by the violence that had touched it. Just like any other Monday morning. A bicyclist rode along the crest through the center of the park. A woman in gray sweats played with a boisterous chocolate Labrador in the middle of one of the sodden fields. Life, it seemed, would go on. Children would run and swing in the playground. Soccer and softball teams would compete in the fields. Violence may very likely touch the place again, and its boundaries—as the cluster of police behind indicated. But Irving Park itself—it was still just a park. Still just grass and trees, benches and picnic tables, backstops and basketball hoops. He followed the path and watched the woman throw a Frisbee to her dog. The dog retrieved it at a full gallop and knocked her over. She laughed and climbed, soaking, to her feet and threw the Frisbee again. The dog ran it down with a bark. As he passed by them, Peter was relieved to find no images of pale legs and newspaper haunting his thoughts. He circled the park, up onto the crest, past the basketball courts and around beside the tennis courts and the playground. Still just a park. And yet, he couldn't bring himself to look down into the playground as he walked by. It was one thing to return to the park. The playground was something else altogether.

The walk provided a chance to ease back a little and contemplate the previous two days. He felt overwhelmed by the seemingly headlong rush from one preposterous situation to the next. The dead woman, cops, reporters, the phone call, the coffee shop—and perhaps another corpse—all because of a single accidental discovery. What did he really have to do with any of it? Suddenly, he knew the intimate secrets of strangers, had TV reporters stalking him. He never should have let himself get caught up in it all. Once Kadash was done with him the previous morning, he should have gone home and talked to no one. No reporters, no one. Chased Abby and family out early. Locked the doors, pulled the shades. Taken the phone off the hook. That would have saved him from Darla, kept him from walking into the middle of this second murder. In another day or so, everyone would have forgotten him.

Still, he felt pity for Darla. On some level, he understood her grief, even identified with it. But he could sympathize with her without getting involved with her. He obviously had to tell Mulvaney what he knew about Darla's mother, but after that, he was done. After that, he really would lock his door, close the shades, toss the fucking phone in the garbage, and hibernate until spring if that was what it took.

He found himself back at the start of Klickitat Mall. Anxiously, he looked up toward the yellow house. Kelly Norris had come up from his house and latched onto some hapless cop—Peter hoped it was the one who'd fucked with him. Or maybe the Public Information Officer had shown up. Another reporter Peter didn't recognize stood off to her side, watching. Mulvaney was still in the yard, talking to Kadash. No way would Peter attempt that gauntlet. He decided to cut along the fence that separated the houses from the park and climb into his own back yard. He headed around a clump of ground juniper beside the path, then stopped, transfixed.

A thin red line trailed out of the bushes to the edge of the path, viscid and stark. He might not have noticed it but for a patch of snow that clung to the roots of the bush. His stomach lurched. He glanced toward Mulvaney and Kadash, but from forty feet away, they didn't notice him. *Let it be nothing. Old spilled paint.* But that couldn't be—old paint on snow. He looked into the bushes. A condom hung looped over a twisted juniper branch, the nipple end swollen and full. Red fluid hung in a long, viscous strand from the tip. The color of the open end was vitreous and uneven. He took a step back in alarm.

He looked toward the cluster of police. They didn't appear to have come this way. That meant they'd probably miss the condom. He wondered if there was some way he could draw their attention without involving himself. He looked around helplessly. *This doesn't have anything to do with me.* But he found his eyes drawn back to the condom. He crouched down to see more closely. Blood had dripped into the curl of juniper roots and frozen. A red thread ran through the roots and out to the edge of the path. Yet it was the condom itself that absorbed him. Somewhere, remotely at first but with mounting urgency, his sense of horror was being overwhelmed by an urge to touch it. To lift it. To carry it away. He pictured the condom in his hand, hanging, glistening in the thin sunlight. Imagined the slickness and flaccid give of the latex. *What would it feel like?* he wondered. *Please, no*, he thought almost as quickly. Yet the urge to take the condom grew and enveloped him—a hot, inexorable, expanding bubble of impulse. He felt his stomach roll, and yet couldn't stop himself as he raised his hand. *This doesn't have anything to do with me.* For an instant, he squeezed his eyes shut, his hand still reaching. In his mind, he'd already grasped the condom, was already walking away. It swung gelatinously, bounced against his thigh and left a greasy red smear on his pants. But he didn't care—it didn't matter. It wasn't a condom anymore, wasn't full and swollen anymore. It was nothing; it was anything—a crystal figurine of an angel, a broken woman's black cap, a co-worker's lunch, a stapler, a twenty-fifth anniversary portrait. Just something that gets taken away. Because things get taken away—that was the way it was, and, sometimes, someone had to do the taking.

He shook his head and opened his eyes, but couldn't pull back. He hated the damned thing, craved it. Longed to carry it away. He gazed sightlessly into the bush. "Don't," he muttered, barely audible. "Don't."

"Whatcha looking at, bud?"

Peter jerked his hand back and looked up to see Kadash and Mulvaney beside him. He hadn't noticed them approach. He felt his face grow hot, and he stood up abruptly.

Kadash looked into the bush. "Oh, shit," he said. "It's a bloody rubber." He crouched down for a closer look and curled his lips. "Jesus Christ, is the blood just on the outside? It looks like—" He reached inside his coat and pulled out a half-crushed pack of Marlboros. He shook one out into the corner of his mouth and lit it with a match.

"Give me one of those, Sarge," Mulvaney said dryly.

Kadash shook his head. "No way. Eric'd have my ass if he found out. And if he didn't, Leah sure as hell would."

Mulvaney didn't take her eyes off the condom. "I need a cigarette," she said. "Eric and Leah aren't here. Give."

Kadash shrugged and handed her the pack. "Suit yourself," he said. "But when they smell it on your breath, keep me out of it." Mulvaney put a cigarette between her lips and lit it with the last of Kadash's matches. She released a tenuous cough as she exhaled. The three of them stared down into the juniper.

After a moment, Peter said, "What does it mean?"

"I dunno—don't wanna know." Kadash blew smoke. "She was just an old woman."

"We don't even know that this has anything to do with her."

"Yeah, sure. Look at all that blood. This ain't no babe's first bump in the park, Susan, and it ain't no period, either. You saw the gut shot that woman took. I think the perp banged her after she was dead. Hope she was dead anyway." Kadash took a long drag on his cigarette. "What kind of a nutcase uses a rubber for something like this anyway? *I* don't even use a rubber."

"That'll be enough, Sarge."

"Sure, fine. I give you a smoke, risking Mulvaney family wrath, and look at how you treat me."

Mulvaney drew on her cigarette and said, "We'll need a rape kit right away. I know the ME said there was no sign of sexual assault on yesterday's victim, but have them take another look as well." Kadash nodded. "And, Sarge. I want to keep this quiet. We'll need to check for a match to the victim's blood, and until we get one this doesn't mean much anyway. But in any case, keep Norris away from here. I don't want this getting out to the public." She thought for a moment, then said, "I'm going to go find Owen and Huxley. They need to see this."

Peter felt a surreal disconnection from the scene around him. For a moment, it appeared Kadash and Mulvaney had forgotten him, and the flood of their conversation, rife with implication and revelation, overwhelmed him. For a long, tenuous moment he felt certain he would throw up, and almost laughed to think of the trend that would perpetuate—talk to Mulvaney, vomit. Kadash, he thought, would probably enjoy it.

Mulvaney turned to him. "What were you doing anyway?"

He peered at her, his face still hot, and shook his head. "I don't know. I just saw it, and ..." He looked away. He didn't know what to say. *Sometimes things need taking*—but he didn't think that would go over so well. Yet he had a feeling she wouldn't let him off the hook with just an *I don't know*. But that's all he could think to say. "I don't know."

"I see," she said. "Well, Mr. McKrall, you better come with me." To Kadash she added, "I'll get some officers to extend the police line to this point, and alert Ident. Till then, you take care of this thing." She pointed at the juniper bush with her cigarette.

Kadash gazed with distaste into the bush. "Right," he said. "Go off and leave me with the bloody rubber." He scratched the cherry patch on his neck with a thorny fingernail. "And you people wonder why you don't like the way I talk."

SEVEN

JAKE HAD TO ADMIT, he kind of liked that Kelly Norris. She reminded him of his sister—what he could recall of his sister. It had been a while. Actually, he hardly remembered Dee-Dee. He still kind of liked Kelly, whoever the hell she reminded him of. On TV, she stood in front of the yellow house by the park and talked into her microphone. The way her lips moved made his left leg tremble.

"...two murders in two days have brought fear to this quiet neighborhood. In the second killing, police believe the assailant may have come upon Regina Cossart while she was outside with her dog. There was no sign of forced entry. The body was discovered in the bushes outside the house shortly after 9:00 a.m. by the victim's daughter, Nora Petersen of Estacada. Police have linked the killing to yesterday's murder through physical evidence found at the scene. However, at this time, they have no theories on the connection, if any, between the two dead women. Detective Richard Owen, investigating officer of the second murder, had this to say..."

The view shifted to a barrel-shaped man with grayish hair, bald on top. "At this point, the only connection we know of is the way the two women were killed and the proximity of the crime scenes. That may be the only connection. However, the investigation is still in its earliest stages. We hope to know more soon."

Kelly reappeared. "The first victim has now been identified as Carlotta Younger of Northwest Trinity Place. How she found her way to Irving Park is unknown, though police say she frequented the 747 Lounge, a tavern on Northeast Broadway just a few blocks south of Irving Park. Police are canvassing the Irvington neighborhood for witnesses to both murders, and hope to have a break in the case soon. A reward has been offered by Mrs. Cossart's family for any information leading to an arrest and conviction. If you have information, call CrimeStoppers at 823-HELP. From Irvington, this is Kelly Norris reporting for Fox 12 News."

"*Call CrimeStoppers at 823-HELP*," Jake mimicked. "What about Peterhead Mackerel? I fucking *gave* him to you! Why isn't he nailed to the wall?" He stalked over to the TV and snapped the channel knob around. On channel 8, they were talking about some congressman's overly friendly tongue. Who gave a crap about Congress anyway? He watched for a few minutes, hopeful, but after the tongue they started in on the weather and he angrily flipped to channel 2. No good. They'd moved on to other stories, too. "What about the coat?" he said. "What about the *goddamned coat?!*" He paced. It had seemed so simple at the time, especially since he couldn't get into Peterhead's house anyway. Place was a fucking fort. Jake had poked around outside, but the windows were barred and the door hard as a brick. He had started to wonder if he couldn't just start shooting through the windows, but then the old lady appeared up the street and a whole new idea formed in his head.

He turned back to 12 in time for *Everybody Loves Raymond* at six o'clock. Nice thing about Monday nights—*Raymond* came back after all weekend with no *Raymond*. He flopped onto the couch. His gun poked into his back as he sat down. He'd forgotten he left it on the cushion when he stood up in excitement over the news story.

"Owww! Stupid piece of crap!" He grabbed the gun and threw it against the far wall. The point of the hammer left a black hole in the plaster. On TV, Raymond was arguing with his big scary brother about who ate the crackers or something. The wife complained about someone making a mess in the bathroom. Ordinarily, Jake would have laughed, but he was thinking about the gun. Suddenly it worried him. He watched movies and cop shows, and he knew they could tell if a bullet came out of a particular gun. It hadn't really worried him the night before, because nobody cared about some old hooker—he knew that from the cop shows, too. But keeping the gun now might be dangerous. Nobody knew he had it—he was pretty sure of that. But that old lady last night—hell, she could be the president's mom for all he knew. The freaking FBI could be looking for him right now. Mulder and Scully. Maybe he should get rid of the gun. Toss it in the river where nobody'd ever find it.

Except he didn't want to do that. Dee-Dee gave him the gun. He'd hid it all these years. He couldn't bear the thought of throwing it in the river. But he also didn't want to get nailed with it. Not after shooting the president's mom—whoever she was. *Heh.* He got up and picked up the gun and held it in his hands. Why the hell hadn't they found the coat? That's what he wanted to know.

If they found the coat, he wouldn't have to worry about the gun. He could keep his gun forever. The Peterhead problem would be solved.

Raymond and his brother started to wrestle on the couch. Jake could never remember the giant brother's name, but so what? He supposed the wife was cleaning the bathroom. The show ended, and Jake decided he needed coffee. He hadn't had coffee in a couple of hours and he was starting to get a headache. He went into the kitchen to run water into an aluminum sauce pan. His coffee cup looked grimy, even though he'd already washed it once. He scrubbed it out while the water heated, then measured four level tablespoons of instant Maxwell House into the cup. He felt generous about the coffee because he'd gotten the wad of dough off the hooker. Her night's pay, *heh*. The water took a while to heat so he wiped the counter with a fresh sponge, brooding all the while. Stupid cops. On TV, they always found the coat.

He rinsed the sponge carefully and propped it on the edge of the sink. Then he thought better of it and tossed it in the garbage can. Let the old whore buy him some new sponges. The coffee water still wasn't hot enough. He glanced at the telephone. Stupid Peterhead. He picked up the receiver and dialed. By now, he had Peter's phone number memorized. It rang and then he heard the hollow click that meant the machine had answered. He'd gotten the goddamn answering machine all day. *"Hi. You've reached Peter McKrall. Please leave a message..."*

"Damn it!" Jake hadn't said anything the other times he'd called, but this time the sound of Peter's toneless recording pissed him off. "You *fucker!* Damn it damn it *damn it!*" He slammed the phone down. Stupid coat. Stupid cops. Stupid sicked-out Peter. Nail him to the wall, monkey fucker. Why had he been looking around that playground anyway? How the hell did he *know?* Jake forgot the water and returned to the living room. *Everybody Loves Raymond* was on again. Channel 12 ran two in a row on week nights. He picked up the gun and started to put the barrel in his mouth. "No!" He didn't want to taste the gun. He wanted to hide the gun. Why couldn't he hide it? He'd hid it all those years and nobody found it. He could hide it again and he wouldn't have to throw it in the river. What the hell was the president's mom doing in Portland anyway? Wasn't the president from Tennessee or Texas or somewhere like that?

He switched to channel 2. They ran a second news at six thirty. But they were talking about the Congress guy. Like anybody cared where some Congress guy put his tongue. He set the gun on the coffee table and went to the kitchen to make his coffee. When he came back he heard the news anchor saying, "Two murders in two days have deeply shaken the residents of the quiet Irvington neighborhood. Could this be the start of a string of serial killings, or has the circle of violence closed? Today, we spoke to area residents…"

He sat on the couch and sipped coffee. More whining. More sicked-out people. He wanted to make it look like they all did it. Maybe like it was a big gang thing or something, except instead of the gang being black guys or beaners, it could be all these white bread types. Wouldn't that be funny? *Heh.* He couldn't figure how to do it though. Better to just pin it on Mister Mackerel. That'd be good enough. Hell, that'd be sweet. And Jake would be safe besides. The newsies finished talking to all the Irvington crybabies and gave their old *call-the-police-or-CrimeStoppers* bullcrap, and then it was on to the stupid budget.

He took another sip of coffee. The caffeine was starting to work on him now. He felt it clearing his head, giving him the edge. He wondered if someone called CrimeStoppers on the tongue senator. That was a funny thought.

Then he sat up.

Hoo-boy! He grabbed the gun, stuck the barrel in his mouth. *Gotta pay attention*, he thought. Sweet little Kelly Norris had been telling him what to do all along, and he'd been too busy watching her lips move to get it.

Just call CrimeStoppers. 823-HELP.

Still sucking the gun barrel, he went into the kitchen. The letters were right there on the telephone. It was so perfect. He wouldn't have to say who he was or anything. Just tell them about the coat and Mackerel could join that senator on the hot seat. He picked up the receiver and read the letters on the dial. 8-2-3 ... H was 4 ... E was 3 ... L—5 ... P—7 ... 823-4357. He dialed.

"CrimeStoppers ... Officer Garrett."

Jake didn't say anything. His voice hung frozen in his throat.

"This is Portland Police CrimeStoppers. Is anyone there?"

Jake hung up. It occurred to him they could trace the call. Maybe they traced all the calls. That's what they did on the cop shows. Maybe they traced it already and they'd call him back any second now and ask him what he wanted. *Just a wrong number*, he'd say. *I messed up.* All there was to it. They'd believe that. Why not? He hadn't said anything. But if he mentioned the coat, they'd want to know who he was. And even if he didn't say who he was, even if he hung up, the cops might even show up *here*. And then ... *and then* ... if something went wrong, if Peterhead wriggled off the hook, they might nail *him* instead, and find his gun, and *take his gun*. That would be bad.

But the idea was good. Calling CrimeStoppers was real good. He just couldn't call from this phone.

There was a pay phone up the street. Only cost a coupla quarters, right? Hell, he could even walk a few blocks to a pay phone that wasn't in the neighborhood. Wasn't raining out. Kind of warmish even, for a change. He wouldn't miss his coat, *heh*. Might even walk all the way across the river—nice night out for walking. He could phone from Peterhead's neighborhood. Why not? Just dial 823-HELP. Mention the coat, say he was a neighbor or something and he didn't want to get involved. Neighbors never wanted to get involved on TV. He just thought it was kinda peculiar the way Mister Mackerel was stuffing that coat in the garbage like that. Looked like a nice coat and all, but maybe all that redness was *blood*, if you know what I mean, Officer. Maybe that was why Mister Mackerel was being so sneaky about it. Just thought it was weird, just wanted to let you know . . . no, don't want to get involved. Just a neighbor. Just doing my citizenly duty and all. Just being a good citizen.

Heh.

EIGHT

"When I first got to Portland, I just didn't get it." Peter sipped from a glass mug. "Coffee from all over the world, everyone arguing over which was better than what. Knife fights in the streets. And hell, espresso, cappuccino, caffè latte, caffè mocha, macchiato. Back home, the only place I saw espresso was in foreign movies on cable TV."

"Lexington, Kentucky?"

"Yep. Kain-tuck-ee."

"I thought I detected a trace of hick in your voice. You're a cracker." Ruby Jane sat backward on her chair, her arms across the back and chin resting on her folded hands. Her own coffee mug sat three-quarters empty on the table in front of her.

"With a name like Ruby Jane, you might watch who you're calling a cracker."

"Touché. So we're from the same red neck of the woods. I'm from Louisville myself, which the last time I checked was practically in the same state as Lexington." She slurped coffee. "I can't believe Starbucks hasn't assimilated Lexington, though."

"Well, it's been a while," Peter said. "Anyway, after I'd been here a few months, a guy I worked with said he wanted to show me the *real* Oregon, the one you don't see on postcards. He took me backpacking one weekend out east of Prineville. The first morning, we woke up on this high desert ridge we'd hiked up to. There was nothing around for miles except mice, lizards, brush, and cow doots."

"I have a picture of a cow doot in my living room."

"Anyway, this guy digs into his eight-hundred-pound pack and pulls out a single-burner stove, a water bag, and a little cast-aluminum espresso pot. Brews himself an espresso there in the middle of nowhere. 'I prefer cappuccino in the mornings,' he says, 'but no fresh milk.' He even had a tiny porcelain cup wrapped up in a T-shirt."

"Your fault for moving to the land of the coffee droids."

"After all these years, I've become one of them. Used to be I'd drink anything you put in front of me. Folgers, motor oil. Now I'll walk for half an hour to make sure my latte comes out of the right kind of equipment."

"You said it takes you half an hour to walk here, so there you are."

Ruby Jane finished her coffee and stood up. She looked out the front window and Peter followed her gaze. The cloud cover had broken late in the day and the first stars were visible in the deep blue-black sky. Peter could hardly believe it was still only Monday—what a day. Off to the west, a thin band of golden fire silhouetted the West Hills. Ruby Jane stretched her arms over her head, drawing Peter's gaze back inside. She wore the red vest from that morning, but a floppy flower-print hat had replaced the beret. The vest swept open as she stretched. She was as supple as a cat, and Peter caught himself gazing at the curve of her sweater under the vest. For an instant, he imagined slipping the vest off her shoulders, sliding his hands over the sweater—but then her arms dropped. He shifted his gaze back to her face. It was a face anyone could get used to looking at. Yet her spirit and spark captivated him even more than her physical allure. During the last hour drinking coffee with her, he felt more animated and at ease than he had for some time, months maybe. He didn't want their time together to end.

Ruby Jane appeared to have other ideas. She stifled a yawn, and said, "I've been on the hop since before dawn. It's closing time for me—"

Peter felt his face go red, as if she'd known what he was thinking and came up with a quick reason to get rid of him. He slid out of his chair. "I'll take off then," he said.

Ruby Jane peered at him and raised her eyebrows. "If you've got to go … but I was thinking you might hang around a bit, tell me all about this murder mystery you're all caught up in. I mean, if you want."

Peter's blush deepened, and he was sure she'd notice. Despite his desire to stay, he almost felt he had to flee to stanch the abashed flow of blood to his face. But Ruby Jane only smiled and he knew he would stay, pink cheeks and all.

Peter had shown up at Uncommon Cup at about five. He'd spent much of the afternoon downtown with Mulvaney and Kadash, describing his conversation with Darla over and over. Then there was Detective Owen, who somehow managed to be even less charming than Kadash. "Tell me again what was going on between you and that rubber." When they had finally finished with him, he'd refused the offer of a ride home. He felt drained and exhausted, yet he wandered around downtown for a while, thinking he'd pick up a bus, or maybe take a MAX train to Lloyd Center and catch a bus from there. But after a while, he got used to walking, to the mindless rhythm of putting one foot in front of the other. He didn't let himself think about anything that had happened. He could barely think anyway. His brain felt wrung out by the endless questions—*let's just go over that one more time.* He window-shopped, fingered paperbacks on the bargain table in front of a used bookstore, bought a hot dog from a street vendor. As the afternoon wore on, he found himself strolling across the Hawthorne Bridge, a warm, southwest breeze at his back.

He paused mid-span and rested his forearms on the rail, peered down into the river. The Willamette picked up glints of blue from the clearing sky overhead and looked surprisingly clean. A couple of small boats were out taking advantage of the mild shift in the weather. Downstream, beyond the Broadway Bridge, he watched a freighter turn with the help of a tug. He decided to continue across the bridge into Southeast and catch a bus from there, or even walk all the way home. He wasn't in any hurry. His feet didn't hurt. The sun was warm, the breeze felt good. He was gainlessly unemployed. What the hell.

He breathed fresh air and watched the in-line skaters in Waterfront Park below the bridge. Other pedestrians, and the occasional biker, passed him, but he paid them no mind. The freighter completed its turn and started downstream toward the Columbia River and, eventually, the Pacific Ocean beyond. Motorboats charged up and down the river, making microbrew toasts to each other as they crossed wakes. When the sun neared the West Hills, he picked up his feet and continued across the bridge into Southeast Portland. He turned north at Seventh and followed it until Sandy Boulevard veered off at an angle toward the northeast corner of town and the Columbia Gorge beyond. The traffic picked up as he walked, lunging forward and screeching to sharp stops. Peter's pace was less expeditious. He strolled up Sandy absently, only half realized he was starting to retrace his walk home from Uncommon Cup that morning. He glanced at the coffee shop twice before he recognized it. Through the window he saw that the place was empty. Ruby Jane sat behind the counter reading a book. He took a few more steps then glanced back through the window. He didn't have anywhere else he had to be, right? Unemployed, and all that. Besides, by her own admission, she made the best coffee in town.

"Toss me your glass," Ruby Jane said. She slid out of her chair and headed behind the counter. She put his mug and hers on a tray full of others, then pushed it to the side and started rapidly taking parts off the espresso machine and setting them on a second tray.

"So you pretty much run this place," Peter said.

"So I pretty much *own* this place." She raised her arms grandly. "This is my domain, almost the whole block. The coffee shop's in the front, my apartment in the middle, warehouse space in the back. *Mine!* Ha ha!" She stopped and faced him, dropped her arms. Shrugged. "Well, mostly mine anyway."

"Only mostly?"

"My brother owns part."

"Does he work here, too?"

She laughed. "Jimmy? Ha! Jimmy won't even make his own cup of coffee, let alone anyone else's. Might mess up his manicure. Besides, he lives in San Francisco."

"That'd be a rough commute."

"He could afford it. He's one of those white guys in dark suits who trades money with other white guys in dark suits and somehow manages to always end up with more than he started with—bitching about taxes all the while. As for actual work—well, he underpays an illegal to clean his apartment and pick up his dirty underwear. He couldn't be bothered pulling a shot or wiping down a table. That leaves it all up to me."

"Must get hard sometimes."

"Oh, I hire help when I can. Sometimes I even keep them for a while. Usually I have someone in the morning, but there's a lot of turnover in this business, and my last barista bailed Christmas Eve. I only need someone in the mornings and at lunch. People want more of a job than that, I guess. Go work for Starbucks I suppose. Problem is, by one o'clock, it gets to be barely worth keeping the place open, let alone paying someone else to sit here thumb wrestling with me. Part-time hours at a nearly minimum wage rate do not an attractive job make, if you know what I mean."

"Why do you stay open in the afternoon, if it's so bad?"

"Well, that's usually when I fire the roaster up, depending on inventory and orders. Besides, if I can make an extra thirty or forty bucks in the afternoon, it's thirty or forty bucks I wouldn't have got otherwise." She paused. "You're not IRS, are you? Oregon Department of Revenue? Something like that?"

He chuckled. "Not a chance."

"Well, to tell the truth, the tips are better in the afternoon, so I generally make out like a bandit in that department. And who reports tips? Not this cracker chick. It's like making double wages. And while I'm racking up all those unreported quarters, I roast, bag beans, work on marketing stuff for new specialty customers, or just read if I'm way ahead of orders and feeling lazy. I provide whole and ground coffee to several specialty shops, so the slow time gives me a chance to stay on top of that. On Saturdays, I open late and close at noon so I can actually have an afternoon, and on Sundays I don't open at all."

"I'd think Sunday would be a good morning for business."

She shrugged. "Every morning is good for the coffee biz, once people know you make the best coffee in town. But I need at least one day off. This is mostly a business area, which means heavy Monday to Friday traffic. That's plenty till I'm ready to expand." She put the drip pots and the filter baskets on the tray with the espresso machine parts. "Be right back!" she said brightly. She grabbed the tray of machine parts and carried it through the doorway in the back wall behind the counter. He heard running water and the clink and rattle of glasses, then a rushing sound he took to be the dishwasher. After a moment, she popped back through the door, her face flushed, a dish towel tossed across one shoulder.

"So what did the cops say when you told them about Darla?" she said.

A prickly sensation quivered across his shoulders and neck. He hadn't avoided the topic of Darla or the killings up to that point, but he didn't mind that the conversation covered other ground. He realized now that part of him had been checking Ruby Jane out to decide if he could trust her. It was one thing to like her cheerful smile and the curve of her sweater. It was another to just open the Pandora's box of the last day and a half to her. After his long afternoon with the grim triumvirate of Mulvaney, Kadash, and Owen, he didn't feel up to another inquisition. On the other hand, Ruby Jane's interest was natural, given her acquaintance with Darla. Besides, he doubted talking about the whole mess with her would be as unpleasant as it had been with the police. Still, his initial instinct was to start slowly and ease into the story. "What do you know about Darla?" he said.

She pulled the towel off her shoulder and grabbed a bottle of cleaning spray from under the counter. She starting spraying and wiping parts of the espresso machine. "I really don't know much more than I told you this morning. She used to come in with the halfway house crowd. Kind of quiet, as I recall. But not incapable of laughing at a good joke, and sometimes even at my bad ones."

"And it was six months ago that she stopped showing up?"

"About. I wouldn't swear to it. Might have been five. Might have been seven. Eight. I'm not really sure. Why?"

He shook his head. "The police don't seem to believe she's real."

"Well I'll vouch for her reality." She turned the steam knob on the espresso machine and blasted the towel from the steam wand, then wiped down the front of the machine.

"That's not the problem, exactly," Peter said. "They already knew who the dead woman was, before I told them. She had a record and they had her fingerprints on file."

"So what's the problem?"

"Well, I show up with this story about her daughter calling me, but there's no evidence she had a daughter. They searched her apartment and found no photographs or letters or anything that suggested any family at all. None of her neighbors ever heard about a daughter. So the cops asked me about a thousand questions. Or more like the same few questions about a thousand times each."

"So they don't believe Darla called you? Or that you met her? Let 'em talk to me. I watched it all happen."

"I think they're willing to consider the possibility that Darla exists. But I don't think they believe she's who she says she is."

"So they hassled you about it."

"Among other things. I was down at the police station all afternoon being hassled."

"Maybe they were pissed you didn't tell them about Darla as soon as she called."

Peter smiled grimly. "Kadash didn't seem to care, but I do think Mulvaney was pissed. Not that you could tell from looking at her. She's very controlled."

"Must be some kind of lady cop thing. So now what happens?"

"Well, they're going to check the corrections system for a Darla Younger. That was her mom's last name. But I have a feeling they're not going to find her. Not under that name maybe. I don't know. It's all so crazy. If I hadn't found the body, then showed up at the second murder scene, none of this—"

"Wait, wait!" Ruby Jane dropped her towel onto the countertop. For the first time since he'd met her, her face showed concern. "What do you mean, second murder scene?"

Peter's blush suddenly came back full force. So much for going slow and easy. "Oh, um. You haven't caught the news today?"

"Jesus! I try to avoid the news while I'm working. And when I'm not working."

The dishwasher went quiet and a hollow silence filled the coffee shop. Ruby Jane gazed at him with her blue eyes. He thought about how easy it would be to get lost in those eyes, but he wondered if she'd give him the chance. Curiosity about Darla and her connection to the murder was one thing. Hanging out with Murder Boy was another. He gazed back at her, at the worried crinkle of skin between her eyebrows, and decided the only thing he could do was tell her what happened and let the chips fall where they may. The burgeoning friendship would either happen, or it wouldn't.

He drew a breath, then described his walk home that morning. Coming upon the murder. Spying Mulvaney, and then Kadash on his front porch. Kelly Norris and Fox 12 News. Fleeing into the park. Then finding the condom. Not the *wanting the condom*, just the *finding the condom*. No reason she had to know he'd *wanted the condom*. "At that point," he explained, "there was no going home." Kadash and Mulvaney kept him at the scene for another hour, cooling his heels till they could talk to him at greater length. When he sprang Darla on them, he thought they were going to arrest him on the spot. They didn't, but they did whisk him downtown and into a drab little room. He was relieved to see there was no mirror on the wall. He sat at the end of the table, Kadash and Mulvaney to either side, Owen in the middle. They were gracious enough at first. Got him a halfway decent coffee. Even brought him lunch—a burger and enough root beer to drown himself had he been so inclined. He had to pay for it, but at least they brought it to him. Even left him alone to eat it, which provided the opportunity to lift a couple of loose pens and Owen's Zippo lighter, which he'd left on the table. Not that he told Ruby Jane about that. After lunch, a general pissiness led by Owen but flanked by Mulvaney overwhelmed the graciousness. Kadash hardly cracked a joke, and Peter quickly realized Mulvaney wouldn't be asking him if he felt okay. Owen snarled and asked most of the questions. When had Darla called? Had he ever met her before? Did he know Carlotta Younger? Had he ever been to the 747 Lounge? He'd answered *never* to that one, figuring the last thing he needed was grief over where he chose to drown his sorrows from time to time. There were plenty of other questions anyway. How well had he known Mrs. Cossart? What time did Darla call? What did she say? Did she mention how long it had been since she said she last spoke to her mother? What time did you say she called? Did she happen to show him any ID? *Yeah, right—a driver's license and two credit cards.* Kadash had actually laughed, but Mulvaney's face remained a mask. Owen said acidly that being a smart-ass was the last thing Peter wanted to do. *No, Peter had muttered, it's actually the first thing I want to do.* Owen growled. At one point, Kadash asked, "What kind of condom you keep in your wallet?"

"None in my wallet," Peter had said. "I keep them in a crate in my basement. A truck delivers them once a month or so." Kadash laughed at that one, too, and even though she might have also laughed, Peter didn't share that exchange with Ruby Jane, either. Finally they left him in the little room again with a fresh coffee but nothing else to steal while a stenographer typed up his statement. The best thing about the whole situation was that the weather had gotten nice while he was inside. That and he had Owen's lighter in his pocket.

Ruby Jane listened to his story impassively. The crinkle between her eyebrows never wavered. He expected at any moment for her to make an excuse—gotta meet the boyfriend or wash the cat, some reason he had to get a move on. But she only drew a breath, shook her head, and said, "Remind me never to find a dead body."

"Whatever you do, never find a dead body."

The crinkle smoothed and the corners of her mouth turned up slightly. "Thanks." She tossed the towel back over her should and picked up the tray of glasses. "I need to get these in the dishwasher."

This was it. She was in the next room thinking him over. Coming up with something to say that would be firm but not too unfriendly. *Peter, I got stuff to do. It's been nice meeting you and all, but...* Something like that. It was too bad, because he really wished they could get to know each other better.

The dishwasher started up and she appeared again. He stood up, ready for the brush off, but she only said, "So now what happens?"

He blinked. "Uh, well, I don't know. What do you mean?"

"With the police. What did they say?"

"Oh. Uh." Her question caught him by surprise. "Um, I don't leave town."

"Really? They said that to you?"

"No. Not really. I think Owen wanted to say it. Actually, Mulvaney thanked me for my help, and apologized for keeping me so long. Not sure she meant it, but she did apologize."

"Mmmm." Ruby Jane looked around. "I still got to mop up front and finish back here."

Peter knew he wanted to spend more time with her, and the fact that she hadn't already sent him on his way emboldened him. "Maybe I could help out. Mop or something."

At first, she didn't say anything. His blush started to return, but then he saw a hint of a smile on her lips. She seemed to be thinking about it. "What do you say?" he said, hoping it sounded like just a gentle nudge. "Maybe we could go get a beer or something afterward."

"I'm not sure I'm ready for our relationship to advance to the point where you're mopping for me." Her eyes twinkled. "We haven't even had sex yet."

Peter's hands dropped to his sides and he opened his mouth, hoping something—*anything*—that didn't sound completely idiotic might come out. Nothing did.

She emitted a short, barking laugh. "Gotcha!" She gestured at a tall cabinet at the far end of the counter. "The mop's in there. The beer will depend on how good a job you do."

Peter stacked the chairs on the tables and mopped the floor while Ruby Jane scrubbed the counter and finished with the espresso machine. She told him to leave the chairs up—she would take the chairs down in the morning before opening. When they finished, he waited by the front door while Ruby Jane went into the back to hit the lights and grab a green canvas coat, then joined him again.

"I don't suppose you have a car lurking around here somewhere, Mr. Man-of-a-Thousand-Footsteps."

He shrugged sheepishly. "We could walk somewhere. Is there somewhere close you like?"

She rolled her eyes. "I'll drive." She pushed him out the door. Outside, she turned and locked up. "Jesus, Pete, I must be out of my mind. If you turn out to be Ted Bundy, I am *so* going to kill you."

Her car, a battered Toyota, was parked around the corner. She drove around for a bit before they decided to head up to Hawthorne for beer and slices of pizza at the Bagdad Theatre & Pub. They sat in the pub and chatted and watched the movie crowd file in for the seven o'clock show. The conversation steered clear of Darla and dead bodies and meandered over more mundane topics. Work, or in Peter's case, lack of work. Mood swings in the Portland coffee market. Movies playing at the Bagdad. Movies in general. Books made into movies. Books that should never be made into movies. When they finished eating, Ruby Jane suppressed a yawn. "Sorry," she said. "I'd love to keep going, but I've been up since 5:30. I'm afraid I'm an early to bed, early to rise kind of girl."

"I'm running down myself. Think I'll leave the phone off the hook tonight."

"Well, before you have to ask and get all blushy again, I'll take you home, since you're so pathetically without wheels."

"Oh, uh, thank you," he said as his cheeks blossomed.

"Blushy anyway," she said, giggling. "I bet you got the hots for me."

"I did mop." His cheeks grew even warmer as they headed for the car.

The evening had remained balmy. A film of high clouds haloed the half-moon and blocked all but the brightest stars. They drove up Thirty-Ninth up through Hollywood to Broadway, then up Fifteenth to Fremont. "Turn left there at the next corner," Peter said as they neared Eleventh. Ruby Jane turned onto the dark street. As they came up to his house, Peter saw the silhouette of a car parked in his driveway. Its headlights shined against the garage at the back of his driveway, and he could make out a figure on his front porch, fist rapping on the door.

"I wonder who that is," Peter said.

"You weren't expecting anyone?"

"No. God, I hope it's not some stupid reporter."

"We could always keep going."

"Well, pull up at the curb. If I don't like what I see, maybe you could drop me at the next corner. I can sneak in the back through the park."

Ruby Jane stopped on the street in front of the house. The figure on the porch turned and came down the steps. A woman. When she moved into the glare of the headlights, Peter recognized Mulvaney. He glanced at the car and saw someone sitting in the passenger seat. Kadash. Had to be.

"Who is it?" Ruby Jane said.

"Cops." He climbed out of the car. Mulvaney came down the driveway and joined him at the sidewalk. He thought of Owen's lighter in his pocket.

"I'm sorry to bother you, Mister McKrall," she said. "Something has come up."

"God, why doesn't that surprise me? Listen, I'm really tired. Can't this wait?" Ruby Jane got out of the car and leaned over the roof.

"I'm afraid it can't," Mulvaney said. She looked over at Ruby Jane. "Who is this?"

"A friend," Peter said with a none-of-your-business edge to his voice.

"I think we can make this quick," Mulvaney said. She turned to her car. "Sarge?" Kadash got out and joined her. "We would like to look in your garbage can."

"My garbage can? What the hell are you talking about?"

"Just a little garbage picking," Kadash said. "Maybe if there's any returnables in there you'll let us have them."

"Mister McKrall, we just came from downtown." Mulvaney's voice sounded terse. "We didn't get a search warrant because we were

103

pretty sure you would want to be cooperative. But if you choose not to be, we will take you into custody until a search warrant can be issued."

"A search warrant?" Ruby Jane said. "Are you kidding?"

Mulvaney turned her head toward Ruby Jane. "A warrant won't be necessary if Mister McKrall gives us his consent," she said.

"If we was the feds," Kadash said, "we wouldn't need a warrant. But rules are a little tighter for the local constabulary. The garbage can, turns out, is within the confines of your curtilage. Means we need your okay, or a warrant issued by a neutral detached magistrate."

"What the hell are you talking about?" Peter said.

"Skin," Mulvaney said. "Please."

Peter felt anger curling around in his gut. He was tired and hardly interested in messing around with the police for God only knew how much longer. But it seemed like the only way to get rid of them quickly was to do what they wanted. "Fine," he said, his voice short. "Let's do some garbage picking." He stalked past Mulvaney and Kadash up the driveway. Ruby Jane followed, the two police officers directly ahead of her.

The back yard was lit by the frosty glow of a security light in the next yard. The garbage can was beside the garage. He hadn't been in it for, he didn't know, days maybe. As a single man living alone, he didn't produce much in the way of trash. "Why do you want to look in the garbage can?" Ruby Jane asked as she and the others came up behind Peter.

"Let's just open it and see," Mulvaney said.

"That means we don't want to tell ya why," Kadash said.

"Fine," Peter said. "Go ahead."

Mulvaney nodded toward the can. "Would you lift the lid, please?" Kadash pulled a long flashlight out from under his overcoat and shined it at the lid of the can.

Peter hesitated a moment, wondering what they thought they'd see. Clearly they expected to find something, and clearly they wanted him to have every opportunity to hang himself with whatever it was. For a split instant, he was tempted to tell them to fuck it and go get their damned search warrant. But of course that would just make things worse, especially if there turned out to be nothing there. *Where'd you put it, Mr. McKrall? ... Where'd I put what? ... We think you know what ...* Lips tightening, he grasped the handle and yanked off the lid. He heard Ruby Jane inhale. Inside, a blue wool coat lay in a heap on top of the garbage, the front soaked with dark liquid. The lining of one pocket had been pulled out, and in the light of Kadash's flashlight, Peter could see a deep, red stain on the white cotton lining. With sinking certainty he knew it would turn out to be Mrs. Cossart's blood.

NINE

PETER WONDERED WHAT WAS happening to Ruby Jane. When the police brought him downtown, Mulvaney had suggested Ruby Jane join them, "just to answer a few questions. Help us clear some things up." Ruby Jane had agreed, but she looked strained and worried. She mentioned she needed to open her shop early the next morning, and Mulvaney promised to be as brief as possible. When they reached Mulvaney's desk, Ruby Jane had been left behind while Kadash escorted Peter to the same drab little room he'd inhabited in isolation for far too long earlier that day. Peter could imagine the questions they were throwing at her. *How long have you known Mister McKrall? Have you ever been to the 747 Lounge? What kind of condom do you keep in your wallet?* Kadash sat with him and cracked jokes. He mentioned more than once that Peter wasn't under arrest or anything, they were just trying to find out how a bloody piece of evidence came to be in his trash, *if ya know what I mean.* Peter tried not to think about the coat. As Kadash yammered, Peter stared at a crack in the paint on the far wall and fretted about Ruby Jane.

After a while, Kadash offered to get him a coffee but Peter declined. He could already feel his heart racing, and he'd had at least twice as much coffee that day as he was used to. "One more coffee and I'll be bleeding from my eyes."

Kadash chuckled, but left him alone. Peter slouched in his chair and waited. He traced the crack in the wall with his eyes, up and down, back and forth, into the corner where wall met ceiling. Water-stained acoustic ceiling tiles. Dusty cobwebs in the corners. The crack was kind of shaped like Florida, he thought. The cobwebs made mangrove swamps. There was Miami. Ft. Lauderdale. Tampa–St. Pete on the other side. And about there was the Magic Kingdom. *Hey, Peter McKrall—you're embroiled in two vicious murders. Now what are you going to do?* "I'm going to Disneyland." He laughed quietly, but without mirth. Of course, Disneyland was in California. So maybe the crack looked like California instead. There was San Diego, L.A. farther up the coast, Bakersfield inland—

The door opened and Mulvaney came in. Owen was with her. He was a squat, burly man with a balding pate and razor-cut sidecar hair. His small dark eyes gazed out from below pale eyebrows and a permanently creased forehead. The fluorescent glare of the overhead lights made his skin look waxy. Peter wondered if he missed his Zippo. He felt sudden concern that they might pat him down, discover the lighter in his pocket. But they seemed to have a different plan. Mulvaney set a rectangular silver device on the table, which Peter recognized as a digital audio tape player. She and Owen sat down across from Peter. Each dropped file folders onto the table. Owen rolled a pencil between the palms of his hands while Mulvaney sifted through her folder. She said, "We have a recording of the person who called in the tip on the coat. I'd like you to listen to it, tell me if the voice sounds familiar to you."

Peter nodded. "Whatever." His cheek twitched and he rubbed it.

Owen cleared his throat and leveled hard eyes at Peter. "Mc-Krall, I want you to understand the situation here. The discovery of the coat in your garbage doesn't constitute direct evidence you put it there—in fact, this recording *suggests* another possibility." He raised his wispy eyebrows on the word *suggests* as if to imply he thought otherwise. "You have not been arrested. You do, however, have certain rights you need to be aware of. This is not a court of law and you aren't under oath. You can choose not to cooperate with us if you want. Do you understand, Mr. McKrall?"

"I never would have told you about Darla if I wasn't willing to cooperate."

"So you say. Now do you wish to have counsel present for this interview?"

"A lawyer?"

"Yes."

Peter sat up. He glanced over at Mulvaney, but she ignored him. "Is there a reason I should have a lawyer?"

Owen's gaze didn't budge. "I can't give you any advice on that. I can tell you that since you have not been arrested, we can't provide counsel to you, even if you don't have the means to pay for it yourself. I can also tell you that—at this point—you are not officially a suspect. You are not a target in this investigation."

"So why the hell do I need the lawyer?"

Owen's brows lowered. He pursed his lips. "I'm not saying you do. I'm saying you have the right to counsel, but if you want it, it'll be on your own dime."

"What you're saying is you're cheap."

Mulvaney snapped the folder down on the table. Owen rolled his eyes. "Mister McKrall," she said, "I understand you're under a lot of stress. This has been a long day for all of us. Please try to remember that we're just trying to find out what's going on. You have been drawn into this, partly by happenstance, but also through the actions of the person who planted that coat. We would like to find out why."

"So you really don't think I put the coat in there."

Mulvaney looked at Owen, then back to Peter. She opened her mouth to speak but Owen cut her off. "I'm not prepared to concede anything," he said sharply. "There are a number of theories under consideration." Mulvaney peered at Owen, but he kept his eyes fixed on Peter.

Peter shifted his gaze back and forth between them. Mulvaney's dry, empty face was unreadable. Owen's was an open book. The prick. Surprisingly, Peter wished Kadash was there. Mulvaney came across as straight and he didn't think she'd lie to him. But could he really be sure? She seemed sympathetic enough, in a reserved way, but she was hard to pin down. Maybe the sympathy thing was just an act, intended to put him at ease so he'd make some kind of slip. Owen, to his modest credit, hadn't tried to hide his ambivalence.

The plain fact was that Peter didn't have anything to hide. "Let's get this over with," he said abruptly. "You want to play a tape. So play it."

Mulvaney took a breath and nodded. "This came in on our CrimeStoppers line. Listen carefully. We can review the recording as many times as you like." She pressed the play button. After a brief silence, Peter heard a beep, then, "CrimeStoppers. Officer Garrett."

"I, um—hello. Are you there?" The voice sounded thin and reedy. Peter could hear the grumble of traffic in the background. As he listened, he pinched his lower lip between the index and middle fingers of his right hand.

"Yes, sir. May I help you?"

"I have something I wanted to tell you."

"Yes, sir. Go ahead, sir."

"It's about them two murders in the park. You know, Irvington Park?"

"Irving Park, sir?"

"That's what I said. Irvington Park. What did you think I said?"

"Just making sure, sir. Please go ahead."

"I'm gonna. That's what I called for. I mean, goddamn."

"I'm sorry, sir. Please go ahead."

"I just saw something, that's all."

"You saw one of the murders?"

"No. Uh, 'course not. Something else. The guy that was on the news, Peter Mackerel. I saw him put something in his garbage can and I thought it might have something to do with the murders."

"What did you see?"

"He was stuffing this coat in the garbage. It looked all bloody. Red, you know. I figured it was blood. This was, uh, last night. Maybe around the time of that killing, you know? I thought it was kind of weird, you know?"

"Sir, could you tell me your interest in this? Are you looking for reward money?"

There was a long pause—so long that Peter almost thought the conversation was over. Then the voice said, "I, um, … I just wanted you to know. I don't wanna get involved. I thought it was kind of

110

weird. Kind of creepy. I thought you'd've wanted to know about it. Sorry for bugging you. Goddamn."

"Just checking, sir. Please tell me how it is you saw all this."

"Um … I was out walking when I saw him. It was that guy, Mister Mackerel."

"You know this man?"

"Yeah. I'm his neighbor, you know. I live right there on, um— on Eleventh."

"Do you live next door to him?"

"Sort of, I mean. No. I mean, I was walking—I saw him with the coat and I thought … Listen, why're you hassling me?"

"I'm not trying to hassle you, sir. I'm just trying to get all this straight."

"He put the coat in his garbage. I don't wanna get involved. It was all bloody and I saw him and I don't wanna get involved. Is that straight enough for you?"

"Yes, sir. How did you—" There was a click, followed by a series of beeps and a computerized voice saying, "7:29 p.m." Mulvaney pressed the stop button. Kadash opened the door and came in. "Your friend is waiting for you outside," he said to Peter. "She said she didn't want to leave you hanging." Kadash winked and Peter felt himself flush. He wouldn't have blamed Ruby Jane for deciding to go home, but he was pleased, if a little surprised, that she chose to wait. Kadash set a glass of water in front of Peter, then leaned against the bare wall behind Mulvaney, ignoring the empty chair beside her. He slid his hands into his pockets. Peter mumbled a thanks and took a long drink. He wondered why Kadash didn't sit down with them at the table.

"Have you ever heard that voice before?" Mulvaney said.

"I don't think so."

"You want to hear the recording again?" Owen said.

Peter shifted in his seat. "In a minute maybe. I don't know." He looked at Mulvaney. "What does all that mean? It doesn't even sound like the guy knows me. I mean, *Mackerel*?"

"Maybe the guy's a fisherman," Kadash said. He looked at Owen as he spoke, as if he expected a response. But Owen seemed not to notice.

Mulvaney shrugged. "We're not sure what it means. That's why we asked you to come in."

They'd hardly asked, Peter thought, but he let it go. Quibbling over incidentals wasn't going to get him out of there any sooner.

"Is there anyone who might want to harm you?" Mulvaney said. "In any way?"

Peter shook his head an emphatic *no*. It sounded preposterous. He hardly knew anyone at all, let alone someone well enough to make an enemy of them. Sure, he'd pissed a few people off here and there, especially at his last job, but nothing *that* serious. Did sticky fingers warrant a frame-up for murder? Since college, he'd found it difficult to get to know people, to get close to them—though Lexington hadn't been as tough as Portland in that regard. People in Portland seemed tighter, more inwardly focused than those in the Midwest. The Mole Person thing, he thought. Maybe the dreary weather caused it. Or maybe all the creepy kale in people's front yards emitted some weird chemical that affected their brains. He didn't know. What he did know was that most people weren't itching to become bosom pals. Ruby Jane stood out in sharp contrast to so many others, which explained at least part of his attraction to her. "I can't think of anyone who would do something like this," he said at last. "It doesn't make any sense."

"Perhaps not," Mulvaney said. "But it sounds like someone is angry at you."

Owen shuffled through papers in front of him with one hand, tapping his pencil against the tabletop with the other. "You mentioned you're unemployed."

"Yes. I am."

"How did that come about?"

"I was laid off."

"Why?" *Tap … tap … tap.*

Peter pushed himself back from the table, ran his fingers through his hair. He didn't understand what this had to do with anything. He looked to Kadash, then Mulvaney, but their expressions were closed and impassive. "You don't read the paper? Last time I looked, the economy was for shit, in case you hadn't noticed."

"Why don't you just tell me about it, pal?" Owen's dark eyes were hard as marbles.

Peter took a sip of water. "I worked as a trust administrator at U.S. Bank. Between computerization and the tighter economy, they just don't need trust administrators like they used to. I was low in seniority, so when cut time came, I was part of it."

"You're sure it was only a lack of seniority?"

Peter began to drum his fingers on the tabletop. "I got laid off, that's all." Owen didn't respond, kept staring. Tapping the pencil. Staring. Behind him, Kadash shook his head slightly. Perhaps he wasn't so impassive after all. He shifted against the wall and glared at the back of Owen's head. Peter took heart from it. He looked at Owen and added, "Maybe I sucked at my job and they wanted rid of me. They canned a bunch of other people at the same time so I wouldn't take it personally."

Behind Owen, Kadash's eyes suddenly flashed. "You musta infected all those others with your lousy work ethic. Had to can the lot of them before you brought the whole company down."

"Maybe they thought I was trying to unionize the trust department." Peter smiled grimly. "Maybe I was planning a big wildcat strike."

"City paralyzed when trust administrators walk," Kadash said. "'Hoffa' McKrall rules mob of angry picketers."

Owen flicked the pencil down sharply. It bounced, then rolled off the edge of the table. No one moved to retrieve it. "There's a reason a man with your years on the force isn't running this show, Detective," Owen barked. "Now shut the hell up." Mulvaney's head snapped toward Owen and her mouth opened, but then she seemed to think better of it. Kadash just chortled. Owen ignored them both and said to Peter, "How do you feel about being laid off?"

Peter's smile faded. "What do you expect me to say? That I felt like going on a random killing spree? Jesus!" He sighed. "Frankly, trust administration is pretty dull. I'm happy enough to put it behind me. I did send out some resumes right after the layoff, but nothing came up and I haven't thought about it in weeks. Does that satisfy you?"

"Not particularly," Owen said. He shuffled though his papers again. He found one he seemed to have been looking for and studied it for a long, silent moment. Peter thought he could smell sweat and wondered if it was his own. He didn't like this line of questioning, didn't really want to get into U.S. Bank and all the rest. But Owen wasn't going to let it go. "Have you considered," Owen said at last, raising his cold eyes slowly and deliberately, "perhaps the reason nothing has come up might be your tendency to take things that don't belong to you?"

The air in the room took on a sudden acrid tinge. Peter felt his bowels go watery and a tight band seemed to constrict across his chest. Owen's lips curled up slightly as Peter shrank back in his chair. He tried to respond, but his voice caught in his throat. *They already knew.* He thought of Owen's Zippo. *They knew all along, were just pushing me to see what I would say.* He shifted uncomfortably and closed his suddenly gaping mouth, spread his hand over the hard rectangular shape of the lighter in his pocket. If Abby knew he'd taken it, she'd kill him. Stealing from a cop. What a fucking idiot. *But how did the cops find out about U.S. Bank anyway?* The whole thing was supposed to be confidential, and it wasn't specifically an issue in his dismissal anyway. They really were laying a bunch of people off. *How the fuck did they find out?*

"Mr. McKrall?"

"What?" The word came out as a hoarse whisper.

"Would you care to comment?"

He slowly shook his head. Kadash and Mulvaney said nothing, actually looked away. But Owen kept staring, kept bearing down. "I'd just like you to help me out here, Mr. McKrall. Like, for instance, did you steal something really important to someone, piss them off real bad? You see where I'm going with this, don't you?"

"It wasn't like that," Peter said, voice barely audible. He looked at his hands.

"How was it then?"

"You don't understand."

"Then make me understand."

Sudden exhaustion settled over him. Peter heard himself trying to explain, speaking in desultory tones through his weariness, tossing out lingo like *impulse control disorder*. It was stuff that surely they already knew about. They were goddamn cops after all. Peter kept insisting the situation at U.S. Bank was nothing, really—no one was ever angry with him. That fudged things, maybe, but close enough. Hell, his boss had made sure the company insurance covered his counseling. Case closed. Owen snorted derisively at that, but then seemed to lose interest and left it to Mulvaney to continue the interrogation. After a while, the questions shifted back to more prosaic topics, like Peter's whereabouts while women were being murdered, and how sure he was that he'd never pissed anyone off. With the return to that subject, Owen abruptly decided to start asking questions again. Peter supposed there was a plan to it all. Let Owen act as the heavy, with Mulvaney going a little easier. Perhaps they were signaling each other. And yet, Mulvaney had seemed genuinely displeased with Owen's manner. In any event, the questions just kept coming, over and over again. *How did he get along with people at work? Did he have any friends outside of work? What sorts of things had he stolen recently? Had he had any big arguments with anyone lately—friends, family or otherwise?* Peter answered in a perfunctory manner, but the fact was, he was close to no one except his sister, and while they'd each wanted to kill the other at various times in their lives, he didn't think either one of them was likely to go through with it. He went down his list of acquaintances with Owen, but no one he knew seemed to be a likely caller of the phone tip—or wearer of the bloody coat.

"This isn't going anywhere," Mulvaney said at last. "Listen, Mister McKrall, we're just trying to find out who would want to do this to you."

"Well, obviously I don't have any idea. I mean, this guy on the phone hardly knows where I live. He doesn't even know my name. McKrall isn't the most common name around, I'll admit, but it's not a goddamned fish."

"Maybe the guy thought he was being funny," Owen said.

"That was hilarious what he left in my trash can."

"A real side-splitter," Kadash said.

An uncomfortable silence followed. Peter tossed down the last of the water. His gaze drifted back to the crack on the wall. San Francisco. Silicon Valley. Owen sorted through his papers again and Kadash scratched idly at his cherry patch. "I could use a smoke," he mumbled under his breath. Finally Mulvaney cleared her throat. "Mister McKrall, there's something I want you to do."

Peter pulled his gaze away from Yosemite Valley. "What's that?"

"I want DNA and hair standards."

"What do you mean? Samples?"

"Yes. Samples."

"Jesus! Why?"

She glanced at Owen, then said, "We hope to get semen from the condom, plus we've got epithelials from under the fingernails of Mrs. Cossart. I want to make sure they're not yours. Let's face it, we did find a blood-soaked coat in your trash—"

"But that's absurd. Even if I had something to do with the killings, why on earth would I put blood-soaked anything in my own garbage can?"

117

"You'd have to be a fool. Maybe you are a fool. I suspect the coat was planted. But I have no evidence of that. Just a suggestive phone call and your assurance you didn't put it there. If I can't find the killer, I'm going to have to explain to the DA why I didn't arrest you. Standards will enable me to say I ruled you out through forensic testing."

"Or nailed me through forensic testing."

"If you did it, yes," Owen said. "Did you do it?"

"*Jesus Fucking Christ!*" Peter snarled. "I didn't do it!"

Owen shrugged and gathered his papers into a neat stack and slipped them into the manila file folder. "You've done plenty of other stuff. Just wondering."

Mulvaney said, "Will you agree to provide the standards?"

"What if I say no?"

She sighed. "I'll have no problem getting a court order, and I'll hold you until I can get one. I will tell you, if the tests are inconclusive, it'll look a hell of a lot better for you if I can get the standards voluntarily."

"How often are the tests inconclusive?"

"Not often."

"Great. That sounds great. Really reassuring." Peter felt nervous and prickly. But he also felt innocent. The tests would at least prove that. Then maybe these people would leave him the hell alone. "Okay. What do I have to do?"

"Just let the criminalist comb your hair and swab the inside of your mouth." She paused, then added, "We may have to take some blood, too, for good measure."

"This just gets better and better." Peter rolled his eyes. "Do I shit in a cup, too?"

Kadash laughed. Mulvaney frowned and said, "That won't be necessary."

Peter pinched his lip again. "How long do these tests take? I mean, how long before you know for sure I've been ruled out?"

"A few days or a week," Mulvaney said. "I don't think you should worry about it."

"That's easy for you to say." He added, "Okay, let's get it over with."

Mulvaney shook her head. "Our duty criminalists are out on cases. You can wait, but it will probably be a while. I think we can take care of it in the morning."

Owen snorted and shook his head. "Jesus, why don't you just buy him a bus ticket." He pushed himself away from the table so abruptly his chair fell over. As he turned his back on them all, Mulvancy drew her lips into a tight line and raised her head. She started to rise from her own chair.

"He's not going anywhere," Kadash said suddenly. "Tomorrow morning'll be fine."

Mulvaney glanced from Kadash to Owen—who ignored her—then nodded. "First thing," she said. "I'll set it up before I leave."

Owen reached for the door handle, then stopped. "One more question," he said. Peter met his eyes, tried to keep his lips from curling into a sneer. "Have you had any more contact with this Darla chick?"

Peter shook his head. "I haven't even been home."

"That wasn't the question."

"Well that was the answer. She called *me*. I have no way to call her back. She didn't leave her card. If she's called, there might be a message on my machine at home, but I haven't been there since I last talked to you guys."

Owen leaned forward over the table, his forehead lowered and menacing. "Tell ya what, pal. Next time you hear from her, you call. You *got* that?"

"Yes," Peter said, looking away. He was glad he hadn't been left alone with Owen.

"Yeah, well, I mean *immediately*. Not after you've thought about it for a while." Owen straightened up. "I'll leave the standards to you," he said to Mulvaney. Without another word, he opened the door and went out. The door rattled in its frame when it slammed.

"Mr. Cranky," Kadash said. He pushed away from the wall and came around the table to clap Peter genially on the back. "I'll take you and your friend home," he said to Peter. "And then, Susan, if you don't mind, I'm going home myself."

"Go ahead. Though I might suggest Mr. McKrall stay at a hotel or with family or friends tonight."

"You think I'm in danger?" Peter said. Acid rose in his throat and he grimaced.

"I think it's a possibility," Mulvaney said. She glanced at Kadash, who shrugged, then nodded agreement. Peter wondered if Owen would have agreed—somehow he thought not.

Peter felt his cheek start to twitch again. "This shit doesn't make any sense to me."

"It's just a precaution," Mulvaney said. "I don't want to unnecessarily alarm you, but I also don't want to minimize the potential risk. Is there someone you can stay with?"

Peter shook his head and ran his fingers through his hair. "I don't know. I mean, no. My sister's in Seattle. I really don't want anyone else involved in this."

"Come on, bud," Kadash said, resting his hand gently on Peter's shoulder. "There are plenty of cheap motels around. I'll help you find a place."

Peter looked up at Kadash gratefully. The bitter weight of confusion and anxiety that had built up over the previous day and a half seemed to bear down upon him. But Kadash, at least, offered something in the way of sympathy. Slowly, wearily, Peter rose to his feet.

"Thanks, Sarge," Mulvaney said. She remained at the table and began sifting through her paperwork as Peter followed Kadash out.

TEN

"Goddammit!" Jake griped. Fucking piece of shit cops. He could tell right through the phone that Officer Garralootie guy hadn't believed any of it. Like it was some kind of trick—*Are you looking for a reward?*—and Jake said no, because, duh, someone who just wanted a reward would make up anything.

The television was on, but he wasn't watching. He'd flipped through the channels, hoping he'd see a *Special Report—Mackerel Arrested*. Maybe even that honey Kelly Norris talking—"Tonight, police nailed Peter Mackerel after finding a coat covered with the dead woman's blood in his trash. Police heard about the coat from an anonymous phone tip. Whoever made that call is a real hero…" Except the *Special Report* didn't come, just reruns of *Friends*.

He paced back and forth in front of the television. Saw a commercial for some kind of fruity nutty cereal. High performance motor oil. No *Special Report*. His gun lay on the coffee table next to an empty coffee mug. He needed another coffee. It would help him relax. He grabbed the mug and headed into the kitchen.

Jake washed the mug and spooned in the coffee crystals. He wiped down the countertop while he waited for the water to boil. Saw the phone. Damned Peter Mackerel—never home, not arrested, not nailed to the *fucking wall*. Why the hell wasn't he ever home? Jake picked up the receiver and punched the numbers so hard he twisted his finger. It rang twice, then, "*Hi. You've reached Peter McKrall. Please leave a message...*"

"Goddamn! Never fucking home, never fucking home—you hear what I'm sayin'? *Fuck you!*" He slammed the phone down. "Never fucking home...never fucking home—" His finger ached. He rubbed it and paced in the narrow kitchen. The water started boiling and he stopped to stare at it for a moment, fascinated by the bubbles and rising steam. He wondered how it would feel if he stuck his finger in the boiling water. Make it feel better, maybe. Might hurt, in a way—but it would be a different kind of hurt. Like the time when he got poison ivy on his legs and they itched so bad he wanted to cut them off. He got a knife out of the kitchen and started to saw away at his shin, and it *did* feel better—in a way. It hurt like nobody's business, but the itching stopped right away. But then his foster mom came in and freaked and took the knife. He got nailed on that one. They made him go to a new foster home. And the worst thing was, once he quit cutting the itch came back.

His finger wasn't as bad as the itch had been, anyway. He poured the water into the mug, stirred, then washed the spoon and put it in the dish rack. Always let them air dry—no germs from some dish towel that way. He carried his coffee back into the living room. The late news was on. That meant it was after eleven. Had to work in less than an hour. He hadn't worked since Christmas day, when he pulled a double shift. They'd given him extra days off because of that, because he was willing to let everyone else stay home. Like who gave a shit. Like Christmas was any different than any other day. Actually, it was different in that he only got about ten customers. He'd sold cigarettes and forties of beer, watched the little TV they kept under the counter all day. They hadn't even made him restock, it being Christmas. The TV-watching was pretty damn good.

The top news story was the stupid congressman again. Jake flipped through the channels and it was all the same. The congressman, or a bunch of eco-whacks all hot and sweaty over some trees. Who cared? There was absolutely nothing about Peterhead. *They'd had hours.* As he watched, Jake slurped his coffee and it was too hot, but he didn't care. He didn't care if he burned a hole right through the back of his head because dipshit Officer Garralootie didn't believe him and now they were going to nail him to the wall. Probably Peterhead had talked them out of it. Probably started whining about how *sick* it was, and they believed him. *Yeah.* That was it. Maybe Officer Garralootie *had* believed Jake, but Peterhead said, "No, I didn't put that coat there it's sick sick *sick!*" And they believed him and now Jake was going to go down hard and it was all Peterhead's fault.

"Goddamn *jerkwad!*" Jake said to the television. He drank more coffee, then picked up the gun and tried to spin it on his finger. The dad used to do that when Jake was little. It was kind of a joke. Jake could hardly remember the dad's face, but he remembered the gun spinning on his finger, like in an Old West movie. "I'm the sheriff, boy!" he used to say with his big, booming voice, "and you're a stinkin' outlaw! If you don't stop yer thieving ways, I'm gonna plug ya right between the eyes." He'd always laughed, but Jake had to admit it kind of scared him. It was funny, sure, but he didn't want to get plugged right between the eyes. Besides, he never stole anything. That was Dee-Dee. But then, Jake often got blamed for stuff Dee-Dee did. That was okay. She always made it up to him. She let him have the gun before they took her away. That made up for a lot. He wondered where she'd got to after all this time. He wondered if he'd ever see her again. Maybe it'd be like old times. The idea of that made his legs tremble. Without thinking, he rubbed the gun against the inside of his thigh. The weather report came on, rain and cooler temperatures returning, but he hardly noticed. He stopped worrying about Peterhead Mackerel, too, for the moment.

After the news, Jake went into the bathroom to wash up. They didn't care much what he looked like at work, but he liked to be clean. Clean skin, clean clothes. He didn't want people to think he was some kind of dirtbag who couldn't take care of himself just because he worked at the Plaid Pantry. He found a jacket to wear in the bedroom closet, then loaded the gun and stuck it into the inner jacket pocket. He liked his coat own better. *Frigging Peterhead.* At quarter to twelve, he slipped out and locked the door behind him.

On the street, Jake felt like people were staring at him. A lot of people were out, even though it was cold and rainy now. All the *chichi-fufu* bars in Northwest were starting to shed for the night, kind of early since it was Monday. Couples staggered back to their cars, laughing a little too loud, clutched arm to waist to hold each other up. Jake tried not to pay too much attention, because they all made him think of *her*. He had a pretty good idea what they were going off to do, but he couldn't think about it because he had to get to work. He didn't have time to use his gun.

He turned west at Burnside, and went up three blocks to the Plaid Pantry. Midnight to eight. He did it all the time, but tonight he felt restless and uneasy. Peterhead could be saying anything to the cops, and there was nothing Jake could do about it. Just trapped in the Pantry, selling cigarettes and breath mints to fuckwads on their way home from Casa U-Betcha. Like the group home where he lived for two years as a teenager—he couldn't leave even though he knew there were things that needed doing on the outside.

The bar crowd was steady until after two. One small, dull sale after another—cigs, mints, cigs, mints. After the traffic died down, he had to restock the coolers. That was okay. It was something to keep his mind on, something other than his seething worry. As the night passed, he sold a few bottles of Thunderbird and a bunch of twenty-twos of Olde English malt liquor. When the guy brought the early edition of the *Oregonian* at four thirty, Jake took a break to go through the paper. There was no news about the arrest of Peter Mackerel. Nothing. Half the stinking night had passed and they still hadn't grabbed him. The killings were front page Metro, under the fold, but the story was mostly about the rising tide of violence in closed-in urban neighborhoods, and how there were no new leads in the case. Please call CrimeStoppers *blah blah blah* and all that malarkey. Well, somebody *had* called CrimeStoppers. Jake felt himself start to get worked up again. Peterhead out there lying to the cops, Jake in the Plaid Pantry sweating like a dead pig in a fireplace. He almost wished he hadn't done the old whore. Almost wished he hadn't done any of them.

He hadn't planned it. After he ran into her that first time, he started following her around. Just seemed to be the thing to do. Follow her, see what she was up to. A few times he even talked to her. At some point, he learned where she lived, and all the rest followed. He went down to Multnomah and got the gun—thank goodness it was still there, all safe and secure, after all those years. He'd hid it pretty good, but you never know. Took some work to clean it up, get rid of years of caked-on dust and cobwebs. After that, he found the apartment and moved in. And then he watched the stupid whore come and go. Sometimes she brought men with her, but Jake didn't dwell on that. He watched, and tried to pretend like nothing was going on. Like those guys were just friends come to visit. But then one night he peeked through the curtains and there she was, right across the alley, her own curtains wide open, lights on, bouncing away on top of some guy. She had his thing right up inside her. Jake could see it, as clear as watching TV. He wanted to look away, but it was as if his eyes were stuck open, glued to the scene through the window. After a bit, the whore rolled off and the guy rubbed his thing till he came. That didn't bother Jake—he rubbed his own thing. But sticking it inside, that was wrong. Dee-Dee had explained how it was wrong—and dangerous. He didn't understand why the old whore would do that.

The next night, Jake followed her to the bar down on Broadway. He watched her go outside with guys and get into their cars, those that had cars. Peterhead didn't have a car, he didn't think—not that Jake had paid that much attention. He didn't yet know how important Peterhead would turn out to be. It was hard to see inside the cars with the windows fogged up, but Jake knew what was going on. She did some of the guys with her mouth. No problem with the mouth. That was how Jake liked other whores to do him, better than rubbing. Dee-Dee said the mouth was fine. But the old whore let some of the men put their things inside her. *Bad wrong bad*, Dee-Dee would say. And Dee-Dee never lied to him about anything.

A couple nights later, Jake went back to the bar, late, after his all-day Christmas shift. He couldn't have said what made him bring the gun. That was the funny thing about the gun—the more he carried it, the easier it got to carry. He waited outside and after a while the old whore stumbled into the street. Through the door, he could see the bar was almost empty, not like usual. The old whore didn't recognize him. It had only been a week or so since he talked to her, and besides, she ought to have recognized *him*. But she smiled and said she'd blow him for twenty dollars, or all the way for fifty. Sounded like a pretty good deal, he said. He got her to walk up toward the park. The night was cold and snowy, but he pretended like he had a place where she could do him. She was stoned or something and followed along. "Where'm I gonna do ya?" she kept mumbling. It made him laugh, because they got to the park and he did her instead. Wasn't that the surprise? He used the gun, just like Dee-Dee showed him, and then he used the old whore's rubbers. Safer, what with all the diseases they talked about on TV. The stupid old whore sure as hell wasn't going to be putting any things inside her anymore, that was for fucking sure.

At seven o'clock, the manager came in to do the bookkeeping. Things got busy the last hour, selling coffee and donuts and cigarettes. Finally, at eight o'clock, his relief arrived and Jake was left with nothing but thoughts of Peterhead and the long, empty day ahead.

Freezing rain had come on during the night. With sunrise it diminished to a fitful drizzle, but the air remained cold and the sidewalk glistened with slick patches. Jake pulled his jacket tight and trudged slowly down Burnside. The solid pressure of the gun against his side comforted him. His eyes felt sandy and raw from the long night under shapeless fluorescent light. It was peak rush hour. Cars on the street crept past hardly faster than he walked. He reached his street, Trinity Place, but instead of turning, he continued straight. He didn't want to go home. He felt too edgy, too consumed with the need to act. The coat hadn't worked for shit. He watched traffic and plodded along, down past Whole Foods and Powell's. Down along the edge of Old Town, past the big pink U.S. Bank Tower and the Rescue Mission. The tramps outside the mission tried to bum change off him, but he pushed past. Normally he would have said something, *get a job, deadbeat* maybe, but this morning he was too preoccupied with the street and the cars, and with Peterhead. The chill rain soaked through his jacket to his skin, but he liked that. The cold kept his thoughts from boiling over.

It wasn't until he reached the Burnside Bridge that he knew where he had to go—back to Peterhead's house. Back during the daylight, when he could see what he was doing. Had to be a way inside. If the stupid cops couldn't take a hint, Jake would take matters into his own hands. Bust into the place, gun blazing, like he should've done Sunday night. Jake was too tired to guess what the hell Peterhead had been up to Sunday morning, searching and staring, staring and searching. Maybe he *was* psychic, or maybe he'd been sniffing around the old whore all along, same as Jake. Watching. *Fucking pervert.* Didn't matter. Jake would take care of things. The decision filled him with a sense of relief. He picked up his pace. He was wet and cold and nervous, but he had somewhere to go.

North of Broadway, not too far from the old whore's bar, Jake began to wind his way through neighborhood streets. The houses were silent. People at work, he supposed. That would be good, once he got to Peterhead's. He didn't want anyone to see him. Not that he had a clear notion yet of what he was going to do. Something would come to him. Whatever happened, happened. *Heh.*

From the outside, Peterhead's house looked empty. Drawn curtains, no car in the driveway. Same as Sunday night. Only this time Jake walked up to the front door and rang the bell. If Peterhead answered the door, Jake wasn't sure what he'd do. He wasn't liable to shoot him on his porch, broad daylight. People in the other houses might just be pretending to be gone. They might be peeking out their windows, waiting for an excuse to call the cops. Peterhead didn't answer anyway. Jake tried the doorknob. Locked, and deadbolted, too. It had been a lot easier with the old lady up the street. She'd been out in the street with her yapping dog when he crept out of the darkness. *Heh.*

Go home, a voice murmured in his head. It surprised him—sounded weird, like someone else. He was tired, and the chill had settled into him now that he'd stopped moving. He'd had his last coffee at six-thirty—that was a long time to go without coffee. He turned and gazed up the street. The houses all looked gray and dead under the overcast. He could walk out to Fremont and catch a bus downtown. *Go home, get some sleep, take care of Peterhead later.* But then he thought of Peterhead searching, staring. *How long had he been watching the old whore, anyway?* Jake smacked the door with his fist, then left the porch and stalked around the side of the house.

The trash can was gone. No sign of it anywhere in the yard. *Cops have it, maybe.* That would be good. Maybe they *had* arrested Peterhead. Maybe they just weren't telling the news about it yet.

That happened sometimes on the cop shows. They had information but they kept it secret so some sneaky newshound couldn't wreck the case.

He went to the back door. Deadbolted. Jeez, this guy was a worrywart. What did he think was going to happen to him? *Heh.* Jake looked around. The park was beyond the back fence, but no one was out there. No one could see him from the houses to either side so long as they didn't come out into their yards. And who the hell was gonna come out in the rain anyway? He took a deep breath and slammed his shoulder into the door.

"Yowch!" The exclamation escaped his lips before he could bite it back. The door didn't budge. Solid Sunday night, solid this morning. He gave it another push, less emphatically. He wasn't going to be pulling any macho crap here. He couldn't shoot the lock out, either. People would hear and then it would be cop central. Too bad he couldn't pick locks like crooks did on TV.

He stepped back from the doorway. The back windows on the main floor all had bars. The upstairs windows were free of bars, but there was no way he could get up there. No ladder, no trees or anything close to the house. He wished he were Spiderman.

"Goddamn butthead," he breathed through his teeth. Then he saw a basement window off to the right of the back door. Weeds had grown up in the window well. He'd missed it Sunday night in the darkness. He bent down and pushed the weeds aside, peered through the glass—three dirty panes, too mucked up to see through. No bars. He glanced around quickly, then put his foot through the center pane.

The clatter of breaking glass was much louder than he thought it would be. He flinched, then cringed against the side of the house, waiting for neighbors and cops to come crashing down upon him. The rain tapped against a few leaves still clinging to a maple at the back of the yard. The sound of his breath boomed in his ears. After a moment, when nothing happened, he relaxed. No one came. Adjacent yards remained empty. *Heh.* With mounting confidence, he kicked out the other two panes, then the wooden slats between them. He picked the shards of broken glass out of the crumbled glazing, then slithered through the opening feet first.

It was a lot warmer inside. The basement smelled slightly of mildew—an odor Jake did not tolerate at home. A washer and dryer stood off to one side, dirty laundry piled in front, and a heap of boxes leaned against the far wall. Jake snorted when he saw the washing machine. "Must be nice." The coin-op machines down the hall from the apartment were usually so dirty that Jake had to scrub them before he could use them. And Jake would never leave dirty laundry piled up like Peter had. He sorted his own into separate bins—whites and colors—as he undressed each day.

Stairs in the middle of the back wall. He crept up tentatively, listening for movement from within the house. The only sound was his own hoarse breathing. The stairs turned at the back door and climbed three more steps to a second closed door. A broom and a dirt-blackened dust mop hung from hooks in the stairwell. Jake put his ear to the door and listened. Nothing. His stomach did a flip-flop in anticipation. He opened the door and slipped into a small kitchen. A dirty glass in the sink, and the stove could use wiping down. Hoo-boy, wouldn't it be nice cleaned up? Twice as much storage as he was used to. Plants on the windowsill, tiny little trees shaped by wire. Neat. He went into the dining room. Even more plants there, a whole wall of them next to the big window that looked out onto the park. The plants were tidier than the rest of the house, carefully arranged on shelves. In the living room he found an actual fireplace. Big soft couch. And what a TV—color, with a remote! Stupid Peterhead didn't deserve such nice stuff. Just the thought of it pissed Jake off. Everything so cluttered. Newspapers piled on the floor by the couch. A cobweb up in the corner near the ceiling. He went through a doorway into a back hall. In the bedroom, the bed wasn't made. And the bathroom—*Jeez*, did this jerkwad ever clean his toilet? Jake took a pee anyway, because he had to, but he wrapped his hand in toilet paper to flush.

Through a narrow door in the hallway opposite the bedroom, Jake found a second stairway leading up. He trudged up to a small, finished attic room with curtained windows at either end. It was dark but felt warm and cozy. There was a bed and a nice big easy chair, and another TV. Not so big and nice as the one downstairs, but still color. The room looked like it wasn't used. The bed was made.

Jake could get used to this. Dust the place up, sit and watch TV. And the bathroom right at the foot of the stairs. Real nice. Of course, *that* would need a thorough scrubbing. But if there was one thing Jake knew how to do, it was scrub.

He sat on the chair. He didn't know what to do. The gun was in his pocket, but Peterhead was somewhere else. Rotting in fucking jail, maybe. Jake eased into the chair. It reclined backward, and a footrest popped up under his tired legs. "*Hoo*-boy," he whispered. What a life Peterhead lived. Fucking millionaire. Jake pulled the gun out of his pocket and licked the barrel heedlessly. He let his thoughts drift. An idea would come to him. It did with the old whore. It did on Sunday night. It would come today. "Inside now,

Peterhead," he said to the tidy little room. "What're you gonna do about that?" *Heh.* He felt so tired. He rubbed the gun against his thigh and yawned. *Let it come.*

ELEVEN

KADASH LED PETER OUT of the interrogation room into a cramped hallway lined with gray filing cabinets. Overhead, a fluorescent tube flickered. Ruby Jane slumped in one of a pair of padded metal chairs across from the door, her jacket pulled tight around herself and her arms folded across her chest. She pushed herself to her feet when Peter appeared. "What's going on? We going to jail?" Her words carried only a hint of perkiness, without much energy.

"Taking you home," Kadash said.

"Even better. House arrest. I got cable."

Ruby Jane stretched and yawned. As she extended her arms up and behind her head, her coat fell open, and her shirt tightened across her breasts. Peter felt a sudden desire to touch her, to run his hands over her. He wanted to feel her skin, to breathe in her scents. The sensation came on with such abrupt intensity that for an instant he trembled. It seemed to him that Ruby Jane and Kadash could hardly help but notice, and a flush rose in his cheeks. Time seemed to stretch out, long and supple as Ruby Jane's allure. Then she dropped her arms and the moment passed. It could hardly have been but a second or two. Peter drew a breath, anxious to shift his thoughts. He mumbled, "I'm sorry I got you into this."

"I've been through worse," Ruby Jane said. "I saw Jewel in concert."

Kadash motioned down the hallway. "Let's get out of here. Got to find this guy a motel, and the night ain't getting any younger."

Ruby Jane's brow crinkled and she looked from Peter to Kadash and back again. "Why do you have to go to a motel?"

"Mulvaney thinks I shouldn't go home tonight." Peter rolled his head to one side and looked away, half embarrassed. "Kadash is going to drop me somewhere. It's no big deal."

"Better safe, and all that," Kadash said. He headed toward the exit, then stopped, waiting for Peter and Ruby Jane to follow.

For a moment no one said anything. Ruby Jane eyed Peter. Kadash waited in silence. Finally she seemed to come to a decision. Her forehead smoothed and her cheeks dimpled. "Listen, there's a motel right up on the street from the shop," she said. "On Sandy about Tenth or Twelfth. You could come for coffee in the morning without having to walk all over hell's half acre."

"I know the one she means, I think," Kadash said. "A Travel-Inn." Ruby Jane nodded. "It's a little seedy, but maybe you're into that sorta thing," Kadash added.

Peter gazed at Ruby Jane. She smiled. It surprised him she was still so genial after what he'd dragged her into. He would have expected her to give him the *nice-ta-meetcha-now-fuck-off* treatment. Yet her face was rosy and inviting, with a hint of sleepiness around her blue eyes that, if anything, made them all the more captivating. "That sounds good," he said. He attempted a smile he hoped wasn't too fervent.

"Let's get going," Kadash said.

"Can we go back to my car?" Ruby Jane said.

"No sweat," Kadash said.

Peter and Ruby Jane followed Kadash to the elevator and down to the parking garage. At the car, an anonymous gray Taurus, Kadash said, "You guys sit in back. House rules." Ruby Jane popped open the back door and slid in. Peter glanced through the front passenger side window and saw a few folders stuffed with paperwork on the seat. Nothing to stop one of them from sitting up front, but Peter didn't quibble. He slipped in after her.

"Mind if I smoke," Kadash muttered as he dug out his cigarettes out of his coat. It wasn't quite a question and he didn't wait for an answer before he shook one into his mouth.

"Could you open your window?" Ruby Jane said.

Kadash grunted and rolled down the window six inches. He felt around his pockets for a moment, then muttered, "Loaned my lighter to Owen a couple of days ago and he still hasn't given it back. Never trust a cop." Chuckling quietly, he depressed the knob on the dash lighter, then started the car and threw it into gear.

A cold flood of recognition spread through Peter. *Never trust a cop.* Peter shook his head, mindful of the hard rectangular shape in his pocket. As the car pulled out of the garage, he realized he felt guilty—not a feeling his small-scale thefts usually elicited in him. The dash lighter popped and Kadash lit up. The smell was at once familiar and comforting to Peter. His father had been a Marlboro man, and even years later Peter still associated the dry, ashy aroma with his dad. He might be strolling around Saturday Market, or seated too close to the smoking section in a restaurant, and he'd catch that scent and half turn in recognition. But cancer had claimed his father years before, and it was always just another Marlboro smoker. When he thought about it, such warm associations didn't really make much sense, given the way things turned out. But all his memories of his father, good and bad, included that telltale aroma. Now those feelings returned disconcertingly. Suppressing a shudder, he squeezed his hand into his pocket and slid the lighter out, dropped it onto the seat. Let Kadash wonder how the hell it had gotten there.

The long day suddenly seemed to assert itself. He could feel the heavy weight of his eyelids, every weary muscle in his legs. He glanced over at Ruby Jane, who looked out her window as Kadash navigated over the Broadway Bridge and past the Rose Garden. Peter felt calm for the first time in days, and without thinking about it, he relaxed against Ruby Jane, leaning gently onto her shoulder, hands loose in his lap. The sensation was at once soothing and electrifying. She turned to him, smiled sleepily, and reached over and squeezed his hand, then turned back to the window. They passed into neighborhood streets, the windows of the houses lit lemon and golden warm. Peter felt listless and comfortable. He found himself wishing the drive could just go on and on. But Kadash finished his cigarette and tossed the butt through the open window. Moments later, they pulled up behind Ruby Jane's car.

"That was a twelve dollar cab ride," Kadash said, twisting around. "But too bad for me, this ain't no cab."

"Thanks," Ruby Jane said.

"Glad to oblige," he said. He turned to Peter. "Ready for the five-star excellence of the Travel-Inn?"

Peter glanced at Ruby Jane. It had come to "good night," but he wasn't ready. His desire to stay near her was like a thread between them; if he pulled too hard, he knew it would break. She'd invited him over for coffee in the morning—he would have to be satisfied with that. Give the thread time to strengthen, to add strands. "I'll go grab some things first." He opened the car door.

Ruby Jane spoke up suddenly. "You know, the motel is right down by me. Why don't I just take you, Pete?"

Peter hesitated, one hand on the car door. He felt both surprised and pleased. "Sure, that would be great."

"Fine with me," Kadash said. "I'm ready to roll into my coffin. Been a long day."

Peter stepped out onto the curb. Ruby Jane slid across the seat and joined him. "Be sure to let us know if you get any more weirdo phone calls, okay?" Kadash said through the open window. "Otherwise Owen'll slap you in chains." He waved as he drove away. Peter watched his tail lights for a moment, then turned to Ruby Jane. "Thank you," he said, for lack of anything more dazzling.

"Aw, shucks. Call it a little *Kain-tuck-ee* hospitality from one expatriate to another."

"I'm not sure they know the word 'expatriate' in Kentucky."

"Certainly not in my corner of the briar patch," she said. "Let's go. I'm beat."

"I should run in real quick and get a couple of things. Toothbrush and stuff."

Ruby Jane peered up at the dark house. She shook her head and shuddered. "I gotta tell you, Pete," she said. "I'm feeling a little creeped out. Maybe you should come back in the daytime."

As far as it went, Peter wasn't particularly thrilled with the idea of going into the house himself. And wasn't that a nice thought?—afraid of going into his own home. He wondered when the coat had been left. Right after the murder last night? He'd been there then. The thought of someone lurking around outside his house while he was sleeping sent a chill through him. It would be a hassle to go without a change of clothes for the morning, but he could deal with it. "Okay," he said. "Let's get the hell out of here."

Ruby Jane's car started with a sound like a lawn mower. As she pulled away from the curb, Peter said, "What did they do with you?"

She shook her head. "Nothing much. Asked me how I knew you. Asked a bunch of questions about Darla. I think they were a little surprised I could confirm your story. At least Mulvaney seemed to be. Owen was basically a dick."

"That was my impression of him."

"They were especially interested in exactly when Darla stopped showing up at the coffee shop. Which, of course, I couldn't tell them. Exactly. I mean, I'm supposed to keep track of everyone's comings and goings? I'd never get a chance to pull a single shot."

"I'm sorry you got involved."

"It's not your fault. True, I could have found something more interesting to do this evening, like sleep, or have a root canal. But the cops were fine. They didn't stick me in a little room for two hours, or triple-team me. Kadash even brought me a glass of water."

"That's something."

"The real question is what happened to you? I'm just the innocent bystander."

Peter took a deep breath. "That's what I thought I was."

Ruby Jane followed Fifteenth south and cut over to Twelfth at Lloyd Center. Traffic was light, except for a knot of cars and moviegoers on foot outside of Lloyd Cinemas. As they drove, Peter told her about the tape and about Mulvaney's request for hair and blood standards.

"You're sure you don't know who it was?" she said when he'd finished.

"Yeah. I suppose I should have listened a couple more times, but nobody who knows me would call me Mackerel, except as a joke. And it sure as hell was no joke."

"So what about Mulvaney? Was she hosing you?"

"About the tests ruling me out? I don't think so. Owen was plenty suspicious. I think he was ready to strap me in the chair and throw the switch. But Mulvaney at least acted like I was just a guy in the wrong place at the wrong time."

"That was the impression Kadash gave me. After Mulvaney and Owen left to chew on you, he stuck around for a few minutes. I think he wanted to reassure me you weren't some kind of serial killer."

That Kadash would make the effort to reassure her gave him a measure of comfort. Owen would have probably done the opposite. Hell, it was a wonder Owen hadn't called a news conference announcing Peter as the killer. In any case, Ruby Jane's friendliness, and her willingness to drive him to the motel, were less surprising. Perhaps that thread between them was a little stronger than Peter realized. It almost seemed that Ruby Jane was giving it a gentle tug herself. If so, he had Kadash to thank for that. "So," he said, "are you reassured?"

"In your dreams, psycho." Peter saw her teeth flash in the afterglow of a passing car's headlights.

Ruby Jane turned off Twelfth onto Sandy and a moment later turned onto Tenth at the Uncommon Cup. She parked in a small lot next to the building. "Home sweet home."

Peter looked around. The street was dark and quiet, no sign of the Travel-Inn nearby. "I thought you were going to drop me at the motel."

She didn't speak at first. She looked at him through the darkness and he saw the silver-blue gleam from a street light reflect off her eyes. "I was thinking there was no need for you to spend money on that place. Besides, it's mostly hookers anyway. You'd probably catch something off the sheets."

Peter felt a trill run up his back. A quickening of his pulse, a fleeting tingle in his fingertips. Tugging on the thread. "Ruby Jane, are you sure about this?" he said carefully, gently tugging back.

She smiled and raised her hand, ran it lightly across his cheek. "Hey, we're getting along. I mean, you do a great job of finishing up my setup lines. Plus, you really like my coffee, right?"

"Best in Portland."

"See what I mean? I admit I feel bad about all this happening to you, but I wouldn't make the offer if I didn't like you." She tilted her head coyly. "Do you like me?"

He felt his face go hot. "Yes or no?" he said. "Check the box."

"Which box do you check?"

"The 'yes' box. I like you, too."

"Great. Come on, then!" She popped her door open, then added, "Besides, it's not like you're not gonna sleep on the couch, perv."

She unlocked the side door of the warehouse and led him back into her apartment. He followed her into a huge room with a double-height ceiling and windows all around at the second story level.

At the near end, a pair of brown plush couches heaped with pillows faced a low table covered with books, magazines, and a mishmash of junk. A wooden stand with a small television on top and a mix of electronic components below stood against the whitewashed wall opposite the couches, a couple of speakers mounted above it. At the other end of the room, a queen-sized canopy bed sat on a carpeted platform with bookcases extending to the left and right at the head of the bed. Off to one side was a small kitchenette. The opposite wall sported a basketball hoop with the key marked off on the concrete floor in silver duct tape, a battered basketball on the floor beneath the hoop. The openness of the space was broken up by colorful hangings suspended from the ceiling girders. A claw-foot tub in the middle of the room drew Peter's attention.

"I only take a bath when I have company over," Ruby Jane said.

"That must make for a very exciting visit."

"Of course, I'm very demure about it. Actually, I have a real bathroom through that door over there." She pointed to a door-way beside the kitchenette. "This space used to be all partitioned off with these shitty plywood walls. When I tore them all out and opened the place up, I left the tub where it was because I thought it was cool."

"This is great. It's all yours?"

"The whole building," she smiled. The place had a homey feel to it. Ruby Jane tossed her coat on the back of one of the couches and looked at her watch. "Jeez! It's after ten! I've got to get ready for bed. Pre-dawn'll be hammering on my eyelids before I know it."

"I could help you out tomorrow," he said. "Pull a few shots, swab the deck, that sort of thing."

She smiled. "You're hired." She went to the door next to the kitchenette. "This is the bathroom. I think there's a new toothbrush under the sink. You go ahead."

He found the toothbrush, still in its box, under the sink as advertised. He suppressed an urge to paw through the cupboard to see what sorts of things she kept there. Instead, he used the toilet and washed his hands, then brushed his teeth and splashed water on his face. When he came out, Ruby Jane had changed into a nightshirt and sweatpants. She stood at the kitchen sink drinking a glass of water. "Ah, tap water," she said as she set the glass on the counter. "The stuff up front in the shop is filtered, but back here it's pure Bull Run."

"You make it sound so appetizing."

She grinned and breezed past him into the bathroom and closed the door after herself. A moment later, he heard the sound of running water.

Peter felt a weird mix of excitement and apprehension. He couldn't help but feel pleased, but there remained a niggling tickle of doubt. He had to wonder what had inspired Ruby Jane to bring him here. Guys had to hit on her all the time. Was this the way she usually responded, or was there something special about him? No reason she couldn't just like him, he supposed. He was a likeable fellow.

Right?

Restless, he paced back and forth below the hoop, contemplated shooting some baskets. After a moment, he sat down on one of the couches instead and wondered how she kept wild shots from smashing her stereo or wiping out a stack of clean dishes on the sink. He gazed at the bathroom door, imagined her inside, washing up, brushing her teeth—or maybe she was pawing through the cupboard to see what she kept there. He shook his head, then nervously began fingering the objects on the table, a candle here, a makeup brush there. A glass swizzle stick with a hand-blown penguin on one end. A palm-sized wooden carving of an Oceanic mask. Thin paperbacks of poetry, the odd mystery novel, and a *Harper's* magazine or two. His hand strayed across a silver pen, slender and elegant and obviously expensive. Her name, *Ruby Jane Whittaker*, engraved on the shaft. He slipped it into his inside jacket pocket, felt a momentary calm.

Yep, she'd like him just fine—until she ran an inventory.

The calm fled as quickly as it had come. He reached back into his pocket for the pen. He gazed at it for a second. Grimacing, he tossed the pen onto the table and then leaned back, releasing a long breath. For a second he just sat there, tense and anxious. *Think about something else. Read some poetry, shoot a hoop, wipe out the stereo.* But he only sat there and breathed. Tried to empty his mind. *Just don't steal anything.* Little by little, he began to relax. The couch was deep and soft and suffused with the faint aromas of ground coffee and fruity soap, perhaps a remnant of her shampoo. Probably he was getting all worked up about nothing anyway. Most likely, she just felt a little sorry for him and would leave him here on the couch till morning. It wasn't like anything else was going to happen. He closed his eyes and let his weariness take hold of him. The air of the room was cool, but he felt a soft warmth seem to rise from the couch and envelope him. His mind began to drift.

He didn't realize Ruby Jane had joined him on the couch until she lightly stroked his hair. The gesture surprised him, but he only opened his eyes and smiled.

"You dozed," she said. She had a glass of white wine in her hand. He raised his eyebrows, and she added, "It's late and I'm tired, but after the evening we've had I was feeling a little wired. I poured you one, too."

He saw the glass on the table next to her pen. "Thank you."

She took a sip. "It's nothing special. Something cheap I picked up at Trader Joe's. Some people don't like white wine, think it's too froufrou or something, so if you're one of them, you're shit outta luck. I have a couple of bottles of red around here but I didn't want anything challenging this time of night." She took another drink and gnawed at her lower lip. "Geez, listen to me chatter. I *am* wired."

"It's been a long, crazy day. I'm glad it's almost over." He leaned forward and took the glass of wine, sipped. "I'm normally more of a beer guy, but this is nice."

"Good. Of course, you seem less wired than me."

"Maybe it was the extra grilling I took from the cops this afternoon. Once makes you wired. Twice makes you tired."

"You're a poet—"

"—but wasn't aware that I am."

She giggled. Sipped again from her glass. Gazed at him from beneath long eyelashes. She looked sleepy, but that somehow made her even more attractive. Neither of them spoke. Peter drank his wine. Ruby Jane gnawed once more at her lip. Peter wanted to gnaw it himself, but now the thought, instead of making him feel anxious, only brought on a sensation of comfortable bliss. After all the tension that had wrung through him while she was in the bathroom, suddenly, with her here beside him, he felt at ease. Something had happened, he thought, when he put the pen back on the table. Something good.

"What are you thinking about?" he said.

She giggled again. "That's what the girl is supposed to say."

"Maybe I'm a woman trapped in a man's body."

She laughed out loud. "Uh-oh. Not sure where I fit into that picture."

He grinned. "Make that a lesbian trapped in a man's body."

Ruby Jane finished her wine. "Pete, you're a curiosity to me. I gotta tell ya."

"Sometimes I'm a curiosity to myself."

"No, seriously." She set her glass on the table, then raised her eyebrows and stared at him. "I get lots of guys into the shop. Most of them are working fellows and they're perfectly nice, but not really my type. I'm sort of this odd mix of easy-going and driven. I work hard here. I have a vision of where I want it to go, but when the day is done, it's done."

He drank the rest of his wine. "Ruby Jane, I think what you're doing here is really great. I think your apartment is great. I think this collection of books and weird little gewgaws on the table here is great." He paused, then added, "You're just great."

"See? See what I mean? You're a curiosity! You show up at my shop, and you're all lost puppy dog and no ambition, and yet full of compassion for Darla and for Darla's mother, all full of giving a damn about people most everyone else couldn't scrape off their shoe fast enough. And you have this knack of saying exactly the right thing. Not just finishing my setup lines, but stuff like, 'Your weird little gewgaws are really great.' That was perfect."

She'd long since shed her floppy flower-print hat and her bangs lay in ringlets against her forehead. Her eyes were as deep as sapphire. He eased over and she gazed at him. The delicate thread he'd imagined between them seemed to have strengthened into a tight strand—seemed to pull him toward her. He was so glad he had put the pen back. He could feel heat radiate off of her.

"A curiosity is good," he murmured. "Definitely a step up. Not so long ago I was a perv who'd be sleeping on the couch."

"You bought that?" She moved closer to him, so close they almost touched. "What a gullible boy you are." Her eyes looked big as half-dollars and soft as silk. She tilted her head toward the bed. "There's room enough for two." He leaned forward and brushed her lips with his own. She laughed quietly as he lingered there briefly, then he pressed his lips into hers. She tasted of mint. After a moment, he pulled back and looked into her deep, shining eyes.

"Ruby Jane, I just have to say this, okay? There's no place I'd rather be right now than in your bed with you—but it's been one hell of a day, you know?" He hesitated, then added, "I just don't want to presume."

"Pete." She gazed at him. "Peter . . . you haven't presumed a thing." She pressed her hand into his own and it felt as warm as a loaf of fresh-baked bread. "Come on," she said. "It's a good bed."

TWELVE

"Ruby Jane, I have a question for you. It's very important."

"Mmmm?" Ruby Jane curled tight against him, back to belly, with his arm wrapped around her and his hand cupped over one breast. She smelled faintly of apples.

"How *do* you keep wild shots from destroying stuff all over your apartment?"

"Silly boy," she murmured. She breathed deeply and seemed likely to leave it at that, but finally she said, "I never miss..." Then she drifted away, and shortly thereafter he followed her into a dreamless slumber.

He awoke in inky darkness. His own bedroom was never so dark, with silvery light always shining around the window blinds from the security light next door. He sat up. The air felt warm and heavy with the scent of sleep. He ran his hands through the sheets, but Ruby Jane wasn't there. He hitched himself up onto his knees and whacked his head against the wooden frame of the canopy above. He saw a flash of stars and slumped back down onto the bed, head wrapped in his arms. As he lay there cursing to himself, the canopy curtains parted and Ruby Jane appeared, floppy flower-print hat propped on top of damp hair, her face framed in warm light.

"Watch your head," she said.

"No kidding," Peter replied.

"I was going to let you sleep, but I see you've taken matters into your own hands."

"What time is it?" he mumbled.

"Ten till six. I've got to finish getting ready. My pastry guy will be here in ten or fifteen minutes, and I generally like to be dressed for the pastry guy. Anyway, I open at seven, so I have to get set up."

"I'll come help you."

"Okay. I left a clean towel for you in the bathroom. As far as shampoo goes, you're stuck with the girly-smelling stuff I use."

"As I'm washing my hair I'll be reminded of you."

She leaned down and kissed him. "I'll be up front."

He showered and pulled on his clothes from the previous day—seemed a little self-defeating. He joined Ruby Jane in the shop, and thirty minutes later, found himself in the midst of his first barista lesson. Ruby Jane showed him how to assemble the espresso ma-chine parts, how to steam milk so that he got just the right amount of foam, how to load the portofilters with ground coffee. With an instruction guide and a free hour, he might have taught himself the basics, at least well enough to produce some steam and maybe scald himself. But Ruby Jane as instructor had much greater appeal.

"Okay," she said, "you insert the portofilter up into the group—that's the hole under the front panel of the machine—and give the handle about a quarter turn. Firm, but not too tight. I have a four-group machine, which means I can pull up to eight shots at once."

"How do you figure that?"

"I have double portofilters, ones with two spouts. If I'm really busy, I use doubles all around and have three or four groups going at once. Since we're the only ones here, and in no rush, I'll just use a single and pull each shot one at a time."

Peter heard a tap on the glass and looked up. Outside the door stood a gray-haired woman wrapped in a mountain of colorful shawls. She smiled and waved, then clasped her arms around herself. Her breath billowed white from her nose.

Ruby Jane glanced at her watch. "Seven o'clock," she said. "Here goes." She pulled her keys from her pocket and walked around the counter to the door.

"Happy Tuesday," the woman said as she slipped inside. "Coffee, please. Nothing fancy—the drip is fine. Just make it deep, caffeinated, and two to go. Room for cream."

The Drip Option of the Day was Sumatra Boengie, a variety that Peter thought sounded either like a ballroom dance step or a daredevil recreational activity. He filled two large cups, with room for cream. As the woman paid Ruby Jane, the door bells jangled and two more women came in. A double tall latte and a short Americana, both to go. The Americana woman added honey. That was how Peter began to think of the customers—the Americana woman, the caramel latte man with the orange cap, the short espresso with capillary lines on her cheeks. Sour cream coffee cake, to go. Initially, Ruby Jane spent half her time fixing Peter's mistakes, but before they'd seen too many customers, he found a rhythm, and in any case she handled the difficult orders. Cappuccino with a marionberry Danish. Large drip coffee. Double latte. *Triple* latte with vanilla. Here and to go.

Around eight thirty, just as things started to slow down, the telephone rang. Ruby Jane answered. He felt no surprise when she mouthed the word, "Police."

He took the phone. "This is Detective Mulvaney. Detective Kadash told me where to reach you. How are you this morning?"

Kadash didn't seem to miss much. "Terrific," Peter said. "Thought I'd give blood."

"Then you're still agreeable about the standards." It didn't sound like a question.

"'Agreeable' isn't exactly the word I'd choose. But I can live with it."

"I'll have Detective Kadash pick you up in half an hour."

Peter drew a breath. "Yeah, sure."

Mulvaney said goodbye and he cradled the receiver. Ruby Jane looked into his eyes inquisitively and stroked his forehead. "Are you okay?" she said.

He shrugged. "I can think of about a hundred things I'd rather do today, but other than that I'm fine. Maybe if it was the Red Cross..."

"You could always pretend. Get Kadash to give you a cookie afterward."

They had a couple more customers—a blueberry steamer in a bow-tie, and a large drip decaf who wanted to buy a morning paper. "There's a box around the corner," Ruby Jane said, "or you're welcome to sit and read our copy." It was quiet after that. Peter fell into his own thoughts, and Ruby Jane didn't try to intrude. She wiped down the espresso machine and began to stack dirty mugs onto a tray to carry into the back. Peter watched her lithe, confident movements with a feeling of contentment and not a little astonishment. The last forty-eight hours had presented him with a dizzying diversity of fortunes. Two dead bodies, the condom, the coat, the anonymous phone tip. And then there was Ruby Jane, with her sapphire eyes and lively spirit. He'd only known her a day and already he felt more connected to her than anyone he'd met since coming to Portland. What few friends he'd had were all at the bank, and now that was gone. Since the layoff, he'd half considered leaving Portland, at least to the extent that he'd allowed himself to consider anything. Abby suggested he move to Seattle, but that idea held all the appeal of a hangnail. More likely he would drift somewhere else altogether. Not anywhere in the Pacific Northwest, and not back to Lexington. Somewhere new. Somewhere clean. Somewhere without a history of Peter McKrall or his sticky fingers.

Then along came Ruby Jane.

How could something so good be so starkly contingent upon such a horrible sequence of events? If he hadn't found Carlotta Younger's body, Darla would never have called and he wouldn't have had any reason to come to Uncommon Cup. And the contingencies only multiplied. *If he hadn't gone to the park Sunday morning… if Julie hadn't lost Patch… if Abby and Dave hadn't come for Christmas.* A series of disconnected events, stretching back as far as he cared to look, and yet all linked, at least in his own mind, by Ruby Jane. As she worked, he gazed at her and wondered—if it were possible to erase the last two days and save the lives of the two dead women, would he do so, at the risk of losing Ruby Jane to the ineffable stream of altered fate?

He was glad it was a question he didn't have to answer.

A little before nine, Kadash's gray Taurus pulled up in front. As the detective climbed out of his car, Peter slipped his arms around Ruby Jane's shoulders and pulled her close. She seemed to fit against him like a puzzle piece, and for a moment he breathed her apple scent and felt the warmth of her skin radiate against him. Then the bells jangled and they disentangled and turned toward the door as Kadash came in.

"Hey, bud," Kadash said. "Hate to break up yer little party, but it's time to, eh, set some standards, as they say. Heh heh."

Peter said to Ruby Jane, "I hope I won't be long."

She grinned. "I'll be sure to wait up."

Peter grabbed his coat and followed Kadash outside. As soon as the door closed behind him, a cold, sharp breeze bit his face and found its way inside his jacket. He paused to zip his jacket up to his neck and turn his collar against the breeze. Kadash stopped at the end of the car. He took his cigarettes from inside his overcoat. Peter grew suddenly alert. Kadash patted his coat, then reached into his pocket and pulled out the Zippo. He stuck a cigarette between his lips and raised the lighter, then noticed Peter watching him and stopped. He waved the lighter and grinned.

"Found it in the back seat of the car this morning," he said. "Ain't that something?" He flipped open the lighter and fired it up, then lit his cigarette. Exhaled with obvious relish. "Damnedest thing, really." He waved the lighter again. It was still burning, and the flames whipped back and forth in the breeze.

Peter swallowed. "How's that?" His feet felt rooted in place.

Kadash snapped the lighter shut and shrugged. "Well, you might recall I loaned this here lighter to Detective Owen, who neglected to give it back to me. Then it winds up in my car. Now the thing is, Owen hasn't been in my car in, I dunno, months probably. I can't even remember when." He drew deeply on the cigarette, released a great billowing plume. The wind snapped it away in an instant. "So how'd this here lighter end up in my back seat do ya think?"

Peter swallowed again. *Cops—always fucking with you.* Kadash knew exactly what had happened. Still, Peter heard himself say thickly, "I don't know." Denial to the end. Never admit anything.

Kadash eyed him. Peter wondered how the scene looked to Ruby Jane inside. Would Kadash suddenly whip out cuffs, spread eagle Peter across the roof of the car? Read him his rights? The moment seemed to hang there between them—buffeted by wind and cigarette smoke. The silver Zippo. Peter suddenly thought of Ruby Jane's silver pen and suppressed a shudder. *I have got to get a grip on this!* he thought. It's what Abby would say to him, but as he gazed at Kadash and thought of Owen and Mulvaney, he couldn't help but think Abby was right, the self-righteous bitch.

Then Kadash raised his hands in an exaggerated shrug. He said softly, "Well, bud, I didn't figure you knew. Not like you ever even saw this here lighter before." He chuckled, opened the back door for Peter, and added, more emphatically, "Not that I give a fat rat's ass anyway. I got the lighter back. Who the hell cares how it got here?" His eyes twinkled and he beckoned Peter over. "Come on, bud. Freeze your tits off out here."

Peter drew a cold breath, trudged over to the car. Hesitantly slid into the back and pulled the door shut as Kadash climbed in up front.

"Gonna try to make this quick," Kadash said.

"Okay. Fine." Peter didn't feel talkative. He wanted to think about something else, let go of his anxiety about the lighter, and his anxiety about the reason for their trip. Peter glanced through the shop window and saw Ruby Jane come through the door from the back. She must have taken the morning dishes to the dishwasher. Probably hadn't even noticed the taut tableau of him and Kadash and the mysterious reappearing lighter. The car started and Kadash pulled out onto Sandy.

"We're going to hook up with a criminalist out at Southeast Precinct," Kadash said. "It's a bit quieter there than the lab downtown. 'Course, we're not talking *CSI* here, just so you know."

Peter shrugged. "Whatever."

"Try not to get too excited."

Kadash smoked as they drove, which in Peter's mind relieved him of any responsibility to chat. He let his mind shift into autopilot, only half aware of things that went on around him. The car seat was cold and seemed to draw the heat out of him, but that was okay with Peter. Gave him something to focus on besides "hair and blood standards." Kadash made his way up Sandy to Burnside and headed east. After that, Peter stopped paying even a little attention, just let his consciousness drift, until the car finally slowed in front of a broad, nondescript gray and cream cinder block building with the words *Southeast Portland Community Policing* in large burgundy letters above a row of windows in the front. Kadash pulled into a small lot to the side past a sign that read *Police Only*. They climbed out of the car and hunched against the cold. Lowering clouds pushed toward them from the north and west and Peter smelled distant rain on the wind. He followed Kadash around to the front and inside.

An older couple sat on a pair of comfortable-looking brown leather sofas in the waiting area. Kadash spoke briefly with a uniformed woman behind the glass-fronted reception desk. She buzzed him and Peter through a door to the left of the desk. They entered a corridor painted soft cream with burgundy fabric wainscoting. The place looked nothing like a police station to Peter, until Kadash led him through a sturdy door into a small, antiseptic room with nothing in it but a steel-frame chair with a cracked green vinyl seat and a short gunmetal cabinet. Peter slumped onto the chair. Kadash leaned on the cabinet. They waited in tense silence.

A few minutes later, a man came in and introduced himself as a criminalist. Peter hardly listened and missed the man's name. Even his face didn't register, just a vague round shape beneath dark hair. The man set a black case on the cabinet. He snapped the case open and rummaged through it. He had Peter extend his left hand, then swabbed the end of Peter's middle finger with alcohol. He expertly lanced the fingertip and drew purple-red blood into two long, slender glass pipettes. When he was finished, he wiped Peter's finger again and affixed a small bandage over the puncture. He capped the two pipettes and put them into a hinged plastic box, snapped it shut and labeled it. Kadash signed the label, then put the case into a padded envelope.

The criminalist then ran a fine metal comb through Peter's hair. Several strands caught in the teeth and the man dropped the hairs into a plastic bag, which he labeled and sealed and handed to Kadash. It found its way into the envelope with the pipettes. Finally, the man took a packet and a glass test tube with a rubber stopper from the case. He tore open the packet and pulled out a pair of cotton-tipped swabs. He turned to Peter and said, "Open." Peter drew and impatient breath, but he opened his mouth and allowed the man to swab the inside of his cheeks. The swabs went into the tube.

There was a brisk knock on the door. Before any of them could react, the door thrust open and Owen barged in, eyebrows creased. "You done?" he said, his voice harsh and too loud for the little room. "I hope you don't think you're done."

Kadash turned sharply to face him. "What are you doing here?" he said. "I said I would take care of this."

Owen ignored him. He looked at the evidence specialist. "Pubics," he said. "I want pubics." Then he glared at Peter. "You're going to have to give up some pubic hair, pal."

"I wanna talk to you outside," Kadash growled.

Owen shook his head. "You're not calling the shots here. This is my investi—"

Kadash put a hand on Owen's shoulder. "I said outside." His voice was low, but as rough and inexorable as falling rocks. The florid patch of skin on his neck pulsed red. He lowered his head and locked eyes with Owen. For an instant Peter imagined that they might charge each other. The air in the little room felt as tight as a drumhead. Then Owen muttered a profanity and looked away. Kadash dropped his hand to his side.

Owen yanked the door open, let it slam against the wall. He thrust himself headfirst out into the hall. Kadash followed and pulled the door shut gently behind him. Through the doorway, Peter could hear their voices, harsh and angry, but he couldn't make out the words. He leaned back uncomfortably. The criminalist glanced at him, then pointedly looked away. Peter drew a breath. Pubic hair. *Jesus.*

The door opened and Peter flinched. But Owen was not there. "Okay, bud," Kadash said, coming in and shutting the door behind him. "This here's the fun part, I guess. Time to give a tug on your short and curlies."

Peter stared at him. "Why is Owen messing with me?"

Kadash rolled his head to one side. "He's the lead on the Cossart case and he's got the ear of the DA," he said. "He wants pubes, and Mulvaney didn't want to argue. She's lead on Carlotta Younger, but she has to work with Owen because the deaths are connected." Kadash drew a breath. "I answer to Mulvaney. What are you gonna do?"

"And if I say no?"

"The DA'll get a court order and you'll give 'em anyway." Kadash dropped onto the other chair. "Listen—you say no and Owen'll make sure you spend some time in a cell. He's that kind of an asshole."

Peter leaned forward and rubbed his eyes. His head felt like it was going to split open. They weren't going to leave him alone. Yet he knew he'd brought at least part of it onto himself. He'd talked to Kelly Norris, against Kadash's advice. And then Darla. And the stunt with the lighter. Cops were going to be cops, especially when you did things to piss them off. Encounters with cops after some of his sticky-fingered indiscretions had taught him that. He squeezed the bridge of his nose and said, "Fine." He stood up and unzipped his pants.

"You don't have to flash us or nothing," Kadash said, sitting up. "Just reach in there and get me a couple of hairs. Try not to enjoy it too much."

The criminalist watched as Peter slipped his hand into his underwear, but Kadash glanced away. Peter pulled out a trio of kinky brown hairs and dropped them into a second plastic bag. Kadash sealed it, labeled it, and popped it in the envelope with the rest. Then he closed up the envelope, signed a form affixed to the front, tore off a carbon for the criminalist. He looked at Peter. "Done."

"Then let's get out of here," Peter snapped.

Kadash thanked the criminalist and led Peter out of the little room. Peter pressed ahead to the waiting area, and then outside. Abruptly he stopped to zip his coat against the frigid east wind. Kadash coughed and pulled out his cigarettes. At the car, Kadash paused to light up and Peter took a deep breath of fresh air before getting into the car. "Thank God that's over," he said. He was anxious to see Ruby Jane. "Can you take me back to Uncommon Cup?"

"No problem," Kadash said. He inhaled smoke and coughed again. "We do got one stop to make before that."

Peter paused, stared at Kadash with exasperation. "Let me guess. Mulvaney? Or another fucking round with Owen?"

Kadash gave him a wry grin and opened the car. "You got your Owen encounter behind you for the moment. To be honest, the reason I brought you here rather than the crime lab is I'd hoped to dodge an Owen bullet. But I might just as well have taken you downtown from the get-go for all the good it did us." He popped the automatic lock on Peter's side. "In any case, Mulvaney's got something she wants to talk to you about."

"Of course she does. It's been almost twelve hours since she talked to me last."

"It shouldn't take long."

"It's never supposed to take long." Peter scowled. "What if I say no? Court order? Or cuffs?"

"Cuffs, I guess. But I'd rather not do that. The paperwork is a bitch."

Peter gazed at him across the roof of the car. For a moment, he was half tempted to force Kadash's hand. But as he thought about it, it occurred to him that arrest could easily lead to a more permanent arrangement, especially with Owen already looking for any excuse to lock him up. With a sigh, he climbed into the car. Kadash flicked his cigarette onto the ground, then slid in behind the wheel. Peter didn't speak during the drive downtown. Kadash seemed content to smoke another cigarette and let Peter stew in silence.

At the Justice Center, Peter found himself once more in the same little room. This time, however, Kadash left him alone less than five minutes, then brought him a coffee and sat down at the table with his own cup. Peter took a sip and made a face—he was already spoiled by Ruby Jane's coffee. He set the cup down and scowled. A moment later, Mulvaney joined them, file folder in hand. "You haven't heard from Darla, have you?" she said by way of greeting.

Peter shook his head. "If that's what you dragged me down here for, I could have told you no on the phone."

Mulvaney leafed through the file. "Dee-Dee Smithers," she said without lifting her eyes. "A.k.a. Darla. Twenty-two. Parents: George Washington Smithers, deceased, and Carlotta Smithers-Younger, also deceased. Her name is still legally Dee-Dee Smithers, but she hasn't used Dee-Dee since the death of her father. We presume she started using Younger after she learned that her mother had remarried. Her current whereabouts are unknown. She used to live in a halfway house in southeast near your friend's coffee shop, but she was relocated a few months ago after fighting with another resident. Now she lives in a facility off Foster and Seventy-Second, but she walked out of there yesterday morning and hasn't returned. Broke the terms of her parole."

"Well, uh ... great. You know who she is."

Mulvaney regarded him, her eyes impassive. "Yes."

"So?" Impatiently, Peter glanced at Kadash, who brooded into his coffee.

"So ten years ago, at age twelve, she shot her father six times with his own thirty-two. This was in Multnomah, where she lived with her family at the time. He'd been sexually abusing her, possibly for years, but I haven't been able to get access to the court records so I'm not sure of the details. Just going off some police reports that didn't get included in the sealed file. Two days ago you discovered her mother shot six times—with a thirty-two. The same thirty-two. It's brought up a few questions."

Peter looked from Mulvaney to Kadash. Their faces were blank masks. "You're telling me that Darla killed her mother?"

Mulvaney slid the papers back into the folder. "I'm not jumping to any conclusions, but I'd have to say that's a likely possibility."

Peter shook his head. He thought back to his meeting with Darla. She'd been defensive, embittered, mistrustful, but also deeply stricken. Could she also have been guilty? "She came to me because she was upset about her mother's death. She wanted to know what had happened. Would she have done something like that if she was the murderer?"

"Maybe she wanted to find out what you knew about our investigation," Mulvaney said. "Talking with you was certainly safer than talking to us, given her history."

"Her history," Peter said, half to himself. He had a history of his own, and he was none too thrilled to be talking to the police. He could only imagine how Darla might feel about it. She killed her father. Had she opted for a repeat performance with her mother? *Jesus...* He pinched his lip, gazed at Mulvaney across the table. The sterile world he lived in had little room for prostitution, sexual abuse, and murder. But he had sat across the table from Darla—Mulvaney hadn't.

"So now what happens?"

"Hopefully we find Darla and clear all this up. In the meantime, there remain a number of questions to be answered."

Peter had a sudden thought, though his stomach lurched to contemplate it. "What about the condom I found? How does Darla fit with that?"

"The blood on the condom matched the Cossart woman's blood," Mulvaney said. "Her blood was also inside the condom, but there was no semen present. Additional microanalysis may yet turn something up, some preseminal fluid perhaps, but at this point, the condom doesn't rule Darla out."

"Maybe it was some guy who couldn't—"

"Pull the trigger," Kadash muttered. He sipped his coffee.

"That's possible," Mulvaney said. "It's also possible the condom was meant as a diversion. The coat was apparently intended as such. The fact is, Darla might be very dangerous. If she contacts you—"

163

"Call you guys immediately. I know." Peter reached for his coffee, then thought better of it. He looked at Mulvaney. "Can I get out of here?"

"I have one more thing I'd like to talk to you about."

Peter sighed with mounting frustration. "Why doesn't that surprise me?" He leaned forward and propped his elbows on the table, rested his chin on his cupped hands.

Mulvaney took a sheaf of pages from the folder. She gazed at it expressionlessly for a moment, then said, "Mr. McKrall, Sunday morning wasn't the first time you found a dead body in a park."

Peter felt one hand drop onto the tabletop with a smack. With his other hand he fingered his lower lip. A tight band of tension played through his belly. "What are you talking about?" he said, his voice suddenly hoarse. Water gathered at the corners of his eyes.

Mulvaney looked up at him. "Your mother, Mr. McKrall. You found your mother's body in a park back in Lexington, Kentucky, a little over four years ago, dead from a gunshot wound. I want you to tell me about that."

THIRTEEN

"MULVANEY GOT YOU WITH the old '*just one more thing*' thing," Ruby Jane said. She and Peter sat by the front window, each with a mug of coffee. "She must be into Columbo." Ruby Jane attempted a smile. "So what did you tell her?"

Peter gazed out the window. A fitful rain had come and gone, and now the sun struggled to break through a hazy cloud-cover. "It's a long story," he said.

"I don't close until six."

He brought his gaze inside. Ruby Jane had pushed her floppy hat up on her forehead. Her brown bangs stuck out under the brim in all directions. Her eyes seemed to search his face, but there was warmth in her scrutiny. It comforted him. "What I mean is I told Mulvaney, 'It's a long story.'" He attempted a laugh. "It *is* a long story, if you're up for it."

"Of course."

The shop was empty, and Peter felt grateful for that. The pre-lunch slump, Ruby Jane called it. They might have twenty minutes or half an hour uninterrupted. He lifted his mug and started to drink, then set it down again. "I think I need something cold—and caffeine-free. I feel like I'm going to jump out of my skin. Maybe just a glass of water."

"Make yourself an Italian soda," Ruby Jane said. "There's a soda water dispenser on the counter and an ice maker next to the sink."

"I probably owe you about a hundred dollars for drinks."

"You can work it off. This morning you did two hours, which, at a buck an hour—"

"I didn't realize I'd gone to work for Nike." He stood and went behind the counter.

"You should have negotiated more aggressively. Still, if you behave, I might toss you the occasional tip."

"I'd just waste it on food and shelter."

Peter mixed an Italian soda, then rejoined Ruby Jane at the window. Outside, the street brightened under a sudden sun break, then just as quickly dimmed to cold gray again. He sipped his drink in silence for a moment, searching his mind for the right place to start. "I studied botany in college," he began. "Everyone thought that was a mistake, but I enjoyed it and I didn't want to end up in trusts like my dad. Worst case, I'd end up in a commercial nursery or maybe with the Forest Service—either of which would be fine. But I really hoped to go to grad school, to do research. Eventually go all the way—get my PhD, become an eccentric professor, wear a bushy beard and muddy boots—the whole shtick."

"So what happened?"

"My dad died. When I was a junior."

"I'm sorry. That must have been really hard."

"Yeah, it was hard. But it wasn't much of a surprise. He'd been fighting lung cancer for a long time." Peter shifted in his seat. "My dad personally supported the tobacco industry, I think. Three packs a day. Mom, too. All of us, really, except my sister Abby. She used to wear T-shirts that said, 'Kill Big Tobacco Before It Kills Us.'"

"Sounds like I'd get along with her just fine."

He bit back a remark and shrugged. He didn't want to get into Abby. "Anyway, I'd borrowed money from my folks for school, and when I graduated, I didn't feel like Mom could afford to let that loan hang out there, especially since I would probably have had to borrow even more money to go to grad school. She had Dad's life insurance, plus savings and some investments, but she had never worked a day in her life and wasn't likely to start at almost sixty. Without Dad, it got tight for her. There were medical bills, too. Dad had health insurance through work, but it didn't cover everything, and Mom was left owing a lot."

"So you decided to forgo the beard and muddy boots. Got a job."

"Yeah. As a trust administrator. An undergraduate degree in botany doesn't open a lot of doors. Or rather, *any* doors. I did get an offer of a graduate assistantship at the University of Cincinnati but the stipend didn't cover everything and there would have been no chance to pay Mom back, even if I didn't have to borrow any more money. I ended up calling some old friends of my Dad's and landed a job at Lexington Savings and Trust."

"The start of a whole new career."

"That's one way to look at it, I suppose. I was able to pay Mom some money, though. I learned my trade, such as it was, and worked my way up a little bit in the hierarchy. It wasn't horrible. It was just—I don't know … it was nothing. A big, blank hole in my life. All I did was go to work and come home. I was never tired enough to sleep well, never rested enough to feel like doing anything. I lived in a tiny apartment and marked time.

"At some point, Hank and John, my two older brothers, moved out of town. Hank's down in Atlanta, selling real estate, and the last I heard, John was in New York or Boston. Editing children's books, I think. He's not big on communication. Abby lives in Seattle now, but at the time she was in Portland with her new husband."

"Didn't you have any plans? Something long term?"

"Well, I've kind of always kept graduate school in the back of my mind. But paying Mom back came first, and to be honest, I just fell into a rut. I'd probably still be in that rut if U.S. Bank hadn't dumped me. But that's another matter altogether, and much later in the tale."

"So what happened to your mom?"

"Well, one day she called and said she'd been to the doctor and there'd been some tests and it was confirmed—she had a large malignant growth on her left lung. The doctor wanted to operate, then start her on chemotherapy. Or maybe the other way around. I don't remember exactly. It didn't look good either way."

Ruby Jane sipped coffee. Her gaze was soft and sympathetic. "It was abrupt then."

Peter shrugged, stared down at the bubbles rising in his drink. "Well, like my dad, it wasn't such a surprise. She really liked her Chesterfields. But, yeah, it was abrupt. I went to see her right after she called. She seemed okay. A little down, but not devastated. I was probably more upset than she was. She'd lived with Dad's cancer for over two years, and maybe she somehow learned to cope with the idea of dying. Hell, Dad had been dead for almost three years, and she'd always been fine. Of course, after two years fighting the cancer, his death was hardly a shock. She grieved, but she didn't fall apart." Peter breathed in through his nose, feeling suddenly stupid and self-conscious. He thought he was being a little mawkish. But Ruby Jane remained attentive. He smiled weakly and went on.

"I decided to take a few days off work to stay with her, so she wouldn't be alone. Outwardly, she wasn't in bad shape yet. Just a cough that never went away. Mostly, I went because I didn't want her to feel abandoned, and because I wanted to spend as much time with her as possible. Abby planned to come out for the surgery, but that wasn't going to happen right away. The doctor wanted... he wanted..."

"Pete?" Ruby Jane said quietly. He looked up at her, half startled. He took a long slow drink of his soda. Most of the flavoring had sunk to the bottom of the glass and he got a mouthful of cherry syrup as he finished it off. He swirled the leftover ice. "I think she'd made her decision before she even told me about the cancer. The morning after I arrived, she got up early and got my dad's gun. It was a thirty-two he'd bought years ago for protection. We never needed it for that—our neck of Lexington was pretty tame. Dad took us all out one time to plink at cans, but other than that, I don't remember ever seeing it. Dad had these hollow point bullets. He said that even though it was a small gun he still wanted it to have some stopping power. He talked about the bullet expanding and tearing up a person's insides. Abby was mortified, but Mom just shushed her. Protection is serious business, my dad said, and Mom was always quick to echo him. I dunno—she grew up with guns on a farm in central Kentucky. It was no big deal to her. Anyway, that morning,

Mom took the gun. Walked down the street to the park, three or four blocks. She used to spend a lot of time there—I guess that's why she picked it. She backed into some trees out of sight. Watched the sun come up. Smoked one last cigarette. Put the barrel of the gun in her mouth. The hollow point performed as advertised."

Ruby Jane's eyebrows narrowed and she reached out to take his hand. "Peter, I'm sorry. I'm so, so sorry," she said in a still, quiet voice. Peter felt his eyes water. Ruby Jane blurred and he blinked. In the gray halo formed by his tears she took on a sudden, striking clarity—an image captured in delicate crystal. For an instant, his mind was absorbed in her round face, by the ringlets of hair that framed it, by the sparkling depth of her blue eyes and the compassion that seemed to radiate out from her. Then he blinked again, and the crystal vanished in a scintillating wash of light. Ruby Jane remained. He blinked and yet she remained. He thought she was beautiful.

"Are you going to be all right?" she said, her voice as clear as flowing water.

He nodded and wiped his eyes with his free hand. "I just don't like to think about it."

She took his hand and gently caressed it. Her fingertips were warm and soft and after a moment the rhythmic motion began to relax him. "How do you feel?"

"I feel . . . better. I'm glad I told you about it." He brushed his hand across his forehead and was surprised to discover a thin film of perspiration. "I didn't tell most of the details to Mulvaney and Kadash. Not that I held back anything they'd find important, I think—just stuff *I* find important. But . . . getting it all out with you was—well, I suppose I feel relieved more than anything else."

She slowly shook her head. "So Mulvaney is digging. Looking for connections."

"Even if they're not there."

She returned her gaze to his face. "You must have found—"

He nodded. "I found a note first—it was on the kitchen counter when I got up. It told me exactly what she intended to do. That's how I know she watched the sunrise. She didn't want to be a burden on her family. She didn't want to saddle us with medical bills. I ran down to the park as soon as I saw the note, but I was just a few minutes too late. Her last cigarette was still smoldering in the grass beside her body. After that, I quit smoking."

She gazed pensively at his hand in her own. "That's why you got so upset when you found Darla's mother," she murmured. "It must have brought it all back."

"Not directly, but my emotions certainly bubbled up. I gave Kelly Norris an earful as a result, that's for sure." He chuckled wryly. "Boy, you should have seen the look on her face. They must have edited out three-quarters of what I said to her."

"You're changing the subject."

"Deft of me, wouldn't you say?" He smiled.

"Not really. But I'll let it slide." She took a long swallow from her mug. "I could use a refill." She headed back behind the counter and started to pour a cup of the Sumatra Boengie, then seemed to think better of it and got a glass off the shelf. She mixed an Italian soda, then asked Peter, "You want another?"

"Only if you let me renegotiate my contract."

She grinned. He brought her his glass and she poured in a shot of cherry syrup, then topped it off with soda water and fresh ice.

"The trouble with making the best coffee in Portland is you drink too much of it. It wouldn't hurt me a bit to cut back by a gallon or so a day." They sipped their sodas quietly, and her expression grew earnest again. "The question now," she said after a moment, "is what did Mulvaney have to say about your story?"

He snorted. "Not a damn thing. The whole time I spoke she just looked at her fax. It must have been a report from the Lexington police and she was just letting me confirm what she already knew from that. When I finished she said thanks and told me—yet again—to call her if I heard from Darla. Then she had Kadash drive me back here."

"What do you think it means?"

"I think it means I'm a suspect, and not just in Owen's mind now. What other reason would she have for digging that story up?"

"But what about the gun? You said it was the same gun in both murders. Who else would have it except Darla?"

"I don't know." He shook his head, shrugged. "But obviously they're looking for connections between what happened with my mother and what's happening now."

"They're grasping at straws."

"I can see why they're asking questions. Think about it—in my life, I've found two dead women, both in parks. The day after I find Carlotta Younger, a woman I supposedly didn't know, I happen to meet her daughter, who provides me with all kinds of inside information. Suddenly I know more than the police do—much as the killer might. Then a second victim turns up just a few houses from my own and, surprise, *I'm* the one who finds a dramatic piece of evidence at the crime scene. And note—the only known connection between the two victims is my own appearance at both scenes—

172

something that vulture Owen is quick to point out, just in case anyone missed it." He pursed his lips in disgust. "Then there's the bloody coat in my garbage, and on top of that, the gun my mother used was the type that killed the other two women. Wouldn't you ask questions, too?"

"Maybe I would. But, Pete, it's all just coincidence. The police must be able to see that. Darla called you, not the other way around. And it's not such a big surprise you appeared at the second murder—it happened practically next door to your house. And so you found the condom, so what? As for the coat, well, that's pretty thin, too—someone is trying to set you up. Maybe Darla, maybe somebody else. And as for the gun, well, there are lots of thirty-twos out there. Besides, the blood tests will rule you out."

He stared into his drink as if trying to divine a message from the pattern of bubbles, ice, and cherry syrup. No new answers emerged. Ruby Jane was right, of course—not only about the blood tests but about everything else. But that didn't make him feel any better about knowing that the police were delving into his own past in connection with a murder investigation. He felt invaded and exposed. It was for him to choose when and with whom he would share his pain—yet Mulvaney usurped that choice without a second thought. What did it take for her to prospect so successfully into his secrets? A phone call or two to Lexington, and a fax in return. Hardly any effort at all. It struck him as ironic that the police needed a warrant to search your home, but evidently they could tread upon the hidden recesses of your soul with nary a by-your-leave. He took a swallow of soda and decided it was time for a clumsy segue. "Do you think Darla could have killed her mother?"

Ruby Jane frowned. "I never would have guessed that she killed her father. Of course, I knew she had problems. You don't end up in a halfway house for no reason."

"You saw her yesterday morning. Did she seem like someone wracked with guilt?"

"My gut says she was more wracked by grief than guilt, but what do I know? I'm a purveyor of fine coffees—not Dr. Phil."

"I know I wouldn't want to be her lawyer. She's gonna need Perry Mason."

The door bells chimed and a couple of guys in grease-blackened coveralls came in. Peter drifted back to the window table with his drink while Ruby Jane served them. He glanced at the clock. It was after eleven, which meant the lunch crowd would start to appear soon. Ruby Jane offered soup and bread for lunch, which kept trade brisk through mid-day. He watched her serve the two men—French press coffees and two soups to go ladled from an electric pot—and he was struck once more by her carefree openness. Her smile was bright and genuine. She jawed readily with the fellows, laughed at their jokes. After she passed them their orders and they paid, they both dropped money in the tip jar. When they left, she rejoined him at the table.

"You're really good with the customers. I bet you have lots of regulars."

She grinned and tilted her head sheepishly. "Aw, shucks," she said.

"I mean it."

"I like people. I like coffee. This is a good business for me." She paused and stared at him thoughtfully. "Pete, I've got a notion," she said.

"What's that?"

"Sometimes there are connections you don't see."

"What do you mean?"

"Well…" She stared at him a moment, as if trying to measure his reaction. "… would you have responded to finding Darla's mom the way you did if you hadn't found your own mom in similar circumstances? Would you have said the things you did to that reporter? And if you hadn't, would Darla have ever called you? And would you now be stuck in the middle of a murder investigation trying to get out?"

"And would I have met you?" he said.

"Well, yeah. That, too. The thing is, I think there *are* connections, even if they're not the ones the police are looking for. They're the connections that mean something to you."

He considered her words, and recalled his own ruminations earlier that morning as he waited for Kadash to pick him up. "Contingencies again," he said. He tilted his head toward her. "How long have we known each other now?"

"You want it to the minute?" she said, grinning. "I'd have to check the clock. Twenty-six, twenty-seven hours. Call it a day, just for the sake of convenience."

"It's been quite a day. I feel like Wall Street." Peter smiled and leaned back and stretched. "I should probably go home and get some clothes—and I have bonsais I have to water every day or they shrivel up, but I'll help you with lunch first."

"Why don't you go now and get it over with? The sooner the better. I can handle lunch. I expect it to be fairly light anyway, it being Christmas week and all. Yesterday I only went through one kettle of soup."

"You sure? I'm glad to help."

"My, you're eager to work. But seriously, go ahead and go. You can help me close."

"Mmmm, mopping."

"Do you want to take my car?"

"The bus is fine. Or maybe I'll walk. The rain's stopped and the air'll clear my head."

She shook her head. "Pete, do you walk everywhere? Don't you have a car?"

"Actually I have an old Land Cruiser in my garage that I bought last summer. I'm sort of restoring it."

"How does one *sort of* restore a Land Cruiser? There's not much to it, right? Sheet metal, an engine, and hard unforgiving seats."

"Well, I put in a couple of soft cushy seats that I pulled out of a junked Jeep Wrangler. That was one of the easier chores. Right now the engine's hanging off a hoist in my garage. I haven't worked on it since it got cold."

"Well, that's an excuse, I suppose."

"I'll get it up and running this spring. Maybe we could go camping."

"I'd like that, if I can get away from this place." She came around from behind the counter and kissed him lightly. "Be careful," she said. "I know it's daylight, but if anything seems funny, just turn around and leave, okay? You can always buy some clothes."

"I'd definitely have to renegotiate my contract in that case."

"I'm serious. Don't take any chances. Your place seems weird in any way, clear out. You got me?"

"I got you. See you soon."

FOURTEEN

THE PLACE SEEMED DIFFERENT. His home for over two years and suddenly it looked like a stranger's house. Didn't take much. A couple of murders, a bloody coat, and everything changed. Peter looked at the houses to either side, seeking commonality, some source of security, something to bring the sense of home back to him. To the right lived an elderly Filipino couple, Jonny and Lily. They barely spoke English and buried their garbage in their back yard. In the warmer weather, he often stood on his driveway and had long, broken, and all but incomprehensible conversations with the old man. Now that it was cold, he hardly saw them. To the left lived a black woman named Doris raising two children on her own. She hadn't spoken more than ten words to Peter in all the time he lived here, but her son, Daryl, now fifteen, mowed Peter's lawn for fifteen bucks a pop and sometimes hung out for hours at a time asking about Peter's plants. Across the street was the pumpkin—painted yellow-orange, with two triangular roof vents and a fascia over the narrow porch that suggested a jack-o'-lantern. The pumpkin was a rental, and Peter had never met the current tenants. Up and down the street were more of the same—transient renters and insular gray homeowners who spent their summers weeding their beds of foxglove, kale, and alyssum and their winters hiding from the rain and each other. Some of the doorways were festooned with Christmas wreaths, but these were only feeble evidence of friendliness or cheer. Just his little pocket of the Irvington neighborhood, except to Peter it didn't seem like a neighborhood, but merely a collection of houses and a gathering of strangers intent on remaining estranged.

Overhead, the Portland sun glared like a glaucoma-lidded eye. After the warmth of Ruby Jane, he felt cold and alone. Now he wished he'd taken her suggestion to just buy some clothes. The plants could tough it out on their own. The house seemed to mock him in its silence and solitude. Back at the coffee shop, he had deemed it more reasonable to come while it was daylight. Bad things didn't happen during daylight. But he hadn't counted on the isolation of his own street, on the quiet somnolence that pervaded the very air. If something bad did happen, would anyone wake? Would they come if he called out for help?

The place looked secure. The front door was closed. None of the windows were broken. The windows on the sides and in the back, the ones that faced Irving Park, all had bars on them. He walked slowly up onto the porch. When he'd left the previous morning, he had expected to be back soon. Nonetheless he'd locked up with his usual care—the spring lock on the doorknob was always secured, and he'd turned the deadbolt as well. He'd even lowered the heat. He didn't have a cat or a dog or even fish that needed feeding. Aside from the plants, there was no reason he couldn't simply turn around and leave, for a day or a week or more. Call Abby from

Ruby Jane's and let her know where he was—pick up a few pairs of underwear and some shirts at Fred Meyer's. Then let Darla call or sneak around all she wanted. It didn't matter.

"Don't be an idiot," he muttered to himself. "Go water your plants and get some clothes." He thought in particular of his bonsais—a few tender ficus trees and a pair of flowering quince that required almost daily attention. He fingered his keys in his pocket, still wavering. Crazy, feeling so anxious about entering his own house. With quick deliberation, he pulled out the keys and unlocked the deadbolt, then inserted the key into the doorknob and turned it. For a second he hesitated, then pushed the door open. He scrutinized the living room and dining room beyond, faintly and curiously surprised to see no one there. He took a deep breath and entered. Without thinking about it, he left the door open behind him.

The living room was filled with a diffuse staleness. Thin light filtered through closed curtains and tinted everything with a somber, funereal pallor. In his mind, the familiarity of the space battled his anxiety. His memory seemed to want to play tricks on him—he recalled a time when this was merely the place where he lived. The couch where he read or watched TV. The dining room that housed most of his plants. The mock Oriental rug where he wrestled with Julie and Patch. But that all seemed so long ago. He breathed the inert air and tried to remember that his last wrestling match with Julie had been just a few days before—that he and Abby and Dave and Julie had eaten a big holiday dinner at the dining room table on Friday night—that the couch was simply his couch, battered and lumpy and purchased through the Thrifty ads only a year before. But his memory remained rooted in the most immediate events.

It was all too easy to recall that Mulvaney had suggested his home might not be safe.

Through the open doorway, he heard the sound of traffic from Fremont. The Sunday paper lay in a heap by the couch where he had left it Sunday night. The empty water glass still sat on the arm of the couch. From the end table, the light on the answering machine blinked on and off. Its mundane familiarity comforted him in a vague way. He unzipped his coat, but decided to leave it on. The LCD on the machine showed fourteen messages. The number bewildered him. He didn't ordinarily get fourteen messages in an entire month. "Abby must be worried," he breathed. She hadn't had a chance to prattle at him for a good thirty-six hours or so. He pressed the playback button and sank into the couch to listen.

The tape rewound and the machine clattered for a long time. Finally it beeped and he heard a moment of silence followed by a sharp click. A hang-up. He shrugged absently as if to say, *Fine—hang up then.* A second hang-up followed, then a third...a fourth...a fifth—a bizarre, empty succession. Was it that hard to leave a message? Abby *always* left messages. He felt his impatience rising when, after the ninth beep, he heard, "You *fucker!* Damn it damn it *damn it!*" followed by the sound of a sharp, plastic-against-plastic whack. A shudder swept through him. The voice sounded remotely familiar. The tenth beep yielded another hang-up, as did the eleventh. Then the machine beeped again.

"Goddamn! Never fucking home, never fucking home—you hear what I'm sayin'? *Fuck you!*"

There was a hollow, breathy pause and a click. Another deep shudder passed through him. *Who was that?* Apprehension mounting, he stared at the answering machine.

The machine clicked and beeped. "Peter, this is Abby. I'm just checking in. It sounds like things are getting really awful down there. We heard about that woman up the street from you—it was on the Northwest Cable News, if you can imagine. Please call me and let me know if you need anything. Julie keeps asking about Patch. We all love you and hope you're okay—*beep*—" He shook his head and ran his hand through his hair. The call from Abby sounded discordant and unreal after the two previous messages—if they could be called messages. The machine beeped one last time and Abby's voice came back on. "Peter, where are you? What's going on? We're worried about you. I don't understand why you haven't called. I don't like this."

He gazed around the living room. Suddenly it seemed more remote and alien than ever. He took a long, slow breath in an effort to calm his jangled nerves. His first thought was to get his things and then get the hell out. Screw the plants. Go back to Uncommon Cup and call Mulvaney about the phone messages. Maybe she could make something of them. He reached down to pop the tape out of the answering machine, but hesitated. His hands were shaking. He squeezed them into tight fists, then shook them as though shaking off water. His eyes shifted to the telephone. *Take a minute and call Abby*, he thought. *She'll piss you off. You'll feel better.*

He picked up the phone. No dial tone. He tapped the disconnect button a couple of times, without effect. Helplessly, he stared at the receiver in his hand. "Shit," he said aloud. But the voice in his head said, *Outta here!*

He heard the creak of a floorboard behind him. "I'm really sorry," a soft voice said. "I unplugged the phone."

Peter lurched to his feet and spun around. Darla stood in the doorway that led into the bedroom hallway. She held a tangled skein of silvery phone wire in one hand. "I gotta talk to you," she said. "The cops tried to bust me. If you talk to me I'll give your phone cords back, okay? Just talk to me."

Peter felt a sensation like flowing water in his arms and legs. He opened his mouth to speak, but no sound came out. He looked toward the open front door. She was closer to it than he was.

"I just wanna talk to you," Darla said again. "Please. I'll give you your phone cords back then." She raised the bundle of wire as if in offering, then withdrew it to her chest.

He gazed toward the doorway again. The door had been locked— he was sure of that—the windows locked or barred as well. Yet here she stood, in his house, with his telephone wires in her hand. He was surprised to find someone inside after all. "How—how did you get in here?" he managed through a constricted throat. His voice sounded thin and reedy and only barely under control.

Darla ducked her head in evident shame. "I didn't break in," she said tightly. "I don't do that no more. I promise I didn't break in." She looked back up at him, but he didn't respond. "The basement window was open. Broken or something. There was glass on the floor." Her eyes seemed to search his face but if they saw anything, it could only be his alarm. "I didn't bust the window. I know you don't believe me—nobody ever believes me—but I didn't do it. I just came in that way. That's all," she finished miserably.

"Darla—why are you here?" he said.

"I *told* you! The cops tried to bust me this morning," she said. "But I didn't do anything! I swear! I can't go back to jail."

With an effort, Peter slowly shook his head. "I can't talk to you."

"Please. I can't go back to jail." She glanced down at the phone cords pressed against her chest. "I got the one off the bedroom phone, too," she said. "I couldn't take a chance you'd just call the cops without talking to me first. I left the answering machine plugged in so you wouldn't miss any messages. I don't want to cause no trouble."

You've already caused trouble. But he kept the thought off his lips. He took a deep breath and looked her over. She wore the same dirty stocking cap and dingy army jacket. Her cheeks were, if anything, more blotchy than the day before, her eyes more sunken and dark. The scar on her jaw stood out in lurid contrast to the unhealthy color of her face. She looked exhausted.

"Please," she said. "You gotta tell me what the cops think. What did you tell them about me?"

The watery sensation migrated from his legs to his gut and he felt that at any second his bowels might simply let go. Darla faced him across a dozen feet of empty space, her face a relief map of pain and entreaty, and he was terrified of what might happen if he said the wrong thing. He stared at her and tried to think of something to do. One misstep—

"Please," she said, "what'd you tell them? I just gotta know." As he gazed at her, he saw moisture gather in the corners of her eyes. A swollen tear rolled down her cheek and caught on the ridge of her scar. A second tear followed. Her eyes looked like bubbles, glistening and fragile. She sighed deeply and a third tear fell. "*Please…*" she whispered.

Something in her voice and in her doleful tears blunted the edge of his fear. Perhaps it was that he heard the appeal of her own fear, or the appeal of some deeper anguish. Part of him wanted to agree to talk to her, but another part recalled their last meeting, and the swiftness with which he had been drawn into two murders. He felt his ambivalence war within him, and through it Mulvaney's face arose in his mind again and again. After a moment, he swallowed and said, "Darla, I promised the police I would call them if you came back. Do you understand that? People are dead—"

She closed her eyes and for a moment her jaw hardened. Then she sighed again and opened her eyes. "I understand, okay? I just want you to tell me what they know. Then I fade and you can call the cops. I understand that. Please just tell me what you told them, so I can get a handle on where I stand. Okay?"

His ambivalence told him not to talk to her. But the haunted desperation of her voice reached deeper. *A little bit won't hurt*, he told himself. *Talk to her for a few minutes, then get away and call Mulvaney. It won't make any difference.* Besides, it might be the only way she would let him go. He wondered if the gun was in her pocket. "I only told them the things you told me. About how you saw your mom at the bar, and going in and out with the men. They already knew she was a—um, that she was a—"

"A *whore*."

He flinched at the knifelike severity of her tone. "Yeah. They didn't know where she'd been Saturday night, though. They didn't know about the bar. I think they were going to check it out."

She slowly and solemnly shook her head. Color rose in her cheeks and her brows narrowed. He could see her mood change as quickly as if a curtain opened. "They was gonna check it out, huh," she said with a voice full of acid. "I can just see it—'How many of you boys scored a knobwax from that murdered pro last Saturday night?' What a fucking joke." He hated to think how she would react if he told her he'd been at that very bar just a couple of nights earlier, that he'd seen a woman there working the crowd. Heaven help him.

She drew air through her teeth. "What else did you tell them?"

"Well, that was it. Just what you told me."

Thunder threatened on her forehead as she considered his words. For a moment, he wished he hadn't said anything. The open doorway continued to lure him, and it occurred to him that if he made a dash for it, she wouldn't be able to stop him. He could probably run right through her. Unless, of course, she pulled the gun. Yet even as he contemplated such an act, the curtain seemed to close on her mood again. Moisture returned to the corners of her eyes. She looked at him and her face seemed to sag. "I bet you told them how I didn't like it that my mom was a whore," she said.

A warning flared in his mind. "Well," he said cautiously, "nobody would." He searched for the words that might deflect her bitterness. "Darla...when I talked to you yesterday it was, uh, pretty intense for me. You were really angry." At those words her eyes narrowed and he quickly added, "But you had a right to be. Your mother had been murdered. Of course you were angry. I understand."

For a moment, it was as if she hadn't heard him. Her eyes were fixed on some empty spot in the air behind his head. Then she seemed to stifle a sob and she brought her empty hand slowly to her forehead. "Oh, god," she said, "I know what you did. You didn't just tell them I didn't like it. You told them I was pissed about it. You told them I couldn't fucking *stand* it!" She slapped her forehead sharply. "Oh, god. They think I did it, don't they? That's why they tried to bust me. They think I killed my mama."

She suddenly buckled over at the waist and held her hands at the side of her head. For a moment he thought she was going to vomit. Her hair hung from beneath her stocking cap like a mat of dried moss. "They think I killed my mama," she murmured, half whimpering. She hung there and he heard the soft, bubbling sound of sobbing.

He took a step forward. "Darla—"

At the sound of his voice she jerked up. "Why?" she said. "Why did you tell them that?" Without waiting for an answer, she turned first to one side, then the other, like a trapped animal. He took another step toward her and she suddenly brandished the wad of phone wire at him like a weapon. "Stay away from me!" she hissed.

"I never meant for them to—"

"To what? To blame me? They always fucking blame me. Oh, god…" She twisted again from side to side, her arms wrapped around her middle. Her eyes took on a feral cast. He struggled to find something to say that would bring some semblance of sanity back to the situation.

"Darla—"

"Listen," she said, interrupting. "I done some bad things in my life, okay? Maybe some horrible things, people might think. But all that's been behind me a long time. I done my time. I even been off smack since my last time in treatment." Her voice bargained, thick with a piteous tone just short of pleading. "Been almost a year since I shot up, okay? I'm clean. That's why I thought I was ready to see my mama again. I'm clean and I just wanted to see my mama. It'd been such a long time, and I missed her, you know? Shit, she didn't even recognize me, but I was clean, and I wanted to see her."

His desperation stretched around him like a great sheet of plastic. Awkwardly, almost desperately, he said, "I think it's good you're clean." His voice sounded muted to him—once removed by the plastic layer of his solicitude.

She nodded tersely, as though only half aware he had even spoken. "Now you gotta listen to me. I didn't do it. I never killed my mama. Okay? I don't care what happened a long time ago. It don't mean I killed my mama, too. The past is past." Her eyes pleaded with his through plastic. "The ... past ... *is* ... *past.*"

The moment stretched, then Peter's stomach lurched with recognition. He realized she was acknowledging, in her own oblique fashion, the murder of her father. A surreal sense of the weight of history bore down upon him. He all but forgot Darla's presence as, in his mind, grim memories of his own father arose unbidden like pictures bound in shrink-wrap. The old man, in his last months, had hobbled around the house pulling his oxygen tank on a cart while his body wasted away and lesions as vivid as bullet holes formed on his chest and back. Peter felt tears form and he clenched his teeth in an effort to beat the memory back. Instinctively, he knew this wasn't the time to face such recollections. But as he struggled with the memory, an image surged into his mind of what Darla's father must have looked like at his own end, a heaving body riddled with bullet holes as vivid as lesions. And Darla, shrunken, younger—a child—standing over him, warm gun in her hand. Desperately, Peter tried to shake the images away. In an instant, the young Darla and her gun faded, but his own father's image remained, merged now with a vision of his mother, smoking her last cigarette on the final morning of her life. The gun hung from her hand, like Darla's gun. Behind her, the sun rose above a landscape covered with sores. Peter shook his head again and squeezed his eyes tightly shut.

I didn't ask to be a part of this horror out of some fucking stranger's past. His own past was awful enough.

Darla didn't appear to notice his turmoil. "I didn't do it!" she insisted again. "You gotta understand that. I didn't *do it!*"

From a remote place at the heart of his dark memories, he heard his voice speak without volition. "Darla, it was your gun that killed your mother. The one you shot your father with." He regretted his words instantly. The very force of their meaning brought him rushing back to the present. The plastic sheet split before him as the words hung in the very air, a palpable force that stunned Darla into momentary silence. She gasped for breath, and he was reminded once more of his father's oxygen tank.

"That can't be …" Her voice faded away and all the color drained from her face. "Oh my god," she whispered. "That means he … it just can't be …" She brought her hands up to her face. A quavering wail rose in her throat as she turned and bolted through the open door.

Peter stood in stunned silence. *I never should have come home.* He felt wrung dry. Then, behind him, the answering machine clattered and beeped, and he heard Abby's voice. "Peter, what the hell is going on? Where are you? Why won't you return my calls? Please, *please* call us. We're worried to death!" For a moment Peter didn't comprehend what was happening. The unexpected sound of Abby's disembodied voice, like the voice of a ghost, sent a chill through his body. "Call us, dammit!—*beep*—"

Then he realized what had happened. Darla didn't want him to miss any messages, she said. She'd left the answering machine plugged in, but no way for Peter to even hear the phone ring before the machine did its thing. Abby's message joined the inexplicable string of hang ups and—

The voice. Mind churning, Peter stared at the machine. Its black surface gleamed dully in the light from the open doorway. As he gazed at the blinking LED, he remembered where he had heard that voice before—Mulvaney's recording. He pressed the Rewind button, then, after a moment, pressed Play.

—*beep*, click—*whir*—*beep*, click—*whir*—

Impatiently, he jabbed Fast-Forward, then hit Play again half a second later.

—*beep*, click—*whir*—*beep*, "Damn it! You *fucker!* Damn it damn it *damn it!*" click—

The voice from the tape. He was sure of it. The person who had called him Mister Mackerel.

—*whir*—*beep*, click—*whir*—*beep*, "Goddamn! Never fucking home, never fucking home—"

A man's voice. Peter ran his hands through his hair, then looked at the open doorway. Too much had happened, too much—all swirling around in his head. The plastic sheet had split, but its shreds fluttered in tatters among his jumbled thoughts.

Darla—

There was something he was missing, some connection he wasn't making. He kneaded the skin of his forehead as though the physical act could jar his thoughts out of their viscid lassitude. *What was the last thing she said?* he asked himself. It came to him with the abruptness of a cough.

That can't be…Oh my god…That means he…it just can't be… The words hung in his mind for a long, stark moment, their meaning suddenly clear.

"She didn't do it," he said.

His voice seemed to resonate in the empty living room. The sound cleared the last shreds of uncertainty and distress from his mind. *She didn't do it*, he thought. She didn't do it, but she knew who did. That was why she ran. It was someone she knew, someone close to her—maybe someone who had been there, at the murder of her father, ten years earlier. Someone who could have somehow gotten ahold of the gun, and kept it, hidden perhaps, all these years. He glanced at the useless phone one last time, then ran out the front door, slamming it behind him.

"Darla!" he called. "Darla—!" He looked up and down the street. She was nowhere to be seen. He ran around the side of the house and into the back yard. He stopped at the fence. Two hundred yards away, at the edge of the playground, he saw a figure—green jacket, black cap. Even in her dolor, she couldn't resist the lure of the site of her mother's murder.

"Darla!" he shouted. "Wait! I think I know what happened! Wait! *Darla—!*" She kept moving. He glanced quickly back at the house, then vaulted the fence and ran after her across the wet grass of Irving Park.

FIFTEEN

JAKE DIDN'T OFTEN REMEMBER his dreams. Most of the time, he simply awoke with a fretful, unsettled feeling, as though he'd done something bad in his sleep. Even before he did the old whore it had been like that. In one of the group homes there had been a case-worker who tried to get him to talk about his dreams. She wanted him to remember them so she could help him. *Help me do what?* She could suck his thing, he told her—that would help. But he wasn't going to talk about his dreams. Eventually she gave up on him.

But sometimes the dreams were more insistent. As the cold morning wore away, he dreamed of voices. In the distance he could make out two silhouettes, but he couldn't tell who the people were. He tried listening to the voices, but they were just sounds—angry sounds. He shrank away, tried to escape, but his feet stuck to the ground. He kept yawning, and he wanted to just sleep. He pulled the covers over his head, but the voices penetrated like small snapping animals. He sat up and tried to see, but the door was only part way open, the light the color of piss. He heard grunting and weeping. Then one of the voices got louder. It boomed through the doorway, it shouted at him. It told him to shut his cake hole and get back to bed, if he knew what was good for him. And the other voice cried, and said *please don't*, and Jake knew it was Dee-Dee. The big, booming voice told her to shut up and take what was coming to her. And Jake looked through the door, and he saw Dee-Dee kneeling face-down at the edge of the bed, arms stretched out, fists beating the mattress. Skirt hiked up. The big, booming voice behind her. She cried and said *please just talk to me…*

Jake tried to get closer, but the big, booming—

He awoke to the sound of a calling voice. The gun was still in his hand, held to his crotch and pressed against an aching boner. He forgot where he was. He sat up with a start and the footrest of the recliner folded down. The room looked strange. Then he remembered. Peterhead's house. Little room at the top of the stairs. Bed and chair and dust and television. And the calling voice. The sound crept in through the windows, muffled by layers of glass and wood. *Darla!* it called. *Darla! Wait!*

Jake was coated with sweat. His jacket and pants seemed to have dried from the rain, but down underneath, he felt damp and clammy. The voice called again, *Darla!* This time farther away. He shook his head and stood up. The light around the windows seemed brighter than when he'd fallen asleep. He listened, and when the voice called again he went to the window opposite the stairs and lifted the curtain.

The rain had stopped, and the clouds seemed thinner, but the world still looked gray and dreary. Below, facing the park, stood a man wearing long black jeans and a puffy navy-blue jacket. One of those down jackets—the kind of jacket that was way too expensive for Jake. The man clasped his hands to the top of the fence and called out again, *Darla! Wait! I think I know what happened! Wait! Darla—!*

The man glanced back at the house and Jake's leg trembled—Peterhead, it was that goddamn Peterhead Mackerel. Jake's hand tightened on the gun and he almost squeezed the trigger. *Ooo, man, that wouldn't do*, he thought. *Wouldn't do one bit.* As Jake stared, Peterhead jumped the fence and ran off through the park.

"Aw, fuck." Jake didn't have a plan, but if he *did* have a plan, he knew it wouldn't include Peterhead running off into the park. Without thinking, he lifted the gun and aimed it through the window. He steadied his hand to fire, but Peterhead was already too far away. Too far, too fast. Jake lowered the gun. What did he think he was going to do anyway? Shoot through the window? The glass would probably ruin the shot, and then Peterhead would know somebody was gunning for him.

Jake thrust the gun into his jacket pocket and turned away from the window. He had to follow. But at the top of the stairs he hesitated. He gazed back at the easy chair, at the television, and sighed. It was a *color TV*. He wanted to sit down and flip it on and watch *The Price is Right*, or maybe *Maury*. But then, as he contemplated the comfort of the chair and the cool glow of the color TV, a grim memory of his dream rose up in his mind. —*big, booming*— He recoiled as though from a dark shadow and choked back a whimper, then turned and scrambled, almost stumbling, down the stairs.

He stopped in the hallway. The living room looked the same, but he detected a chill in the still air that drew his eyes to the front door. Peterhead had been here. Jake was sure of it. And now Peterhead was gone again, out through the park, out into the world. *Getting away.* As Jake stood, hesitating, he sensed a looming darkness behind him at the top of the stairs, the lingering shadow of his dream. He shook his head and suppressed the urge to cry. He felt for the gun, just to make sure it was still there, then went to the door. He pulled it open nervously, half expecting to see someone waiting for him on the other side. But the porch was empty. He went out and shut the door behind him. It half registered in the back of his mind that the deadbolt hadn't been locked. Peterhead was in some kind of hurry.

Jake went around the side of the house to the back fence and scanned the open fields. A few cars rolled by on Fremont at the north edge of the park, but Jake saw no one on foot. No Peterhead, nobody.

Anger boiled at the edge of his thoughts. "Damn it!" he hissed. Fucking fall asleep, fucking miss your chance. He was there, Peterhead was *there.* And Jake had missed him. The urge to cry returned. Sucking air in frustration, he climbed the fence and started across the field, angling vaguely in the direction of the playground. His anger fluttered fecklessly like an old crow. But he pushed it aside, because suddenly the playground lured him toward it, drove other thoughts from his mind.

It wasn't hard to know why. Jake shoved his hands into his jacket pockets and pressed hard against his lower abdomen through the fabric. He walked up off the soccer field onto the path that split the park. He knew they would have taken the old whore away, but a part of him fantasized about finding her there in the big tube just as he left her. The bullet holes would be darker now, deeper and blacker and rimed with frost. He pressed harder against his stomach as an anxiety of need swelled in his groin. He almost forgot Peterhead.

The playground was as empty as a cemetery. He knew it was Christmas break, but there weren't any kids anywhere. Maybe they were afraid of the place now—didn't like old dead whores. He drifted toward the swings, then past the dry wading pool filled with dead leaves, up to the ring of pipes. He continued to scan the park in the raw yet aimless hope that Peterhead would appear, but more of his attention was focused on the pipes, on the old newspaper and leaves, and, finally, on the black stain he found inside that one big tube. The old whore's big tube. *His* big tube. He took a deep, shuddering breath and crawled inside. His stomach clenched and quaked. He lay down on his back and stared up at the curve of concrete above him. He tried to imagine what it was like for the old whore. The holes all over. *Did it hurt?* he wondered. Shit, it had to hurt. Something like that couldn't not hurt. But did it also—? Could it have—?

Did it—?

Did it *feel*—?

—*good?*

He grasped the gun in his pocket and rubbed it against himself. Somewhere far away the rising wind passed through the upper boughs of the cedars and made a sound like falling water. Jake breathed in cold air, and the wind rushed. The holes filled up his mind, bloody and black. They consumed him. They made him think of Dee-Dee, of their times together. It had been so long, so long ago. He wanted her, wanted to see her face. Wanted to touch her—

He remembered how it started. She lay on her bed, and she was rubbing herself, and she let him watch. She told him to touch it, to rub it, just like that—*that's right.* "It's okay to put your fingers in-side, but not your thing," she said. She smiled, but it was a kind of a nervous smile—she was worried about something. But then she reached out and unzipped his shorts and grabbed his thing. "If you put your thing in, something bad could happen," she said, and she squeezed it till it almost hurt. "Daddy said so. That's why he never puts his in. He makes me put it in my mouth." She giggled, but it was a nervous giggle. She stopped squeezing so hard—started rubbing and it felt good. "Rubbing's okay. The mouth is okay." The concrete was above him and the bloody black stain was beneath him, but the memory of Dee-Dee filled him up. He rubbed his thing with the gun and imagined Dee-Dee was rubbing it and imagined the holes in the old whore. It felt so good he hardly noticed when he came. He didn't even care that he had made a mess in his pants. It just felt too good. Almost like Dee-Dee was with him again. Almost like—

He heard voices.

His hand froze and in an instant his thing collapsed in on it-self like a snail slupping back up into its shell. He listened, but at first he couldn't quite make out what was being said. Were they coming closer? Were they going to catch him rubbing his thing? He jerked his hands out of his pockets. He twisted himself around and crept to the end of the tube where he could hear the voices over the sound of the wind.

"—tell Detective Kadash you're back?" a voice was saying. A man.

"You probably ought to. Skin can stop by any time today. Got plenty to do around the house so I'll just wait right here for him." Another man. Older. Old man.

There was a pause, then the first voice said, "This is all so crazy."

"You take it easy, son. You're doing fine. Now just you go on. You tell Skin I'm waiting for him. But don't dawdle. He'll skin *me* if I keep you any longer."

"Thanks, Andy."

"You're welcome. Now get moving."

They don't want me, Jake thought. They didn't have anything to do with him. But something about the first voice made Jake want to just see. Skittishly, like a mouse creeping from its hole, he stuck his head out the end of the tube. The wind brought a chill to his cheeks. At first he didn't see anyone. Then he caught a blur of motion on the far side of the fence that bordered the park. A big yellow dog nosed back and forth in the back yard of a small house. Up on the porch, Jake saw an old man standing motionlessly and gazing off to his left. When Jake followed the line of the old man's gaze, he saw Peterhead Mackerel walking away from him down the street that dead-ended there at the edge of the park.

As Jake huddled, staring and transfixed, Peterhead disappeared beyond a laurel hedge. Jake felt a sensation like electricity surge through him. He popped to his feet and wended his way out of the jumble of pipes. The old man on the porch turned his head and stared, and for a moment Jake had the uncomfortable feeling of being scrutinized. Then the old man looked away and clapped his hands. The dog barked once and bounded onto the porch. The old man held open the back door for the dog and both disappeared inside.

Jake trotted to the opening in the fence where the path joined the sidewalk beyond. Peterhead was at the corner, about half a block away, and moving briskly. He turned left. Jake followed after him at a quick pace, glancing uneasily at the houses to either side to see if anyone was watching. He saw cars in many of the driveways, but if anyone was home they didn't show themselves.

At the corner, Jake saw that Peterhead had gained some distance. He glanced at the street sign. Ninth and Siskiyou. He wondered if Peterhead was going to turn at Eleventh and go back to his house, or continue elsewhere. *Go home*, he thought. *Go home!* He didn't have a plan, but if he could get Peterhead back to his house he would probably think of something. Probably just shoot the fucker. Stop beating around the bush. But when Peterhead came to Eleventh he continued straight and Jake felt the acid bite of frustration rise in his throat. At least Peterhead didn't look back. He would probably think it was strange to see some guy trotting along after him. Might scare him. Not that the thought of that bothered Jake. He kind of liked the idea of Peterhead getting all scared. Maybe, really, that was his plan. Make Peterhead scared. Make him really scared. Make him so scared he'd cry and wet himself. That thought made Jake chuckle and he stopped feeling so frustrated. But he also picked up his pace. Peterhead wasn't looking.

Jake gained ground between Thirteenth and Fourteenth. As he neared Fifteenth, Peterhead slowed. He took a couple of steps onto Fifteenth and gazed up the street to his left. The house on the corner blocked Jake's view of what he might be looking at. Peterhead returned to the sidewalk and stood waiting at the corner.

Jake slowed to a stroll. He didn't want Peterhead to get a good look at him, but he also didn't want Peterhead to get too far ahead. Peterhead needed to move—stopping wasn't part of the deal. Jake couldn't follow him if he stopped. That was fucking Peterhead for you. Didn't get busted from the coat, didn't get busted from the phone call. Didn't hang around his house so Jake could shoot him.

He wrecked everything. Why the hell was he just standing there? As Jake edged closer, he looked around for some clue. Cars went by on Fifteenth, but not often enough to keep anyone from crossing. So what the hell was Peterhead gonna do? Stand there and pick his nose? Then Peterhead reached into his jacket and removed a card. Something about the card seemed vaguely familiar, but Jake couldn't place it.

He heard a loud metallic squeal from up Fifteenth, the brakes of a big truck or a bus. A moment later, the bus stopped at the corner. With a clatter, the door opened. Suddenly he recognized the card in Peterhead's hand—*bus pass.*

Jake lunged forward, then halted just as quickly. He realized Peterhead would see him if he got on the bus, too, but if Jake didn't hurry, Peterhead would get away. All kinds of people rode the bus, right? Business guys and housewives and bums. Jake wouldn't stand out, would he? Just another working guy. Probably—hopefully —Peterhead wouldn't even notice him.

The bus door closed and the engine revved. "Wait!" Jake yelled. He dashed up and the bus door popped open again. "Thanks," Jake grunted as he trotted up the steps. The bus driver grumbled something indecipherable. Jake dug into his pocket and came up with quarters to feed the change collector, accepted a transfer from the driver. He lowered his head and moved up the aisle, grasping the overhead handrail for balance as the bus surged ahead.

The bus was half full with a mix of midday riders—women with big hair and long overcoats, clumps of high school kids swearing and pretending to spit on each other, one or two blank-eyed old men with a week's growth of stubble and clothing that looked as though it had been slept in. Jake couldn't imagine allowing himself to ever look so untidy, no matter how old he got. He shook his head and sat on the bench seat behind the driver that could be folded up to allow space for wheelchair riders.

He glanced furtively around the bus. He spotted Peterhead sitting toward the back across from the rear door. He was staring out the bus window, his eyebrows slightly pinched. After a moment, he brought his gaze back inside and met Jake's eyes with his own. For an instant, they looked at each other as panic rose in Jake's chest. Then Peterhead looked back out the window again, his face untroubled by any hint of recognition. Jake lowered his head.

"Hey, bro," a voice said. He looked up and saw a trio of teenage boys across from him. They wore high school letter jackets and ripped jeans. One of them grinned at Jake, a long shock of blond hair dripping into his eyes. "Right space, wrong handicap?" he said. Jake stared at him without comprehension. The boy started laughing and pointed at the handicap sticker above the bench seat. "Right space, wrong handicap, dumbass," he said. "You look like you can walk to me."

Jake glanced at the sticker, then back at the boys. They were all grinning. He suddenly felt hot. They were—they were saying he was retarded or something. That's what the boy meant. *Right space, wrong handicap*. He wanted to tell them he wasn't retarded. But he could tell by their faces that they wouldn't care.

"You're making fun of me," Jake said.

The boys burst out laughing and turned away. Jake felt blood rush to his face and he slid his hand into his coat pocket to grasp the gun. *Shoot you*, he thought. *Fucking shoot the crap out of you.* He hunched his shoulders up tight and tried to imagine the holes. He knew he couldn't start shooting on the bus. They'd nail him to the wall for that, and then Peterhead would get away. But the boys kept whispering to each other and snickering, and he wanted to make them dead. He wanted to fill their stupid grinning faces with bullet holes, see if they laughed then. He sat simmering miserably as the bus lurched down Fifteenth. He hardly noticed as the bus made several brief stops, though once or twice he glanced back to make sure Peterhead was still aboard.

The bus jerked to a halt and the bus driver announced, "Lloyd Center," over the intercom. The boys stood up and filed toward the front door. The one with the blond hair gave Jake the finger and laughed, then ambled off the bus. Jake gritted his teeth and told himself to stay cool. But he turned and watched the boys disappear into the stream of people coming and going from the mall. He imagined following them and catching them alone somewhere. He imagined his gun could shoot a hundred bullets instead of just six and he'd just shoot the boys over and over and over and they'd make the pain face like the old whore, and then maybe Peterhead would show up, like he thought he was going to rescue them or something, and Jake could shoot him, too. Maybe it was *two* hundred bullets and Jake could use the first hundred on the boys and the second hundred on Peterhead all by himself. Reduce the stupid buttwad to a jelly red smear on the pavement.

The bus started rolling and Jake turned to glance back at Peterhead and imagine what he would look like full of holes. *Pretty damn funny*, Jake thought.

Except Peterhead was gone.

Jake scanned the bus in a panic. "Oh no," he muttered. Peterhead was fucking gone—gone gone *gone*. He turned to the bus driver.

"Wait!" he hissed. "I need off." He jumped up and grabbed the side rails behind the driver's seat. "I need off," he said again.

"Sweet Jesus, buddy," someone said from behind him. "Stay on the ball and you wouldn't miss your stop."

"Please," Jake said, as the bus picked up speed. "I need off now."

The bus driver shook his head. "I'm rolling. Next stop in a couple blocks."

"But I need off *now!*" Jake said. He looked through the windows for Peterhead, but there were too many people on the street. Kids everywhere. Stupid laughing teenagers. Fill them with holes. "I need *off!*" He gripped the bus driver's right shoulder and squeezed. The driver grunted and twisted in Jake's grasp and pulled his right hand off the steering wheel. The bus shuddered as he tried to steer one-handed. Jake squeezed harder.

"What's going on?" someone said from the rear of the bus.

"I … need … the fuck … *off,*" Jake said. The driver pressed his foot against the brake pedal and the bus slowed. He shook his arm free of Jake's grasp as the bus came to a stop.

The driver turned and rose from his seat. "Then get the hell off," he said through clenched teeth, "before I call the cops." He thumbed the door switch. Jake didn't look at him as he headed down the steps, but the driver pushed him from behind and he stumbled onto the street.

"Get the hell out of here!" the driver said.

Jake squeezed his fists tight. "I'll shoot you, you creep!" he yelled. But instantly he felt panic rise in his chest. *Stupid, stupid!* Talking about shooting in front of the whole world. They'd bust him all over the place. He turned and ran into the crowd around the entrance to Meier & Frank. People bumped into him from all sides and made it difficult for him to run. A bell rang somewhere, and for a minute he thought it was because of him, but then he saw a Salvation Army bell ringer standing beside his red kettle. Jake squeezed through the press of people and finally broke free beyond the doors to the department store. He ran up the sidewalk away from the bus. A moment later, as he neared the intersection at Thirteenth and Multnomah, he glanced back and saw the bus moving away. No one seemed to be following. Distantly, he could still hear the Salvation Army bell.

He stopped at the crosswalk. Cars went past on Multnomah, or turned into the parking garage at the corner. Shoppers bustled all around him. Jake gazed at them blankly, looking for a face—*the face*—but not seeing it.

Peterhead Mackerel was gone. The numb realization settled on him as inexorably as falling stone. The bell rang and shoppers strolled and he was stunned by his own stupidity. He'd let the bus boys bother him and now Peterhead was *gone*. He gritted his teeth and fingered the trigger of the gun. The longing to hunt down the boys swelled within him. Peterhead probably put them up to it. *Make fun of that guy*, he'd have told them. *Call him a retard, so I can get away.* And now they were gone, too. Somewhere in the mall, sure, but there were a million people in the mall. He wanted to sit on the curb and cry. All his long morning, walking to Peterhead's, breaking into the house. So close, so close … *stupid*—

The light changed in front of him and without thinking he crossed Multnomah and headed into Holladay Park. Just a block square, dotted with huge elms and walnut trees with a small fountain at the center, it was mostly free of pedestrians. The Lloyd Center MAX stop was on the far side of the park, and Jake decided to take the train back across the river and walk home from Old Town. He didn't have to work that night, but he felt like he probably ought to get some more sleep anyway. Not that he couldn't drink coffee, but he always felt better if he got enough sleep.

The MAX station was more crowded than the park, mostly with shoppers far too cheerful for Jake to tolerate. *Shoot them all.* He moved to one end of the platform to wait. He still had his bus transfer, so he didn't need to buy a ticket from the machine. But he half wanted to anyway, even if it was a waste of money, just to have something to do with his hands. Working at Plaid Pantry wasn't ever going to make anyone rich, though, and the old whore's money wouldn't last forever. In mounting frustration, he edged closer to the end of the platform and watched the traffic come and go. A long line of cars waited to turn south onto the Banfield overpass at Twelfth.

He saw a couple of figures waiting at the crosswalk to head down Twelfth. He paid no attention at first—they were little more than indistinct shapes huddled against the cold wind that blew sharply down the Banfield corridor from the northeast. But then, abruptly, as the light changed and they started across, Jake realized that one of them wore long black jeans and a puffy blue coat.

"Holy guacamole," he said. "Ho-lee-gua-ca-mo-lee."

He didn't have a plan, but if he *did* have a plan, he knew it sure as heck would include finding Peterhead again. He patted his gun in its pocket once more, just to make sure. He felt like he did that morning a few weeks before when he decided to go see if the gun was still in its hiding place after all those years, and, holy-*fucking*-guacamole, there it was. And now it was in his pocket and Peterhead was crossing the street a hundred feet away. And Jake was going to shoot him. That simple. Without another thought, he darted across the MAX tracks toward the intersection. The light changed as he reached the crosswalk, but that didn't matter now. He could see Peterhead walking south on the Twelfth Street overpass, and there weren't any butthead teenagers to distract him here. Cars rushed past or turned left, but Jake just kept his eyes on Peterhead. Before he reached the end of the overpass, the light changed again and Jake trotted after him.

Now it was easier for Jake to follow. Peterhead wasn't moving too quickly, so Jake could hang back without fear of losing him. At an easy gait, he trailed Peterhead past Benson High School, then past a bunch of tennis courts. Peterhead walked like he knew where he was going. They passed a big soft drink bottling company and Jake wondered if all the high school students went there during lunch to get soda pops. One of the warehouse doors stood open and Jake saw a pallet stacked with two-liter bottles of RC Cola right next to the door. Jake could have reached in and grabbed a bottle if he wanted. No one was around. But Peterhead kept walking, so Jake continued after him.

Peterhead stopped at the intersection where Twelfth crossed Burnside and Sandy. It was a big, confusing intersection, with traffic coming in five different ways. Peterhead waited a long time for the light to change in his favor, and Jake hung back the whole time. Then, as Peterhead crossed, Jake ran up behind him and crossed at the same time. It was a chance. Would have been safer to wait for the next signal, but the cycle was too long. Peterhead might have time to get out of sight, and Jake wasn't going to let that happen again.

Peterhead never looked back. He followed Sandy as it headed southwest at an angle from the intersection. A couple of blocks down, Peterhead entered a white building with a glass front and a teal awning. *Uncommon Cup—Fine Coffee* in white letters on the awning. For several minutes, Jake just stared at the place, waiting. Peterhead didn't come out.

"Hurry up," he muttered. The place didn't look like much. Just a little coffee shop, couple of tables with chairs sitting out front. How long did it take to get a cup of coffee? Jake edged closer. Cars and trucks drove by on Sandy. In the bushes across the street, Jake noticed a couple of bums sitting with their backs against a wall, passing a paper bag. Just like his neighborhood. The door to the coffee shop pushed open and someone came out. Not Peterhead. A guy in greasy, gray coveralls. He walked down Sandy in the opposite direction, cup of coffee in his hand.

Jake slipped up to the window and looked inside. He saw two guys at a table, each with a mug of coffee. Peterhead was behind the back counter, a telephone pressed to his ear. A woman stood beside him, staring at him with a concerned look on her face.

He came all this way to use the phone? Jake thought. That didn't make sense. There was a phone in his house. Jake watched him talk, nodding his head and pinching his lower lip with the first two fingers of his right hand. After a minute, he hung up the phone. The woman reached up and touched his face, and he grasped her hand with his own.

So that was it. This was the Darla. Jake remembered when he called Peterhead's the other morning. He hadn't said anything and after a minute Peterhead said, "Darla?" and then something about seeing her soon. And then, back at the house this morning, Peterhead had been yelling *Darla! Darla!* So now he'd found her, here. It was the girlfriend or something. She worked here.

The two guys at the table stood up. They said something to Peterhead and the Darla. She smiled at them and waved, and they waved back. Quickly, Jake turned away from the window. He didn't want the Darla and Peterhead to see him. The two men came out and walked passed Jake around the corner of the building. One of them said something and the other laughed, and a moment later they were out of earshot.

Jake didn't have a plan, but if he *did* have a plan, this would be the time to spring it. They were alone, Peterhead and the Darla. Who cared about the Darla, really, except maybe Peterhead? The thing, really, was that they were alone. And Jake had the gun. He didn't have any rubbers, but he had the gun.

What could they do? Right?

Nothing. Fucking A nothing.

He went to the door. Inside, he could see them talking. He stood there and watched them for a long moment. They didn't notice him. A tremor of anticipation ran through him and he pulled the door open at last. Bells on the door chimed. Behind him, the wind seemed to pick up, but maybe that was his imagination. The Darla looked at him and smiled. She was used to serving customers—she smiled at everyone. He saw her mouth move, like she was talking, but all he could hear was wind. A great rushing sound, it filled up all the space around him. He felt a smile twist his lips, a smile to match hers. Peterhead looked on expressionlessly, without recognition. Didn't matter. He put his hand in his pocket and felt the gun.

Six bullets. Three shots each.

He'd shoot the Darla first. That was the plan. He'd known something would come to him, when the moment was ripe. Like the old whore, leading her up to the park—like that old lady with the dog. Heck, even like that whining bald guy—god, that seemed ages ago now. The plan always came.

Yes, he'd shoot the Darla first, then laugh at Peterhead while he shot him, too.

What a plan. *What a fucking great plan.* Just thinking of it made his dick hard.

SIXTEEN

PETER STARED UP AND down Seventh, barely aware of the rose bushes and maple trees, or the shrub-lined lawns. A chill breeze blew his hair and urged him to zip his coat. A biker trailing a plume of vapor from his nostrils rolled past heading toward Broadway. Down the street Peter saw two older black women talking to each other across a short cedar fence between their front yards. Darla was gone.

He'd thought he would catch up with her at the playground, that she'd slow down as she neared the place where her mother died. But she'd just kept running, on past the shelter house and down the slope beyond the tennis courts to Seventh. Now she was ... who knew? She'd probably gotten good at evading over the years, running from cops and whoever else. She could have gone anywhere—down a side street, between a couple of houses and through someone's back yard. The two black women might have seen her, but so what? By now she could be blocks away, in any direction. That realization defused the energy with which he'd pursued her through the park. He felt deflated and empty again. He began to doubt the guesses he'd made in his living room. If somebody else did have her gun, what was Darla afraid of? Her flight only served to make her seem guilty after all.

He needed a phone, but Darla had eliminated his house in that regard. Mulvaney would probably prefer that he seek out the nearest pay phone, but he decided he'd rather call from Uncommon Cup. He wanted to let Ruby Jane know what had happened, and besides, a few minutes with her might make the inevitable trip down to the Justice Center and the little room with the crack on the wall more bearable.

He turned and walked back into the park, the shortest route to the bus stop on Fifteenth. A jogger passed by on the path beside the tennis courts, the only sign of ambulatory life. The jogger went up the path toward the basketball courts and disappeared over the crest of the hill. Peter felt half tempted to follow. A good run might be just what the doctor ordered. Get the blood flowing, clear the mind, wash away his anxieties in a rush of endorphins. But he kept walking, his thoughts too bootless to provide the impetus to overcome the inertia of his pace or trajectory.

He cut across the playground toward the park gate at Ninth. Nobody was out playing today. He wondered what it would take for people to overcome their fear of this place. Catching the killer might do it, he supposed. Until then, Peter suspected that parents would have their children play at home. He kicked through some dead leaves, and gazed at the swings, the slide, the concrete wading pool as he walked. The only sounds were his own footsteps against the damp ground. For a moment he felt a brief splash of rain, but it passed as quickly as it came.

"Hey, bud. Did ya find that dog you was looking for? Paunch or some such?"

Peter recoiled at the sound of the voice. He looked across the fence at the edge of the park and saw the old man who'd spoken to him Sunday morning before he found Carlotta's body. The man stood on his back porch, wearing an ancient gray cable-knit sweater and corduroy trousers. For a moment, Peter didn't answer, but then he realized there'd been only friendliness in the man's tone. "Oh. Patch," he said. "No—no sign of her, I'm afraid."

The old man shook his head. "Sorry to hear that. What'd she look like? Maybe I'll see her running around the neighborhood."

Peter shrugged, amused by the question. "Patch is small, lumpy, battered, and made of cloth. She belongs to my niece."

The old man chuckled. "Yep, had a feeling it was something like that. Didn't sound like no real dog when you was talking to Bo that morning. Old Bo, he thought you was a piece of work. Loopy." At the sound of his name, the big yellow dog trotted up onto the porch from the yard and sat down next to the old man.

Peter smiled. "How was the fishing?"

"What's that?" Bewilderment crossed the old man's face. Then he said, "Oh, that's right. The fishing. Well—" He patted Bo on the head. "Good and bad, I guess. Good 'cause me and my old dog had a high time. Bad because I forgot my fishing pole."

"How'd you manage that? You remembered your hip waders."

"So I did. Guess I must like wadin' better'n I like fishin'." He threw back his head and laughed. *What a kook*, Peter thought, but he laughed, too. There was a warmth and humor about the old man that reminded Peter of Ruby Jane. "Well, it occurs to me that you know my dog's name, but you don't know mine. I'm Andy Suszko, and have been for as long as I can remember—which isn't all that long when it comes to some matters."

"It's nice to meet you, Mister Suszko. I'm Peter McKrall. I live over on the east side of the park there." Peter waved his hand vaguely over his left shoulder.

"Ah, so we have a back yard in common. Call me Andy. I've been retired too long for anyone to be calling me mister anymore." He chuckled mildly.

"Okay. You can call me Peter."

"I was planning on it," he said. "So you must be pretty determined to still be out here looking for Patch after two days. Don't it seem like it might be time to try somewheres else?"

"Probably," Peter said, shrugging. "Actually, I've about given up on Patch. I was just passing through. Thinking." It suddenly occurred to Peter that Andy might not know about the murders. If he left right away Sunday morning, he would have been gone before the police arrived.

"Thinking's good," Andy nodded. "Not a lot of that going on nowadays. But then that's the kind of comment old folks always make, eh? You thinking up anything good?"

Peter hesitated. He remembered that Mulvaney said she intended to talk to Andy after Peter had mentioned their conversation on Sunday morning. But if he'd already left, she wouldn't have had the chance. Andy might have seen or heard something on Saturday night, something to shed light on Darla's guilt or innocence. Peter knew he should leave it to the cops, but suddenly he wanted to hear what the old man knew. "Actually," he said, "I was thinking about what happened here Sunday. I don't know if you've heard yet, what with your trip. While I was looking for Patch I ... found a body. A woman was shot to death."

Andy seemed to consider for a moment, his prunish old face scrunched and contemplative. "That would explain why Skin Kadash left a note in my screen door. Wants me to call." He thought for another moment. "Maybe you should come inside where it's warm. I'll make you a cup of oil drum coffee and you can tell me all about it."

"Okay," Peter said, even more curious now. He walked through the park gate and across the sidewalk into Andy's back yard. As he climbed the steps onto the porch, he asked, "Do you know Detective Kadash?"

Andy pushed open the back door and let Bo in ahead of him. "Oh, yeah. Skin Kadash was good pals with my sister's boy growing up. Used to have their water fights right here in my back yard, the little cretins. Not that I was against joining in, mind you. But sometimes they flooded my peppers." Andy laughed quietly as Peter slipped inside.

He found himself in a small, well-ordered kitchen. The walls were red cedar, darkened by years of steam. A line of colorful trivets hung on the walls just below the ceiling, and a rack of copper bottom pans hung from the ceiling over a central butcher block. Andy took down a kettle and filled it from the kitchen tap, then set it on the stove. "I call it oil-drum coffee because that's what most people say it tastes like. Not that I can tell. I drink it so hot I've long since scalded my taste buds." That generated a chuckle from his warbly old throat. He took a couple of mugs out of the dish rack beside the sink. Then he dumped ground coffee into the kettle and fired up the burner.

He indicated a stool at the butcher block, and joined Peter on a stool of his own. The dog laid down on the floor at Andy's feet. "I make my coffee the old fashioned way—boil the grounds. Sorta the opposite of that soda pop—all the bitterness and twice the caffeine."

Peter wondered what Ruby Jane would think of that. Probably hold out her mug and ask for a fill-up. "I've never had coffee made that way," Peter said.

"Count your blessings." Chuckle. Andy eyed Peter for a moment. "So you know my old pal Skin Kadash."

Peter half shrugged. "Barely. I met him because of the killing."

Andy nodded. "He's a good cop. Knows his duty, I think. But—hell on wheels. Always in trouble for going his own way—that's why he's risen no higher than he has. He'd have a hard time at a tea party."

"At first—to be honest—I didn't like him. But I guess he grew on me."

"Skin's like that. You know why they call him Skin, don't you?"

"I can guess."

"Yeah. My nephew started all that. Hell, them boys can't have been more than seven or eight years old. Skin lived up on Siskiyou. I'd seen him around, but there was lots of kids around, and I wasn't so interested in kids in those days. Probably too busy thinking about women." Andy grinned. The kettle started ticking as it heated. "My sister came to visit for a few days from Seattle with her boy. She was planning to move back down here—her husband had died recently and she was feeling, well—lost. My nephew, Tommy, was as irascible and foul-tempered as a goat. Hurt, really—missed his dad. When he saw Skin, he started giving him hell. Calling him

Berry Patch and Chicken Skin. These days that'd be nothing, but in 1960, they was fighting words."

"So what happened?"

"Skin told him, 'My name is Tommy, not Chicken Skin.' And Tommy, *my* Tommy, said, 'My name's Tommy, so you *can't* be Tommy, Chicken Skin!' Well, it wasn't too long before Skin up and beat the hell out of Tommy. Bloodied his nose, purpled both eyes. Good fight, really. I watched the whole thing from my front porch. My sister was pretty mad at me for letting it happen, but I told her it wasn't Skin's fault he had that thing on his neck. If Tommy was going to make fun of people, he needed to learn to take his lumps." Steam started to shoot out of the top of the kettle. Andy stood up and looked into the top. The rich aroma of coffee filled the tiny kitchen. "Few more minutes yet," Andy said.

"So how did the water fights come about?" Peter said.

"Well, my sister and I grew up in this house, and she wanted to come back. I wasn't married yet, so she and Tommy moved in. Tommy started up at Irvington School. He and Skin circled each other at first, but they were a lot alike—quick to anger, quick to laugh. They found their way to each other after a while. And Skin, well, it seemed like it was easier to not have two Tommys, even to him. Not that just anyone could call him Skin. He got in a lot of fights—but most of the time, later on, he had Tommy's help."

"Are they still friends?"

"Well…" Andy hesitated. "… maybe, maybe. In a way, I suppose they are. In '71 they went off to Vietnam together. Only Skin came back, I'm afraid."

The atmosphere in the tiny kitchen seemed to thicken perceptibly. Peter glanced at the steaming kettle, then back at Andy. "I'm sorry," he said quietly.

"Eh?" Andy said distantly. "Oh, yeah. Thank you, son. I appreciate it. It was hard on all of us. I was married by then, of course, and Patty had moved into her own house. But she'd lost her man and now her boy, and she didn't live much longer herself. Yeah, it was hard on all of us, but especially her."

"And Detective Kadash?"

Andy nodded. "Oh, yes. It was hard on him, too. They were best friends."

For a moment, Peter felt as though he were in a spell formed of steam and the sound of the boiling kettle. The very air felt thick and oppressive. Then Andy stood up and the spell broke. Peter drew a deep breath as Andy peered down into the kettle.

"Sludge is ready," Andy said. He lifted the kettle from the burner and set it on the stove top. He filled one of the mugs with cold water from the tap and poured it into the kettle. Then he whapped the kettle sharply with a spoon, peered inside, grunted with satisfaction. He filled the two mugs, brought them to the butcher block. "Cream? Sugar?"

"Uh..." Peter peered down into the oily black liquid in the mug before him. "What do you recommend? I mean, am I going to be able to handle this stuff?"

That produced a bark of laughter. "Don't be afraid, son. Puts hair on your chest."

"I suppose you drink it black."

"This stuff? Hell no! Cream and sugar all around!" He got a carton of half-and-half out of an ancient Frigidaire and a sugar bowl off the counter. Peter added each generously.

"Ah!" Andy said. "Cowboy ex-*presso*."

Peter took a sip and made a face. "Well. It's not as bad as I thought it would be."

Andy laughed and slapped the top of the block. "That's right. Makes Folgers Instant seem like stagnant water."

Peter took another sip. He'd had better, but he had to admit that he'd also had worse. He breathed in the aroma steaming from his cup. Ruby Jane would enjoy hearing all about this—then he looked up. Thinking of Ruby Jane reminded him that he had a phone call to make. "Andy—?"

The old man set his mug down. "I know, I know. I distracted you with my coffee and foolish tales. It's an old man's vice. But you've got something more important on your mind." He took a deep breath and said, "Let's not quibble—you found a dead body all but in my back yard. You're wondering if I know anything about it."

Peter sighed. "Well—it's all gotten very complicated. A second woman was killed on the other side of the park, and the killer seems to be trying to make it look like I did it."

Andy's eyes widened at that, and he turned his gaze to the kitchen window. After a moment, he propped his elbows on the counter top, chin in one hand and coffee mug in the other. "Irving Park used to be different. All of the parks used to be, I suppose. But this is the only one I've ever lived near, so it's the only one I worry about. Anyway, used to be, you could walk through the park any time of day or night, no worries. Not anymore. Oh, by daylight it's okay—mostly.

But at night—well, I never been a gambling man. Testing the park at night is bad odds, with a weak return at best."

"I know what you mean."

Andy nodded. "I suppose you would, at that, living up against the park yourself. You ever been in the park at night?"

Peter shrugged. "I built a snow fort in the park with my sister and my niece when we had that big snow last winter. We worked on it well into the evening. But there's a big light in the park near my back fence."

"Right. Don't bet you went up to the basketball courts though, did you?"

"No. Wouldn't do that."

"Of course not. That seems to be where the bad stuff happens, when it happens at all. Which isn't always, I admit. I've heard 'em set off firecrackers over that way a lot, but I also know sometimes it's not firecrackers. This morning wasn't the first time I've come home to find Skin's card in my door."

"Did you hear anything Saturday night?"

Andy nodded sharply. "Here," he said. "Look out this window."

Peter turned and peered through the glass. He could see out into the back yard and the playground, from the swings at one end to the pipes at the other. As he scanned the scene, the jogger he'd seen earlier trotted by on the path, returning the way she had come. Peter felt a tremor of excitement pass through him. He turned to Andy. "You saw it, right? You saw it happen?" He gazed at Andy, suddenly breathless with the thought that real answers might be at last forthcoming.

But Andy shook his head slowly. "No. Not that easy, I'm afraid. I heard firecrackers. Some time after midnight. They sounded close to the house this time, not like usual. I came into the kitchen and looked out this window. I saw a young man standing there by them concrete tubes—boy, how the children love them tubes. This fellow was just standing there, with his back to me, and I thought he was waiting for another firecracker to go off. Then he raised his hands in the air and I could see he was holding a gun. I immediately left the window and went into the front room. Bo and I was packing our stuff for our trip, so I just went back to it. I wanted to get an early start the next morning."

"Why didn't you call the police?"

"A couple of reasons, I suppose." Andy blew air through his teeth and drank from his mug. "First of all, boys who shoot off guns and firecrackers in the park don't tend to wait around for the police to arrive. Second of all, I don't have a phone—can't abide by 'em, frankly, ringing, ringing, 'Let me save you money on long distance.' Had the damn thing yanked years ago. But that's beside the point. I could have walked next door and woke up Mrs. Jenkins, used her phone. But I have a policy of not going out of doors when people with guns is out there. And third, someone else would probably call, and the police would drive by on Seventh and shine their big lights up into the park and this fellow would be long gone, because that's the way it always is."

"But, the woman. I mean, she was shot. If you'd called, maybe…"

Andy didn't speak for a long time. He shifted his gaze from the window to his coffee cup and back again. Took a sip from his mug. Finally, he sighed. "Son, I gotta tell you. I made an agreement with my situation here. My situation is that I live at the edge of a park that gets some pretty lively action from time to time. My agreement is that if I leave it alone, it'll leave me alone. Now I'll be the first to admit it's a foolish agreement, because it's one-sided. Just me contracting with myself for a false sense of security. Someday it's bound to backfire on me. Maybe it backfired last Saturday night. I don't know. What I do know is I never saw a body. I never heard a scream. I just saw a young fellow with a gun. My agreement with myself dictated my reaction."

Peter's coffee had lost much of its heat. He held the mug in both hands as though he could squeeze warmth back into it. "It's been a long time since I bothered to call the cops myself," he said.

They sat together in silence. Andy drained his mug, and Peter followed suit a moment later, tepid coffee and all. Finally Andy said, "How'd you get involved in this?"

Peter laughed wryly. "I just found the body." For a moment, that was all he intended to say. In spite of the morning's revelations, the situation remained confusing, and he couldn't imagine Andy would be interested in his troubles. But Andy gazed at him with a ready, inquisitive look and Peter found himself spilling the whole sordid tale—the discovery of Carlotta Younger's body, meeting Kadash and Mulvaney, and Kelly Norris; his first, serious mistake—taking the call from Darla without telling Mulvaney about it. "After that, things seemed to mushroom," he said. Andy nodded. Peter described his tempestuous meeting with Darla, and his subsequent, more peaceful encounter with Ruby Jane. Then the second killing, the bloody rubber, the interrogation. Peter let it all come out, and Andy listened patiently. He talked about his growing relationship with Ruby Jane, and his worry that he had dragged her into the middle of the terrible mess when she ended up being present for the discovery of the bloody coat. Andy listened quietly, intently, nodding from time to time, but not interrupting. He grunted when Peter described the recording of the phone call to the police regarding the coat, and his eyes widened when he heard that Peter had heard the same voice recorded on his answering machine at home. But otherwise he simply listened through to the end. When Peter finally finished with his pursuit of Darla across the park, and subsequent return back through the playground, Andy sat quietly for a moment. Then he said, "Does Darla have a brother?"

Peter nodded, unsurprised by the question. It ran along lines similar to his own half-realized thoughts. "I don't know. I'm sure that's something the police can find out."

"Yep, I'm sure it is."

"You think this brother took the gun, and he's the one who committed the murders, who's—calling me?"

And shrugged. "Just speculating. But it fits. Man been bugging you on the phone. Man called the police on you. Man was in the park with a gun. Maybe it was Darla's brother. Maybe she killed the father, and he killed the mother. How you fit in, I can't say though."

"I found the body. Carlotta's body. That's why Darla called me. Maybe it's also why the killer, whoever he is, has picked me to mess with."

Andy nodded, one finger tapping rhythmically on the butcher block. "Maybe. No way to tell, of course, without asking him."

"You're sure it was a man out there?"

Andy shrugged. "As sure as you can be this day and age. The fellow had short, dark hair. Not a big guy. Had a coat on, of course, so I can't tell you his exact build."

"Wasn't it dark out? How could you see him so well?"

"There's a security light in the playground. It's one of them mercury lights, so that colors were all wrong, but I could see him fairly well. I'm pretty sure it was a man."

"Darla wears a black knit cap. Maybe it was her and she tucked her hair tucked up under the cap."

Andy chuckled mildly. "You make a good devil's advocate. But it wasn't no hat I was seeing. I'll tell you—I'm eighty-five years old. I only got half my hair, three-quarters of my bowel function, but, thank heavens, just about all my eyesight. That boy with the gun might have been a mannish girl, but it wasn't no girl with her hair stuffed under a cap. I'll wager it was male all the way down to the middle leg. And you can quote me to Skin on that."

At the mention of Kadash, Peter felt a squirm of anxiety in his gut. "I really ought to call him," Peter said. "Him and Detective Mulvaney." An urgency suddenly took hold of him, and he wondered how long he had been sitting there. He looked around the kitchen for a clock, and spied one on the old Hotpoint stove. It read twenty-five minutes to eight. Andy followed his gaze. "Sorry, son, but that's one of those clocks that's only right twice a day. But I don't think it could be much past noon."

"I should have found a phone as soon as Darla got away. I'm glad I talked to you, but now I'm feeling nervous about the delay. Detective Mulvaney will be pissed off that I waited so long."

"Darla would have been long gone in either case. You said so yourself. Besides, Skin'll be glad to know I'm home. I have to admit that if you hadn't have come by, I might not have bothered to get in touch with him for a day or more. Scaring up a telephone is just too damned inconvenient."

"What about Mrs. Jenkins, next door?"

"She works. So does most everyone on the block. I couldn't have asked anyone till this evening. And maybe I wouldn't have bothered. I get caught up in my own things sometimes."

Peter stood up. "I know I should find a pay phone, but I still want to see Ruby Jane before I start down the merry path with the police, if just for a few minutes. Even with the bus, it'll take me twenty or thirty minutes to get to her place."

"You should get going then."

Andy led him out onto the back porch, old Bo at his heels. As he headed down the steps, Peter said, "Do you want me to tell Detective Kadash you're back?"

"You probably ought to. Skin can stop by any time today. Got plenty to do around the house so I'll just wait right here for him." Andy stuck out his hand, and Peter took it. Andy had a firm grip. He smiled at Peter reassuringly.

"This is all so crazy," Peter said.

"You take it easy, son. You're doing fine. Now just you go on. You tell Skin I'm waiting for him. But don't dawdle. He'll skin *me* if I keep you any longer."

"Thanks, Andy."

"You're welcome. Now get moving."

Peter headed down the street toward Siskiyou and the bus stop beyond on Fifteenth. He felt a curious exhilaration. He was no cop, but he wondered if this was how cops felt when they had a breakthrough. Without even intending to, Peter was helping them to zero in on the killer. All the police had to do was find out who else was present when Darla's father was killed, someone who could have taken the gun. Find that person, find the killer. That simple. There had to be names in a file somewhere. Then Darla would be off the hook, and Peter along with her.

SEVENTEEN

"SHE WAS IN YOUR *house?*" Ruby Jane said, "You must have wet yourself."

"And me still without clean underwear."

"Well, don't sit down," she said. "I run a sanitary establishment." Peter smiled. He felt inordinate relief at seeing her, as though her mere presence pushed the anxieties of the last few days into the background. "So what happened?" she said.

Peter filled a glass from the tap. "We talked—sort of. She told me the police tried to arrest her—she didn't say where or how they found her. She was very upset and kept asking for my help. She claims she didn't have anything to do with the killings."

"Do you believe her?"

"I didn't at first, or at least I didn't consider it—I was more worried about whether she was going to pull a gun on me." He sipped his water. "She ended up running away through the park—took the cords from my phones with her."

"Cheaper than going to RadioShack, I suppose. Why did she do that?"

"She didn't want me calling the cops until she had her say." He took another sip of water. "In any case, after she ran off, I learned something that makes me think she's innocent." Ruby Jane raised her eyebrows. Peter drank down the rest of his water and set the glass on the counter. "There's this old man who lives on the edge of the park next to the playground," he continued. "I saw him in passing on Sunday morning before I found Carlotta's body. This morning I ran into him again after I tried to catch Darla in the park. His name is Andy and he makes terrible coffee. But you'd like him anyway."

"At least I wouldn't have to sweat the competition." Ruby Jane smiled slightly. "Did he see something? Why didn't he call the police?"

"He heard gunshots—or firecrackers, he thought at first. He looked out his back window and saw a man with a gun, but no one else. He didn't call the police because he thought it would be a waste of time. He's used to stuff like that going on in the park." Peter shrugged with resignation. "So am I, for that matter."

"Nice way to live." She shook her head slowly. "So you're going to call Mulvaney?"

He hesitated. "Kadash, I think. He knows Andy, it turns out, and I think he's less likely to give me a big lecture about not calling quicker. I wanted to see you first." He looked at her and felt a rush of warmth in his cheeks. "If he chews me out, it'll be worth it."

Her own cheeks colored. "Pete, you're still a curiosity, but I like you that way. Lucky for me you don't carry a cell phone." She tilted her head to one side and met his gaze. With her blue eyes peering from under her floppy hat, she looked so lovely he had no choice but to bend down and kiss her. She leaned against him, warm and soft. For a moment, he forgot Darla and Mulvaney and Kadash. Just basked in the aura of warmth that surrounded her. Then, abruptly, the sounds of whistling and clapping broke the spell. Peter looked up and saw two men sitting at one of the front tables. They smiled and raised their coffee mugs to Peter and Ruby Jane. "Bravo!" one said. Peter hadn't noticed them when he rushed into the shop, he'd been so intent on talking to Ruby Jane.

Ruby Jane grinned. "Thanks, fellas. Always eager to please my fans." She turned back to Peter. "Okay," she said, "go on and call Kadash. You can give me all the details when the police are done with you, assuming you can still talk."

He dug through his wallet for Kadash's card. He found Mulvaney's first, and felt a momentary twinge of guilt as he kept searching. It wasn't that he didn't trust her—he felt more comfortable with her than he was ever likely to feel with someone like Owen. But Kadash had taken on an added dimension for him, a more human aspect, and not just because of what Andy had told him. Kadash was less distant, projected an element of warmth, even if he was irreverent and impudent at the same time. Peter found his card, then grabbed the phone and dialed his cell.

"Kadash."

"Hello, Detective. This is Peter McKrall."

"Calling to check on those tests already?" Peter heard a low, raspy chuckle. "Sorry, bud. Yer not out of the squeezer yet."

"Actually, it's something else—I ran into Darla again."

He heard Kadash take a breath. "Where'd this happen?"

"In my house. I went there to pick up some things and she was inside."

Kadash whistled lightly through his teeth. "Well, it doesn't sound like she shot you." Chuckle. "Are you there now? Where is she?"

"I don't know. She ran off, and I came back to Ruby Jane's. Darla said you tried to arrest her, but that she didn't have anything to do with the murders."

"It wasn't me personally who tried to arrest her, but, yeah, an effort was made to pick her up down at one of the missions in Old Town this morning." Kadash *tsk-tsk*ed. "She, er, *evaded arrest* is the official term. Busted the nuts of a careless probie, I hear." Another chuckle.

"Detective, there's more. There were messages on my answering machine, pretty nasty stuff—it was the person from the tape. I've talked to Darla a couple of times now, and it definitely wasn't her voice. It was a man's voice."

"You sure about that?"

"Yeah. It's still on the tape—you can check it out."

"We'll do that. But I don't think it'll get Darla off the hook."

"Well, how about this? I also ran into a friend of yours. Andy Suszko."

"You know Andy? He's been gone. I've been trying to get in touch with him."

"He's back. And he was home on Saturday night. He heard shots in the park. When he looked out his back window, he saw someone with a gun. It wasn't Darla—it was a man."

Kadash was silent. Peter ran his hand through his hair. Ruby Jane served a man at the counter, and Peter saw him leave out of the corner of his eye. Kadash said, "You've had a hell of a morning, bud. We got a lot to talk about. You're at the coffee shop, you say?"

"Yeah. Ruby Jane's—Uncommon Cup."

"Hang on—" The line took on an anechoic quality that suggested Kadash had put his hand over the mouthpiece. A moment later, he came back on. "Mulvaney's here. She wants to talk to you as soon as possible—Owen, too, I suspect, once he hears. I know he's around somewhere, pissing in someone's coffee, more than likely. I'll come pick you up."

"Okay." Mention of Owen caused Peter's stomach to clench, but there was probably no getting around it.

"Be there in a few minutes."

Peter cradled the receiver. "Lucky me," he said. "Owen'll be there."

Ruby Jane gently caressed his cheek. "I'll be thinking about you," she said. He reached up and took her hand. He wanted to kiss her again, but at that moment, the two guys at the front table stood up. "See ya later, Ruby Jane!" one of them said. "Keep up the good work!" She grinned at them and waved, and they waved back. The bells on the door jingled as they went out.

Ruby Jane laughed, then kissed him quickly. "I guess you'll just have to come back after working hours—we're less likely to be interrupted then."

"The tribulations of entrepreneurship."

"That's right. I don't have time for all this unprofessional behavior. So why don't you tell me more about what happened this morning before Kadash shows."

"Okay. But it's a confusing mess."

"I'll make you a latte to take with you," she said. "I'll even make one for Kadash—doubles your chances of avoiding a lecture."

"Mulvaney'll probably lecture me anyway, if Owen doesn't arrest me first." He quickly ran through the morning's events, from the voice on the machine, to the appearance of Darla, to his realization that someone else present at the time of the murder of Darla's father must now have the gun. Ruby Jane steamed milk and drew a couple of shots while she listened.

"So you think Darla knows who the killer is."

"She acted really strange when I told her the same gun killed her father and her mother. She said something like, 'That means he—' and then chopped off her sentence. She ran off a second later. My question is, who's '*he*'?"

"Well, the father's dead, so it couldn't be him. Unless, of course, this turns out to be an *Unsolved Mysteries* rerun."

"I doubt this is Robert Stack material."

"Maybe there was a brother."

"That's what I'm thinking. The brother took the gun, hid it or something, and now he's—"

The door bells jangled sharply and Peter looked up, expecting to see Kadash. Instead, a slight, dark-haired man stood in the door frame with his left hand on the open door. His right hand was thrust tightly into the pocket of a tan jacket. He took a step or two into the shop and stopped. The door clinked shut behind him. For a moment, he stared at Peter, his eyes dark and sunken against ruddy, wind-chafed cheeks. His hair was cropped close to his head and damp with the day's intermittent rain. He looked like he was wearing a skullcap.

"What can I get for you?" Ruby Jane said.

He didn't say anything. Peter saw that he was shaking slightly, and he wore a thin-lipped smile. Peter felt a sudden discomfort. *He's gonna ask for money,* he thought. There weren't many street people in his own neighborhood, but he knew they frequented the area around Uncommon Cup. The St. Francis Dining Hall was a couple of blocks away, and it attracted large numbers of the homeless. Peter never felt sure how to deal with street people. They hadn't been common in Lexington while he still lived there, and he'd been stunned by the large numbers he encountered once he moved to Portland. At first, he'd given whatever spare change he had to any he met, but as time passed he learned to avoid eye contact and to move quickly past. Nevertheless, he attended all these encounters with a certain amount of vague guilt, uncertain of the right thing to do. Now he felt especially uneasy—behind Ruby Jane's counter, he didn't have the option to avert his eyes and keep walking.

The man took a short, reluctant step. He put his left hand to his head for a moment, then lowered it to his side again. His gaze remained fixed on Peter.

Peter took a quick glance at Ruby Jane. She smiled stiffly, and he sensed her tension. "It's cold out," she said quietly. "Would you like something hot to drink?"

The man glanced at Ruby Jane. For a moment, his smile seemed to widen. "I want—" he began in a low, hoarse voice. "I've got—" He looked back at Peter and his smile faded. His eyes narrowed. "I want to—hundred times—"

Peter saw him press his right hand down deep into his pocket. *This guy is about to rob us,* he suddenly thought. He turned to Ruby Jane and reached toward her just as the young man began to pull his hand out of his coat.

The bells jingled. Peter twisted his head toward the door. Kadash stood there, half in, half out, holding a lit Marlboro outside. A faint whiff of smoke drifted in through the door.

"Well?" he said. "You ready to go, or what?" He looked the young man over quickly, but with obvious thoroughness, then turned his gaze back to Peter and Ruby Jane.

The young man turned around and looked at Kadash. At the sight of the detective, he seemed to contract in on himself like a deflating balloon. Peter suddenly realized he was small, almost boyish in form. He glanced quickly over his shoulder at Peter and Ruby Jane, and for an instant, the look on his face was one of tortured frustration. "I can't right now!" he blurted. He pushed past Kadash and dashed away around the side of the building.

Kadash gave Peter a quizzical look. "What the hell was that about?"

Peter let out a long slow breath. "I don't know," he said. "For a minute there, I thought he was going to rob us."

Ruby Jane looked startled, then shook her head. "I don't think so," she said thoughtfully. "He probably just wanted something hot to drink, but didn't have any money." She looked at Kadash. "I bet he could tell you're a cop. That's what made him run away."

Kadash grunted. "And I thought it was the smoke." He glanced at the hand he held outside. He seemed momentarily indecisive, then he quickly flicked his butt into the street and came in, letting the door close behind him. "You get a lot of that kind of action?"

"Some," she said, shrugging. "Comes with the territory, I think, with St. Francis around the corner. I learned early on that I had a choice—be afraid, or come to terms. So I donate tea bags and coffee to the Dining Hall, and a lot of the regulars there know that. Sometimes they come in with their own mug and a tea bag they've been nursing, and I'll give them hot water and a fresh tea bag or maybe an instant cocoa packet. It doesn't happen a lot, but I'm used to it now."

Kadash shrugged absently, already disinterested. He said to Peter, "The inquisition awaits. I ran into Owen as I was leaving and he's got God's own hard-on. You ready?"

Peter took a deep breath. "As ready as I'll ever be." He turned to Ruby Jane. "What are you going to do if that guy comes back?"

"I'll suggest he head over to St. Francis. It's getting close to serving time there. Don't worry about it, Pete. I know how to handle these situations."

"But what if he was going to rob you?"

She shrugged. "The people who stay around here know who their friends are. Nobody's going to rob me."

Peter felt unconvinced. "Well, please be careful." He tried a halfhearted smile, and she grinned back.

"You're just wired by what's happened today," she said. "Everyone must seem sinister. Except me, of course."

"Of course."

"You two gonna stop billing and cooing any time soon?" Kadash muttered. "I wanted to see this kind of shit I'd go home and watch the *Love Boat* marathon on TV Land."

Ruby Jane stretched up and kissed Peter lightly. "Go solve the case," she said, "and come back soon." Peter headed around the end of the counter. "Oh, and Pete?" She raised two cups. "Don't forget your coffee."

EIGHTEEN

"*STUPID FUCKING MONKEY SHIT!*" Jake hissed.

He sat on a bench in St. Francis Park, a couple of blocks over from the coffee place. As he mumbled to himself, he gazed down the slope to a brick-lined wading pool, where a group of four or five men sat huddled on the ground, passing a cigarette around. They were all wrapped in blankets, and behind them, off to one side, were a couple of shopping carts filled to overflowing with bags full of clothing, old shoes, and aluminum cans.

"Coulda just done it," Jake grumbled through clenched teeth. He rocked back and forth as he muttered, his arms wrapped around himself against the cold. "Coulda just done it—*shoulda* just done it. Stupid!"

"Amen, brother!" one of the men called up to him from the wading pool. "Just do it!" He and the others laughed, blew smoke, gave each other high fives.

Jake froze. He hadn't realized he was talking loud enough for them to hear. The sounds of their laughter suddenly infuriated him.

"Shut up!" he shouted. "Just shut up, buttheads! I'll use the g—" He stopped. *I'll use the gun on you*, he thought. But that was stupid. Peter Mackerel was who he should be thinking about. Jake had been there—he'd been *right there*, and he blew his chance. Coulda got Peterhead and the Darla at the same time. But, no—

"Hey, motherfucker! Who you calling a butthead?" Down the slope, the man who'd spoken stood up, dropped his blanket on the ground. "You talking to me?" he said. He was tall on his feet, but very thin, with gaunt sunken cheeks darkened by several days growth of beard. His hair hung long and lank from under a black cap, and from afar, his eyes looked dark and forbidding. He stepped out from the circle of the others and started up the slope. "You think you're gonna fuck with me? I'll take you apart, motherfucker."

Jake felt tears spring to his eyes. He stood up from the bench, looked at the man as he approached. Started to back away. "I'll do it," he said, his voice hoarse.

"Say what? What you saying? You gonna fuck with me?" The man wore fingerless gloves, and Jake saw him clench and unclench his fists rhythmically.

"Hey, Snort!" one of the others called. "Leave that dipshit alone. Come have a drink."

"Yeah, come on, man," said another. "Don't be getting into this shit."

Snort waved a hand behind him dismissively, and advanced on Jake. "I'll drink when I'm done fucking this guy up!" he said.

Jake shoved his hands into his pockets. He felt his stomach turned over, and he looked for a way to run. His legs felt like jelly. "Don't come no closer!" he said. "I can do it!" His voice sounded weak and whiny, and he saw Snort grin in response.

"You ain't gonna do shit. I'm the one's gonna—"

Jake pulled the gun out of his pocket. In a heartbeat, the scene around him seemed to solidify. Everyone froze.

He hadn't meant to take it out. He didn't want to use Dee-Dee's gun on some dumb creep named Snort. But his hand was in his pocket and it felt the gun and it pulled the gun out. It didn't even aim the gun. It just held it there, pointed off to the side.

Snort's eyes widened, and the tableau cracked. Down the slope, the other men scrambled out from under their blankets and scattered in all directions. "Jesus—" Snort croaked, then he was running, too. He stumbled and cried out, then he found his feet again and was gone. Jake couldn't even tell where they'd all got to. In hardly a blink, he was alone.

He looked down at the gun, hanging from his hand. He shivered, as though the men's fear of the weapon was somehow transmitted through it into his own body. He felt pleased at the sight of it, at the power it had over other people. Snort was bigger than he was, but the gun made him afraid. Jake liked that. But then he had a sudden thought.

"They'll try to bust me," he whispered, realizing the truth of his words even as he said them. The men were afraid of the gun, the men ran away—the men would call the cops. Shuddering, Jake jammed the gun into his pocket and turned around. He felt suddenly open and exposed. The park was a block square and bordered by stunted cedars on three sides. Cars rolled by on the streets to either side, but didn't seem to notice him. At the north end of the park stood a brown, slat-sided building—some kind of school or something. For a moment, Jake gazed up at the building, expected to see someone looking out one of the many windows, phone pressed to an ear, frantically dialing 9-1-1. But the windows looked lifeless and empty. The park itself had a few benches, a dry fountain with a brick-lined channel for water, in warmer weather perhaps, to run down the slope to the wading pool. The park was empty, except for abandoned shopping carts and blankets.

Get outta here, he thought. He headed around to the left of the school, back in the direction of the coffee shop. But he wasn't thinking about the shop, or about Peterhead. He just wanted to get away. He crossed the street and trotted up the sidewalk on the far side, beside the long brick wall of a building that ran the length of the block, windowless, doorless. He kept glancing over his shoulder, expected to see a cop each time. But no one was there. He was in a weird part of town—lots of broad low buildings with few doors and fewer windows. No people hardly at all. A couple of cars passed without stopping. He came to the corner of the building and turned left.

As he rounded the corner, he collided with an old woman. She looked up at him, startled, through thick-lensed glasses, then smiled when she saw the dismay in his own face. Her teeth were edged with green. "Excuse me," she said. "I didn't realize you were there." Her breath smelled strongly of mint.

"Whatever," he muttered, tried to push past.

"Wait, sir?" She grasped his arm with an old, clawlike hand. He tried to pull away, but she was surprisingly strong. He felt the fear return to his gut. *She's holding me for the cops.* But the old woman only smiled at him and said, "Can I ask you a question? Please?" He stared at her, baffled, and didn't answer. The scent of mint threatened to overpower him. After a moment she asked, "Young man ... are you happy?"

He didn't like the question. He pulled away from her. He needed to get away before they busted him bad. He was wasting time—the cops would come, they would nail him to the wall. Yet the woman's grip was firm, and the question suffused through him. *Are you happy?* No one had ever asked, no one had ever cared. He thought of Dee-Dee, all those long years behind him, lost, lost … As the moment hung by a thread, the question worked a sea change on him. He felt his breathing slow, grow more calm. He gazed at the old woman, breathed her aroma of mint, and he whispered, "No."

The woman's eyes widened with unmistakable satisfaction. She smiled and patted his hand. "It's not too late to find joy," she said softly. "Open your heart to our Lord Christ in heaven and accept His saving grace, and He will grant you peace, happiness, and life everlasting." As she spoke, she shoved something into his hand, a little booklet with a black-and-white drawing of Jesus hanging from the cross on the cover. *He Died For Our Sins*, read the headline, *And Lo, We Are Saved!*

People had tried to give him tracts like this before. Usually he blew them off. This time the words of the headline connected with an old memory, and he murmured, "Jesus loves me." It was half statement, half question, said to himself as much as to the old woman.

"Yes! That's right, honey. Jesus *does* love you!" she asserted. "He does indeed!"

Jake looked up into the diffuse gray sky. He remembered the foster home, the one where the woman wouldn't let him saw his leg off. That woman made the whole family go to church every Sunday, made them all sing songs. She never gave a liquid shit for whether he was happy. Just say the prayers and sing the songs, and don't saw your legs off, you little prick. He felt an itch in his shin, and without thinking he started to sing under his breath, "*Jee-zus loves me, this I know—For the Biii-ble tells me so...*"

"Oh, what a lovely song—"

It sounded crazy to him. That woman in the foster home, she was practically queer for Jesus, but she was just a fucking bitch—sing the songs and say the prayers and then shut the hell up. *Get to bed, don't make no noise, you'll eat when I'm ready to feed you.* Jake looked at the old woman, felt her hand on his arm, felt the gun in his hand. He pulled the gun out of his pocket. "Will Jesus make the itching go away?" he asked, his voice quiet and matter-of-fact, as though he already knew the answer.

The woman gasped, and released his arm. "Don't..." she murmured. She pushed away from him. A clutter of pamphlets dropped from her hand. Jake watched her flee down the street, emitting panicked chirps as she ran. He dropped the tract she'd given him. For a moment, he imagined using the gun on her, but then he grew thoughtful.

"Hey...gonna nail me to the wall," he said. "Jesus gonna nail me to the wall." He put the gun into his pocket. The gun was for Peterhead, not the old lady. But he was glad he'd run into her, even if she did run and call the cops. She asked the question no one ever asked, and, to his sudden surprise, he found an answer he hadn't known was there. No, he wasn't happy. He was pissed off, he was frustrated. Fucking Peterhead. He'd been fine until he saw Peterhead in the park. Fine, but not happy. The thing was, there'd been times when he *was* happy, if he'd only noticed. With Dee-Dee, yeah, way back when. And now, long after Dee-Dee, he could be happy again. Dee-Dee had taught him how. *Just use the gun.* When he used the gun on the old whore, and then the president's mom, he felt happy. And he would have been happy using it on Peter and his Darla. But he'd looked Peterhead in the eye, and run away, gun still in his pocket. Like Snort and those guys in the park, he'd been afraid.

But it wasn't too late. That's what the old woman had said—it wasn't too late to find joy. He was only a block or two from the coffee place. He only had to return, and take out the gun—point and shoot. It would be beautiful. Solve all his fucking problems right there.

He trotted down the street in the direction the old woman had gone. At the far corner she'd turned left, but he crossed the street and turned right, headed up toward Sandy. He felt a thrill in his gut, and he pressed his hand against his pants, felt his thing grow hard. At the next intersection he saw the big white building attached to the back of the coffee joint. He crossed the intersection catty-corner and slipped up alongside the long white wall. He passed no one on the street, but he could see cars drive by up on Sandy.

At the corner of the building, he stopped to catch his breath. He didn't want to be all out of breath when he went inside. He peeked around the corner, saw the line of tables under the awning. All empty. He nodded with satisfaction. Then he heard the jingle of bells and the coffee shop door opened. A woman came out with a steaming cup in her hand. She saw Jake and startled, then turned and walked away in the opposite direction. He saw her glance over her shoulder at him as she headed down the sidewalk. Jake grinned to himself. Maybe he'd use the gun on her some day. Not right now, though. Right now was Peterhead's time.

He edged around the corner, looked in through the glass. Place didn't seem to get much business, but that was just as well. He didn't see Peterhead, but the Darla stood behind the counter. Maybe Peterhead was in the back or something. Should he just go in, or wait till Peterhead returned? His legs trembled with anticipation. He could always start on the Darla, but save some shots for Peterhead. And maybe shooting the Darla would bring Peterhead running. That might be fun—he might get to see the look on Peterhead's face when he saw the girlfriend shot full of holes, right before he got some holes himself. Jake shook his head. He wished he'd brought more bullets with him, or had the hundred-shot gun. That would be great. Too bad bullets didn't grow on trees. He chuckled to himself at the thought.

Six would have to do.

He hesitated a moment longer, then went to the door, pushed it open. He heard the bells jingle. The Darla looked up as he stepped inside. He saw a troubled look pass over her face as she caught his eye, but then she smiled. Jake stepped up to the counter, his gun hand trembling in his pocket. He felt a grin cross his face.

"It's pretty cold out there," she said. "Would you like a cup of tea?" She smiled at him as if she didn't know he was going to shoot her.

"I don't like tea." He didn't know why he said it—maybe he wanted to tease her a little, make her think he was a real customer. He almost giggled, he felt so sly. Her smile narrowed. He saw a pinch appear between her eyebrows.

"Well, if you've got a mug, I'll fill it with hot water. You can get a cocoa packet over at the St. Francis kitchen. But anything else you have to pay for, I'm afraid."

"I got money."

"Oh," she said, her face growing uncertain. "Well then, what would you like?"

Jake didn't answer. He realized he couldn't wait for Peterhead, didn't really care if Peterhead showed up at all. The gun seemed to pulse in his hand, and his thing was a straining stone between his legs. A shudder passed through his entire body, and for a moment he closed his eyes. Without thinking, he pressed his free hand against his crotch, and a moan of pleasure escaped his lips. Then, he heard movement and he opened his eyes.

The Darla was gone.

He stared at the empty counter space, and a feeling of panic rose in his chest. He lunged forward and put both hands on the counter, looked back and forth. The floor behind the counter appeared to be empty, but then he heard a rustling sound, followed by a muted series of beeps. He grasped the far edge of the counter top and pulled himself across. The Darla was on the floor, squeezed up against the backside of the counter. She had a telephone in her hands. When she saw him, her eyes bulged.

"Somebody's here!" she shouted into the telephone. "Please, help me. I think he wants to—"

Jake pulled himself onto the counter top. The Darla dropped the telephone and screamed. She reached into the counter space behind her, groping wildly, and came up with a heavy glass mug. She brandished it at him as he swung his legs over the edge of the counter. He started to laugh, but suddenly she heaved it at him with brutal force. The glass struck him in the forehead. A spear of pain lanced into his head and he slumped backward. Distantly, he heard the glass hit the floor in front of the counter and shatter.

"Goddamn fuckerhead poop hole!"

He put his hands to his head and moaned. His forehead felt like it had been branded, but he was more worried that she'd called somebody on the phone. Maybe the cops, maybe she called the cops. They'd nail him to the wall, damn it. They'd nail him all over the place.

A whimper escaped through his teeth. He wanted to cry, but he tried to fight it. He didn't want to cry in front of the Darla. This whole stupid day just wasn't working out. First he went all the way to Peterhead's house and missed his chance. But then after following him across the whole fricking town to this stupid coffee shop, when it came to the point, he couldn't close the deal. He'd run away, like some kind of stupid girl. Now the fucking Darla had hit him with the glass—*she'd hurt him.* He'd felt so good when he walked in the door. His thing was big and hard, he had the gun in his pocket—he was going to be *happy.*

He groaned, leaned against the counter. Dimly, he saw the Darla on the floor. He lowered his hand from his forehead, and caught a glimpse of red on his palm. His stomach lurched at the sight, his own blood. This was nothing like the old whore, or the president's mom, or even that guy a couple of weeks ago. None of them had known how to fight back.

"Stay away from me!" he heard the Darla hiss. She scrambled along the floor beneath him. He reached out with one hand, tried to grab her. She slithered to the side and eluded his grasp. He realized he oughta get the heck out. If he stayed, he'd get nailed. But it felt so close—even when the glass struck his head, his boner didn't go down. He felt it pulsing between his legs, swollen and urgent. He couldn't just run away. He couldn't waste it.

Maybe if he was quick he'd have time. At least he could use the gun. That was the thing—use the gun. Show Peterhead he was the one with the power, the one who knew what it took to be happy.

The Darla clambered to a doorway in the back wall, pushed it open. "Hey!" he cried out. She shot him a furious glare, then crawled through the door. He reached into his pocket for the gun. It felt good in his hand, felt strong. He pulled it out and aimed as her legs slid through the door. He knew he was going to miss, but he squeezed the trigger anyway. He wanted her to hear the gun. He wanted her to know what was coming next.

The sound of the shot rattled the front windows. The bullet hit the door jamb near her foot, threw splinters into her ankle. He heard her shriek, and the foot vanished. Jake laughed. He liked the sound she made. He strode to the door and flung it open. It felt good to fire the gun. He stopped worrying about the time. He was using Dee-Dee's gun. It was wonderful.

The Darla scrambled away down a narrow hallway. He laughed again. She tried to get to her feet, slipped and stumbled against the far door. Her hand found the doorknob as he brought the gun up and aimed. She screamed and pushed on the door. It started to open, and Jake squeezed the trigger. The bullet hit the door beside her and she flinched to the side. The door swept open before her with a bang and Jake fired again. This time, the bullet hit the Darla in the thigh as she stumbled through into the next room. A shrill cry escaped her lips and she fell. Behind her, the door slowly began to swing shut.

A great rush of heat swept through Jake's face and hands. He lowered the gun and breathed, basked in the tingling warmth. She wouldn't get far now. He could afford to take a minute and just enjoy it. He walked up the hallway. He felt like he was walking on a springy turf. Through the door, he could hear her whimper, and he laughed. The old whore had whimpered, too. Didn't know what was good for her. He reached the door and pushed it open with the palm of his hand. He looked into a big room, some kind of bed to one side, kitchen stuff to the other, couch and TV straight across. There was a bathtub right out in the middle, no walls around it or anything. The Darla was on the floor near the tub, trailing a stream of blood. She'd clamped one hand over the hole in her leg, pulled herself along with the other.

"Where you think you're going, Darla?" he said.

She looked at him and screamed, "Help! Somebody help me!" She began to crawl again, blood dribbling out from around her clenched hand and pooling on the concrete floor beside her. No one came to save her. Jake chuckled with glee, pressed his hand against his thing. He was safe, he'd used the gun, and he could use it again if he wanted to. He decided not to worry about Peterhead for right now. Obviously he was gone, so Jake would have time to go get more bullets if he used them up on the Darla.

Laughing, he lifted the gun and fired at her, just a pot shot really. Not even aiming. The bullet struck the foot of the tub, broke off a piece of the porcelain. She shrieked, rolled onto her side. "Stay away from me," she hissed. "Stay the hell away from me."

"Ha! Forget you!" He aimed and fired, more carefully this time. The bullet hit her in the side, low, around stomach level. That was a good one. The one in the leg—it was okay. But the one in the stomach was real good, just about perfect.

He could hear her crying. She didn't try to crawl any farther. Hard to do with a hole in your side. The perfect hole. He walked across the room and stood over her. She gazed up at him with eyes wide, her face pasty white. Sweat glistened on her skin. She was pretty, he thought. Like Kelly Norris, only in a different way. He drew in a long deep breath, pressed the gun against his crotch. He let out a sigh of pleasure. This was joy, he thought. Fuck that old lady with her little books. This was what it was all about.

He gazed down at the Darla, rubbing the gun against his thing. She tried to squeeze her legs together. Hard to do with a big hole in her thigh. What did she think he was going to do? Not that way. "Keep your pants on, Darla," he said. He laughed. It'd be different if she was Dee-Dee—but then if she was Dee-Dee, he wouldn't be shooting her. He'd rub her on the outside like he used to, and she'd play with his thing, put it in her mouth, and they'd both be happy. He grinned, unzipped his pants, let his thing come out. He rubbed the gun along the shaft, felt the warm barrel against his skin. He looked down at the Darla's blood as it leaked out on the floor, so slippery, so wet. Smooth as cream. He wished he had one of the old whore's rubbers. That would have been great. But he could do the hole without one.

At the sight of his thing, the Darla began to squirm. Jake giggled as he watched her. Stupid girl. What did she think she was going to do with a big old hole in her side? But suddenly, she let out a loud shriek and brought her good leg up with driving force, smashed her foot against the shaft of his thing. Jake felt himself rise with the strength of her strike, and he stumbled backward as she rolled onto her side away from him.

For an instant, there was no pain. He stood motionless, his mouth open in anticipation of a cry—but the pain hesitated, made him wait. It seemed to hang out here in space before him, a horrid tease. He rolled his eyes toward her and saw a hint of satisfaction in her pain-wracked face. He almost dropped the gun—almost.

Then, the room around him was filled with a flood of light, so hot it burned him to the very center. He felt the howl in his throat more than heard it. It wasn't pain like the cut of a knife. It was pain like the rumble of thunder. He staggered on his feet, fell against the side of the tub. Bile rose in his throat, followed by a sudden stream of puke. The hot, bitter stench of the vomit flooded his nostrils and tears sprang from his eyes. Between his legs, his thing sagged like a withered slug.

"Hey, what the hell—?!"

Jake's head rolled on his neck in the direction of the voice. Somewhere, off to the side, he heard the Darla gasp, "Please stop him." A man stood at the door that led back into the shop. At first, Jake thought it was a cop, but he didn't have a uniform on. Hard to tell really—Jake couldn't focus his eyes very well. *They're here to nail me to the wall.* He tried to stand, but another wave of nausea swept over him and he almost vomited again.

He had to get away. It was all ruined, but it would be even worse if they made him go away. He had to escape before it was too late. Desperately, he pointed the gun in the direction of the man. The gun felt too heavy, his arm felt loose in its socket, but somehow he managed to squeeze the trigger. The report echoed throughout the room. The man threw himself backward into the hallway, cried out in fear or pain. Jake couldn't tell if he'd hit him or not. Didn't matter. Had to get away. He squeezed the trigger again, but now the gun only clicked. All six shots, down the drain.

He pushed himself to his feet, tried a step. His foot slid on blood or vomit, he wasn't sure which. Beneath him, the Darla whimpered.

He pointed the gun at her one more time, squeezed the trigger. Just in case. *Just in fucking case.* Click. Click.

Off to the side, he saw a door. He hoped it led outside. No way to tell. He lurched toward it, slipped again, fell. Landed face down on the floor, felt the cold concrete against his limp dick. The Darla clawed him and he pushed himself up, scrambled away. He found the door, felt for the knob. There was a deadbolt latch, and he flipped it, then turned the knob and pulled. The door came open and cold air rushed past him. He stuffed the gun into his pocket, grabbed the top of his pants and pulled them shut. Couldn't escape with his thing hanging out. Over his shoulder, he took one last look at the Darla lying by the tub, surrounded by blood and puke. *I hope you die, cunt*, he thought. Then he slipped through the door and fled.

NINETEEN

"All right," Owen said, "Let's run through this one more time."

Peter felt himself slump lower, if that were possible, in the metal chair. He had been two hours now in the little room with the crack on the wall. Mulvaney sat directly across from him, Kadash to her right, Owen to her left. Peter felt alone on his side of the table, talking, talking, answering questions, talking. His head hurt and his eyes felt as dry and hairy as a couple of old tennis balls. Two long hours of telling the story again and again—Peter goes to his house . . . Peter listens to the messages on the answering machine . . . Darla appears and they talk, argue, whatever . . . she flees and he stops to listen to the tape again and *just so happens* to come to the startling conclusion that she's innocent . . . he chases her through the park—unsuccessfully, but *just so happens* to run into Andy Suszko (surprise witness, ahem) and learns the killer is evidently a man—couldn't possibly be Darla after all. *But, of course, you're a man, aren't you, Mr. McKrall? Maybe it was you this Suszko saw.*

"It wasn't me."

"I would expect you to say that," Owen said.

"You understand that Mr. Suszko's sighting isn't conclusive of anything," Mulvaney said. "Irving Park sees its share of young men with guns. It could have been anyone—the gun doesn't automatically make him our killer."

Peter shifted in his seat. "At that time and that place? Come on."

Mulvaney looked to one side at Kadash, then across to Owen. Kadash shrugged. "They're bringing Andy in. We'll talk to him," he said. "Try to nail it down."

"And what will he tell us?" Owen grumbled. "He and our friend here have already had plenty of time to get their stories worked out. They could be colluding with Darla, too, for that matter."

"Andy don't collude with nobody," Kadash growled. "Why don't you take the goddamn cob out of your ass?"

"Sarge," Mulvaney said. "Skin. That'll be enough."

A tense silence followed. Peter had felt certain they'd greet his tale as a significant break in the case. But for the most part, all he'd gotten was a skepticism that seemed to increase as he hashed over the details of his meetings with Darla and Andy again and again. Even Kadash seemed reticent. They showed a little interest, sure. The long grilling indicated that much. They'd even sent a patrol car, with his keys and his permission, to retrieve the answering machine tape. But Darla remained their chief suspect, and—in Owen's mind at least—Peter wasn't off the hook, either.

"I have a question," Peter said.

"What's that?"

"Does Darla have a brother or not?"

Mulvaney met his stare. Since that first morning, she'd grown increasingly inscrutable. She gazed at him with a dark, empty expression. The moment seemed to stiffen, and Peter shifted again in his seat. Maybe there was no brother, no cousin, no male figure out of Darla's violent past to fill the role that Peter had in mind for him. "What does it matter, Susan?" Kadash said at last, breaking the silence. "He ain't the guy. Darla? I dunno. But he definitely ain't."

Owen blurted, "I'm not ready to concede—"

Kadash slapped both hands on the table's surface. "Owen, for once why don't you just shut up!"

The top of Owen's head burned sudden crimson and his eyebrows seemed to grow into one over his glaring eyes. He opened his mouth, but at first the only sound that came out was an angry strangled noise. Finally he growled, "You're not running this investigation."

"But you're sure as hell hindering it." Kadash leaned forward and fixed dark, angry eyes on Owen. Mulvaney put a hand on Kadash's forearm, but he shook it off.

Owen pushed himself to his feet. "Always the problem child, aren't you, *Detective*?" he spat. "Well, you've stepped in it again. I guarantee you haven't heard the last of this."

"I'm quaking in my boots, Dick."

A sharp rap sounded at the door. Owen gave Kadash a withering look before turning and yanking the door open. An officer stood in the hall, a folder in his hands. "What is it, Parker?" Owen barked.

"We're back from the canvass, Detective," Officer Parker said. "Thought you'd want to take a look at this." He waved the folder.

"Can't it wait?" Owen puffed, impatient.

"I think it's pertinent."

"Okay." Owen turned to Mulvaney. "I'll be right back."

"Don't do us any favors," Kadash said. Owen ignored him and stalked out, slamming the door behind him.

Mulvaney opened her mouth to say something, but Kadash cut her off. "I don't want to hear it, Susan. He doesn't have a fucking clue."

Mulvaney looked at Kadash, restrained ire evident on her face. "You're sure of that, are you?"

"Aren't you?"

Mulvaney's face remained dour and closed. Finally she sighed. Turned her gaze back to Peter. "Darla had a younger brother named Jacob Smithers—Jake. He would be twenty now. He drifted through the Oregon juvenile system until he was eighteen. Foster care, group homes, that sort of thing. The last address we have for him, now two years out of date, is in care of a Quik-E Mart up in Battle Ground where he got a job shortly after he left state care. We know he's not there any longer. We don't know his current whereabouts."

Peter felt himself fill with relief as Mulvaney spoke. The existence of a brother at least made his own theory plausible. "Well, there you go," he said. "Find him, I bet you find your guy. Like I said, maybe he took the gun, hid it before the police came."

"That would be only speculation at this point," Mulvaney said.

Peter started to respond, but was interrupted by another knock at the door. Mulvaney nodded to Kadash, who got up and pulled the door open.

Officer Parker stuck his head in. "Detective Owen asked for you," he said to Mulvaney.

Mulvaney closed her eyes, then nodded shortly. "Excuse me a moment." She followed the officer out and the door closed behind them.

Kadash sat down again and leaned onto his forearms. "Sorry you had to be here for that," he said, "I got a habit of speaking my mind, you mighta noticed."

"Didn't bother me a bit," Peter said.

Kadash chuckled. "Didn't think it did." He leaned back and scratched at the patch on his neck. "Mulvaney's out there now listening to Owen fulminate. She's trying to decide if she's going to defend me this time, or just get out of the way."

"I take it this has happened before."

Kadash bobbed his shaggy eyebrows. "Once or twice."

"She's not just going to let Owen have his way, is she?"

"She might have to. She's got a career to consider. I'm just a crusty old loner whose mouth is bigger than his brain." He stood up, tilted his head side to side. His neck cracked.

"This just gets crazier and crazier," Peter said, shaking his head. "I thought you all would be pleased with this new information, even Owen. But it seemed to piss him off even more than usual. It's like he isn't even willing to consider the possibility I'm innocent. He just wants blood. Mine, yours—he doesn't even seem to care."

"You up and complexified things for him." Kadash smiled grimly. "Bud, you got to understand, someone like Owen—well, guilt or innocence don't much come into play. It's about building a case, and if he can build a case, close a file, then he's done his job." Kadash looked at Peter and shrugged. "I may not like Owen, but I gotta tell you, he closes a lot of cases. He's damn successful. Whether you really did it or not, well, he doesn't care. He's a cop. His job is to gather and then puzzle the evidence into a plausible narrative."

"And the truth be damned." Peter didn't try to disguise his disgust.

Kadash snorted. "Police work ain't about tracking down the truth. It's about building a case that'll stand up in court. As it so happens, most of the time building a case coincides with finding the truth. Evidence suggests a guy did it, more'n likely the guy did it. But given the choice between the truth and a good case, a cop like Owen's going to take the case every time."

"What about you?"

Kadash didn't speak for a moment. He stepped away from the table, scratched his neck. "I've lived my whole life knowing that appearances can be deceiving. That's what I know. It's not always as simple as building a case the way it's laid out in front of you."

"Where does Mulvaney stand in all this?"

"She wants to close her files, but she's not as quick to jump to conclusions as Owen is. Plus, she adheres to that mossy, old ideal, 'to serve and protect.' Owen wants an arrest record, a closed-case record, a high conviction rate—hell, he wants to be chief. But it's different for her. She's ambitious, but she understands that opportunities are a lot more limited for her than someone like Owen. It gives her the luxury of being able to focus more on the police work. But mark my words, if she thinks she can close a case against you, she will."

"So you're the only thing I got going for me right now."

Kadash chuckled again. "Well, that, and the fact the evidence is more and more starting to fall in your favor. Consider yourself lucky. Even Owen is having a hard time hammering the pieces together to nail you."

The door thrust open. Mulvaney started through, but Owen pushed past her brusquely. He came to the table and slapped an eight-by-ten photograph down in front of Peter. "Look at the picture," Owen barked. "You recognize anyone?"

Mulvaney came in. "Slow down," she said.

"I'm tired of pussyfooting around!" Owen said. He glared at Peter. "Tell me who that is."

Peter glanced at the photo, but Owen's presence dragged Peter's attention away from the image. The detective leaned forward, his hands planted on the tabletop, his small eyes dark and staring, almost greedy in their intensity. His lips drew back from his teeth, his forehead glistened with beaded sweat. Peter looked to Kadash for support, but the detective, his salty eyebrows high on his forehead, seemed off-balance himself.

Nervously, Peter turned back to the photograph. It was a head-on mug shot of a woman, make-up heavy and obvious, eyes sunken and dark. Peter drew a breath. "It's Carlotta Younger," he said.

"How did you recognize her?" Owen said sharply.

"This is the photo from the newspaper."

"You're sure that's the only place you recognize her from?"

"What are you talking about?"

Owen stood up straight and folded his arms across his chest. "Ever been to the 747 Lounge? And this time, I want a straight answer."

The air in the little room developed an abrupt, oppressive weight. An acrid scent Peter realized must be his own sweat filled his nostrils. The apparent wisdom of feigning ignorance of the 747 suddenly revealed itself as folly. His previous narrative collapsing, Owen had turned to a new one, with Peter still at the center. And Peter had made it easy for him with his foolish evasions. "Why do you want to know?" he said, knowing the answer already.

"The 747 Lounge," Owen snarled. "Have you ever been there?"

Peter looked away. "Once or twice," he muttered.

"So look at the photo and just try and tell me one more time the newspaper is the first place you saw her."

Kadash said to Mulvaney, "What's going on, Susan?"

"I want to hear Mr. McKrall's answer," she said, quietly.

Peter felt lost. One foolish choice after another. The only thing he could feel grateful for in this whole great misadventure was that he'd put Ruby Jane's pen back on the table. One good choice amid a string of bad ones. He gazed at the photo, knowing already he couldn't give Owen the answer he was looking for. It had a vague kind of familiarity to it, but he couldn't be sure from where. He hadn't seen her face Sunday morning, hadn't been able to bring himself to remove the newspaper that hid her upper body. But that didn't mean he hadn't seen her before. Darla's revelation in the coffee shop, Owen's interest in the 747 Lounge—the picture could certainly be of the woman from the bar. She'd flirted with Peter. She'd flirted with everyone.

"I was there one night last week—"

"Thursday night, in fact," Owen said.

Peter shrugged uselessly. "I had a lot to drink. I barely remember it."

"Well then let me refresh your memory." Owen slapped another photo onto the table, this time a color frame capture from Peter's interview with Kelly Norris. The image was pixelated and grainy, but clear enough. They'd caught a moment with Peter in full bluster, mouth open, eyes wide. "The bartender remembers *you*," Owen said. "Sitting at the bar, telling your sad tale of unemployed woe. Drinking cheap vodka. He remembers you real well, especially after he saw this shot. He saw the news story." Owen sat down across from Peter, thrust his jaw out in evident satisfaction. "Am I jarring your memory any?"

"Jesus," Peter muttered. He pinched his lower lip. "Jesus."

"He remembers Carlotta, too. It was a busy night for our dead hooker, and it turns out you were one of the people she was busy with."

Peter shook his head. "I was hung over for two days. My sister gave me endless shit about it." Peter rubbed his eyes, ran his hand through his hair. His skin felt clammy to the touch. "I just don't remember."

Owen shook his head sharply. "This ain't a congressional hearing, pal. That answer ain't gonna cut it."

"I don't know what you want me to say!" Peter's voice suddenly raised. "I'm not going to help you make something out of nothing."

"You call this nothing? How about when you trotted out of there with ol' Carlotta hanging on your arm, laughing and happy? Was that nothing?"

Peter sat back. His recollection of that evening was so murky. It was possible, certainly possible. Peter couldn't imagine himself going with a prostitute, but it wouldn't be the first stupid choice he'd made in his life. He did remember the woman, remembered enjoying the feeling that she liked him. Was it possible he'd left with her? Was it possible he'd actually paid to screw a hooker? He knew there was less money in his wallet the next morning than he expected. But … Darla's mother? *Jesus.*

Peter placed his hands flat on the tabletop. He wanted to turn to Kadash, but he sensed that Kadash could do nothing for him, and perhaps wouldn't even try after this revelation. The only thing, it seemed, was to come as clean as possible, and hope for the best. After what Kadash had told him about Owen, however, there didn't seem to be much call for hope. *Fucking cops.* But, of course, he couldn't really blame the cops for this one.

He drew an uneasy breath. "This is what I remember. I went into the bar on a lark. I'd gone out for something to eat. I was feeling anxious. My sister and her family were coming for Christmas and I wasn't really looking forward to their visit." His voice shook at first, but as the words started to flow he felt himself steady. "I saw this bar and it seemed, I don't know, alluring somehow. Not the kind of place I usually go to. Dark and anonymous. A cheap drink seemed like a good idea. Just one, I thought. The next thing I knew, it was lots of cheap drinks. I vaguely remember a woman, and I remember talking a lot. But not much else. At some point I was outside and a cab was there. Maybe someone called it for me, or maybe it just showed up at the right time. I don't know. I showed him my driver's license so he'd know where to take me. I remember I couldn't talk real well. I went home, puked in the yard and again in the toilet. Took a long shower. And that's it. That's what I remember. You say the woman was Carlotta, but I didn't know her and I don't remember leaving with her. And that's it!"

Mulvaney stood expressionlessly by the door. Kadash leaned against the wall, arms folded across his chest. Owen said to Peter,

"I'm supposed to believe that. You lied about having been there. What else are you lying about?"

"Nothing. Jesus!" Peter raised his head, glared at Owen. "I knew you would act this way. You've been on the rag for me since the beginning, and for no better reason than you're too damn stupid to look at what's really happening. I was in that bar two days before Carlotta was killed, and home with my fucking family the night it happened! I'm sitting in this room because my niece lost a stuffed animal. The person you're looking for is someone else, and he's still out there, and for all you know he's going to kill again while you're sitting here jerking my chain!"

Owen pushed himself to his feet, turned to Mulvaney. "I'm ready to make an arrest. No fucking way is he walking out of here again."

Mulvaney sighed. "Dick, we need to talk to the DA—"

There was a knock at the door. Kadash moved abruptly and yanked the door open before Mulvaney or Owen could say anything. Parker stood in the doorway, a surprised look on his face at the sudden attention from the three detectives. "Uh, Detective Riggins needs to see one of you. He said it's urgent."

"Now what?" Owen muttered.

"I might have said the same thing a few minutes ago," Mulvaney said. "Detective, why don't we both go? We can discuss this matter further in private, and give Huxley a call. Detective Kadash can wait with Mr. McKrall."

"Fine," Owen said. He glared back at Peter. "Don't think you're getting out of this, you little prick." He stalked out the door past the officer. Mulvaney followed.

Kadash trudged heavily away from the door and slumped down in the chair opposite Peter. He could feel the detective's penetrating gaze upon him, but he didn't want to look up. "Well," Kadash said quietly. "You sure know how to step on your dick."

Peter closed his eyes, leaned forward. "I don't remember leaving with her."

"Bud, I've done my share of drinking, and I know what a blackout is, so you don't have to tell me. But it was pretty damn stupid pretending you hadn't been to that bar. You'd have been upfront about it from the start, Owen might've let it go, or had less of a hardon about it when the details came out."

Peter drew a trembling breath. "It was embarrassing. Abby had already given me a hard time about going there—not like I could hide a two-day hangover from her and she has a way of weaseling things out of me. The last thing I wanted was even more of a hard time about something I figured was irrelevant anyway. And besides, I didn't want to even think about the possibility I had met Carlotta before. It's not like it changes anything. I'm still just a guy who went looking for a toy and found a fucking nightmare instead."

The door opened and Mulvaney stuck her head in. "Sarge? I need you out here." Kadash threw a look at Peter, grunted, then followed her quickly.

When the door closed, Peter took a deep breath. They'd brought him a glass of water, but he hadn't touched it. Now suddenly his throat felt dry and tight. In one quaff he drained the glass. His stomach was turning over, and the water helped a little. He folded his arms on the tabletop and laid his head upon them, indulging himself in the warm darkness behind his eyelids. By rocking his head gently from side to side, he ameliorated the pain in his forehead. Thinking about the look on Owen's face when Kadash told him off helped a little, too. Better to think of that than the look on Owen's face as he went about jarring Peter's memory.

The door opened and Peter looked up. Kadash stood framed in the doorway. For a moment, he didn't speak, and Peter was struck by the unsettling feeling that Kadash had somehow changed in the intervening moments since he went out. He seemed shrunken somehow, his face drawn. "I need you to come with me," Kadash said quietly. He waved his hand vaguely through the door.

"Why? What's happened?"

"Mulvaney and Owen have gone ahead. They're probably in their cars by now. Susan told me to bring you with me." Kadash took a long slow breath, didn't meet Peter's gaze. "I tell ya," he muttered to no one, "I think I could use a butt about now."

"Wait a minute!" Peter said, his voice rising to meet the disquiet in his chest. "What the hell happened?" He leaned forward in his chair, then realization struck him. "It's Ruby Jane, isn't it?" he said. "That guy came back."

Kadash gazed at Peter for a long moment, then nodded sharply. "I ain't the right person for this," he said in an abrupt rush. "I never been good at this. That's part of why I work with Susan. She knows how to say the right thing—just lets me hang back and do police work. But she told me she thought you'd gotten most comfortable with me, so I should be the one that broke the news. Jesus. I'm sorry."

Peter pushed himself roughly out of his chair. Kadash looked momentarily alarmed, the expression surprisingly out of place on the detective's craggy face. The cherry patch on his neck fluttered almost imperceptibly. "She's not dead," Kadash said quickly. Then his voice softened. "She's not dead. But I have to tell you, she's in pretty bad shape. She took a button in the gut. They've got her at Emanuel."

"Oh, Jesus," Peter whispered.

"Listen," Kadash said quietly, his voice constricted, yet edged with sympathy. "Emanuel has one of the best trauma units in the whole goddamn country. They know what they're doing there, okay?"

Peter heard a hollow rushing sound in his ears. "We should have stayed. We should have brought her with us. God, you saw that guy—"

"Listen, she asked the paramedics if we could bring you to the hospital. Mulvaney and Owen are on their way there now. She wants you to come."

Peter stood paralyzed. Inexplicably, the crack on the wall caught his attention. It seemed to swell and widen, and for an unsettling instant he peered into black depths and imagined himself falling. He felt himself start to sway.

Kadash reached out with his right hand and caught his arm. "Peter," he said softly. "Peter … She wants you to come."

TWENTY

KADASH LED PETER THROUGH the Justice Center toward the parking garage. The corridors felt tight and claustrophobic, overcrowded with police officers and men in disheveled suits, women in utilitarian skirts, empty-faced loiterers. Kadash guided him with a hand on his upper arm, almost as though he were in custody, but Kadash's grip was gentle. He spoke quietly as they walked, and Peter listened from a distant place. "She was able to talk to the paramedics and a couple of uniforms at the scene. She told them it was the same guy you and I had seen there. That's why we found out so fast. She said, 'Tell Detective Kadash it was that guy he chased out of the shop this afternoon.' Otherwise, Mulvaney and I might not have been informed for hours. The case wouldn't have fallen to us. You probably would have found out before we did. But she told them you were with me and Mulvaney at the Justice Center, and that we should bring you."

Peter nodded vaguely and followed along. At the car, Kadash had him sit in front. He didn't comment when Kadash asked to take a smoke. He struggled against the urge to ask for a cigarette himself, and against the wave of memories that came with the smell of Kadash's Marlboro—other trips to other hospitals, years before, with his father attached to an oxygen tank. Something told him it wasn't right, wasn't fair, that he should think of such long-past events now, not with Ruby Jane the one in an ambulance, Ruby Jane the one whose life hung in the balance. She needed all his attention right now, all his energy. His father was long dead, but Ruby Jane wasn't beyond his help—not yet anyway.

"Mulvaney's gonna try to talk to her before she goes into surgery, see what she can find out. It's not really our case, Susan's and mine. I think it fell to Riggins and Davisson. Not sure, but it's been a busy end of the year. Too many fucking bodies, if you ask me. The rotation's all fucked up. So much for the holidays, eh? Anyway, Susan wants to talk to her because she knows Darla and she knows you. We gotta look for connections wherever we can, you know? Don't worry though—Susan'll keep that cockbite Owen away from her."

Peter felt dimly grateful, not just to Mulvaney for holding Owen off, but also to Kadash, for blathering on, filling the otherwise empty silence, and for continuing to refer to Ruby Jane in the present. She wasn't dead, she wasn't beyond his help, and she wanted him to come. Peter felt himself start to chafe at every traffic light, at every left turn with oncoming traffic that forced them to wait. Somehow, incredibly, they turned at last into the Emanuel campus. Kadash drove past the outpatient parking lot and straight for Emergency.

Owen met them at the door. "Mulvaney's inside," he said, "talking to Riggins. Davisson's back at the scene with a couple of witnesses. The woman's in surgery."

Kadash glanced at Peter. "What's the story?" he said to Owen, voice clipped.

"Two slugs," Owen said. "Gut and leg. Leg's dicey. Nicked the femoral artery. Don't know much more than that."

"What happened?" Peter said. He hated having to ask Owen that question. He felt as though he were talking out of a hole, but they seemed to hear him anyway.

"We're still filling in the details," Owen said. "Got a garbled 9-1-1, situation uncertain, at 3:12 p.m. We dispatched a car, but what saved her was two civilians, a man and a woman, who went into the shop around 3:15 for coffee. Place was empty, no one behind the counter. There was a broken glass on the floor in the front, and that got them worried. They thought about leaving, then heard a noise from the back. The man walked through a hall and came upon the assailant and victim in a big room. The assailant had his pants open, dick in his hand. When the witness came in, the assailant turned and fired a shot—a gun in each hand, you could say. He missed. Tried shooting some more, but his gun was jammed or out of bullets. He fled through a side door, pulling up his pants as he ran."

Peter listened from inside the hole. "He raped her?" He felt Kadash's hand on his arm.

"Well, we don't think it got that far," Owen said. "The witnesses busted up the fun before he could get to the good part."

Peter pulled his arm free of Kadash's grip and threw a balled fist at Owen's face. The move was reflexive, and Peter hardly had time to think about it before the punch landed on Owen's cheek and jerked his head back. Owen's mouth popped open and he took a step back, a livid red welt on his face. Peter glowered at Owen and hissed, "Shut up. Just shut up, goddamn you."

Kadash thrust himself between Peter and Owen.

"You're taking your cues from the wrong cop," Owen snarled. He leaned forward and puffed himself up. "You just made a very serious mistake."

"You're the only mistake around here," Peter said coldly.

"Oh, yeah? Well, you're about to find out about mistakes, pal. You and your buddy, Kadash, here. The only reason you're not in a cell already is because another one of your bimbos took a slug at the wrong moment." Owen ran a hand over his bruised cheek. "Nobody strikes a police officer and gets away with it."

Kadash leaned into Owen until his weight pushed Owen off balance. "I didn't see anyone strike a police officer, Detective," he said softly, but with restrained menace in his voice. "Just the three of us standing here, talking. You being too mouthy and full of shit, as usual, but that's it. I do think we've heard the last of this."

Owen took a step back. He stared at Kadash in astonishment. "I'm a police officer, and he's just a damned petty thief who also happens to be a susp—"

"Be quiet!" Kadash snapped. "You got all the couth of a dog turd at a tea party and I'm sick of listening to you."

Owen bristled. "I'm not going to let you protect him, Kadash. You're in enough trouble as it is. I don't think you—"

"How many times a day do I have to tell you to shut the fuck up? Come on, bud, let's go find Susan." Without waiting for a further response, he pushed past Owen and headed into the emergency waiting area.

Mulvaney and Riggins weren't in the emergency room, but a nurse directed Kadash to surgery. Peter followed him through a maze of corridors deeper into the hospital. As they walked, the full impact of the encounter with Owen settled onto him. He realized with dull surprise he was shaking. They came to an elevator, and as they waited Peter felt a wave of lightheadedness sweep over him. Kadash chuckled.

"First time slugging a cop?"

Peter smiled weakly.

"Couldn't have happened to a nicer fella."

Peter sucked air to clear his head, then followed Kadash into the elevator. "What will he do about it?" he asked as the elevator started to rise.

Kadash shrugged. "He could be a pain in the ass if he wanted to. On the other hand, Owen's not the type to readily admit to being cold-cocked by a civilian, and even if he does I'll make sure everyone knows why he deserved worse. I wouldn't sweat it."

That didn't sound all that reassuring to Peter, but he only said, "Thanks." He followed Kadash out of the elevator. The tension of the encounter still warmed the base of his neck, but when they found Mulvaney and Detective Riggins waiting outside surgery, his thoughts turned to Ruby Jane.

There was no real news. Mulvaney confirmed what they already knew. She'd talked briefly to Ruby Jane before she went into surgery, but could add only that Ruby Jane was sure it was the same man she'd seen earlier with Peter and Kadash. "She also asked if you were coming," Mulvaney said to Peter. "I told her Detective Kadash was bringing you."

All they could do was wait. Riggins left to return to the scene, but Mulvaney and Kadash stayed behind. Peter found a seat in the waiting room and gazed blankly at the television mounted on the wall. An old *Looney Tunes* was on, the frenetic humor unable to pierce his dark mood. He watched anyway, hoping to distract himself from thoughts of Ruby Jane in surgery, and of Owen. An animated *Batman* followed that was so somber Peter couldn't stand to watch it. He looked out the window into the parking lot, watching people limp in from their cars, towels wrapped around bleeding heads or clutching an oddly twisted arm to their chests. The news came on next and there was mention of a shooting at a Southeast Portland coffee shop. Perpetrator still at large. Peter shivered to think they might have video, but evidently the news was too recent—they promised a detailed report in the next hour. Peter promised to be elsewhere by then.

After a while, a woman in green scrubs came out of a set of double-doors and spoke to Mulvaney and Kadash. Peter climbed wearily out of his seat and slipped up behind them. "—could have been a lot worse," the woman was saying. "Just the surface of the femoral artery was damaged."

"When will we be able to talk to her?" Mulvaney said.

"It's going to be a few hours, at least. I'm going to have her in ICU at least through the night. If she wakes up and seems okay, I might be able to give you a couple of minutes. But I'm not making any promises."

"Me first," Peter said. "I talk to her first."

The doctor looked at him, her gaze stern. "And who are you?"

"This is Peter McKrall," Mulvaney said, moving aside so Peter could slip between her and Kadash. "He's Ms. Whittaker's—"

"Yes, I know," the doctor said shortly. "She mentioned you before the surgery. Fine, you're first. But like I said, I'm not making any promises. It will probably be tomorrow."

"But she's going to be all right?" Peter said.

The woman's gaze softened. "Her condition is stable, but serious. She's not out of danger. But she's strong and seems well-conditioned, and that gives me hope. Unfortunately, it's still too early to say much else." She turned to Mulvaney. "You can wait in ICU reception if you like. I'm afraid I've got to get going." She turned and disappeared back through the double doors.

"She's being cautious," Mulvaney said as soon as the doctor was gone. "Ruby Jane was clear-headed before the surgery and seemed to be holding up fairly well, considering everything."

"Thanks," Peter said.

"Why don't you go up to ICU with Detective Kadash. I'm going to go see how things are going with Riggins and Davisson. I'll try to be back before she wakes up. Later on, after you've had a chance to talk to her, I'd like you to come down to the Justice Center and look at some mug shots."

Peter nodded tightly.

"Come on, bud," Kadash said. Once again, Peter followed him through the corridors and up another elevator to a small, dimly lit waiting area. The obligatory TV hung from the wall, but the sound was turned down and the whimsical imagery of a candy commercial seemed strangely surreal in the hospital setting. Kadash checked in at a nurses' station across the hall from the waiting room, then joined Peter.

"How you doing, bud? Need anything?"

Peter shook his head.

"You let me know, okay?" Kadash said.

Peter closed his eyes. His thoughts seemed jumbled. "How come Detective Mulvaney calls you Sarge?" he said, looking up at Kadash. "It really seems to piss Owen off."

Kadash dropped down into the seat beside him. He sat quietly for a moment. "A while back, Owen sat for the sergeant's exam. Some guys on the detail talked me into taking it, too, just to tweak him. It took some finagling, but I got a spot." He chuckled. "I ended up scoring higher than he did."

"But you're not sergeants, are you?"

"No. I probably never will be. Owen's waiting for his slot." Kadash shrugged. "He'll get it, soon enough. Meanwhile, I'm Sarge to certain folks, especially if I happen to be within earshot of everyone's favorite homicide dick."

"That's why he's such an asshole to you."

"He's an asshole to everyone. I'm just a little more special than most." Kadash's eyes twinkled. "You too, now."

Peter smiled thinly and leaned back. "I guess I'm in good company... Sarge."

Kadash grinned and patted Peter gently on the shoulder. "Hope you got yer waiting shoes on, bud." Kadash gestured toward the TV. "You care for *Seinfeld*?" he said.

"Go ahead."

Kadash flipped the channel selector and turned the sound up slightly. Peter settled onto the couch. He half watched the TV, noted Kadash's mild chuckles at intervals. An episode of *Friends* followed *Seinfeld*, and *The Simpsons* followed that. For a while, Peter closed his eyes and let his mind drift. He didn't think about anything except Ruby Jane. Not the shooting, not Darla or the hypothetical brother, not the killings—not even Owen. Definitely not Carlotta and the possibilities created by too much cheap vodka. Just Ruby Jane—in her shop serving lattes, in her beater car driving through Northeast Portland, at the Bagdad drinking beer. These thoughts kept more somber images at bay. At some point, his weariness caught up with him and his thoughts became vivid dreams. But, for the moment at least, they remained merely dreams—the potential nightmares stayed away.

"Mr. McKrall?"

Peter jerked awake. Kadash and a white-frocked nurse stood in front of him. "She's awake," the nurse said. "Doctor said you could see her for a few minutes."

Peter pushed himself out of his chair. "Where is she?"

"This way," the nurse said.

"I was just about to go out for a smoke," Kadash said. "But I'll wait here for you. Find out what you can, in case she isn't up to talking to me, too."

Peter nodded, then followed the nurse. She led him past the nurses' station to a row of glass-fronted rooms. The first door stood open. "She may have fallen back asleep," the nurse said. "If she has, just come back out without disturbing her."

Peter took a deep, uneasy breath, then slipped into a tiny, dimly lit room. The back wall flickered with LEDs and lime-green read-outs. Ruby Jane lay quietly on the bed, her arms at her sides on top of the sheet. IVs dripped into the back of each hand, and a clear plastic tube looped across her face under her nose. She was very pale, with deep channels under her eyes. Her lips were dry and chapped, and he could see a blue vein pulsing in her temple. He felt himself tremble as she opened her eyes.

"Hey, Pete. How ya doing?"

He swallowed. "Hell of a lot better than you."

She showed him a hint of teeth. "I told the paramedics what I could, and I talked to Mulvaney for a few minutes right before surgery. But I bet they want to talk to me more."

"Kadash is with me. He's chafing for a cigarette, but he won't go outside until he can talk to you."

She increased her thin smile. "He can wait. I want to talk to you. I want to tell you what happened."

Peter stood silently, afraid to try to say anything, afraid his voice would crack. His stomach felt as tight as the head of drum, and his eyes kept blurring as water gathered at the corners. From somewhere, through a confusion of humming machinery and distant, faint voices, he heard a steady beeping he realized must be her heartbeat, signaled again and again on a monitor. The sound was reassuring, a continual, independent reminder that she was alive.

"How do you feel?" she said.

"Me...?" The question seemed strange. How he felt seemed hardly important. He was more concerned with how she felt. But he gazed at her, at her sunken face, and he recognized what she wanted. She wanted to know where he stood, what his reaction to what she was about to tell him might be. She required his honesty—he couldn't hide his anger, or his fear, in some vague hope of sparing her. "I want—I want to find the man who did this to you. I feel like I want to kill him."

She closed her eyes. For a moment, he feared he'd said the wrong thing. But then she opened her eyes again. "I understand," she said. "That's what I wanted you to say. But, Pete—" She lifted her hand toward him and he reached out and took it. "Pete, I don't want you to kill him. Wanting to is enough for me. Okay?"

Peter took a long deep breath. He felt he should appear sure and steady to her in this time of pain. But her words unlocked something in him and tears suddenly flowed down his cheeks. He tasted them at the corners of his mouth.

"Sit down," she said softly. "Sit on the edge of the bed. I want you close to me."

Without releasing her hand, he lowered himself carefully onto the bed. Through his tears she seemed soft and fluid, the dark, battered cast of her face made smooth again. She breathed in with difficulty and said, "Pete, I have to tell you, I wasn't really there for most of it. I think I missed the worst parts."

"You were unconscious?"

"I don't know. Not exactly. I was awake, but it was like I was somewhere else. I felt as though I was out of my body, watching. But not even that. Not really watching, except out of the corner of my eye. I didn't really want to see. I think I went away to protect myself. But I'm back again."

"What happened?"

"He shot me, Pete. He came for me and he chased me and shot me, and he would have killed me if he could. I ... I know he would have. Those people came in just in time."

"You don't have to say any more."

Her nod was so slight as to be almost imperceptible. She closed her eyes and drew a shuddering breath. He squeezed her hand, tried to send her strength and reassurance through her skin. She kept her eyes closed and he sat there, quietly, waiting. He stared at her face, his gaze settling first on one feature, then another and another. Her eyes were sunken—he wished he had the power to will them back to normal, make them quick and mischievous, full of light again. But she lay with her eyes closed, lids purple and lined with veins. Her dry lips were drained of color, her cheeks pale. He could see her pulse at her throat, slow but steady. That was something, at least. "Pete?" she said suddenly, without opening her eyes. "If you could do anything you wanted in the whole world, what would it be?"

The question caught him by surprise. He shifted on the edge of the bed. "I don't know." He hesitated. "I guess I haven't really thought it about."

She shook her head slightly, and opened her eyes. The whites had a yellowish cast that reminded him of his father's during his last few months. "Yes, you have," she said. "Everybody has." She tried to smile. "Come on, it's me, Ruby Jane. You can tell me."

The strength in her words belied the weakness of her voice. The real Ruby Jane was still in there, undaunted by her damaged shell. Peter swallowed and tried to be undaunted as well. His fingers found his lip for a moment, but then he dropped his hand. "I guess I would get my Land Cruiser fixed up, and then just go in it," he said quickly. "What about you?"

"Not yet, buster. You gotta give me more than that."

"You don't want to lie there listening to me blab."

"You are required to indulge me—I'm injured. Where would you go?"

He sighed, and then chuckled quietly. "I don't know exactly. Lots of places, I guess." Her stare told him she expected more than that. He paused to think for a moment, then said, "When I was in junior high school, my mom and dad took all the kids on a big vacation. We were never vacation types, really. Dad's two weeks off in the summer he spent futzing around in the yard more often than not. But Hank was a freshman in college and John was set to go. Abby was thinking more about her friends than her family. Mom wanted us all to do something special together before we split up, went our separate ways for good. So we packed the car and spent three weeks in Yellowstone National Park."

"You want to go to Yellowstone?"

Peter felt himself blush. "Not exactly. I mean, it was a beautiful place. It inspired me. We did all the main stuff, of course. Old Faithful, the bears, and all that. They say ninety-five percent of the visitors see only five percent of the park, and not necessarily the best five percent. I always thought I'd like to go see the ninety-five percent I missed the first time. Take my time about it, you know. Months, if I could. Camp a lot, hike a lot. Then go south, explore the Tetons. Maybe I'd head east, cross the Washakies and the Bighorns, go see Devil's Tower, the Black Hills. Maybe go on to the Badlands. Or go the other way, through Utah and Nevada, basin and range, basin and range. Follow the path the Donner Party took through the Sierras. I don't know. Maybe end up in Yosemite, or even the Grand Canyon. That's something else I always wanted to do—raft down the Colorado River through the Grand Canyon." He stopped suddenly and gazed at her, surprised at his own volubility.

She continued to smile. "I was hoping for something a little more specific," she said.

He didn't say anything. Something about his abrupt expressiveness seemed foolish to him, even with Ruby Jane. Perhaps it was just that he was out of practice, sharing his dreams. No one else had been interested for so long. Ruby Jane just smiled and breathed slowly.

"So, Pete," she said. "Why haven't you just gone? And don't say it's because the Land Cruiser isn't done yet. I want a real answer."

"I don't know. I guess I just figured I'd get around to it when I got around to it. There always seemed to be plenty of time."

Her smile faded. "I don't think so," she said. "You know, people talk about what they learn about life when they come close to death. I'm not sure what I'll learn. But I can say the one thing I know right now is that your time can run out any second." She inhaled deeply and for a moment her eyes grew troubled. "It hurts to take deep breaths," she muttered.

Peter felt tears return to his eyes. "I'm sorry, Ruby Jane. I really am. I never should have left you alone."

She shook her head and the tube strapped to her nose quivered. "There was no way to know what would happen. If you'd have been there, he would have shot you, too."

"Maybe with both of us, he wouldn't have come back. Maybe he would have been too scared to come back—"

"Pete, he would have come back. Listen —" She swallowed thickly and coughed, and he saw her wince. "—he definitely would have come back. Pete, he called me Darla."

Peter closed his eyes briefly. "It was him, then. It was the killer."

She nodded. "That's what I think."

A wave of calm suddenly settled over Peter. At first it surprised him, but then he realized it came from the understanding that the killer was no longer a faceless enigma, a ghost made of vapor and fear. He was real. He'd been seen—he could be caught. "So now we know what he looks like, and maybe we even know his name, if he is Darla's brother. We can find him. Do you think he called you Darla because he doesn't remember her? It's been a long time, maybe, since they would have seen each other."

"I don't know, Pete. I don't know. He wasn't—" Her voice caught in her throat and tears brimmed in her eyes. "He wasn't normal," she finished.

"We just have to catch him," Peter said. "We know what he looks like. Even Kadash knows. We'll just catch him. Then we'll be safe. Okay?" He gently stroked her face, wiped away her tears.

"Okay." She tried to smile again, but the effort seemed beyond her strength. He knew he would have to leave soon. But there was one more thing he felt he needed to tell her. Peter gazed at her, and was struck all over again by her beauty, and by her independence, her playfulness and humor. He wanted to make her safe, to protect her. He wanted to be there for her, for as long as she'd have him. But she had to know the truth about him. He couldn't hide behind smart-assed comebacks with Ruby Jane. He looked at her, and tried to think of how to say it. Simple and direct, he thought. That would be best. *Ruby Jane, I'm a thief.* The words came to his mind, but he couldn't speak them. *My mom died and I started stealing things because it was a way I could feel alive, feel in control, but now you make me feel...*

"Ruby Jane," he said, "I—I'm..." He felt his thoughts trip and veer. He opened his mouth again and the words just fell out. "I—I love you."

Her eyes darkened and her gaze focused somewhere in the distance behind him. "Peter..." she murmured. "People love. They love, but—" She sighed, deep and slow, then closed her eyes. "I think Darla loved her mother very much."

Peter felt blood rush to his face. "I'm sorry," he whispered in a sudden rush. "I shouldn't have said that. That's not what I meant to say. Too much has happened."

She didn't respond. He waited for her to come back. She breathed heavily, brow creased. The wrinkles in her forehead softened and he realized she'd fallen asleep. The LEDs flashed around him and the metronomic beep of her heart monitor continued to offer electronic reassurance. He hardly felt reassured. What would she say when she awoke again? *People love, but—* Would she mutter that maybe they needed some distance, that it had gotten too intense too fast? He sighed and gazed at her pale but lovely face. *I'm sorry*, he thought, *but it's true. I just shouldn't have said it.*

The nurse came in and touched his forearm. He looked up, startled.

"Sir, it's time to go," she said quietly. "Don't worry. We'll take good care of her."

He stood up. "Do you know when I can see her again?" he said. "Can I call you?"

The nurse nodded. "Just ask for ICU—"

Peter heard Ruby Jane stir. He turned back to her. Her eyes were narrow slits. "Pete?" she said hoarsely. "You leaving?"

He leaned down close to her. "The nurse asked me to go."

"It's okay," she said. "I think I need to sleep." She swallowed thickly. "Listen, Pete. You have to find Darla, okay? She knows who he is, and maybe even where to find him. And you know she won't talk to the police. You've got to make her talk to you, okay?"

Pete glanced at the nurse, who stood beside him frowning. "I'll do what I can," he said to Ruby Jane, "but I don't even know where to look."

Ruby Jane's eyes closed and she took a deep breath. She nodded slightly. Then she drifted off and didn't speak again.

Kadash greeted him at the nurses' station. Kadash thanked the nurse and left his card, asking for a call when Ruby Jane could have visitors again. Then he led Peter to the elevator. "You used up all the time, didn't give me my chance. Susan'll have our hides."

Peter didn't answer and Kadash nudged him. "Hey, bud? Lights are on—anybody home?"

The elevator door opened. Peter shook his head to clear it. "Sorry." They went into the elevator and Kadash pressed the button for the ground floor. "He called her Darla. I don't know what that means, exactly, except the obvious. It was the same guy who killed Darla's mother and Mrs. Cossart."

Kadash nodded, unsurprised. "Yeah, well, I had a feeling. Mulvaney and I already requested a comparison of Ruby Jane's slugs with the ones from the killings."

Ruby Jane's slugs, Peter thought. He wondered what she would think of that. *Aww, heck, I was just borrowing them.* He followed Kadash through the hospital. The lights in many of the hallways had been dimmed. The hospital was on night watch, slumberous and hushed. Yet an alert tension remained in the background, like a hum just at the level of hearing. He saw nurses and orderlies moving around with quiet purpose. Peter sensed all around him that people were in pain, some even fighting for their lives. And some, perhaps, just fading away, their fight worn down. *God, please don't let Ruby Jane be one of those.*

In the car, as they left the hospital grounds, he said to Kadash, without first thinking about it, "Sarge, if you could do anything you wanted in the world, what would it be?"

"Where the hell did a question like that come from?"

"Just curious. What would it be?"

Kadash grunted and shrugged. "I don't know. Guess I never thought about it."

"That's what I told Ruby Jane. She didn't believe me any more than I believe you."

Kadash chuckled. "I see. Well, I gotta tell ya, I ain't a young man anymore, and to be perfectly honest, I don't think you'd've ever called me a dreaming man. I've always been a cop, and I expect I'll be a cop till they make me quit. Which if Owen has his way'll be tomorrow." He chuckled again.

"What about when you retire? Do you have any plans then?"

Kadash pulled his pack of cigarettes out of his jacket pocket. He shook it a moment, then crumpled the empty pack and tossed it into the back seat. "Shit," he muttered. He drove silently for another moment, then said, "Bud, you and me're in different places. I came to terms with my mortality a long time ago. So here I am. I like being a cop. I suppose you'd say I'm happy being a cop. When I stop being a cop, I hope I find a way to like doing whatever I do then, but I don't intend to worry about that till I get there."

"Oh." Peter gazed out the window, vaguely dissatisfied.

Kadash glanced his way. "Listen, bud, you just had a hard look at something you probably hadn't thought you'd have to deal with. I know you went through your folks' deaths, and that was hard—especially your mom. But you expect your parents to die before you do. This is different, right? She almost died and she's young, like you. She's special to you and she almost died."

"Yeah. I suppose."

"I'll tell you, I learned years ago that your time can run out at any moment. It's not a pretty lesson. But I gotta tell ya, this time, for you, it didn't run out. She's still alive."

"I just met her on Monday," Peter said. "I told her I loved her."

"Do you? Or were you just saying that to make her feel good?"

"I think I do," Peter said. "But it wasn't what I meant to say—it just came out."

Kadash looked thoughtful. Peter realized they were already across the Hawthorne Bridge, coming up to the Justice Center. *Time for mug shots*, he thought. Ask him a week ago, he never would have guessed he'd ever be looking at mug shots.

"You really afraid it was too soon? Or maybe not soon enough?"

Peter looked at him. Kadash was staring out the front window. "Do you think she'll make it? Will she be all right?"

"A babe with that much spit in her? Yeah, she'll be all right." He chuckled again as he pulled into the Justice Center parking lot. "You're the one's gotta hang in there."

Peter got out of the car. Kadash was right, and Ruby Jane was right. Peter was only mildly surprised that both had used the same words—*your time can run out at any moment*. Peter recalled Kadash's friend Tommy, dead in Vietnam, still a teenager—not a pretty lesson. Ruby Jane was battered, tubes coming out of her body, but her lesson hadn't been fatal. Her time hadn't run out. And he'd said the right thing, even if he'd meant to say something else. He did love her, and he wasn't afraid to tell her. Far worse to wait, and have it be too late.

He followed Kadash inside. *Mug shots*, he thought. Then find Darla. He wasn't sure where to look, but he'd think of something. It wasn't too late.

TWENTY-ONE

PETER THRUST HIS HANDS deep into his coat pockets against the night's chill. The apartment building was typical Northwest Port-land—buff-colored brick with a dingy gray lintel over the entryway. A marble-faced stair climbed a dozen steps up to a wide oak door set with beveled glass. To the right of the door on the wall hung an intercom box so old Peter wouldn't have been surprised had it been crank powered. Penciled on a piece of masking tape beside the doorbell marked #3 were the letters Y–O– –N–G–E–R, the U faded to obscurity. He'd found Carlotta's address in the phone book.

He looked the building over. Multiple layers of grime encrusted the front steps. The brass doorbells were corroded black, and the cracked, funnel-shaped mouth piece of the intercom hung by a sin-gle screw. A couple of small craters pitted the glass pane in the door, perhaps the work of a pellet gun. Through the glass, Peter could see the hall carpeting was worn thin, though the paint on the walls looked fairly fresh. It wasn't so different from buildings Peter had checked out for himself before his sister and her husband moved to Seattle and he ended up renting from them.

He tried the door. It was locked, felt sturdy. If he'd been Kadash, he'd probably just press the button marked *Manager*, assuming the manager would answer the door at five o'clock in the morning. But, of course, if he was Kadash and Darla was really here, she wouldn't talk to him. She'd evade arrest, maybe bust his nuts for his trouble.

Peter went down the steps and back out onto the street. It was quiet. His breath billowed behind him as he moved. A dry, light snow had fallen while he looked at mug shots with Kadash, just enough to coat the city with grime. Now, the snow blew along the sidewalks before a bitter wind, a marching army of whirling crystal dervishes that broke against his legs below the knees. No one was out—others had more sense than he did. He should have been in bed. He'd almost fallen asleep gazing at the endless rows of mug shots before Kadash finally insisted they stop for the night. But that left Peter with an uneasy choice—to go home, or back to Ruby Jane's? He had her keys, given to him by Mulvaney when he and Kadash returned from the hospital. They'd returned his own keys as well, informing him they'd taken the answering machine tape and inserted a new one in case the mysterious caller tried again. Neither Ruby Jane's home nor his own appealed to him. Both had been invaded, both no longer felt safe. Yet a motel room seemed no better—sterile and empty, it would only accentuate his anxiety and loneliness.

Ultimately, he'd had Kadash drop him at Ruby Jane's. But once inside, his exhaustion had been supplanted by restiveness. In a fit of nervous energy, he cleaned up the shop, trying to remember the closing routine he'd helped Ruby Jane with the night before. He'd probably missed a lot, but the place was at least presentable. When he was done, he went back into the apartment. The place seemed cold, as much for a lack of Ruby Jane as for heat. He cleaned up the blood and vomit, then paced back and forth, stopped from time to time to examine a bullet hole next to the door that led to the shop. The police had removed the bullet, but hadn't fixed the hole. Maybe he'd take care of it before Ruby Jane got out of the hospital. He tried lying down, first on her bed, curtains closed, then, when the bed seemed too lonesome, on one of the couches. Sleep wouldn't come. He considered shooting baskets, but the imagined effects of an errant shot dissuaded him. He started to run a bath in the big claw-foot tub, but then rejected the idea and pulled the drain plug. The tub seemed too intimate, too suggestive to him of shared privacy. He missed her too much to take a bath alone.

What he really wanted to do was find Darla, no matter that it was the middle of the night. But he didn't have the slightest idea of where to start. He couldn't picture himself traipsing from homeless shelter to rescue mission, scanning the rows of forlorn faces for that one perhaps more forlorn than the rest. And where else to look? She was living outside, Mulvaney had said. He often saw people sleeping under bridges downtown, or in sheltered places in parks around the city. But there must be hundreds of such locations, most of which he'd probably never think of. Any search would be doomed from the start.

Maybe she just went back to my house, he thought. *It's warm and dry and she knows how to get in.*

He got up and paced some more. The likelihood of Darla in his house actually seemed pretty slim, given the speed of her exit earlier that day. The shelters and missions were equally doubtful with the police looking for her. To Peter, it seemed most likely she'd go to ground, find a place to hole up out of sight and stay there. But where would that be? The problem was that Peter's knowledge of her constituted a grim, but painfully short, list—she'd killed her father, she'd been in and out of jail, struggled against drug addiction, refused to become a prostitute, liked caramel lattes and smoked cigarettes with a smoldering chip on her shoulder. And loved her mother, or at least the idea of her mother, very much.

There were huge gaps in his knowledge, but the things he knew were striking nonetheless. Darla obviously hadn't spoken with her mother in a long while. But how long? Darla had said Carlotta didn't recognize her. How long did it take for a mother to forget what her daughter looked like? Ten years perhaps—since the murder? If that was the case, how had Darla found Carlotta again? He recalled Darla had said her mother lived over in Northwest, but how had she learned that? By accident, or had Darla sought her mother out?

He went to the telephone stand at the end of the kitchen counter. The phone book was on a small shelf at the bottom, buried underneath a stack of coupons from Pizza Schmizza. He flipped through the pages to the Ys.

YOUNGER, Carlotta 28 NW Trinity Pl #3.

That simple. Darla could have found her from any public phone. He looked on the map in the back of the phone book, found Trinity Place between Nineteenth and Twentieth in Northwest, not far from downtown. Darla could find it. He could find it. The only question was, when he did find it, would he find Darla as well? Was Carlotta's place as easy to get into as his own?

He took Ruby Jane's car. The streets were free of traffic in the pre-dawn hours, and the cold seemed to have driven the street people into hidden places. He headed up Burnside, over the bridge into Old Town, and then past the Park Blocks, past Powell's, over the freeway, counting streets as he went. Trinity Place was a narrow street only a block long, lined with apartment buildings and cars. He had to circle the block to find a parking space, and finally ended up walking down to Carlotta's building from a space he found on Everett.

So now that he was here, how to get inside? If it had been day-time, he might have simply waited until someone went through the front door, then darted inside before the door closed. But at 5:00 a.m., nobody was coming or going. Perhaps there was another way in. Number 3, he thought, would have to be a ground floor apartment. He walked along the sidewalk in front of the building, gazing at each ground level window. These windows weren't lintelled like the windows above, and they were narrower. He wondered if the apartments beyond rented for any less than those higher up.

He stopped at the corner of the building, considered the alley between it and the next. Perhaps there was a back or side entrance, an older, looser door he could card open. The alley was black with impenetrable shadow and stale with the aroma of garbage. He had a hard time picturing himself working a door in the darkness. He wasn't made of the same stuff as Philip Marlowe or Matt Scudder, despite this attempt at early morning investigation. He turned and walked back to the entry. When he reached the steps, he looked up.

Darla stood in the doorway. Her face was a mask of bitterness, her lips drawn into tight lines, her eyes shrouded in shadow almost as impenetrable as the alley. "I seen you walking back and forth out there." Peter didn't say anything. He'd come to find her, but now he was surprised to see her. "You don't know shit, do you?" she said after a moment.

"What do you mean?"

"These buildings—" She waved vaguely around. "—they're the easiest thing in the world to get into. But you just keep walking back and forth in the cold like a dumbshit."

"I wasn't even sure you were in there."

"Then what the hell are you doing here?"

He shrugged. "Couldn't sleep. Thought I'd get a little air."

There was no response at first, then the corners of her lips curled slightly. "You're gonna freeze, you stay out there. Come on."

Peter climbed the steps and slipped past Darla into the foyer of the apartment building. "You gotta be quiet," she whispered as she led him down the hallway to a stairwell that led back down to ground level. "I ain't supposed to be here."

"I'm probably not, either," Peter said.

"Yeah? Well, keep it down. I ain't gonna get busted because of you."

The bottom floor was slightly below ground level. Darla led him into a dimly lit hallway with a painted concrete floor. A large bank of mailboxes hung on the wall directly across from the stairs. Carlotta's apartment was at the corner of the building. Darla had left the door very slightly ajar, and she opened it quickly and ushered Peter inside. The room he found himself in was dark, the air warm and heavy. He could make out Darla's dark silhouette as she moved across the room and dropped down onto a long sofa.

"How about some light?" Peter said.

"How about we're not supposed to even be here."

Peter hesitated a moment, wondering how he would get past her agitation. He decided to try reason. "Darla, it's after five o'clock in the morning. Nobody's awake around here. A light isn't going to give us away."

As answer, he heard a faint rustle of cloth and the crackle of cellophane. A moment later, the scratch of a match accompanied a red flare and Peter caught the scent of cigarette smoke. Darla pointed the cigarette at him. "This is all the light I need."

Peter felt uncertain about how to proceed. The only thing he knew for sure was that he didn't want to stand around in the dark, no matter what Darla thought about it. He ran his hand along the wall by the front door until he found the light switch. When he flipped it, a dim, jaundicy light filled the room from an overhead fixture.

Darla sprang up off the couch. "What the fuck are you doing?!"

As she surged toward him, he imagined the police officers she must have gone through to evade arrest the previous day. He felt a split second of fear, but in an instant it was overwhelmed by anger. For all his uncertainty, he knew he hadn't come here to be bullied by Darla. "Don't come any closer," he said. Halfway across the room, she stopped.

"You're gonna have the manager here in a minute. Or maybe he'll just call the cops."

"I'm not afraid of the cops."

For an instant they locked eyes, and he thought she was going to fight him. She balled one fist at her side repeatedly. Then she turned away from him and went back to the couch. She took a deep, aggravated drag on her cigarette. "We're not supposed to be here," she mumbled through smoke.

He decided to let her stew while he collected his thoughts, took a quick look around. If no one showed up at the door demanding answers and threatening cops, she might relax enough so that he could talk to her.

The room was a confusing mélange. Miscellaneous furniture and junk jammed every inch of wall space, from a television on a rickety stand to a chrome chair-mounted hair dryer to a neat yet precipitous stack of newspapers in one corner. The couch where Darla brooded was upholstered in dark green and dimpled by cigarette burns. Behind her, an orange-and-blue-striped sheet curtained the only window. At one end of the couch was a battered end table, clam shell ash tray, and a stack of thin grocery-store romances on top. Between the end table and the corner stood a ceiling-high wooden armoire. Along the next wall a steno chair sat before a dark, walnut table with spindly legs and drop sides. A tall lamp stood between the table and a narrow bookshelf stuffed with odd pieces of fabric. On the wall hung an intricately patterned quilt. Gazing at it, he realized it presented a figure-ground illusion—first, a large fish in calico and blue, then, when he blinked, a red gingham fisherman in a boat on a blue lake. The pattern was subtle, and striking. It captured his attention at once, so stunningly out of place in the otherwise mundane little room. Then something in his mind clicked, and he looked from the quilt, to the shelf full of fabric, to the spindly table. He recognized scraps of the same fabrics in the quilt on the shelves. The table, he realized, was a sewing machine cabinet. He gazed up at the quilt again.

Carlotta was a seamstress, a quilt-maker. She made the quilt.

Peter suddenly realized he had come to think of her as an abstraction. She was a prostitute. A murder victim. The realization that she had created something artful didn't fit with either of those views. On Sunday morning, he'd been horrified by the callousness and relative disregard with which the police and the press had approached her murder. To Mulvaney and Kadash, she was a body—the point of their job. To Kelly Norris, she was a story, a chance to put another notch in her journalistic pistol grip. This quilt, this sewing machine, this shelf full of fabric suggested more. And he mustn't forget what Darla's very existence meant. Mother, Quilt-Maker. Peter began to wonder what else. He went to the armoire and opened the door.

"What are you doing?" Darla said, stubbing out her cigarette.

"Just looking."

"What fucking business do you have going through my mom's stuff?"

"None." The cabinet was jammed with quilts in various stages of completion. As he reached out to touch one, Darla appeared at his side.

"Keep your hands off."

"You didn't tell me your mom could sew."

"I didn't tell you a lot of shit. Get out of there." She reached past him and slammed the cabinet door. "It ain't none of your fucking business."

Peter turned on her. "Hey, *you* dragged me into this mess," he barked, surprised by his sudden anger, but unable to stop it. "I reported a crime and that should have been it. *You* called me, not the other way around. Hell, you broke into my house. You *made it* my business. Now you better get used to the idea that I'm here and I'm not leaving until I get some answers." The sudden outburst blew out of him like air from a balloon. Yet as he spoke, Darla flinched and he felt his ire begin to deflate.

She slumped back on the couch. "I never wanted it to be anybody's business. I never wanted it to happen at all. I don't care that she was a whore." She pulled her knees to her chest and rested her face against them. Tears stained her jeans. "All I want is my mama," she murmured. "It was too damn long."

He'd been awake too damn long. His nerves were frayed raw by everything from the voice on his answering machine to Ruby Jane's attack to Owen's implication that Peter himself had known Carlotta more intimately than he liked to consider. Drawing a breath, he sat down beside Darla and gently rested his hand on her shoulder. She jerked at the contact, then settled back again into quiet sobbing. She was far more a victim than he was—though with that thought an image of Ruby Jane shot through his mind. "Darla, I'm sorry for snapping at you," he said. "I came here because I need your help."

"I don't know nothing," she sniffed. "I ain't seen the gun in ten years, since I—I mean, since I …"

He'd been afraid to bring up the gun himself. "I understand that. But it's the gun that killed your mother. It also killed a woman who lived up the street from me. And something else. Darla, do you remember Ruby Jane?"

She lifted her head. "From the coffee shop? She got killed, too?!"

He shook his head sharply. "She's not dead. But … she did get hurt. A man …" He swallowed, caught his breath. "A man shot her. The police haven't confirmed it's the same gun … but, Darla, the man who did it called her by your name."

"Oh, shit, ohhh, *god …*" She pressed her face into her knees again.

"Darla, there's too much I don't know. I'm trying to understand, but without your help, I won't be able to."

"I don't know—I don't know what to say..."

Peter took a deep breath, aware before he spoke that he was heading into murky territory. "Darla, why don't you just start at the beginning. Tell me about your family, about—about who else might have taken the gun. You had a brother didn't you? Jake—"

She shook her head vigorously. "I haven't seen him. I don't know where he is. I don't know nothing. I haven't seen the gun since the day I—"

"Darla, please, just tell me about him. Anything you remember. If you think there's even a chance he took the gun, you've got to tell me."

She continued to shake her head. He felt her body tremble as she wept. He stroked her shoulders gently and waited. After a few minutes, her trembling eased and she drew in a couple of deep breaths. "He was a bad man," she mumbled.

"Who? Jake? Jake was a bad man?"

"Jake was just a kid." She looked up, her face blotchy. "I need another cigarette." She felt in her coat pocket, pulled out a cigarette pack and shook it. Crumpled it into a ball and threw it on the floor. "Shit." Abruptly she stood up and headed for a closed door opposite the front door. Peter followed her into a second room, a bedroom. A beat-to-hell dresser stood against one wall, an unmade double bed sagged against another. She went to the dresser and pulled open drawers. He watched for a moment, then flipped the light switch beside the door. She glared at him, then continued to search.

The bedroom was as jammed as the front room. An easy chair sat under the wall-mounted light fixture. Boxes overflowing with scrap fabric lined the walls between the furniture. There were two

291

windows, one over the dresser and one opposite the bed. The window across from the bed was curtained like the one in the front room. But the window over the dresser was covered with another quilt, a pattern of interlocking arrowheads in pastel blue, yellow, and pink. Peter went up to it to examine it more closely.

Behind him, Darla muttered in relief as she found what she was looking for, a half-empty pack of generic cigarettes in one of the bedside table drawers. He turned and watched her light up with sharp movements of her hands. As she inhaled, some of her tension seemed to drain out of her. She pushed past him toward the bedroom doorway, but he didn't follow.

"That help?" he said.

She looked at him, drew on the cigarette again, exhaled a plume of smoke. Nodded.

"Think you can talk now?" In answer, she dropped into the easy chair. He went to the bed and sat down. She avoided his eyes. "Who was the bad man?" he said. "Your dad?"

She sighed smoke, then nodded.

"How was he bad? What did he do to you?"

She rolled her eyes. "He was bad in all the ways they talk about on the talk shows."

"He beat you?"

"Duh." She shifted in her chair, nervously flicked ashes on the floor. Peter waited. He didn't want to say anything to agitate or distract her. She smoked in silence, gazed at the coal at the end of the cigarette. "He wasn't my real dad. I only called him that because I never knew my real dad and he was around for as long as I could remember. George Washington Smithers. Called himself the president of the family. Used to say he was exercising his veto when he wouldn't let me go out and play or something. Jesus, what a fucking jerk."

"Where was your real father?"

"Who the fuck knows? He was a customer. Some guy who had enough money to buy more than a suck and my mom had missed her pill or something. Back before people worried about AIDS and rubbers and all that happy horseshit. George was a customer, too, I think." She snarled the last few words, and Peter wondered what she would say if she knew Owen thought he might be one of Carlotta's customers, too, and that Peter couldn't remember enough one way or another to dispute the charge. She took a final drag on her cigarette and rubbed it out against the sole of her shoe. "You gotta understand, a lot of this I had to pick up listening to them fight in the next room. Nobody ever told me shit."

"What about your brother? Was George his dad?"

She shrugged, took out another cigarette, rolled it in her fingers. "I think so. Probably. He knocked him around like he was his dad, so it doesn't really matter, does it?"

"I guess not."

"Actually, George tried to get my mom to stop turning tricks. Not because he thought it was wrong or nothing. He'd bang a whore quick as anyone else. He just liked to be calling all the shots. But I guess she liked it. She'd slip out to do some guy in his car or somewheres. George'd freak when he found out. Scream he was gonna nail her to the wall. That was another favorite saying of his. *Gonna nail ya to the wall!* Of course, he liked the money she made—he *always* took the money. But she'd just go out again while he was at work or off drinking. Sometimes she'd bring her tricks to the apartment. More than once they was slipping out the back window while George was coming in the front door."

She paused to light her cigarette, inspect the smoldering tip. "Shit, I ain't smoked this much at one time in months. This is the second pack of hers I found, you know." She inhaled with evident satisfaction. "I could get used to this real quick."

"Tell me about Jake."

She blew smoke toward him. "I don't wanna talk about Jake."

"How about…" He hesitated, trying to gauge the extent of her willingness to talk. "What about your dad?" he tried. "Why don't you tell me more about him?"

"You talk like a shrink." She laughed without humor and shook her head. "I told all these stories before, you know. To caseworkers, psychologists, whatever. Cops probably got files a foot thick."

"I'm not the cops."

"Yeah, well, that's pretty fucking obvious." He didn't respond. She sighed. Seemed to think for a moment. "I tell ya, you kill your dad when you're twelve, they don't just throw you in jail… It's all homes and therapy—one-on-one therapy, group therapy, gimme-a-hug therapy. You get real tired of it, I can tell you. Idiots asking questions. How do I feel about wetting the bed? What are my dreams? Do I have sexual feelings about older men? Bunch of bullshit." She suddenly flashed her eyes at him. "I don't *have* no sexual feelings, about no older men nor anyone else." She cocked her head at him in obvious challenge.

"I see," he said quietly, not sure where she was headed.

Her lips twisted into a sneer. "I bet you do. My crotch ain't been wet for no one or no thing in longer than I can remember. What do you think about that?"

A sudden image of Carlotta in the 747 Lounge popped into his head, and he wondered if it was an actual memory, or just imagined. He shook his head sharply and the image faded. "I, uh—"

"You ain't used to talk like that, are ya?" she said.

He tugged his lip and drew a deep breath. "I guess not. It's a bit outside the range of my experience." He tried a chuckle. It came out as a choking sound. He wished he hadn't said anything.

"You talk real pretty, but sometimes you sound like a dipshit." She blew smoke rings at him. "When I was about sixteen this boy kind of liked me. I'd see him at meals and stuff, laugh at his jokes. Guess he thought I liked him back. Tried to grab my tit in the back hall of the home. I broke his fucking hand. I don't *have* no sexual feelings, you see."

Peter crossed his legs, uncrossed them. Someone with more experience at this sort of thing might have known what Darla would do once she started talking. All Peter knew was that moments before he'd felt he had some small measure of control over the situation, and now that was gone—if it had been anything more than an illusion to begin with. Darla, for all her fragility, had an instinct for psychological self-preservation.

"Don'tcha wanna know why?" she said.

"I don't know if—"

"Hey!" she snapped. "You asked, right? '*What about your dad?*' you said. So I'm telling you, okay? You came here. *You* asked *me*. Now you're getting the whole goddamn story."

"Darla, I'm just trying to—"

"I know. I fucking know. You're wondering about Jake, wondering if he took the gun after I killed George. You're wondering what he might be like, right? Could Jake be shooting people now, ten years after all my shit? Am I right?"

"Well, yeah. I mean, that's part—"

"So that's what I'm telling you, damn it. I ain't got no sexual feelings and I killed George with his own gun. Shot the fucker fulla holes. You want to know why, or what?"

Peter didn't speak. He'd unlocked it. He'd insisted, and now she was going to make him pay the price. He sat on the edge of Carlotta's bed, and tried not to think about what must have gone on there.

"President George wanted to fuck my ass," Darla said. Peter felt blood rush to his face. Darla smirked at him. "That's right. Oh, George hit me, sure. But that was just a side thing. I hardly noticed. What he was really interested in was jamming my ass—not a normal fuck even, since he was afraid I'd get pregnant. But I wasn't gonna let him." She laughed without humor. "I told him I'd suck him or jack him off, but I wouldn't let him fuck my ass. And that wasn't good enough for George. He kept pushing and pushing till finally I didn't know how to say no no more. I mean, hell, I was just a kid myself, right? That's what they told me in all my therapy. No way I could hold out for long against a grown man that knowed what he wanted and wasn't afraid to come get it. Right?"

Peter kneaded his lips between his fingers. He could think of nothing to say.

"So finally he did it. And when he was done, laying on the edge of my bed and grunting like a pig, I went and got his gun. Me and Jake knew right where he kept it, even though he thought he had it hid. Kids're like that. They learn all the secrets. So I got the gun and emptied it into him. Assassinated the fucking president. Jake was there, in the apartment. Hiding in the next room. He knew what was going on, but he was just a kid himself. What was he gonna do about it? He came in at the sound of the shots though, and he saw what I done." She hesitated, sucked on her cigarette in short, shallow drags. "Jake wanted to know what happened and I told him that's what happened to you when you fucked someone's ass even when they said no no no nonono*nooooooo*—"

She dropped the cigarette and bent over on the chair. Peter pushed himself off the bed and went to her, thinking to step out the burning butt as he crouched at her side and put his arms around her shoulders. Gimme-a-hug therapy. He smelled the acrid scent of tobacco and stale sweat, the warm wet smell of tears. She shuddered in his arms, and he said the only thing he could think to say. "Shhhhh. I understand." He didn't really understand at all. Outside the realm of his experience wasn't the half of it. Didn't have a fucking clue to save his life. If he'd been asked, he might have guessed only something horrible could drive a twelve year old girl to shoot her father, or step-father—anyone. But he never could have guessed at the extent of the horror. "It's okay," he said. "It was a long time ago. It's over."

She sat up suddenly and pushed him away. "You don't understand," she hissed. "It's not over. She's dead and he's out there. He's got the gun and he's shooting people. It's not over. It's never over!"

"We'll find him," Peter said. "We'll end it."

"There's more," she gasped. "You gotta hear it all. A lot of it's in the files, I bet. But I didn't tell them everything. They may not know about thi—"

"Darla, it's okay. You can help us find him—"

"No! You gotta understand. I don't have no sexual feelings. But there was a time when I did. I had sexual feelings for Jake. Way back. I don't know how—George got me started, maybe. Or watching my mom. I don't know. But Jake and I—we did things. Sometimes it was stuff George made me do to him, sometimes it was other stuff. I mean, I wouldn't go all the way with him, but just about anything else…I don't have sexual feelings anymore. But I can't see him now. I can't help you find him. It's been a long time, but I can't see Jake and have it all come back."

She crumpled against him. For a moment, Peter didn't know whose trembling was greater—hers, or his own. She cried and he wanted to cry with her. It was all so much more than he was prepared for. When he'd come, he'd wanted nothing more than a little concrete information. *Where might he find Jake? What did she know about Jake? Had she seen Jake recently?* But she'd surprised him again. Three times now he'd met with her, three times now she'd dragged him through territory so grim, so foreign, so full of despair that his most basic assumptions had been rocked to their foundations. He thought of his own despairs. Father dead of cancer, mother dead by her own hand. Those bare facts had haunted him for years, yet how could his paltry suffering approach the reality of Darla's life? He lost his job—he didn't get along with his sister. It was so awful he had to drown his sorrows in cheap booze and perhaps even a hooker's bartered affection. His pain seemed trivial held up in the harsh glare of her history. His parents had loved him. His sister annoyed him, but he knew she loved him, too. None of them had ever done anything to harm him. His parents were dead, and that hurt, but his pain was tempered by a lifetime of warm memories. Where were Darla's warm memories? What had Darla known of love?

"I'm sorry, Darla," he whispered. It sounded hollow, even to him, but somewhere inside he knew it was heartfelt. He hoped she would understand that. "I'm so very sorry."

He felt her nod. "Thanks," she mumbled. "What the hell, life goes on, I guess." She lifted her head, disentangled herself from him. He moved to the edge of the bed, and she slouched back in her chair. She looked surprisingly calm, her face smooth if mottled and moist. *Learned her lesson—life goes on,* he thought. At one time, Peter would have thought that a positive lesson, but now, coming from Darla, it was tainted with bitterness.

He stood up and went to the window, lifted the orange and blue curtain. He gazed out for a moment, then pushed the curtain aside. He knew he shouldn't be so cavalier about standing in front of the open window, but he needed a distraction, and he didn't think there was much danger anyone would see him—at least, not anyone who'd know or care that he wasn't supposed to be there.

"Jesus, you are a retard," Darla said. She didn't sound very angry, though.

"There's no one out there," Peter replied. He glanced at his watch. "It's barely six o'clock in the morning."

"Somebody could walk by."

Peter shrugged. "Let 'em, I guess. You're not going to be able to hang out in here much longer anyhow. They'll rent this place in no time."

She didn't answer, but he heard the scratch of a match, smelled sulfur and fresh smoke. "At least turn the light off," she muttered. He heard her get out of her chair and a moment later the room fell into darkness.

Peter gazed out the window. It was still dark out, the only illumination the gleam of a street light. A meager snow fell, too wispy to stick. The snow matched Peter's mood—frigid, inchoate, quiet. He breathed a whiff of cold air that leaked in around the window frame. He didn't feel tired, but the chill breath added an edge to his wired alertness. The window faced an alley. Peter saw another building not five feet away with a window that matched the one he looked through. He half expected to see himself looking back, a forlorn man in the mirror. A thief. A pathetic thief with no clue what pain really was. But the other window was dark, the curtain closed.

"So when was the last time you saw Jake?" he said.

"I ain't seen him since the day I shot George. Shit, I'd almost forgot him till you told me in your house yesterday about it being the same gun."

"So you think no one else could have the gun?"

"Are you kidding me? Anybody else could have the gun. I just left it there. It could have been Jake, but for all I know it was a cop, or one of them social workers that come swarming in like goddamn buzzards."

"Were you aware at the time the gun hadn't been recovered?"

"No." She drew noisily on her cigarette. "Listen, I don't remember a whole lot about that time. It was all a kind of blur. I know they didn't exactly arrest me. I know I went to a court once or twice, but mostly it was just social workers and shrinks and living in the home. Like a dorm, but with heavy wire in the windows. Later I figured out my mom was gone, and I suppose I thought Jake went with her but I don't know. I never knew."

Peter nodded. "We've got to find Jake," he said.

"I can't help you with that!" Her exasperation beat the air like the thrumming of a tightly stretched wire. "I don't know where he lives. I can barely remember what he looked like then. I sure as hell don't know what he looks like now."

"I know what he looks like," Peter murmured.

"Then you don't need me."

Outside, the light changed as the first hint of sunrise tinted the sky to the east. In the window across the alley, he saw a vague, formless shape lying on the window sill. It stood out in drab gray against the darker curtain. For a moment, Peter fixed his eyes on it, half curious, half hypnotized. He turned and looked at Darla, who'd moved to the edge of the bed, directly across from the window.

"Darla, do you know if your mother was the type to leave the curtains open?"

She blew smoke. "What do you mean?"

He glanced back across the alley. "Was she likely to have left the curtain open while she, uh, worked?"

She looked at him, eyes blank. "How am I supposed to know that?"

"I don't know," he said absently. Two or three fewer vodkas and perhaps he wouldn't have needed to ask. The shape in the window remained formless, but as he stared at it, his hackles raised. "I'll be right back," he said.

"Where you going?"

He didn't answer, but went back through the front room and out the door. Darla followed closely. "Where the hell you going? People could be getting up in other apartments. They'll know where we are."

"If you're coming," he said, "don't forget to close the door behind you."

She hesitated, then returned and pulled the door shut. He didn't wait. He headed up the stairs and out the front door. A blast of cold air hit him as he reached the street. At either end of the block, traffic on Burnside and Everett was starting to pick up. He headed to the corner of the building and looked down the alley. The alley was shrouded in shadows, but Carlotta's window was first from the corner, and well enough lit by the street light and the sunrise. He went to her window and looked inside. The bed was framed by the window. He backed up against the building opposite. Even with the bedroom in darkness, he could still make out the bed. Whoever wanted could watch whatever show Carlotta put on from across the alley. Assuming, of course, that Carlotta was the type to leave the curtains opened.

"What the hell are you doing?" Darla hissed. "Get the hell away from there."

"We're outside now, Darla. No one's gonna bust us here." Peter turned and looked through the window behind him, then shivered as recognition hit him. "Oh—"

"What is it?" Darla hissed.

He glanced at her, then back down through the window. On the sill lay a small, stuffed dog—battered, gray, and mottled, mostly furless from a little girl's lifetime of affection. "Patch," he said. "I've found Patch."

TWENTY-TWO

PETER STEPPED AWAY FROM the window. His shoe slipped an inch on pavement coated with black ice. Somewhere down the alley he heard a sound like the dripping of water. He could see his shadowy reflection in the glass, a vague form in black jeans and blue jacket, a befuddled face. Darla hissed at him from the mouth of the alley, but he didn't respond. The dripping grew louder, seemed to demand his attention—but he just stood, listening, feeling the cold, absorbed in the growing light of morning. The meaning of Patch seemed to have less importance—and to be more starkly obvious—than the sensations of the alley around him. He felt calm and coldly present as he made the connections in his mind. Patch in this window, across from Carlotta's window—*how?* There could be only one explanation. Jake was here—this was his place, his window. He'd watched his mother across the alley for God-only-knew how long. And then, when he could no longer stand what he saw, when the pressure grew unbearable—

"What the hell is Patch?" Darla growled.

He looked at her. She seemed shrunken in the cold, her face made raw by the wind. "I told you about Patch," he said. She stared at him without comprehension, her eyes narrow. "I was looking for her in the park Sunday morning when I found—" He stopped. Darla's mouth dropped open, and her eyes lost their focus. Behind him, the dripping sound resolved itself, became the sound of movement, the sharp slap of feet against concrete. Wide-eyed, Darla gaped past him up the alley.

A cry rose out of the shadows, a swelling ululation as the footsteps slapped nearer. "Nooooooooo!" Peter turned and saw a shape charging toward him, the figure of a running man. In the dim light, he saw the man reach out toward him. A flash of orange blossomed from the man's hand, followed by a sharp report like the sound of a tree limb breaking under the weight of snow. Something whistled past Peter's head, followed by an abrupt rumble of thunder that he only distantly realized must be the beating of his own heart.

He shot at me—

Darla screamed. The sound echoed in and out of the alley in waves. Every fiber in Peter's body shrieked *flee flee fleeeee*—but as he turned he slid and slammed down on his hands and knees in the mouth of the alley. A bitter lance of pain stabbed up through his forearms. He scrabbled against the cold pavement. His shoes could find no traction. The ululation boiled behind him, "Nooooooooo, *stuuuupidddd Peterrrrheaddddddd!*" Darla grasped his shoulders, pulled him up. He found his feet as she pushed him out of the alley.

"Run," she hollered. "*Run!*"

He ran, his feet skidding on the icy sidewalk. Odd details seemed to register in his mind—the cold, the sound of his feet hitting the pavement, the smell of car exhaust. His vision distorted, contracted to a narrow view of the path immediately before him. He bolted past parked cars on one side, Jake's apartment building on the other. He didn't see either. Behind him, he heard the crack of another gunshot—and footsteps, pursuing, pursuing. Darla cried, "Jake! Please *leave him alone, Jake!*" His mind recorded the words, but Peter couldn't process them. He could only run, his blood like boiling water in his veins, his eyes rimmed with frozen tears. He looked for a place to hide, but the street was nothing but apartment buildings and parked cars. He realized dimly that he was heading toward Burnside. That meant traffic, people, motion—even this early in the morning. People meant help—someone would help him, someone out there—

"*I nail you to the wall, Peterhead Mackerel!*"

A man stood at a bus stop at the corner, a heavyset fellow in a black jacket, dark hair and glasses, an open book with a bright green cover in his hands. Inexplicably, the book emblazoned itself on Peter's mind. The man looked up as Peter raced down the sidewalk toward him. Peter tried to scream for help, but only a strangled cry came out. The man lowered the book and opened his mouth, and Peter heard another sharp report. A red-black bloom appeared at the man's throat and a bemused expression crossed his face. Then he dropped, as abruptly as a sack of potatoes. Peter slowed for an instant, but the footsteps kept coming. The green book skittered into the street. Someone screamed, perhaps Darla, perhaps someone else—perhaps even himself. Peter turned and ran up Burnside toward Twenty-first. A car rolled past him on the street and Peter lurched toward it. He slapped the glass of the passenger side window. "Help me! Please—" The driver gave him the finger and shouted something, then the car squealed away.

"I get you, *get you!*" came the hoarse cry from behind. Peter flung a glance over his shoulder, saw Jake rounding the corner—bare steps away, it seemed—waving the gun. Thunder rolled in Peter's ears as he tried to find more speed. Narrow shop fronts lined the sidewalk, a tavern, a plumber's supply, a costume shop, all dark and empty. He passed them by and charged across an intersection without hesitating, looking for lights, people, anything. He saw a Plaid Pantry up ahead, shining like a phosphorescent beacon under the dim predawn sky. Somebody would be there, somebody would help him—

A white car slammed to a stop in front of him and he smacked into it, doubled over across the hood. Flashing red and blue lights suddenly blinded him. The driver's door flew open, and Peter saw a uniformed figure appear. A cop—he'd run into a police car.

"What the hell's going—"

Peter reached out to the officer. He felt a sudden searing pain in his outstretched hand, followed by a sound like cracking ice. A yelp burst from his lips and he fell against the car door, slid down hard. His head smacked the sideview mirror and light seemed to cascade around him. He rolled to the side, landed on his butt beside the car.

"Hey—*GUN!*" the cop shouted. Peter watched him draw his own pistol. Details swelled up around him—the fire in his hand, the wet cold of the pavement against his ass. The metallic scent of blood. The world tinted gray and red, the colors of a Portland winter morning. A dozen paces away, back down Burnside, Peter saw Jake. He recognized him instantly, the man he'd seen in the coffee shop the day before. Jake raised his gun and aimed. The light blossomed and Peter felt fire in his cheeks. The cop was shouting, he was shooting. Peter heard the rumble of the thunder in his chest and the whip-cracking reports of gunfire. But Peter was falling away. He saw Jake spin and stagger, then turn. Start to run. Then a black hand reached out and covered Peter's eyes, and he was gone.

TWENTY-THREE

JAKE SAT HUNCHED OVER on the toilet seat and tried to breathe. His forehead rested on his right hand, elbow propped on one knee. His left hand curled, trembling, against his chest. The air in the bathroom seemed both cold and stifling hot. It caught in his dry throat. Jake knew that was just him feeling afraid, feeling the pain. An involuntary shudder shook him and he winced as agony spiked across his chest. A drop of blood fell from his curled hand and hit the floor between his feet. Another tremor surged through him and he groaned. *It hurts.* He couldn't remember anything that ever hurt so much. Another drop fell, joined the growing pool of blood between his feet.

He couldn't fucking believe that stupid cop had shot him.

Too many images chased through his head for him to keep it all straight—the old whore in her bedroom across the alley; the icy cold park late at night; his bloody coat on a heap of trash in Peterhead's garbage can. And more, more—Peterhead staring through the window—*his* window. The cop yelling, shooting. A cold-hot blow to his chest, heavy as a hammer, sharp as a knife. Turning, running. The blood, the blood on his chest, the blood on his hand. The blood on the bathroom floor.

And Dee-Dee. He kept seeing Dee-Dee in his mind. Dee-Dee in the alley, Dee-Dee yelling, *Jake! Please leave him alone, Jake!* What was Dee-Dee doing there? What was she doing, talking to Peterhead? *Helping* Peterhead? Didn't she love him anymore? Had it been so long that she'd forgotten him?

He watched a drop of blood fall. *Can't stay here,* he thought. *Peterhead'll come.*

But he couldn't think of anywhere else to go. He was in bad trouble, and the cops would come any minute and take him away and it would all be over, forever. He wondered if they'd shoot him. On TV, they always shot the guy, filled him with holes. Jake had always got a boner at the sight of the holes in those scenes, but now he wondered. He didn't think he'd get a boner when they filled him with holes. He certainly didn't have a boner right now.

Drip ... drip ...

The blood. He knew he'd lost a lot of blood just running from the stinking cop. As long as it kept dripping onto the floor, he was losing more. It had slowed down, but he knew that for every drop that fell, still more soaked into his shirt and jacket. He had to stop the bleeding. Had to find a bandage, plug the hole up. He'd been taught first-aid in school once, long time ago. Hadn't paid attention. Boring. He couldn't remember much, but he remembered, or just knew instinctively, that you have to stop the bleeding first of all.

Jacket off first. Had to see what it looked like. He pushed himself upright. His one arm wasn't working so well, the left one. The hole was up near his shoulder, and it hurt when he tried to move that side. Slowly, he unzipped his jacket with his right hand, peeled the coat away. He whimpered as the pain twisted through him, steely electric wires running through his flesh. He recalled the Darla, whimpering on the floor beside her bath tub.

The jacket was drenched. He thought he'd gotten used to blood. His own blood though, it seemed different. Looked different. Red, but kind of a special red. His own special color of red. *Jake Smithers Red,* he thought, like they might call it on the painting show on TV. He would have laughed at the thought, but it hurt so fucking bad he couldn't stand it.

He dropped the jacket into the tub, let his blood drain away. Getting the shirt off was harder. It was a pull-over. Used to be white, but now it was Jake Smithers Red. The hole in the cloth was pretty small. Didn't make sense to Jake, really. How could it be so small, when it hurt so fucking big? He started to cry. Everything had been fine. He'd found the old whore, followed her home. Watched her. Did her. *Did her, and got clear.*

And then the gloves turned up missing, forgotten, left behind. He returned to the park, and there he was. Peterhead Mackerel. That's when it all started to fall apart. Suddenly Peterhead was everywhere, foiling Jake at every turn. With the old whore at the bar, searching her out, staring at Jake in the park—*knowing something.* On TV saying all that stuff about how Jake was a sicko, about how he should be nailed to the wall. Always getting away. Slithering out from under the coat, sneaking off through the park. Over and over again, he got away. Every time Jake got close, Peterhead slipped through his fingers.

Every fucking thing went Peterhead's way. Jake never would have got shot if Peterhead hadn't come along.

And the blood. It kept coming, dribbling out of the hole, dripping onto the floor. He was able to use his left arm enough to slip his right arm out of its sleeve. He had to wait a minute after that, breathe, let the pain subside. Then he lifted the shirt over his head, slid it off his arm. He quickly wadded it into a ball, pressed it against the hole. That was something he remembered from first aid. Press something against the hole to stop the bleeding.

Fucking Sunday. Maybe Jake should have just left Peterhead alone. Maybe he should have stayed away from the president's mom, kept his coat out of the garbage.

Gasping, he pushed himself up off the toilet. He had to find a bandage. He looked into the bathroom mirror. His face was white. The cut on his forehead the Darla had made when she threw the glass at him had closed up. *Why couldn't the bullet hole close up, too?* A wave of dizziness passed through him and he almost fell. He put a hand on the counter, looked down into the sink. A drop of blood fell, stark against the white porcelain.

Why couldn't Dee-Dee be helping *him?* He was the guy who needed help, not Peterhead. *Everything* worked out for Peterhead. He didn't need no fucking help. Jake was the one who needed help. Couldn't she see he was bleeding? God, he might even be bleeding to death.

"Dee-Dee! Help *me!*"

His voice resonated in the narrow confines of the bathroom. But Dee-Dee didn't come. She didn't love him anymore. Tears dripped into the basin, mixed with blood. He drew a trembling breath. Alone.

He'd always been alone. Dee-Dee was gone. She was putting Peterhead's thing inside her now. She didn't love him anymore.

Weeping, he opened the cabinet behind the mirror. There were Band-Aids—useless. Aspirin, Tylenol. A prescription for something called Xanax. *What the hell was that?* With a sudden spasm of rage, Jake swept bottles from the shelf. "Damn it! Stupid jerk!" The effort sent a spear through his chest and threw a broad splash of Jake Smithers Red across the sink. He was past caring. Dee-Dee loved Peter now. The place was a mess, but *so-fucking-what.*

He staggered out of the bathroom and into the bedroom. With his good hand, he jerked open the dresser drawers, flung clothes onto the floor. Shirts, underwear, socks. He didn't care. Make a mess. Who gave a fuck? Not Dee-Dee—she was probably off somewhere *sucking that creep's dick.* There was another mirror over the dresser, snap shots slid between the frame and the glass along the sides. With his good arm, he started ripping down the photos in a frenzy. Then he saw himself, saw his pasty face, his bare chest covered with blood, left arm awkwardly curled up to hold the blood-soaked shirt against the hole. He looked frightening, even to himself.

"They'll kill you if they find you here," he said to his reflection, his voice dull and flat. He didn't know where the thought came from. But suddenly it sobered him. He looked at himself, imagined more holes all over his body. The thought didn't give him a boner.

"Maybe I want them to kill me." His reflection didn't respond. Down inside, he felt that wasn't really true, because he knew the way they'd kill him would be to shoot him full of holes. That would hurt so bad. Maybe if they shot him in the brain first it would be okay, but he couldn't count on that. And even if they didn't kill him, he might die anyway. He had a bleeding hole in him. A bullet, down inside. He couldn't go to the hospital. They'd bust him for sure if he did that. All he could do was try to stop the bleeding. But the bullet, he realized, might kill him anyway.

He didn't care. He could hardly believe it, but he just plain didn't care. He'd tried to be happy, to find joy like the minty old lady said, but that hadn't worked. The Darla had busted his nuts. Peterhead got away. The cop shot him. And Dee-Dee didn't love him, so nothing else mattered. Suddenly, dying didn't seem like such a big deal.

But not here, not full of holes. That was the only thing he didn't want.

He bent over, picked up a clean shirt from the floor, wiped the worst of the blood off his chest. He tossed the shirt to the side. Then he got another clean shirt from the floor, set it on the dresser. With his free hand, he carefully folded it into a thick pad, then dropped the bloody shirt and pressed the fresh one to the hole. Pressure to stop the bleeding, he remembered. He spent a moment to catch his breath, then he went back to the bathroom, looked in the medicine chest again. He was feeling calmer, though tired and light-headed. That was because of all the lost blood, he knew. But it was okay. He was going to stop the bleeding, then figure out what came next.

He found a roll of white adhesive tape on the top shelf. He grunted when he reached up for it, but the pain wasn't so bad as before. Maybe it was knowing he was going to die that did it. Hard to worry about a twinge in the chest when it was all coming to an end. He rolled out a long strip of tape, stretched it across his chest over the pad and down under his arm. That freed up his left hand, and it was easier to add more strips with two hands, even if one was kind of gimp. He made sure the pad was secure, then tossed the tape to the side. Already a thin line of Jake Smithers Red showed along the edge of the pad, but that didn't matter anymore. Dee-Dee didn't love him.

He needed a place to hide, a secret place. He looked into the mirror, into his pale, sweat-slicked face, and it came to him. The perfect place, secret, comfortable. If only he could get there. It would be hard, with a bullet in him. But if he made it, he'd be okay. He'd be comfortable. He could die, if that's what came next, in peace. He tried grinning at his reflection, just to show he could still do it, bullet and all. It didn't look like much of a smile.

He chose a button-up shirt from the closet. Easier to put on. Then he went into the living room, hoped to find another jacket in the front closet. Going through a lot of coats these days. *Heh.* He'd left the gun on the coffee table, and at the sight of it he felt the tiniest twinge of recognition between his legs. He smiled, picked up the gun. It felt so good, so heavy. He slid the barrel into his mouth, tasted burnt powder. A warm feeling spread through him, and he knew he had to take it with him. He'd need it if they tried to bust him.

He went to the bookcase, tumbled books onto the floor. He got the box of bullets, opened it. Only two left. He put the empty shells from that morning in the box, then returned the box to its hiding place. As he shoved the books back onto the shelf, one of the titles caught his eye. *As I Lay Dying.* It made him laugh.

After he loaded the gun, he went to the window, pushed aside the curtain one last time. Across the alley, the old whore's window looked back at him. He could see the bed where she let the men put their things inside her. Took a deep, labored breath. He didn't care what anyone thought. Not Peterhead, not anyone. He'd done the right thing.

He started to drop the curtain, but stopped when he saw the little dog on the window sill. He reached out and stroked it. At the park, trying to get away, the old whore had grabbed crap off the ground and thrown it at him, dirt and pieces of junk. He got rid of most of it, but for some reason, he'd kept the little dog.

He gazed at the dog, battered and threadbare. Stupid thing, just some kid's dumb toy. Like it could actually hurt him. Yet staring at it brought the tears back to his eyes. His breath caught in his throat. He left the dog, left the window. Left the apartment for the last time.

TWENTY-FOUR

Peter's arm hurt—a dull, throbbing ache that echoed the beating of his heart. With eyes closed, his body seemed to roll as though caught in a wave. Despite the pain in his arm, he felt warm and comfortable—half awake, half asleep. He'd been dreaming, was dreaming still, a little. A nightmare. Chased, unable to get away. An image of Jake loomed in his mind. Fire blossoms grew from his hand. Peter sat helpless on the ground, and Jake fired at him, a duck in a shooting gallery. In an instant, a shuddering wave of terror passed through him. He could still almost feel the cold wet pavement against the backs of his legs, almost smell the bitter tang of gunfire on the morning air. He couldn't remember ever being so frightened.

He opened his eyes. He lay on a hospital gurney with a sheet over his legs. Right arm across his chest, immobilized from fingertips to elbow by a swathe of bandages. A surgical lamp hung from the ceiling above, oxygen and gas valves protruded from the wall to his left. He heard the muted sounds of activity from beyond a closed door to his right—voices and movement. He was in Emanuel Emergency, he suddenly recalled, in a treatment room. He dimly remembered being brought in—by the police, maybe—and talking to the doctor who had stitched him up. Trying with little success to sign paperwork with his left hand. He'd been so tired, it was easier just to drift away.

Detective Mulvaney sat in a chair at the foot of the gurney. She seemed preoccupied, but stirred when Peter moved his arm and groaned at the subsequent pain.

"Don't worry. You're okay," she said. "The damage was relatively minor."

"What happened?"

"The slug passed through the flesh between your thumb and palm on your right hand. It severed a couple of small arterials and broke the first metacarpus. You'll have physical therapy, but that's the worst of it. You still have your hand." She took a short breath, then added, "I know you're unemployed, but I hope you have insurance."

"I'm still covered by U.S. Bank, I think," Peter said absently, "till the end of next month. Lucky me." He raised his hand, winced, looked at the thick bandage. He expected a cast, but there appeared to be only a splint that held the thumb and index finger stationary, wrapped in gauze and secured by an Ace bandage. "So it was only this?"

"Well, your shirt and coat didn't make it. They were soaked with blood and they cut them off looking for additional damage. Detective Kadash brought you a T-shirt and a sweatshirt to wear. Then there's your face—though that's not too serious." At first Peter thought she was making a joke, then he lifted his left hand to his cheek, felt Band-Aids. Mulvaney continued. "No stitches there. The slug struck the fender next to your head and you were hit by metal fragments. The doctor doesn't expect any significant scarring."

Peter swallowed thickly, felt a tremor pass through him as he imagined the significant scarring caused by a slug that hit just a few inches closer. "What—what about Jake?" he said. "The police officer was firing, but—"

"Your assailant is not currently in custody. We believe he may have been wounded, however." She paused. "Are you certain it was Jake?"

"Pretty sure. Darla screamed his name when he started shooting—" He stopped. Had he thought about it ahead of time, he might not have mentioned Darla so casually. Now it was out, and that meant questions and more questions. He didn't feel ready for questions.

But Mulvaney didn't comment. She gazed at him from the end of the gurney, her green eyes expressionless and impenetrable. Since that first morning, she'd been almost like a ghost. She haunted him uneasily during their various encounters at the Justice Center, asking uncomfortable questions and displaying little or no reaction to his answers. In light of all that, it felt strange to him to see her now. He would have expected Kadash.

"Darla wasn't present at the scene of the shooting," she said. "My understanding, however, is that you were running from some other location. I presume you left her there."

"Yeah. You didn't see her then."

"No."

"He must not have hurt her. She must have got away." He shook his head slowly, remembering his headlong flight down the street, the sound of footsteps and gunfire behind him. He was surprised at just how abruptly the situation erupted, at how quickly he'd been overcome by his fear. One moment talking to Darla, calm, fresh in the realization of Patch. The next, Jake came crashing down with the sound of thunder and cracking ice. Peter didn't feel ready to process it all—just coping with the throbbing in his hand seemed as much as he could take. And yet one thing prodded at him, demanded attention. He looked at Mulvaney. "There was a man, on the corner. I tried to scream. He—"

Mulvaney pursed her lips, looked down at her hands. "He's dead, I'm afraid. The bullet hit him in the throat. Officer Belson didn't even know he was down there. By the time anyone got to him, he'd already lost too much blood."

Peter closed his eyes. The man had probably never known Carlotta, or Jake. He'd just been standing there, reading, evidently waiting for the bus.

"He'll never know how the book came out," he said, eyes still closed.

"What?"

"He was reading a book. I remember the cover." He pictured the book in his mind, the bright green cover. He recognized it, knew the title, the story. "By Robert Parker. I read it myself, not all that long ago. I probably even read parts of it while I was waiting at bus stops. He'll never know how it came out."

She didn't say anything. Peter opened his eyes.

"What was his name?"

"I don't know. I can find out for you. Why?"

"I want to send his family something. Flowers, maybe. I don't know. Something."

"It wasn't your fault."

Of course it wasn't his fault—he was just a man running for his life, past another man standing in the wrong place at the wrong time. Whose fault wasn't the point. He closed his eyes again. He forced the stranger and his book out of his mind. Mulvaney remained. Quiet. Aloof. Inexplicable. "Can I ask you a question?" he said.

"Of course."

"Why are you here, and not Detective Kadash?"

She seemed to consider for a moment. "The answer to that is less complicated than you might think. He's out having a cigarette. I was upstairs with Detective Davisson talking to your friend about what happened to her. Detective Kadash waited with you while you slept. I came down here when I was finished with your friend and he asked me to wait while he went out to smoke. The doctor thought you might wake up any time."

Peter felt dissatisfied with the answer. He remembered the sensation of her hand on the back of his neck Sunday morning as his stomach lurched. She seemed to empathize with him then. Something had drawn any warmth out of her since. He thought of the blood tests. Still no results. "Do you think I killed those women?" he said.

"No, not now."

"But you did, at some point."

She shrugged. "I had to consider that possibility."

"What about Detective Kadash? Did he ever think I killed those women?"

"Perhaps you should ask him that yourself."

"I'm asking you. You're his partner—you would know his feelings on something like this, right?"

She hesitated, looked away. "Sometimes I regret giving up cigarettes." After a moment, she seemed to come to some decision. Narrow lines appeared at the corners of her mouth and eyes and she returned her gaze to his own. "Skin and I don't work quite the same way. He is, ah, more guided by instinct, and intuition, than I am. You might say I'm more methodical, more by the book, and he's more inclined to follow his hunches." She nodded as though reluctantly agreeing with herself. "Perhaps I'm overcompensating for the fact I'm a woman in a job that's traditionally a man's." She brushed an unseen hair away from her eyes. "Perhaps I could allow myself to be more intuitive. I don't know. I do what works for me, and Skin does what works for him. He is a very effective investigator, for all his … idiosyncrasies. I'm glad he's my partner."

"So are you saying he never thought I did it?"

"I think you should ask him that."

Peter reflected upon her words. He wondered how often she had openly made such an admission, especially to someone who was effectively a stranger. Not often, he'd bet. Part of him appreciated her candor and the professionalism behind it. She had a job to do and knew how to do it. She didn't let her feelings get in the way. It probably made her a better cop. But another part of him—the part that simply hurt over all he had seen—wanted her to empathize with him again. Wanted her to ask him how he was. Wanted her to acknowledge that, for whatever she'd grown accustomed to in the course of her work, she felt for his own fear and pain. He met her eyes with his own. Maybe it was there. Maybe, in that moment, her cool green gaze wasn't so distant. But he couldn't be sure. Perhaps her admission would have to be enough. Anything else might be, after all, too much to ask.

"How is Ruby Jane?" he said quietly, allowing his mind to drift elsewhere, to what was, after all, a more pressing worry.

Mulvaney seemed relieved by his question. "She's improving. She's worried about you. She was very alarmed by what happened."

It hadn't occurred to him they might have told her about it. He started to push himself up with his left hand. "I want to go see her. Let her know I'm okay."

Mulvaney shook her head. "She knows. I told her. And besides, she's asleep again. The nurse up there chased Davisson and me out. She'll still be there later. Right now, I think you and I should talk. I need to know what happened."

"Yeah," he sighed. "I know." He settled back against his pillow, caught his breath. He was tired. Whatever sleep he'd gotten was not enough. For a moment, he listened to the pain in his hand, to the whoosh of conditioned air through the vents, to the muted noises that filtered through the door at his side. He recalled all the things Darla had told him. *You've got to make her talk to you*, Ruby Jane had said. *She won't talk to the police.* In his mind, he heard Darla's voice, her tears, the sound of her screams as she cried for Jake to stop. The sounds echoed in his mind. Loudest of all was the crack of the gun, reverberating in rhythm with the beating of his heart. But it was not a memory of that sound—it was the sound imagined, the sound made ten years earlier, when a girl held the gun and pulled the trigger.

Mulvaney's hands were folded in her lap. He wondered, given what she had said, how she would react to Darla's story. He thought, perhaps, that he shouldn't tell it all, should retain some measure of Darla's privacy. Catching Jake was what mattered now, not dragging Darla back through a painful past she'd already paid dearly for. "What, exactly, do you want to hear?" he said.

Mulvaney stared at him, her green eyes as shiny as glass. She seemed bemused by his question. "Everything, of course. Everything since you left the Justice Center last night. I need to hear it all."

TWENTY-FIVE

AROUND HIM, PETER HEARD the murmurs of ICU—the beeps of heart monitors, the shuffle of nurses in thick-soled shoes, the whisper of the respirators. From down the corridor he heard the faint burble of a television—that would be Kadash in the waiting area, watching *Wheel of Fortune* and chafing for a smoke. Peter stood at the foot of Ruby Jane's bed, watched her sleep. She looked peaceful. The color had mostly returned to her face, and her eyes appeared less sunken. Peter felt an inexplicable pressure in his eyes and throat—he wanted to cry, but he wasn't sure why. She was getting better, after all.

"She's doing well," a voice said from behind him. Peter turned and saw one of the nurses, a heavyset women who seemed to be all cheeks and uniform. "I believe she'll be moved off the unit this afternoon."

Peter took a breath, nodded. "That's good," he said.

"You're Peter?"

"Yes."

The woman nodded. "She mentioned you earlier." She motioned toward his bandaged hand. "You two have been through a lot the last few days."

"Her more than me."

"Of course. But that's not your fault, is it?"

Peter looked at her without responding. It was the kind of thing Kadash would say, or Mulvaney, but it surprised him coming from a stranger. Of course it wasn't his fault—Jake was the guilty one. But did he really believe that? He could drive himself crazy analyzing the contingencies, and in the end be no less convinced of his own culpability. Perhaps sensing his discomfiture, the nurse smiled, patted his arm. "She'll be fine. We wouldn't move her off unit if the danger wasn't past. That's all you need to think about."

"Thank you," he murmured. The nurse slipped away, and Peter turned to watch Ruby Jane breathe. The rhythmic rise and fall of her chest reassured him more than the nurse's words, but an edge of anxiety remained. What would she say the next time they spoke?

He sniffed the now-familiar scent of Kadash. The detective slipped quietly up beside him, glanced at Ruby Jane. "We should get going," he said. "Mulvaney's waiting. We got bad guys to catch."

Peter's feet felt rooted to the floor, his eyes fixed magnetically to Ruby Jane. "I feel kind of crazy when I look at her. But I'm not sure why." He shrugged listlessly, his arms as heavy as stone. "I guess I'm worried about what comes next."

Kadash looked at Peter's face, one shaggy eyebrow raised. "You always had such a hardcore habit of fretting about what comes next?"

"It was never important before."

Kadash blew air. "It's always important. You just gotta keep your view of it in balance. Right now is pretty damned important, too. But if you're worried about her—" Kadash pointed a callused thumb at Ruby Jane— "I think it'll take more than a declaration of love to scare that one off."

"How about a bullet in the stomach? Think that might scare her off?"

"Don't recall it was your finger on the trigger." Kadash ran his hand through his thin hair. "Jesus, bud, you're about as subtle as a backhoe in a flower patch. I ain't one to argue you shouldn't beat yourself up, but you oughta at least have a beating due."

Peter forced a shrug, his eyes on Ruby Jane. He didn't speak.

"It's clear as top-shelf gin you've spent a lot of years just trying not to have any actual feelings," Kadash said. "Seems like you got a lot tied up in that, especially when it comes to your mom, or to shit that reminds you of your mom—like Carlotta Younger's body in the park." Peter felt his gut tighten, but before he could say anything, Kadash plunged on. "A lot of people remind me that what I don't know could fill a library, but one thing I do know is sometimes it hurts worse *not* to hurt than to just let it happen. Feelings can bite—I don't deny it—but it's seldom fatal. Maybe it's time you got on with feeling what you need to feel about your mother's death. Pissed off, sad, whatever the hell it is. But feel it, and while you're at it, stop holding people at arm's length by pinching their trinkets. Then maybe you can get a handle on just how responsible you really are for Ruby Jane's situation. Which, in my opinion, is not one stinking bit."

Peter stared at Kadash with open-mouthed astonishment. It was as long and ardent a speech as he'd heard from Kadash. "I almost stole her pen," Peter murmured. "It was in my pocket, but then I put it back on the table."

"I bet she's got a thousand pens," Kadash muttered.

"It's been a really long time since I was able to do something like that. Put something back on my own." His voice sounded to him like it was coming from far away. "It was a really nice pen."

Kadash shook his head, a look of wry amusement on her face. Finally he laughed and said, "Bud, I think you're gonna be all right."

Peter looked at Kadash through eyes that felt moist, yet hard and tight at the same time. "It's been a tough couple of days," he said quietly. It seemed the only thing left to say.

"That's a fuckin' mouthful." Kadash smiled, and the fire retreated from his thorny visage. "You're not a hopeless case yet. Sappy, with an irritating streak of self-pity, but not incurable." He pulled on Peter's shoulder, led him away from Ruby Jane's room. Peter followed compliantly, but with one last look over his shoulder at her. "C'mon," Kadash said. "She'll still be here later, probably eager to talk to you. Right now, I need a smoke, so the therapy session's over."

Peter followed Kadash down the corridor. "Am I going to have to face Owen again?" he said.

"Detective Owen is, uh, going to be pursuing other aspects of the investigation, in light of new information received this morning."

"And to think, all it took was me getting shot to get him off my back."

Kadash scratched his neck. "I should try that." He chortled. "Maybe I can contrive to get in Jake's way when the big bust happens."

"Do you have any idea where Jake is?" Peter said.

"We're close. I gotta tell you, your little adventure this morning really opened things up. Mulvaney said she'd have your statement typed up by the time we got downtown. Once you sign, we'll include it in the affidavit we're preparing for the search warrant for that apartment. Hopefully that'll be enough. It'd help, of course, if it was actually Jake's place."

"It's not? Whose is it?"

"Nobody any of us have heard of. Actual tenant ain't been seen in a while. Curious, don'tcha think?" Kadash chuckled grimly. "Turns out Jake rents a one-room rat hole in a building south of Civic Stadium. Unfortunately, he ain't home. Don't look like he's been there in a while, either, but we got it staked out. I'm not so worried about catching him now—we know who he is, where he lives. He'll turn up. I'm more worried about building the case. Catching him don't count for shit if we can't convict him."

Peter found the news strangely anti-climactic. He was mildly surprised by the fact that the police had found Jake's apartment, considering they hardly believed Jake existed a day or two before. But aside from that, he felt more absorbed by his own inner turmoil than by the possibility of finally nailing Jake. In the car, Kadash lit his much-craved cigarette. Peter stared out the window through the smoke and tried not to think about his tumult of feelings. With dull eyes, he watched the city roll by. A thin sun shone through featureless clouds overhead. It was near noon on a holiday week Wednesday, but the day seemed cast in dreary shades of gray. People on the street walked with their bodies hunched against the cold, seeming to avoid eye contact with those they passed. New Years was only a few days away, but Peter felt no anticipation, no sense of renewal or beginning. In his mind, he struggled to hold at bay images of his mother, of Carlotta, of the bloody condom in the park. It seemed he could only brood over what was past. Even thoughts of Ruby Jane were troubled by images of her hospital bed.

They crossed the river on the Burnside Bridge and turned south on Second. Around him, the city felt soft and sad. The storefronts were dim, lifeless. Peter was glad when they turned into the Justice Center lot.

Kadash stubbed out his cigarette as he parked. "Honey, we're home," he muttered, followed by a wet, rattling cough. He issued a raspy chuckle. "One of these days, I'm gonna have to quit." Peter winced at the words—his own father had joked thus, even as he pulled the oxygen tank on its little cart after himself through the house. Kadash led Peter in to the elevator. The ride up to Homicide seemed interminable.

Mulvaney was waiting for them at her desk. Peter greeted her with a wordless nod, and she nodded back. "Our boy's feeling a little worn out," Kadash said. "Been a tough day."

"That's no problem." Mulvaney held up a couple pieces of paper held together with a paper clip. "Here's your statement. Read it through, make sure it's complete. Once you sign it, you can go. Get some rest. We'll let you know what turns up, if anything."

"Fine," he mumbled. He took the statement from her and quickly read it—a description of his encounter with Darla in Carlotta's apartment and the subsequent discovery of Patch in the window of the apartment across the alley. The appearance of Jake with the gun, the chase. Back at the hospital, Mulvaney had been typically thorough, going over the details of his story again and again. The statement, as presented, was concise, but covered everything. He nodded as he read it, then accepted a pen from her to sign. "You'll have to pardon my handwriting," he said as he fumbled with the pen in his bandaged hand.

She took the pages when he finished and gave them a glance. "It'll do." She thanked him and suggested he get some rest. He nodded in answer, and turned away.

"Come on, bud," Kadash said. "Give you a ride."

Peter started to accept, then found himself shaking his head. "No, thanks," he said. "I think I'd like to walk."

"Colder 'n a witch's tit out there."

"Yeah—" Peter smiled wanly. "I guess I'm just used to walking."

Kadash shrugged. "Well, we'll give you a call. Gonna be home?"

"Sooner or later," Peter said. He added, "You'll only be able to leave a message until I can replace the phone cords."

He left the Justice Center, thoughts adrift. He hoped to just walk, let the rhythmic motion of one foot in front of the other clear his mind. He found himself on the gray street, a chill east wind in his face. Kadash's sweatshirt was hardly adequate, but Peter ignored the cold. Without thinking, he walked down to Waterfront Park, his feet tracing an aimless path over the grass to the railing at river's edge. A handful of people on their lunch hour strolled through the park, coffee cups or hot sandwiches in their hands. Peter felt his stomach rumble at the sight of food, and he bought a falafel sandwich from a sidewalk vendor. He stood for a long while and stared out at the river as he ate. The water was black and choppy, and Peter found its movement hypnotic. He hardly tasted the falafel, but it landed well in his stomach. Overhead, seagulls circled, squawking demands for a share of his sandwich.

"Get your own sandwich," Peter said, but he tossed the last couple of pieces of pita bread into the water, then headed up the waterfront as the gulls fought over the scraps.

He wandered past the Salmon Street fountain, cascading in spite of the cold, then cut back into town. He felt warmer as the buildings closed in around him and broke up the wind, but around him other pedestrians still walked with their chins pressed into their chests. He zigzagged among the streets, following no particular path, crossing against lights, peering into shop windows or up at the gray sky. He bought a latte at the Starbucks in Pioneer Courthouse Square. Merely adequate compared to Ruby Jane's. As he sipped the coffee, he remembered her car, still parked over near Carlotta's. He gulped the last of the latte, tossed the cup in a trash can. He decided to go get the car. He could return it to Uncommon Cup, or maybe drive to the hospital and check on Ruby Jane. Maybe she'd be awake. Maybe she could talk. He wouldn't worry, for now, about what she might say.

He headed up Tenth and crossed Burnside at Powell's. After a moment's debate, he went into the bookstore, mostly to get out of the cold for a bit. As he warmed up, he spent a few minutes scanning the fiction shelves, fingering the odd mystery, no intent to buy. He lingered at the Robert Parker novels, thought about the man at the bus stop. *Paper Doll*, that was the book the man had been reading when Jake's bullet found his throat. A Spenser novel. Peter idly recalled the story, about a woman who'd been brutally beaten to death, seemingly the victim of a random killer. As it turned out, it hadn't been so random after all. There'd been secret reasons behind the killing, hidden meaning ultimately discerned by the inimitable

Spenser. *Not like real life,* Peter thought. For the man at the bus stop, there were no secrets, no hidden meanings discerned by street-savvy private eyes. Just a random bullet, and death.

Peter left the store and went up Eleventh to Everett. Traffic thinned after he crossed the highway on the Everett overpass. The neighborhood shifted to small businesses and apartment buildings. Cars parked bumper-to-bumper on both sides of the street.

At the corner of Everett and Trinity Place he paused. The car was a half block up on Everett, but he turned onto Trinity instead. He knew he should stay away, but he felt curious about whether Mulvaney and Kadash had gotten their search warrant, and if so, what they had found. He stopped opposite Carlotta's building, on the far side of the street, and gazed down the alley between her building and the one next door—Jake's building, he thought, no matter who really lived there. In the afternoon light, he could see all the way through the alley to the next street, the sinister shadow of early morning banished. In front of the apartment buildings, the street was parked up, and he saw no immediate sign the police were there. Part of him wanted to cross the street, check the window again, confirm it was really Patch that he'd seen. But he knew it was time to leave it in Kadash's and Mulvaney's hands. He'd found Darla, learned her secrets, discovered Jake's apartment. The rest was up to the cops.

Kadash came out of Jake's building. He looked at Peter and frowned, shook his head vigorously. Peter's breath caught in his throat as Kadash raised his hand and impatiently waved Peter over to him.

"What in hell are you doing here?" he said as Peter crossed the street and joined him.

Peter nodded up toward Everett. "I left Ruby Jane's car over here. I came to get it."

"I don't see you climbing into no car and driving off."

"Well, I guess I got curious. I wanted to see what was happening."

"That so. If you asked me, I'd guess you just got stupid. Maybe you forgot the last time you were in the neighborhood our friend Jake was taking pot shots at you."

Peter found Kadash's irritation unexpected. "That's why I stayed across the street."

"Good point. I never knew a bullet to make it all the way across the street."

Peter swallowed. Hoping to divert Kadash's attention, he looked at the building, motioned toward it with his head. "Did you find Patch?"

Kadash shook his head and glared at him. "I get it now—you *wanna* get shot." Peter tried a weak smile. Kadash continued to glare, then after a moment, he gave an exasperated laugh. "We're still talking to the building manager." He sighed noisily. "You better come on inside. You can wait with the manager while we check out the apartment. ID the teddy bear, so long as you're here."

"Patch is a dog," Peter said.

"Right. Teddy dog. Come on."

Kadash led him inside, past a couple of uniformed officers who waited in the foyer. They went down the corridor to a first floor apartment in the front corner opposite Jake's, or whomever's, in the basement.

Mulvaney was inside, talking to a short, dark-haired man in a white sleeveless T-shirt and black slacks over scuffed loafers. The man turned and stared at Peter through dark eyes set too close together. Peter noticed yellow sweat stains on his T-shirt. Another uniformed officer stood off to one side. Mulvaney looked up as Peter and Kadash entered. "What's going on, Sarge?"

"He left his girlfriend's car over here this morning. Was coming to get it, decided to snoop. Not too bright."

"I see." She gave Peter a long, appraising stare. Her face was closed as always, and he couldn't guess her thoughts. "I suppose he can wait here with Mr. Heisler and Officer Jefferson while we check out the apartment."

"Who is this?" said the dark-haired man, presumably Mr. Heisler.

"This is Mr. McKrall," Mulvaney said. "He found Mrs. Younger's body."

"Ah, well. I see." Heisler shook his head. "I really don't know how any of this could happen," he said. "It makes no sense to me. Certainly this is an apartment building, with many who come and go, many strangers. Most are quiet, very courteous. I admit that I have to evict people on occasion, generally over failure to pay. But this—this is … so distasteful." His hands fluttered as he spoke, and his head jerked from side to side. Peter felt himself growing nervous just watching him.

"Perhaps we should just go take a look at the apartment, Mr. Heisler," Mulvaney said. "If you remember anything, you can tell us when we're finished. Do you have a key?"

"Of course," Heisler said. He went to a narrow cabinet by the front door. Several dozen keys hung from hooks inside. He selected one and handed it to Mulvaney. "Shall I let you in?" he asked.

"If the man we're looking for is in there, he may be armed. I think it would be best if you waited here. Officer Jefferson will wait with you." Heisler seemed relieved by the answer. He nodded sharply and glanced from face to face. Mulvaney went to the door.

"Hopefully this won't take long," Kadash said to Peter. He clapped Officer Jefferson on the shoulder, who nodded, then followed Mulvaney out of the apartment.

Peter went to the window and lifted white lace curtains, looked out. Down the street, near Burnside, he saw three police cruisers and Kadash's gray Taurus parked in a truck-loading zone. He wondered if they parked so far down in order to avoid drawing the attention of anyone in the building. Behind him, Heisler cleared his throat.

"Would either of you like some tea?" Peter heard Officer Jefferson grunt, "No thanks." Peter turned and shook his head. Heisler paced in a narrow path between a low, winged sofa and a highly polished coffee table. The carpet there looked worn. Peter figured Heisler must make a habit of pacing.

"I don't know this Jake the police asked about," he said. "That apartment is rented to Mr. Anderson. Regis Anderson. He lets me call him Reggie." He added with a nervous laugh, "Though only after he has been drinking."

Peter couldn't think of anything to say. He didn't want to chat anyway. He returned to the window, looked out without seeing anything. He felt no anticipation, no impatience. During his long walk, he managed to find some balance to his anxieties. Perhaps he'd come to some resolution that hadn't surfaced yet. More likely, it was simply that he'd convinced himself not to think about anything for a while. In either case, for the moment, his mind felt untroubled, distantly placid. He idly wondered if they would let him take Patch when they were through. Julie would be pleased to see her.

After a few moments, he turned away from the window. Heisler caught Peter's eye and took it as an invitation to talk. "You must understand, Mr. Anderson looks nothing like this Jake they describe. He's much different. Not unhandsome. He is forty years old, perhaps forty-one if I've missed his birthday. His hairline has receded, almost to the back of his head." Heisler smiled and ran his hand over his own thick hair. "Somewhat heavy, mostly in the belly."

Heisler offered Peter tea again, his earlier offer apparently forgotten. Peter didn't bother to decline. "His wife was the thing, you know," Heisler went on, unconcerned about the tea. "He lived alone, but he wanted his wife to come back to him. She was much younger, I think, and grew alarmed when he seemed to age faster than she. I don't know. I haven't seen her. He keeps a picture of her, and she does look young. Attractive. But the picture is several years old, and Mr. Anderson looks rather attractive in it himself."

Peter heard a knock. Jefferson opened the door. Kadash stood there, his face pensive and uninformative. He looked at Peter. "Come on," he said. Peter followed without a word. He wondered what Kadash would show him—Jake, in custody, or something else? Heisler clung closely behind him, Jefferson after. They went quickly to the stairwell and down, passing an officer at the foot of the stairs. The basement hallway was indistinguishable from the one in Carlotta's building—gray painted concrete floor, rack of mailboxes on the wall. At Anderson's door, Kadash turned to Peter. "I want you to identify the dog. But look around, see if anything else grabs your attention."

"He's not in there," Peter said.

"No, but he's been here. There's blood on the floor in several locations, and evidence that someone tried to bandage a bad wound in the bathroom. I don't know where he got to, but he didn't stay here for long. He might try to go back to his own place, but I doubt it. We've got a team back over there if he does."

Kadash entered the apartment. Heisler said, "It's hard for me to imagine that Regis would involve himself with a killer. He was very quiet, worked hard, was very well-read—"

Peter ignored him and entered the front room of the apartment. Against the long wall was a bookshelf made with flat boards layered between milk crates. A small black-and-white TV on its own milk crate sat beside the bookshelf, across from an old couch and cheap pine coffee table. A blanket printed with New York Jets logos lay folded on the couch. A black vinyl beanbag chair lay on the floor near the window. The walls were bare—no paintings, no photos. The only picture in the room was a small framed photo on top of the bookcase—a man and woman whose faces meant nothing to Peter. Probably the not-unhandsome Reggie and his much younger ex-wife. Two doorways, one at each end of the couch, led into other parts of the apartment.

"Don't touch anything," Kadash said.

Peter took in the entire room at a glance. Tidy and spare, the room was the antithesis of Carlotta's apartment. It was all but barren in its austerity. "Holy Lord above," Heisler muttered behind him. "I have never seen this place so clean."

Kadash stood near the window. "What do you mean?" he said. Mulvaney appeared in one of the doorways at the end of the couch, her face attentive.

Heisler took a few steps into the center of the room, his eyes rolling from one object to the next. "I've never been in here when it was not piled up with newspaper and pizza cartons. Soft drink containers. Good Lord, has he turned over a new leaf?"

"Perhaps it's the people he associates with," Mulvaney said.

Heisler looked startled at her suggestion, but for once he didn't have a response.

Kadash went to the window, pushed the curtain aside with the back of his hand. "That your dog?" he said as Peter joined him.

Patch lay on the floor beneath the window beside a small, oblong blood stain. "Yeah. That's Patch. He must have moved it. It was on the window sill this morning." He reached down to pick up the battered little dog, but Kadash stopped him.

"We need to let the evidence team examine it. They're on their way."

"Oh." Peter raised up again. "Will I get her back? I mean, my niece—"

"I think so. But if Jake carted this thing from the first murder scene, it may have evidence on it. We need to check it out."

"I see." Peter stepped back. He'd hoped they'd let him take Patch with him. He drifted away from the window, aimless and uncomfortable.

Kadash went to the bookshelf, looked at the picture of the man and a woman. "That Regis?" he asked Heisler.

"Yes, that is him. With his ex-wife. She left him but he is still moony over her."

"Yeah, I heard." Kadash turned his head, stared at the photo. "This guy looks familiar to me. I'm thinking about a stiff we pulled out of the river couple of weeks back. John Doe, shot in the back, dropped in the drink. Riggins and Davisson's case."

Mulvaney suddenly looked interested. "You think it could have been Anderson?"

Kadash shrugged. "Don't know. Maybe. Worth checking with them."

The idea of another body added to Peter's discomfort. How far back did Jake's grim hand reach? He wanted to get out of there. Head over to the hospital to see Ruby Jane. He cleared his throat. Mulvaney and Kadash looked up. "I should probably go," he said.

"Oh, yeah. Right," Kadash said. He nodded to Mulvaney. "We gotta get Riggins or Davisson to take a look at this picture. Maybe get Heisler here down to the morgue, see if he can ID the John Doe."

Heisler started to shake his head. "Oh, I don't really think—"

"Come on, bud," Kadash said to Peter, ignoring Heisler. He led Peter to the door.

"I'm sorry for being any trouble," Peter said when they reached the hallway.

"Eh, don't sweat it. I don't blame you for wanting to know what the hell is going on. Poking around over here was dumb as toast, but you lived."

"Yeah, I guess I did," Peter said. He smiled gratefully.

Kadash put a gnarly hand on Peter's shoulder, squeezed it. "So how you feeling?"

"About all that stuff you said earlier—?"

"About anything."

"I don't know. It was, like … well, at first, I didn't want anything to do with it. But I kept getting drawn in. Kelly Norris, Darla, the coat in the garbage. I could have backed away from any of it, at least at first I could. But it was like I was a bystander who secretly wished I wasn't always a bystander. I think that's really why I met with Darla on Monday morning. I didn't have to go—I wanted to."

"I know."

"I got accidentally dragged across the edge of the situation, and then took every opportunity to jump in deeper." He shook his head. "Am I crazy?"

"Certifiable." Kadash shrugged. "So what?"

Peter laughed quietly. "I think I wanted to be the one who caught him. But instead it's all just—this." Peter motioned toward the apartment. "Trace evidence. Fingerprints. Bullet comparisons. I don't know. I suppose I wanted a shoot-out."

"You already had your shoot-out," Kadash grunted. "This is how you build a case. You ask questions, gather lots of little pieces, tie them to the perpetrator, present them in court. It's exciting, but not like TV. You've helped, in your fumble-thumbed way, for what it's worth."

"I didn't want to find an empty apartment."

"We'll get him. Odds are he'll stagger into some emergency room or clinic and we'll grab him."

"No shoot-out expected, huh?"

"Doubtful. But you never know. And these days—" Kadash rolled his eyes, "it'll probably get caught on amateur video, so it's not like you'd have to miss it."

TWENTY-SIX

THE GRAY LIGHT OF late afternoon was waning. Peter drove nervously through a rush hour he'd grown unaccustomed to in the month he'd been out of work. As he reached the west end of the Broadway Bridge, he decided to go home and shower before returning to the hospital. He was beginning to notice his own funky aroma, and he realized it had been more than two days since he'd last put on a fresh change of clothes, Kadash's sweatshirt notwithstanding.

He fought traffic across the Broadway Bridge and up Weidler. Start and stop, wrestle into the next lane, stop again. Horns blared and other cars seemed to condense around him as he passed the Rose Garden, saw on the marquee that there was a Blazer game that night. He found it hard to shift with his bandaged hand, and he didn't like having to deal with pushy Portland-née-Californian drivers while trying to cope with the shift lever. "Should've come another way." He struggled through the Rose Quarter and finally turned up Seventh into his own neighborhood, out of the heavy traffic.

Irvington was as somnolent as ever. Snow lay in tenuous pockets on scattered lawns, graying the rhodies and azaleas. The undifferentiated overcast muted both color and sound, made everything look sunken and old. Cars seemed to sag on their springs, houses on their foundations. Holiday wreaths on front doors already felt anachronistic only a few days after Christmas. The only color came from stalks of kale in the flower beds, and from the few houses with Christmas lights winking in the early twilight. Peter's own house was dark when he pulled into the driveway, except for a single light that glowed dimly in the front window. His lone holiday decoration had been a small tree he'd taken down after Abby, Julie, and Dave left on Sunday. Now he regretted not having a string of lights on the rhodies in front, or garland in the windows—something. The house looked almost forbidding. He intended to shower quickly and get the hell out.

Peter didn't recall leaving the lamp on in the front room. Perhaps the police had switched it on when they came to swap the tape in the answering machine. Although it had only been a day since he was last home, it seemed like months. He half expected to find the place covered in a layer of dust, cobwebs draped from the ceiling. He felt empty and unresolved as he looked around the once-familiar room. He distantly remembered sitting on the couch, watching TV, talking on the phone, napping—the sound of rain splashing on the eaves. Less than a week before, in some other life, he'd roasted a turkey in the kitchen, served the meal to his sister and her family in the dining room, opened gifts. *This place isn't mine anymore,* he thought. *Jake stole it from me.* Memories of his former life came to him in soft focus—more clear in his mind was the image of the bloody coat in his garbage can, the stark contrast of the condom in the juniper bush. Even Jake's sinister messages on the answering machine had more presence than the two years Peter had lived in these rooms.

From the end table, he saw the flashing red indicator on the answering machine. Thank goodness the damned machine was still hooked up. Wouldn't want to miss any calls. He went to the table and pressed the playback button, morbidly curious to hear Jake's latest. The tape rewound and the machine clattered. Peter sat on the couch to listen.

—*beep*, click— "Peter, what in God's name is going on? I wish to hell you had a cell phone ..." Abby. She was pissed, and his gut instinct was to match her mood. But when he thought about it, he couldn't really blame her. He wondered what would she think about Patch crossing town in Jake's hands? Maybe he wouldn't tell her. Run Patch through the wash and pretend nothing had happened.

Sure.

—*beep*, click— "Mr. McKrall, this is Kelly Norris. I realize you and I got off on the wrong foot Sunday. I'm calling to ask you to consider another inter—" He stabbed fast-forward. Kelly Norris would have to find someone else to fuck with. Maybe he should give her Abby's number.

—*beep*, click— "All right, Peter, this has gone on long enough. I'm coming down there. I've discussed it with Dave, and we both agree. Something very serious is going on and if you're not going to call us, we feel we have no choice. I'm on the four o'clock Horizon flight. I'll grab a cab from the airport, and who knows how long that will take, but I should be there by five thirty or six."

The machine beeped and went silent. *They* felt they had no choice?—more like Abby felt *she* had no choice. Dave would be content to let Peter make contact in his own time, on his own terms. Peter shook his head, rubbed his eyes, checked his watch. Almost six.

"Shit." Wearily, he got to his feet and went to the front window, pushed the curtain aside. No sign of a cab. If she got bumped or her flight was delayed, he might have time to shower and split before she arrived. Perhaps he could skip watering the plants. Most would be fine, but the bonsais dried out quickly. He went into the dining room to check them out. The quince looked okay, but the ficuses were drooping, and one had started to drop leaves.

He brooded. For the bonsai plants, he usually filled a pot with lukewarm water and then let it sit a while so the chlorine could evaporate. Abby was sure to arrive by the time he went to that much trouble. Leave her a note, he decided. *Abby, sorry I missed you—no time to explain. Please water the bonsais.* She knew how to prep the water. She'd be pissed about it, but he didn't care. Teach her to show up uninvited.

He went into the hall, toward his bedroom for clean clothes. As he passed the bathroom door, he reached in and flicked the light switch. Then he stopped. He heard something, a faint murmur barely louder than the hushed background noises of the house. A voice outside, one of the neighbors? He listened, head cocked to the side. In the light cast from the bathroom, he saw the door at the end of the hall that led upstairs standing open.

Peter had slept upstairs during Abby and Dave's visit. He was sure he'd closed the door after they left—no need to heat the upstairs. Immediately he thought of Darla. She'd probably gone up there the day before, perhaps looking for more phones to unplug.

Couldn't be too thorough. Could she have returned? While she obviously knew how to get into the house, it seemed unlikely she would come back—too risky.

He went to the half-open doorway. "Darla?" he called. "You up there?" The only response was the muted titter of a laugh track, followed by an emotive sitcom voice. At the top of the stairs, Peter saw the flickering glow of the TV screen. Perhaps Darla had waited up there for Peter to come home, left the TV on when she came down.

He shook his head and turned away. *Just get in the shower, get dressed, and get out.* Then he saw a black leather case on the floor at the foot of the stairs. It was Abby's overnight bag, dropped with obvious carelessness. She must have already arrived, though he wasn't sure why she hadn't answered when he called upstairs. He sighed. Weary-legged, he trudged up the stairs.

Abby sat hunched on the floor in front of the dresser, knees to her chest, fists clenched at her sides. She locked eyes with him and opened her mouth, but didn't speak. Above her, the TV sat on the dresser top, facing the twin bed and the easy chair under the window. Jake lay on the bed, propped up on a couple of pillows. In his right hand, he held the gun pointed at Abby. In his other hand he clutched the TV remote to his chest like a talisman.

"That's close enough," Jake rasped. "You stay right where you are."

Peter stood in lock-jawed silence. The air bled from his lungs and he deflated, an empty bag of wind. His hand throbbed in its bandage. The moment seemed to thicken around him like glue. Abby's presence, unexpected, could at least be explained. But Jake—Jake was the last person he expected to find.

"Do you watch movies?" Jake said. His voice sounded thin and reedy, yet it lacked inflection. From the floor, Abby whimpered. Peter reached out with his uninjured hand as if to touch her, but he was afraid to move any closer. Heat crawled up his back like a swarm of ants. "Do you watch movies?" Jake said again. "I want to know."

Peter found the question incomprehensible. Desperately, he turned to Abby. Her cheeks were wet with tears, but her lips looked pinched and dry in the spectral light of the television. She stared back at him, wild-eyed, and gasped, "Peter, why is this happening?"

"I don't know," he whispered.

"Don't talk to her!" Jake blurted. "I asked you a question."

Peter's eyes darted back to Jake. He suddenly felt the need to grasp the railing to keep from falling. Jake stretched his gun hand toward Abby, and in the ripple of the tendon along the back of Jake's hand, Peter found an answer. "Uh, yeah. Yes, I do." His voice was a hoarse croak. "I like movies."

"Me, too." Jake nodded, then winced. His face looked strained and tight in the flicker of the TV. He shifted his eyes to the television screen and lowered the gun. "I watch a lot of movies. The bad guys always get caught. They shoot 'em up at the end." He stared at the television with a kind of longing. After a moment he said, "You're Peter Mackerel."

Peter nodded blankly. There didn't seem any point in correcting him.

"I like your plants," Jake said.

"Uh ... okay." Peter drew a breath. Abby began to cry, sound rising from her throat like the yowl of an injured dog. "Peter!" she cried, "why is this *happening? Why did you let this happen?!*"

"Shut *UP!*" Jake shouted. A spasm of coughs burst from him and he lunged off the pillows. The gun shook in his hands. "I'll shoot you, bitch!" Abby screamed and cringed back against the dresser.

"Wait!" Peter blurted. "Wait. Please wait!" He took a step and Jake suddenly pointed the gun at him. He stopped.

"Let her go," he said quietly. "Please."

Jake didn't respond. He kept the gun pointed at Peter, but after a moment he sagged back against the pillows again. "She shouldn't be screaming," he said.

"She's scared," Peter said. "Please let her go."

"She'll just call the cops." Jake shook his head. "Nobody's going anywhere."

"Please—"

"You shut up, too. I gotta think." Jake coughed again, a deep rattling sound, and turned his attention back to the television. His eyes took on a vacant cast, but he held the gun steady and unwavering, aimed at the center of Peter's chest.

Peter looked at Abby. Tears streamed from the corners of her eyes. *I'm sorry*, he mouthed silently. Out the windows, the dusk deepened until the only light in the room came from the television. Its glow was cold and blue, and it cast stark bounding shadows against the walls. In Jake's hand, the gun seemed to alternately swell and contract in the radiant shimmer. Peter felt himself shiver as he gazed at it. Earlier, when it had pursued him down the street, he hadn't really seen it, hadn't absorbed any of its detail. Now it consumed his attention. Even in the obscure light, he could see the indentions on the cylinder, the smooth arc of the trigger guard. It was a stubby, anonymous gun—if he hadn't heard from Kadash and Mulvaney that it was a thirty-two, he wouldn't have had any way to know. The hole in the end of the barrel seemed so small, inconsequential, yet Peter couldn't helping remembering the man at the bus stop. From the television, he heard jingling bells, and a chorus of voices offered, *"All the best to you and yours in this holiday season, from all of us at Channel 12."*

"How come you got two TVs?" Jake said.

Peter blinked.

"I got no TV at all," Jake continued, his voice querulous. "I been staying with a guy the last couple of weeks. I mean, he was gone—it's not like I'm queer." He shifted uncomfortably on the bed. "The guy's got a black-and-white TV. But you got *two* TVs. Nice big one downstairs, and this one, and both of them are color. How come?"

He gazed at Peter, his face empty and without guile. It was almost as if he didn't realize that he held a gun in his hand, or that twelve hours earlier he'd tried to shoot Peter on the street. "This one belongs to my sister," Peter said uncertainly. He flicked his eyes toward Abby. She was staring at him.

"Is that your sister?" Jake said. Peter nodded. Jake scrunched up his face in indignation. "It ain't fair. I ain't got no TV at all."

"I—I'm sorry—" Peter struggled to find words. The gun interfered with the movement of his thoughts. "I think you should have a TV," he finished.

"They cost too much money. Is it my fault I have to work at the Plaid Pantry?"

"No, of cour—"

Jake emitted a harsh string of coughs. He lowered the gun, curled the hand with the remote up to a large dark stain on his chest just below his shoulder. Without thinking, Peter took a couple of steps toward him. In the light of the television, Jake looked pasty and

348

white—but Peter thought he might look that way in any light. Kadash had said they found a lot of blood in the Anderson apartment. Peter took another step. He was almost between Jake and Abby when Jake saw the movement, raised the gun again. It shook in his hand. "Don't come no closer!" he growled.

"You're hurt," Peter said.

"Stupid cop. Fucker shot me—!" He coughed again, pressed the remote against the dark spot on his chest. In the light of the TV, the stain glinted a liquid black, but Peter knew it could only be blood. Inexplicably, he recalled Dan Halley that first morning in the park when Peter said the puddle of Carlotta's blood was black— "Sometimes is," Dan Halley had said. *Sometimes is.* It didn't look to Peter like Jake had done too good a job with the bandage. Blood seemed to be seeping across his chest.

"You should be in a hospital."

"I can't go to no hospital," Jake groused petulantly. "They'll nail me to the wall—all they wanna do is nail me to the wall."

What do you expect? Peter thought. But he said, "Jake, you need help—"

"How the *hell* do you know my name?!"

Abby gasped. The atmosphere in the room suddenly grew as tight as a drum. The black blood glistened, and Jake trembled like a leaf. The tendons flexed on the back of his gun hand. Peter realized dully that the moment hung by a thread. The little hole in the end of the gun seemed to orbit in space before him. "You have a sister, too, like me," he said, hoping it was the right thing to say. "I talked to her."

Jake's eyes grew wide and he held Peter in a tight stare, his brow pinched. Then his features relaxed and he looked away. "I saw her," he said with a quavering voice. "I saw Dee-Dee this morning, outside the old whore's bedroom." Suddenly tears sprang to his eyes. "I ain't seen her in so long, but she just ran away." He looked at Peter again, his gaze plaintive and vulnerable. "Do you know why she ran away?"

Vaguely, he wished Darla were here with him to answer the question. Or maybe that Darla was here instead of him. "You were shooting. She was probably scared."

Jake shook his head. "I'd never shoot Dee-Dee. I love her."

"I—she didn't know that. She was afraid."

"Why would she be afraid of me? I never hurt her. I'd *never* hurt her." He waved the gun at Peter. "She let me take this, after she took care of the dad. She left it for me, and I took it and hid it before the cops came. I thought I was hiding it for her, but I never saw her again. I kept it. Then I met the old whore and I knew why Dee-Dee had left it for me. After all those years I still had it, so I could take care of the old whore, too."

"I don't—" Peter began, but he couldn't find the words. Though he'd guessed much of what Jake had revealed, the implications behind the revelations were more than he could handle. He groped for understanding.

"You had to ruin everything," Jake continued, ignoring him. "I should've done that old whore the first night, the first time she told me to put my thing inside her. I told her it wasn't right, but she kept saying my thing was so big and would I put it inside her. I told her no, but she kept saying I wouldn't have to pay extra, so please do it. That's what she kept saying, please do it. I ran away. Lots of the hookers told me I could put it inside, but I didn't care about any of them. Besides, they never tried to make me. They'd take my twenty dollars and use their mouths and that was that. But the old whore, it was like she *wanted* me to stick it in her. Is that crazy, or what?"

Peter didn't want to say what he thought was crazy. He heard laughter from the television, the voice of Raymond telling his folks he wished he were adopted. From behind, he felt Abby's presence, but he didn't know if she was listening, if she *could* listen.

"Dee-Dee took care of the dad. She stopped the big voice, and she kept him from putting his thing inside her. It was my turn to do it to the mom. She was just some old whore who'd let *anyone* put their thing inside her. I told her no, but she just kept saying please do it, please do it, please do it. God, it was like she didn't even know who I was."

Peter felt himself start to weep. At first, he wasn't even sure why. The words spilled out of Jake in a torrent, and, somehow, Peter had hoped there'd be some sinister plot revealed, a dark and twisted evil. He'd expected something palpable, something physical, a force of nature, a spirit of wickedness taken human shape in the world. What else could drive a man to kill the way Jake had? As his tears flowed, Peter realized he had wanted a devil. A devil, he'd hoped with a dull yet swelling ache, which could account for a mother shot full of holes in the park, and might account for his own mother in her own park, so many years away. But there was no devil here. Only a desperate, damaged boy whose mother didn't recognize him.

"I saw you," Jake said abruptly. "I saw you leave the bar with her, and I saw you find her in the playground. How did you know she was there?"

Peter had no answer. But the cold realization struck him like a blow—not only had the bartender seen Peter leave the 747 Lounge with Carlotta, but so had Jake. Sunday morning, as Peter searched for Patch, what must it have looked like to a boy who'd left a body in the park, who recognized Peter's face as one among so many?

Jake coughed and then grimaced. "I watched her a lot, you know," he said. "I followed her and found the apartment across the alley so I could watch her. I had to make the guy who lived there leave so I could watch. But it was stupid. If I'd just done her that first night, it would have been somewhere else, far away. You wouldn't have even known. You wouldn't have been able to find her."

"Jake—" Peter's face felt cold and wet. He thought he was going to vomit.

"You ruined everything. Dee-Dee doesn't love me anymore because of you. Dee-Dee loves you."

"Jake, Dee-Dee loved her mother," Peter said. "And you killed her."

"*I did not!*" Sudden wrath twisted Jake's features and Peter knew that he had gone too far. He shrank backward, his bandaged hand groping along the railing, as Jake gibbered. "Dee-Dee said it was good! She pointed at the holes on the dad and told me that sometimes you have to do it—!" Jake coughed again, and started to wail. "It don't make no sense. I shot the gun and I called CrimeStoppers and I made the old whore's bedroom dark. I saved her! But you came along and made *Dee-Dee not love me no more!*" He pushed himself up and pointed the gun and squeezed the trigger.

The sound was like a physical force in the small room. Abby shrieked and Peter pitched toward her, instinctively hoping to intercept the bullet if it was aimed at her. For the long length of a heartbeat, he waited for the blow to fall, for piercing pain before never-ending darkness. But the bullet didn't hit him. He collapsed against the dresser with Abby beneath him. He felt for her hand

and squeezed it. She squeezed back. "Get behind the dresser," he hissed. "Get behind the dresser and stay down!"

She didn't answer, but he felt her crawl away. He slumped into the space she vacated and waited for the next shot. The air in the room was full and acrid and burned in his nostrils.

"I only got one bullet left," he heard Jake whisper.

Peter opened his eyes and looked up. Jake sat on the bed, eyes wide, his face coated with sweat. He looked at the gun as though he was seeing it for the first time.

"Jake—" Peter began.

"I can't go to no hospital. I can't get nailed to the wall."

"Jake, listen to me—"

"I just missed, that's all. It's not like there's something really special about you. It's just easier when you ain't hurt, you know? Or ain't running, like this morning. I'd've hit you this morning if I wasn't running. There's nothing special about you. But now I got only one shot left. I don't think I can walk anymore." He fell back against the pillows and drew his legs up, his face twisted with pain. The TV remote dropped out of his hand onto the bed, and he gazed down at it, his eyes wistful and lost. He scrabbled at it, but couldn't seem to pick it up. A long, deep sigh came out of him.

After a moment, he looked at Peter, his face suddenly hard. "I only got one bullet left," he said again. A rattling spasm of coughs shook him and he curled up more tightly. "But I don't even care, you know?" The gun quivered, then the spasm subsided. He shook his head. "My shoulder hurts. I can't move too good. Haven't been to the bathroom all day. I think I wet the bed."

"Let me call an ambulance."

"I don't want you to." Another coughing spasm. "A brain shot's the only way. I'm not sure what it will actually do."

"Jesus, I know what it will do. Please—"

"I think you should look the other way."

"Wait, please—"

Jake turned the gun and stuck the barrel in his mouth. Before Peter could move, Jake's eyes grew wide with panic. "*Wait—!*" Peter lurched forward. A long, hollow moment stretched before him, and his mind flashed to an image of his mother in the park.

Jake's finger strained against the trigger, but nothing happened. Peter reached him and groped for the gun. Jake made the faintest effort to resist, but his grip was as weak as a child's. "You don't have to do this," Peter whispered as he slipped the gun out of Jake's grasp. His mouth hung open loosely as the gun barrel slid free. To Peter it looked like a wordless cry of pain.

Peter sagged, dropped to the floor beside the bed. The gun fell somewhere out of reach, immediately forgotten. He knew he should go to Abby, or call the police, get help. But tears came upon him with the abruptness of a Portland rain shower and washed the thought away. For a surprised moment he fought them, demanded release from their spell. A voice in his mind shouted for him to remember—remember the bloody rubber in the bushes, remember the phone calls and the coat in his garbage can, remember the bullet holes in Carlotta, in Mrs. Cossart, in himself. Remember what had been done to Ruby Jane. The voice shouted for him to remember those things, to find the devil in it all. But in Peter's mind, as he lay curled in a tight knot in the deepening darkness, a tinny laugh track issuing from the TV, the only thing he could think of was the frantic look of fear in Jake's eyes as he tried futilely to pull the trigger.

EPILOGUE

JAKE DIED AS PETER lay on the floor of the spare room. Peter heard a final rattling cough and then a long exhalation. Then nothing. Peter lay still for a timeless span, gazing into the darkness under the bed, dreaming conscious dreams of the people he'd lost and those he'd found. At some point, he crawled over to Abby. She grasped him desperately at first, and he held her as she wept. "You're safe," he murmured. "He can't hurt us anymore." He stroked her forehead and heard himself shushing her over and over, calmly, like a refrain. After a bit, her sobs quieted and she leaned against him. In the background, the TV chattered on, steadfast and self-possessed.

At last she said, "Peter, what happened here?"

"I don't know," he lied. He actually laughed a little, surprising himself. "I came home to shower and water the plants. I wasn't expecting company."

"Who was that?"

"His name was Jake. That woman I found in the park—he was her son. He killed her."

"Why was he here?"

Peter shrugged. "I guess he had nowhere else to go."

She pushed away from him. In the light of the TV, he saw her creased brow, knew she was coming back to herself. Abby, ever perturbable. He felt a strange pleasure in the knowledge of her overbearing reliability. "Why didn't you call us? I left tons of messages, and you just ignored me—"

"Abby, shush. I was busy, and I haven't been home much."

"That's not an answer. I was worried about you."

"I know, and I appreciate it. But I needed you to butt out for a change." As her eyes widened and she opened her mouth to respond, he added, "Live your own life, Abby. Let me take care of living mine."

He heard a sound, a familiar voice. Kadash calling his name. Footsteps at the foot of the stairs.

Abby shrank against the wall in sudden alarm. "Who is that?" she hissed.

"It's all right," Peter said. He called out, "Sarge, we're up here."

He rolled onto his knees as the detective grunted up the stairs. Kadash paused at the landing, drew in a sharp breath. "Jesus Christ, bud—you all right?"

Peter nodded. His eyes grew warm and swollen. It felt surprisingly good to see Kadash. "This is my sister, Abby," he said. "She arrived unexpectedly." Kadash dipped his head to her, then looked around the dark room, at the TV flickering and muttering on the dresser. His eyes settled on the bed. For a moment, he seemed transfixed by the sight of Jake's body—the blood-soaked sheets, the wound in Jake's chest. He scratched at the cherry-patch on his neck. "You find him like this?" he said.

Peter shook his head. "When I got home he was up here...he had the gun on Abby. I came up and tried to get him to let Abby go. He took a shot at me." Peter pointed at the wall behind Kadash, though he couldn't make out the actual bullet hole. "Then he put the gun in his mouth and tried to pull the trigger. I stopped him—not that it matters."

Kadash looked at him with wry appraisal, then turned his gaze to Abby. "How about you?" he said. "You all right?"

She lifted her shoulders and said, "I guess so. Confused, more than anything else."

"No reason things should be any different for you," Kadash said. He turned back to Peter. "So he tried to kill himself and you stopped him." He shook his head, seemed to think for a moment. "Hell, I'd've probably helped him finish the job."

Peter's chest tightened suddenly. Images raced through his mind of the condom in the juniper bush, of Darla's watch cap, of Ruby Jane's pen—of a whole host of past petty thefts. Tears gathered in his eyes. "Sometimes things get taken," he said. The words snapped with astonishing severity. "Maybe I figured it was time I stopped doing the taking." He pushed himself to his feet. A sense of urgency arose within him. "I need to go see Ruby Jane."

Abby rose as well. "Who's Ruby Jane?"

Peter ignored her. He blinked the tears from his eyes and headed toward the landing.

"Whoa there, fella. I'm gonna have to call this in, get people over here," Kadash said. He shook his head. "This is a mess."

Peter placed his bandaged hand on Kadash's forearm. "I need to see Ruby Jane—I can't take any more chances, you know? No more stops along the way. I have to go."

Kadash stared at him for a long moment. He seemed to reach a decision. He turned to Abby and said, "You mind going downstairs? We need to talk privately."

She opened her mouth to protest, but Peter cut her off. "Abby, please. Go make yourself some tea or something."

"Peter—"

"Don't start." His voice carried a note of authority he wasn't accustomed to using with her. "Just go downstairs, please." She hesitated a moment longer, then said, "Fine..." Without another word, she slipped past them. She threw Peter a grim-faced glare before stamping down the stairs.

Kadash walked over to the edge of the bed and leaned down. A moment later, he came up with the gun. "You touch this?"

Peter nodded. "Yeah."

"She see you touch it?"

"I don't think so. She was hiding behind the dresser by then."

"Make sure of that. When you leave here in a few minutes, you're gonna take her with you. Mulvaney'll catch up with you later, like it or not. That girl can't have a different story to tell or we'll both have our nuts in a vice."

"She'll be fine."

Kadash pulled a handkerchief from his pocket and carefully wiped the gun. Then, still holding the gun with the handkerchief, pressed it into one of Jake's hands and let it fall carelessly onto the bed. He grunted with satisfaction. "No point in bringing up messy questions about why Peter McKrall's fingerprints are on a killer's gun, eh? Since you were never here, after all. Now later on, when they question you, you have to tell them you asked me to stop by here, check the place out for you. You were scared, because Jake was still on the loose. You gave me the key so I could look around. Okay?"

Peter nodded. "There's something else I wondered if you could do."

Kadash eyebrows bobbed. "Figure I'm in a generous mood?"

"I suppose so." Peter gave a tentative smile. "I just wondered—do you think you could lay off Darla? She's been through enough."

"Think so?" Kadash shrugged. "Well, that'll be tougher. Not my decision, but I'll see what I can do," Peter turned to go. Kadash stopped him with a hand on his shoulder. "You better give me the key before you bug out. And call me later—you know, to check in."

Peter nodded. He fished in his pocket, pulled out his keys, handed them to Kadash. He still had Ruby Jane's keys on a separate ring. He started down the stairs, then stopped. "Sarge?"

Kadash was staring at Jake again. "Eh? What is it?"

"How did you know to come here?"

For a moment, Kadash peered at the mess on the bed. "Just got to thinking is all. Jake here killed Regis Anderson, dropped him in the river, moved into his apartment. He was living there like it was his own damn place. Considering the attention he'd been giving you, it occurred to me he might try the same stunt twice." He ran his hand through his thin hair, patted his coat as though looking for his cigarettes. Gave up, sighed noisily. "Frankly, when I came in and it was all quiet and I smelled cordite, I thought you were a goner. Pleased to see otherwise."

Peter felt a grateful smile creep across his lips. "I'm glad you came. Thank you."

Kadash grunted, waved a hand dismissively. He started to turn away, then seemed to think better of it. "You're welcome," he grumbled. "Now get the hell out of here."

"Okay. See you later." Then he paused. He looked back at Kadash. "Sarge?"

"Jesus, bud, now what is it? You're like a goddamned broken record."

"I just wanted to say I'm sorry…" Peter swallowed. "I mean, I'm sorry for lifting your lighter the other day."

Kadash gazed at him. His face grew suddenly soft. "Ah, well, uh…thank you, bud. I appreciate hearing that."

"It won't happen again."

"I know it won't, son," Kadash said. "I know it won't."

Peter went down the stairs, his mind already looking ahead. Hopefully, Ruby Jane would be out of ICU by now. He felt like they had a lot to talk about, and he hoped she felt the same.

"Hey, bud!" Kadash called. "Peter!"

Peter looked back up the stairs. Kadash met his gaze, smiled. "When you call, drop the Sarge, all right? Call me Skin."

The End

ACKNOWLEDGEMENTS

I want to offer thanks to Captain George Babnick of the Portland Police Bureau Training Division for including me in the Portland Police Citizens Police Academy. The Academy offered a wonderful look at police training and procedure, as well as provided insight into the philosophy of the Portland Police Bureau. I also want to thank Sergeant Kris Wagner for her assistance with homicide investigation procedure, and Officer Michael Schmerber for his insight into the day-to-day work of a patrol officer. To the extent there are errors in procedure and methods in *Lost Dog*, the fault is mine, not these fine members of the Portland Police Bureau.

Thank you also to Janet Reid, agent extraordinaire. I hope *Lost Dog* is the first of many for us!

Thanks also go out to Ted Olson and Melanie Pryor, who graciously allowed me to hole up in their lovely cabin in the woods for days at a time to write.

I owe an inestimable debt of gratitude to my good friends and fellow writers Candace Clark, Andy Fort, Corissa Neufeldt, Claudia Werner, and Yung Yu-Ma, who read multiple drafts of *Lost Dog* and offered invaluable critiques. I'll be gladly contributing to their coffee habits for years to come.

If you enjoyed *Lost Dog*, read on for an excerpt
from the first Phil Riley mystery by Mark Combes

Running Wrecked

COMING SOON FROM MIDNIGHT INK

ONE

I wonder what the shrinks back in the States would say if I told them I was dreaming about a marlin swimming the Serengeti? Ah, fuck 'em—I'm not crazy. I've seen crazier things in my life than some fish where it ain't supposed to be. Hell, I've seen a *little girl* where she wasn't supposed to be and the damn shrinks didn't believe that, either. Besides, what can dreams tell you anyway?

Lost in that phantom conversation with myself, I almost miss it. But Chubby sees her—a beautiful Beneteau sailboat, maybe forty feet stem to stern, off to starboard. I pull back on the throttles and ease the boat over on her starboard chine, making a tight circle back to the sailboat. I'm drawn to the boom as it slams back and forth, the main sheet too slack to keep the heavy hunk of aluminum from pitching to and fro with the waves. Watching the boom from my boat, I'm reminded of a crazy, out-of-control metronome. It strikes me that the sailboat looks sick, or lonely, if a sailboat can look like either. Something is wrong.

When we pull up behind her, the *Miss Princess*, that strange feeling wells up—the one you get when you walk into an abandoned building. You sense the life that was once there but now only lingers in erratic, weak energy. You become aware of it when those pinpricks on the back of your neck start. Combining that feeling with the sound of the sails flapping in the wind and the boom out of control, I know, before I even hail her, that she is abandoned.

Nevertheless, I shout through cupped hands, "Hello, the boat! Hello, the *Miss Princess!*" No response.

Chubby and I look at each other simultaneously and shrug. I pick up the marine radio and hail, "*Miss Princess, Miss Princess. This is Tortuga One.*" Nothing. I repeat my call and still no response. Maybe this is a charter out of Grenada and they don't know their boat name. "Sailboat at South Gap off Isla Tortuga, please respond." The sailboat is picking its way into the wind, tacking back and forth in the same manner that a novice might set his boat to heave to. It's like a wounded animal fleeing.

"Now what?" Chubby asks.

"I have to go aboard and see what's going on. We may have to take her in. I need to let Callie know what's going on." I turn my back to the wheel of my boat to shield me from the wind and shout into the radio, "Callie, Callie, this is *Tortuga One*. Callie, Callie, this is *Tortuga One*. You there, kid?" I wait what seems like thirty minutes, and I feel Chubby moving the wheel under my butt. He nudges the throttles a bit, to keep us in line with the sailboat. I wonder, *where the hell is that kid?* He should still be at the shop working on the air compressor and he should be able to hear the radio. I look in the direction of my shop, Dive Tortuga, some seven miles around the southern end of the island. I envision Callie sleeping out on the dock while my voice bellows over the radio. I chuckle to myself, knowing it isn't true, but I am still curious about why he isn't answering.

The wind has shifted and is blowing through the South Gap from the southwest. The South Gap is a quarter-mile-wide passage between the main island of Isla Tortuga and the small pinnacle known as South Point Island. The passage acts as a funnel for the wind between the high cliff of the mainland and the smaller, sheer pinnacle. It is like standing in a wind tunnel with the fan on high, and we would have to head into that wind tunnel to get home.

Chubby's impatience escapes its always-tenuous bounds. Acting his role as the impatient fifteen-year-old, it's clear he can't understand why we have to go to such effort for this abandoned boat.

"Isn't this government business?" he asks.

"We just can't let an expensive sailboat wallow out here."

"Anchor it," he demands.

"Dammit, Chub, you know how deep it is here. I doubt that they have seven hundred feet of rode."

He rolls his shoulders. "Where is Callie?"

To move the project along for Chubby, I'm about to give up on raising Callie when the radio squawks, "*Tortuga One, Tortuga One*, this is Dive Tortuga. Come bauk, ya read. Over."

"Dive Tortuga, this is *Tortuga One*. Have Bill meet me at the pier. I'm bringing in a sailboat we found out here by South Gap. Seems to be abandoned. Over."

"Abandoned? Overboard?" Callie questions.

"Yeah, just tell Bill to meet me. We'll be back in about a half hour or so. *Tortuga One*, out."

In deference to Chubby I shut the radio off before Callie can come back. I'm annoyed with him for not answering fast enough and don't want to get into it right then as to why he was so slow in responding to my hail. Actually, I'm annoyed at the whole situation—Chubby's impatience, Callie's inattentiveness, and this damn sailboat owner's recklessness.

Isla Tortuga sees its share of bareboat charters out of Grenada, so I've seen a lot of dumb stuff in my short tenure on the island. Bill refers to these bareboaters as "credit card captains" because anyone can be a captain if their card is platinum. It's amazing that more of these guys don't get themselves killed, considering their skill levels. The sea can be an unforgiving place and Isla Tortuga is an especially unforgiving, strange little island surrounded by jagged pinnacles that, at times, rise feet from the surface like teeth on a saw. I've learned great respect for the waters around this island. They have taken many ships and many lives and I don't want to be another stat on a form, another soul lost at sea. So to see a boat this close to shore, its mainsail cracking like gunshots, and no one responding to my calls makes me more than a little concerned. Clearly, something is not right. I need to do something, as inconvenient as it might be to both Chubby and me. "Look Chub, I just want to get back to the shop and have a beer." A gust of wind reminds me that we need to get moving. "Let's just do this."

I quickly go over the plan with Chub, telling him to take the wheel of the *Tortuga One* as I prepare to jump aboard and investigate.

When on board, my plan is to take a cursory look belowdecks and see what, if anything, I can find. I really don't expect to find anyone—we've been behind the boat for some five minutes now, shouting and calling on the radio with no response. The boat is abandoned.

After that, I figure I'll motor the sailboat around the point and back to Pelican Bay. Sort it out there in the calm of the bay, with a cold beer in hand. And that will allow Chubby to drive *Tortuga One* back to the shop and let him get on with his oh-so-important life.

Really, I shouldn't be so hard on the kid. He's worked his ass off this past week in some pretty rough sea conditions with some fairly unpleasant French divers. Yesterday was their last day of diving so Chubby was looking forward to having today off, but I pressed him into service, making him help me with a dive site marker buoy that had a frayed line. I was concerned that the line would snap and we would lose the buoy.

Plus, I haven't been sleeping very well lately. Weird dreams.

The short version is last night I dreamed of Africa. I was alone on safari, wandering the bush, hunting big game. I came across a pride of lions in the open savannah. There were at least six lionesses with cubs. As I drew closer, I saw they were feeding on a fish, a very large fish, maybe twenty feet long. It looked like a shark, but the curve of the tail was beautifully formed, a sickle. It was a marlin. The lions looked at me with little concern, as if they were expecting me. Then I woke up.

And it's been variations on that theme for a couple of weeks now.

The *Miss Princess* is wallowing badly, as boats do that are at the mercy of the wind and currents. My plan is to board her from the swim platform. It will be tricky; Chubby will have to inch up slow and close so that I can jump from the bow of the *Tortuga One* to the swim platform, and all of this when the two boats are in a hollow of a wave so that the platform will be relatively level.

The odds are good that I'll get wet. I do. Chubby does his part, gets me up close, but just as I pounce, a shore-reflected wave tilts the platform, effectively swatting me into the sea. I bob to the surface to see Chubby looking over the side of *Tortuga One* with an obnoxiously broad smile on his face.

You try and do a good deed, I think to myself as I sidestroke to the sailboat. I pull myself up onto the platform, slog my way up to the companionway and poke my head down the opening. "Hello. Anyone home?"

No answer, just the sound of sails and hardware rattling and banging as the boat pitches in the confused seas. So with both hands I push my too-long bangs back over my head and make my way toward the mast. Holding onto the portside stay, I discover the mainsail halyard winch is jammed. Smashed, actually, with the wire halyard miserably wrapped and kinked in the broken winch. It looks like someone has been at it with a sledgehammer. I know I'm not going to get the sails down with it looking like that. Not easily anyhow. From where I stand on the coach roof, I can tell that the jib is badly furled on its roller-furling headstay, bumpy and offline. The jib sheets, the ropes that control the sail, are chopped off, unraveling in the wind, flying like crucified snakes at the clew of the sail. What is going on here?

Hell, I muse, just run the damn thing in and be done with your Good Samaritan deed for the day.

I retrace my way back to the stern of the boat when an unexpected gust of wind rolls the boat and makes me reach for the wheel for support. I then notice—I'd walked right past it before—that the wheel is bound with rope, very distinctive rope. It is polyethylene, with red and blue threads wound around a white core. I've never seen this kind of line on a boat before. It looks like thick clothesline. Strangely, the rope binds the wheel to the compass binnacle, a very rudimentary autopilot, especially for such a nice boat. My eyes drop to the throttle, fully forward—wide open. The transmission lever is down, forward for a sailboat. My eyes scan the gunwale for the fuel gauge and I sink when I see it reads empty. Someone set this boat off motoring full steam ahead and it ended up here, at South Gap, when it ran out of fuel. My great plan of motoring the boat in is shot now, and I can't sail it in with the all the hardware out of commission. The only other option is to tow it.

I turn my attention back to the rope securing the wheel. *Man, this is strange*, I think to myself. I look back at the gunwale. The boat is equipped with an electronic autopilot, so why the rope? Didn't the owners or charters know how to use the autopilot? Unlikely, but possible.

I pull my Leatherman tool out of its sheath, open the serrated knife and begin cutting the rope. As I saw away, I yell to Chubby, "Hey buddy. Bad news."

His head drops to one side, registering his frustration. "What?" he says, plaintive as a small child.

"I'm sorry, but we've got to tow it in. It's out of gas and it's unsailable."

"Can't we call someone? Can't the police tow it in?"

A good idea, but the weather isn't cooperating. I'm not too thrilled with the prospect of waiting for relief on an uncontrollable boat. It could easily end up smashed on the rocks, and I'd be swimming before help would arrive.

"I'm sorry. I don't think we can chance it. We should tow it in. I'll make it up to you. I promise. Hey, dinner on me at the Beachcomber, huh? How does that sound?" *Pretty damn generous to me,* I think. It seems to soothe him. He doesn't respond. With Chubby, I've learned that no response is a tacit agreement. "Start setting up a bridle for towing. Use the dock lines in the back bench." I finish cutting through the rope on the wheel, and as Chubby searches out lines, I decide to check belowdecks.

I skip down the four steps of the companionway into the salon area, and realize suddenly that this is the first time I've been below. I'm surprised at myself, slightly, for not checking there first. Someone could have been hurt below, but I presumed no one was aboard when I shouted down earlier. I didn't see the need.

"Hello!" I shout. I'm right, no one at home.

It smells musty below, like a damp cellar. The sliding companionway roof is pushed forward and the protective boards at the steps are not in place—the boat is open to the weather. I notice salt stains on the sole, irregular white blotches, evidence of intruding saltwater. A good storm with high enough seas could have downflooded the boat and possibly sunk her.

The companionway stairs put me almost directly in the middle of the boat. From this vantage point, I quickly scan the area. Nothing unusual. Everything seems in place. The navigation table is directly to starboard; I think that a good place to start. I can at least get an idea where the boat is from by reading their charts.

I find nothing. I lift the lid to the navigation table, not a single chart or note. In fact, not even a set of parallel rulers or dividers. Odd. Whoever was sailing the boat, no matter their skill level, would need to have these basic navigational tools. And they would want the charts of the area out and ready. Hell, I know these waters pretty well after six months but anyone new to the waters would use—no, need—a chart to avoid the ever-present pinnacle or sandbar. I open the cabinet above the table and find three charts rolled neatly in tubes. I pull out the one on the left, unroll it, and find that it is a sectional chart of the area, but with no course plotted. In fact, the chart looks brand new, never used.

"Hey boss? I'm ready up here!" Chubby yells from the *Tortuga One*.

"OK!" I yell back. I can hear the wind whistling through the rigging topside and I quickly calculate that with towing we are about an hour from the bay and a safe harbor. I decide that a thorough search of the boat will have to wait until we got back into calmer waters. I roll the chart back into its tube and latch the door of the cabinet.

When I pop back up on deck, Chubby is staring at me.

"The weather, boss," Chubby says.

I look at the water and the tops are starting to blow off the chop. We need to beat it around the point. There, we will be protected from the wind, in the lee of the island.

"OK, toss me the line." He tosses me a two-inch line that is about twenty feet long—just long enough to allow the *Miss Princess* to settle behind the wake of my boat. Good choice. The sailboat won't get tossed considerably in the wake so we can chance running at a faster speed. Chubby is thinking. But then, despite his age, Chubby is an experienced seaman.

I find what look like brand new dock lines in the starboard lazarette and then walk the towline up to the bow of the sailboat as Chubby putters alongside. I tie off the *Miss Princess*'s dock lines to the base of the mast and lead one starboard, one port. I lead them around their respective bow cleats and then make them fast to the towline. Chubby keeps some slack, being careful not to foul our props with the dangling line. I need to get back to my boat and it is clear I'm going swimming. I strip my T-shirt off and catch Chubby's sidelong glance at the scars on my chest and shoulder, and I reflexively cover myself, hands crossed at the wrists, wet shirt swinging slowly. He turns away, ashamed, and I stuff the shirt into the back of my cargo shorts. As I brace myself to dive in, I hear a crash belowdecks directly beneath me.

I decide I better go back below deck to secure as many things as I can to limit the amount of stuff that will get tossed as the boat pitches and wallows during towing. "Just a minute, Chub." I move quickly back down the side deck to the companionway.

As I half jump down and half slide down the stairs, the door to the main cabin at the stern of the boat swings open and slams against the wall. The noise startles me so much I nearly fall into the salon as I spin around. The Beneteau has a double stateroom layout: one cabin in the bow, the other cabin astern. From topside, I heard the noise in the forward stateroom, but the door to the rear compartment just swings there, open and close, open and close, periodically slamming violently into the wall, as if it were waving me to come in. I step to the door and grab it on one of its closing cycles and hold it half open. Curiously, I lean against the door and the jamb of the door, my modest six-foot frame just fitting into the opening, and peer into the cabin. The bed is made, and everything, like the rest of the belowdecks area of the boat, seems in order. Something catches my eye.

As if someone flicked it out with a finger, I see a pacifier roll out from the far side of the queen-size berth. The pacifier is opaque blue and with every passing wave, it lolls back and forth on its hilt, like it is waving to me. It is a halting sight, and an even more halting realization. There had been a baby aboard this boat.

ABOUT THE AUTHOR

Bill Cameron lives with his wife and poodle in Portland, Oregon, where he also serves as staff to a charming, yet imperious cat. He is an eager traveler and avid bird-watcher, and likes to write near a window so he can meditate on whatever happens to fly by during intractable passages. His stories have appeared in *Spinetingler*, *The Dunes Review*, and *The Alsop Review*, as well as the upcoming *Killer Year: A Criminal Anthology*.